HALF CRAZY

HALF CRAZY

A NOVEL

• • •

J. M. McDonell

LITTLE, BROWN AND COMPANY
BOSTON   NEW YORK   TORONTO   LONDON

Copyright © 1995 by J. M. McDonell

First Edition

The characters and events in this book are fictitious.
Any similarity to real persons, living or dead,
is coincidental and not intended by the author.

Library of Congress Cataloging-in-Publication Data

McDonell, J. M.
    Half crazy : a novel / J. M. McDonell. — 1st ed.
        p.   cm.
    ISBN 0-316-55560-6
    1. Novelists, American — New York (N.Y.) — Fiction.   2. City and
town life — New York (N.Y.) — Fiction.   3. Models (Persons) — New York
(N.Y.) — Fiction.   4. Friendship — New York (N.Y.) — Fiction.   5. Gay
men — New York (N.Y.) — Fiction.   I. Title.
PS3563.C35845H35   1995
813'.54 — dc20   94-33348

10   9   8   7   6   5   4   3   2   1

MV-NY

*Published simultaneously in Canada
by Little, Brown & Company (Canada) Limited*

Printed in the United States of America

For Marla

Daisy, Daisy,
Give me your answer, do!
I'm half crazy,
All for the love of you!

Henry Dacre

PART ONE

. . .

1

• • •

MIRANDA. MIRANDA. MIRANDA. I really loved that girl. In fact, I was, for a while, *in love* with her, which is odd, to say the very least, since I am a homosexual. Card carrying. Fag. Fairy. Pansy. Shirtlifter and all those other really nasty names. Always have been, since I was a tiny child and could summon no interest in looking up the skirts of my mother's friends. I am old: thirty — and celibate in this day and age when sex equals death.

I can't check into a monastery because I'm antireligion, and I can't drop out and go west because any cowboy who isn't queer himself, hates queers.

So I stay right here participating in the collapse of what was once the best city in the world, New York, and refining the art of compromise.

Living with one's passions does, after all, mean living with one's sufferings — and that's exactly what this story is about. But it's not about me. It's about Miranda.

The first time I saw her was August. I'd just returned from a midafternoon margarita at my neighborhood bar, The Shamrock. Everything shimmered in temperatures well over a hundred, and a relentless breeze only made the heat worse. Other places have names for this — Sirocco in Italy and the Mediterranean Islands, Khamsin or Simoom in the Middle East, and Santa Ana, the devil wind that blows across Southern California and out to sea.

People in these places take to their beds in dark rooms with cold rags on their foreheads when the weather goes wild; nobody runs around tempting evil spirits which both superstition and common sense recognize to be riding the torrid air currents.

New Yorkers, of course, ignore the barometric descent; we're far too frantic to notice anything short of nuclear disaster or, worse, a plummeting stock market. But something always happens when it gets this hot.

It was a Wednesday — the most forgettable day of the week. I mean, Monday's child is fair of face, Tuesday's child is full of grace. Wednesday's child is — what? Who can remember? Who can ever remember the middle, the mean, the average. No one. We only remember the beginning, the end, the best, the worst, the sky on fire, the final flood.

And that's why I remember this particular Wednesday in August as though it happened five minutes ago. Or five seconds ago.

• • •

She was walking slowly, lugging a huge and dilapidated plastic suitcase. A big white dog danced along behind her, attached by no discernible leash.

To say she was beautiful is like saying Van Gogh was a good painter. Incandescent is a better word — but I've used it before in my books. I write romances. What can I tell you — it's a living.

By the way, anybody who still thinks writers are guys with a message or a mission should forget it. Most fiction writers are actually cowards, egomaniacs, or control freaks. That's why all this is so hard to put down on paper — because it's true. The process is easy but the facts remain immutable, making me powerless to effect a single change.

I will tell you one thing: I'm never writing a true story again. In exchange for a single revision of historical fact, I'd erase from my memory every word I ever thought or said about fate and philosophy. I'd quit playing god and start believing in God so I could sell my soul to the devil in an even trade. That done, I'd retell this story and give it a happy ending. Now you don't want to read any further? *Tant pis.*

As I started to say, Miranda was so beautiful that somebody who fancied black women exclusively, or Brazilian women exclusively, or even (as in my case) men, might make an exception. She wore a short blue jean skirt with a cutoff T-shirt and an Arkansas Mockingbirds (whoever they were) baseball cap. And no makeup. She wasn't particularly tall, but she looked tall. She was very slender, with big breasts and long, tanned legs, delicate ankles, graceful hands, and those killer eyes. Those slanting, silver-blue eyes — the color, no doubt, of original sin.

Anyway, there she was, finally standing in front of me. She dropped the bag and held out her hand.

"Hi. I'm Miranda," she said. "I'm moving into the garden apartment."

I don't know how to explain this. Maybe I'd been sitting out on the stoop in the heat for just a little too long — maybe because my life was a mess, my unconscious mind was dicking me around — maybe it was the fact that her hand was cool and dry. But when I looked into her eyes that first time, I suddenly became light-headed and I could actually *feel* my heart beat. Most bizarre of all, I started to get a hard-on. As the guy in the deli says: Go figure.

But don't worry; this isn't about my conflicts. I'm grown up now, and my story is about struggle and disappointment. About the dreaded middle, the cruel gray light.

Miranda's story is all black and white — love and death, sex and betrayal. Part of it made the headlines. Maybe you remember.

● ● ●

Christ, I thought, the garden apartment. An appropriate name for a place with a dirt floor, though probably not what she had in mind. For once, I was at a loss for words. But that didn't stop me from jumping in with a non sequitur.

"It's not usually this hot," I said.

"I'm glad to hear that," she said. "Because it sure is hot around here. Like hell's a mile away and the fences are down. So what's your name?"

Her voice was a surprise, with its husky edge and the deeper register of someone older.

"David," I said. "I live upstairs — here, let me carry your suitcase."

As I picked up the bag, I forced myself to look away from that incredible face framed by long, shining, silver-blond hair. Malone, the

actor I loved, who just left me for somebody else, had blond hair —
and I remember thinking with vicious glee, that no matter how much
herbal oil he soaked in or how many blow jobs he traded with Henri,
or Jean-Claude or Abdul for the latest, lightest, brightest golden
streaks, he'd never come close to that magic no-color color.

"Thanks," she said. "It weighs a ton. I drug it the last block because
the taxicab driver told me this is a dangerous neighborhood and he
wasn't about to go any farther. He said somebody got killed near here
just last week in broad daylight. Is that true?"

Did she actually say *drug?* Not to mention the fences being down. I
never heard anyone talk that way except in the movies. So what was
my reply?

"Yes, I think it's true. Is this your dog?"

"Oh yeah. Pete, shake a paw."

The dog obediently sat on the pavement and lifted his right paw.
Like many city boys, I am not terribly comfortable around large
animals.

"He's friendly," she said. "But you don't have to shake hands with
him."

I laughed and took Pete's paw for a quick instant.

"This neighborhood doesn't seem so bad," she said looking
around. "Windows have glass in them . . ."

"Where do you come from?" I asked.

"Arkansas."

Of course, I thought, and found myself staring into those eyes.

"Where in Arkansas?" I actually said.

"You been out there?"

"No."

"Then you never heard of it."

"What brings you to New York?" I asked like an asshole.

"I had a job at an insurance company in Fayetteville this past year,"
she explained. "I was the only one who could work the new computer,
so I got to be the senior vice president's assistant. Fayetteville's the
second biggest city in the state."

She paused. I waited. She had said the word insurance with emphasis on the first syllable.

"A few months ago," she went on, "I met these people who were
making a movie — well, it was a student film — about an insurance

investigator, and the director used me for a part. He ran out of money because the producer hired a caterer who cost more than the cameraman — so I never got paid, but the director gave me a portfolio of pictures. Of myself. He said he was sure I could go ahead and be a model in New York City."

"I'm surprised some magazine didn't find you in junior high and slap you right on the cover."

"I was ugly then."

"Oh come on," I said.

"I mean it," she said. "I looked like a boy — and I wanted to be a boy — and besides I wasn't around school too much — not that we had very many star searches where I lived. But guess what. I am going to do it, I'm going to get my face slapped on those magazine covers, and on TV, and anyplace else they pay, and I'm going to save up the money and then — "

"Then what?" I asked.

"Then what do you think?" she said. "I'll be free."

She ran a hand through her hair and shifted her weight from one foot to the other.

"Do you suppose we could go inside?" she asked. "I've got a key."

"Sure."

But just as I lifted Miranda's suitcase, Juliana, the neighborhood bag lady, whose several long skirts dragged behind her on the pavement, shuffled up to us, crazy eyes lit with curiosity.

"Miranda," I said, "this is Juliana, she's our neighbor. Juliana, this is Miranda, she just got here from Arkansas."

Miranda extended her hand.

"Hi, Juliana," she said. "How're you doing?"

"Storm Warning," was the reply.

Except for a fast glance at the clear sky, Miranda retained her equanimity.

"Really," she said.

I hadn't time to prepare Miranda for the peculiar fact that Juliana's entire language consisted of the names of racehorses. Style and syntax depended entirely on who was running on the card of the day. No past, no future, and nothing outside the tristate area.

"Well," I said, "we're going inside now."

"Aces and Eights," said Juliana by way of farewell as she headed toward the corner where some kids had pried open a fire hydrant, which was spilling hundreds of gallons of fresh, cold water onto the overheated street.

To me, the unfinished dirt floor of the "garden apartment" was no more startling than the lead paint, asbestos insulation, and substandard I-beams in half the other buildings in New York. I was resigned to the city. Miranda had just arrived.

But she accepted what must have been the shock of the dark, the dank, and the dirty with amazing calm, a trait in her I would get to know and fear as the events that lay ahead took us over.

I decided to wait with the bad news about our landlord, the schizo scumbag who had a Cambodian fuck-chair in the middle of his living room and was rumored to torture small animals for sport. I never really believed the last part. Mark Douglas (Dark Mouglas to his tenants) was too busy torturing people.

But maybe I looked worried even in the shadows. She lit a cigarette and said, as if to comfort me:

"Hey relax, this ain't no hill for a stepper. I've seen a lot worse."

"Like what?" I asked.

A smile fooled around the corners of her lips, making me think she was scanning her memory for the most shocking thing she could say.

I didn't know her then and intuition is hardly my strong suit.

"I slept in the woods once for about a month when I was eight," she said.

"That doesn't sound so bad," I responded, imagining some fragrant bed of evergreen boughs.

"In the winter."

"Oh."

"I'll get this place fixed up," she said. "I hope the shower works. Do you know where it is?"

"In the kitchen."

"Where's the kitchen?"

"We're in it."

"Uh huh . . . now I see."

In one corner of the big, mostly underground room was a hot plate, an under-the-counter refrigerator, and a tiny sink. A few feet away there was a battered fake-Chinese screen, behind which I guess was the john; and next to the screen, a tub, with one of those hand-held shower attachments.

I watched all that silver-blond hair catching what little light there was in the room as she marched over to the tub. She turned on the hot and cold faucets and the shower spray. A torrent of rusty water gushed out, dark as blood.

We watched in silence as the grimy liquid turned clear.

She turned off the shower part and the hot water and held her wrists under the cold-water tap.

"This is a quick way to cool off," she said. "Come here, try it."

I tried it.

"No, no," she said. She leaned close and turned my hands.

"The idea," she said, "is to put your wrists under the water. So it hits your veins."

She smelled like rain.

I closed my eyes for an instant and entered a deep, magic forest where at the end of the story the prince winds up with the princess. I longed for a childhood I never had; I felt searing tears start somewhere behind my eyes.

"Is it working?" she asked.

I nodded.

"Good," she said as if she meant it. "I'm going to go for a run now. I bought a map at the airport that tells the best routes in the city. If I don't move around I feel really bad. . . . Hey, what's your favorite book?"

Favorite book. My mind went blank.

"Fiction or nonfiction?" I asked.

"Doesn't matter."

"Like what would I take to a desert island?"

"Uh huh."

"Eliot. *The Collected Works of T. S. Eliot.*"

"Thanks," she said, scribbling the title in a little notebook. Then she waved as I ascended out of the soft semidarkness into the glaring light.

A few minutes later I watched from the stoop, where I was pretending to read the *New York Times*, as she jogged off into the heat with

Pete right behind her. I was pleased to see that it was she rather than the dog wearing the pink bandanna.

• • •

She had an instant career. In a world where life begins at twelve, and superstardom can be attained by sixteen, Miranda was definitely unusual, like an elderly primagravida, at nearly twenty. Her dazzling looks and mysterious grace opened the necessary doors and made up for lost time. The old pros saw an enduring beauty. Good bones make all the difference. And the young hustlers, too frenzied to articulate a thought, simply saw whatever it takes to sell beer, or magazines, or the idea that a size twelve butt could look good in a pair of skintight jeans. She had it, and they wanted it.

In a day, she signed with the hottest agency in the city. In two weeks she'd gotten half a dozen assignments; at the end of a month, she was turning down work, and by the second month she'd bagged her first television commercial. She was still several years away from being a household word with the attendant big bucks and megastatus. But she was on her way.

• • •

Seventy-two hours before Thanksgiving (I always think of time this way when I'm on deadline), I was supposed to be wrapping up the last chapter of my latest effort, *Midnight Desire,* but was temporarily stuck for a way to save Cassie, the heroine, who was trapped in a burning building while Zack, the hero, was a hundred miles away and blind. In a hurricane.

The ringing phone was a welcome distraction. The caller was not. Johnny Ferris, executive assistant to Clementine Sheffield, owner of Clementine, the agency Miranda had joined, had never acknowledged my existence before — but I knew, of course, that he was a former lover of Roland Tarbell, the decrepit gossip columnist for whom Malone had left me. Malone, who once divided all people into two categories: the young and beautiful and the old and terrified. More about that later.

"Where's Miranda?" Johnny demanded.

"I have no idea," I said.

"That twat," he said. "And why don't you know her schedule?"

"She's not a twat," I said, "and why *should* I know her schedule?"

"All the girls do a form for the office," he said. "They give us a person to call in an emergency. And you're it," he added in a tone suggesting I might be a bichon frisé or a fringed ottoman. Never mind.

"She's got a *Harper's Bazaar* shoot this morning," he continued, his voice rising. "It's only Cat Kelly's *third* cover and she's taking a big chance on an unknown — and the fucking unknown doesn't show and doesn't call. Clementine is *furious*."

"I'll check her place and get back to you," I said.

I ran down the stairs and knocked at Miranda's door. Mark Douglas, our sleazy slumlord, had certainly not repaired the bell. There was no reply except for Pete's barking. I knocked again — then pounded on the door.

Pete barked louder and finally she let me in. She looked, for her, like hell.

"David," she said in a voice barely more than a whisper. "I can't talk right now. The lights went out."

Since at least one lamp was on, I didn't understand what she was talking about, but said nothing as she climbed back into bed and placed a damp tea bag on each of her puffy eyelids. There was a pile of books on the table beside her, all open, facedown, in some stage of being read. *Ethan Frome* was on top.

I sat on the edge of the bed and looked around. She'd been too busy to do much to the pit. But she had put down round pieces of faux granite linoleum on the packed dirt floor from the bed to the tub, from the tub to the kitchen corner, from the kitchen corner to the makeshift closet. Kind of like a garden path. She'd cleaned what was cleanable and filled the place with flowers and books. Lots of books.

Today the room was dim, the linoleum was askew, and the flowers were dead.

"Are you sick?" I asked. "Johnny Ferris said you're meant to be at a *Harper's Bazaar* shoot this morning and Clementine is — "

"Really pissed off." She sighed profoundly and turned her head to the wall.

I patted her foot under the blanket. I'd never touched her before — except when we first shook hands.

By the way, I look like a regular guy. I'm tall enough, stay in shape, and have all my hair. I've got a chipped tooth from where my mother threw me into a table once, and gray eyes. Women like me. The ones who understand sex guess my story pretty fast, or sometimes I tell them. Others never understand why I don't call them back or ask them out. That's their problem.

Miranda must have known, although I never identified Malone by gender in the brief history I gave her.

Pete, seeing, smelling, or sensing me so close to his mistress, growled from somewhere in the shadows.

"Shut up, Pete," Miranda said into her pillow, and the growling stopped.

Touching even her foot had an unsettling effect on me, which I tried to ignore. Here I'd spent my entire life coming to terms with being a fag only to feel, if not exactly turned on, then moved, by a beautiful young girl.

She began to cry — first silently, but soon big gulping sobs shook her shoulders under the wrinkled sheet and ratty blanket. I held onto her ankle like a lifeline — then moved up the bed, not knowing what to do next. Not knowing where this pain of hers was coming from or how to stop it.

She sat up, and as she did, the shawl she'd wrapped around herself fell away, revealing bare shoulders and a nightgown thin as tissue. Even her pale nipples were on view through the transparent fabric; but only for an instant. She put her arms around me — and I held her tight. Then I kissed her. Oh God, she smelled like rain. I think at that moment my soul could have left my body — floated up and away in a golden cloud, if it hadn't been anchored by a stone-stiff cock on the verge of coming right there in my pants.

This was bizarre. I had never kissed a grown-up woman before. My heterosexual experience stopped with spin the bottle.

The kiss ended, but her tears didn't. I put my hand in my lap, surreptitiously pushing at my penis like it was a nagging puppy. She set her hand lightly on my hand.

"It's okay," she said.

"I'm sorry," I said. "Do you feel like telling me what's wrong?"

She moved away from me, put her feet on the floor and her head in her hands.

"I feel," she said, "I feel like in a storm, when the lights go out . . ."

She started crying and laughing at the same time.

"It's the weather," she said.

"The weather," I repeated like a fool.

"I mean this happens to me every fall. When the days get shorter, I start feeling bad. When they get really short, I feel like total shit. I cry all the time and I can't sleep and I can't eat and I think . . ."

"What?"

". . . I think nothing's any good; nothing's ever going to work out. This time I think here's my chance and I'm going to blow it."

"But everything's been working out from the minute you got to New York," I said. "You know how hard it is to get any work at all, let alone with Clementine. You know what the competition is . . . I'd say you've been pretty lucky."

"This sounds so stupid," she said. "I know the stuff you said's true, but I feel bad anyhow: I can't help it. It's like the lights really *are* out and I can't see straight in the dark. And I'm so scared if I let up for a day or a week, everything'll be over and I'll be dirt poor my whole life. But then I get disgusted with myself because what I do is a lie. Put this shit on your face and you'll look like me."

"I don't think anybody," I said, "would actually believe they could look like you under any circumstances."

"But suppose," she said, "I did make some forty-or-fifty-year-old woman think she could have twenty-year-old skin. Or how about buy this jacket and the old man'll come home again . . ."

As I considered and rejected giving a brief lecture on commerce, cynicism, and the notion of the objective correlative, her eyes filled up with silver tears.

"When the lights go out," she said, "the bad feeling just takes over, and it always gets worse in November and December. Today I was thinking about Thanksgiving and being alone . . ."

The sobs began again.

"Is that it?" I asked. "The whole thing? I mean, you're not sick then — not hurt?"

"That's it."

"When do the lights go back on?" I asked. "Do you get better in the spring?"

"Sooner than that," she said. "I start feeling better on December twenty-first."

"You can predict the exact date?"

"Sure. It's the shortest day of the year. Right afterwards, little by little, the days get longer. By February, they're really long — February's much better than, say, October, because even if there's exactly the same amount of light, the days are getting shorter in October and they're getting longer in February."

"Miranda, you're depressed."

"Everybody in New York's depressed."

"No," I said. "I mean you're officially depressed — *clinically* depressed."

"Well you don't have to sound so happy about it."

"I'm not *happy* about it — but I am relieved it's not some weird thing nobody ever heard of. There's a name for what you've got — I know other people who have it too. I've read about it — it *is* about the light."

"Like I told you," said Miranda.

I started to run around flipping switches. Just what she needs, I thought, a cellar to live in.

"You've got to keep all of these *on*," I said. "And get rid of *Ethan Frome*."

"Clementine said it was the best book she ever read."

"Trust me on this," I said. "Read it in the spring. And as far as Thanksgiving's concerned, just plan to spend it with me."

"What are you going to do?" she asked.

"Shit if I know."

We both laughed, and for that instant the darkness disappeared.

•   •   •

I didn't see this happen, but like Clark Kent, Miranda somehow transformed herself, because according to my now-deceased friend Perruchio the stylist, when she finally made it to work that morning, she was filled with energy and looking great.

The usual crowd, from the famous photographer to the seamstress's assistant, was flapping around a large studio trying to get back on the schedule that Miranda's tardiness had disrupted.

But with the shoot finally well under way and moving smoothly, a pipe broke, sending cascades of water onto the floor from above. The garmentos went wild, and work stopped again while somebody summoned a plumber, who appeared miraculously not only the same day but in less than thirty minutes.

According to my friend Perruchio, Miranda hated her makeup, which she said made her look like the tail end of hard times. So while the lensman and the makeup man were having a line in the loo, Miranda scrubbed her face, removed a couturier bustier (said it was choking her) from under her diaphanous shirt, and stood on the plumber's shoulders like a barrel-rider while Sally Gall, a rock photographer who was passing by to see her boyfriend, fired off several rolls of film.

The *Harper's* editor, Cat Kelly, recently arrived from London, took quite a risk when she nixed the pictures taken by her big-bucks contract photographer and went with one of Gall's shots for the cover. That issue of the magazine was banned from the Bible Belt — but it leapt off the stands everywhere else. People (at least those who think about such things) still talk about Miranda's cover being the pivotal factor in establishing Kelly as a permanent presence on the American fashion scene.

● ● ●

The night before Thanksgiving, Miranda got home from work around ten, and because the wide avenues of Hell's Kitchen are, if not menacing, at least desolate, I offered to go along when she took Pete out.

A high wind came up as we walked the turf once ruled by Irish street gangs like the Hudson Dusters and Battle Row Annie's Ladies Social and Athletic Club. At that time, herds of roving pigs served as a primitive method of, shall we say, human waste removal.

Resisting gentrification, the neighborhood hasn't changed so much over the years. The Hudson Dusters and the pigs are long gone, but we still have slums and the slums still house immigrant families. The Irish have moved on, and now the people tend to be West Indian, Puerto Rican, Filipino, or Greek. Though the same edginess has been in the air every day for a hundred years, the police aren't afraid to come around anymore. They're simply too busy, too overworked. Unfortunately, misery and poverty abide, and we could probably still use a few roving pigs.

Miranda wanted to know what everything was, including a building with a facade of polychromatic brick, and another with arched

ironwork and crumbling fishscale slate. I couldn't say, though I remember pointing out the local firehouse and a couple of abandoned
piano factories.

Hell's Kitchen used to be the animal butchering center of the city,
so there are a number of ancient slaughterhouses around. When I pass
them, I just walk a little faster, like I would near a cemetery. Therefore
I picked up the pace when we approached the nearby abattoir. Former
abattoir; it's renovated. But like an old athlete with muscle memory (I
mean a quarterback's arm *never* forgets how to throw, even if the guy
attached to it is eighty and gaga), an old slaughterhouse can never
shake off the memory of blood.

"These streets are always empty," Miranda said as we headed
toward home after Pete did his doggy business.

"I guess so," I said. "If you don't count the pimps, hookers, and
junkies. Plus there aren't any subway stops."

"I like the space," she said. "You can see what's coming."

I wish.

•   •   •

Thanksgiving Day slid in on icy rain that turned to sleet by afternoon.
At two, I saw Miranda go out running with a shiny slicker over her
sweatsuit. Pete trotted beside her in derogation of the leash law, as
usual.

At two-thirty, craving a Bloody Mary, I dropped by The Shamrock,
which stays open three hundred and sixty-five days a year.

Ben the bartender is a former wrestler. He's short on both charm
and conversation, which suits me fine. His beady obsidian eyes miss
very little, so he couldn't have failed to notice Juliana the bag lady
scurrying into the restroom one step ahead of the Salvation Army or
the Soup Troop or some other do-gooders. Maybe the holiday spirit
had got hold of old Ben that day, because in an uncharacteristic
gesture of generosity, he claimed not to have seen her and shooed the
Good Samaritans out. As I pretended to read the *New York Times,* he
surreptitiously placed a double shot of Harvey's Bristol Creme at the
end of the bar. Eventually, Juliana ambled out of the bathroom,
slugged down her drink, and said, "Cranberry Crown," on her way to
the door. I imagine that meant thank-you-and-Happy-Thanksgiving,

though I had long before stopped trying to interpret her racetrack gibberish. And so had Ben, who ignored her departure but snapped to as I ordered another Bloody Mary.

Around four, I banged at Miranda's door and was unpleasantly surprised when that dirtbag Mark Douglas opened it. His long thin hair was pulled back from a high forehead in a skanky ponytail. Despite the cold, his shirt was open down to the fourth button, revealing a collection of tacky gold chains and medals against the soft flesh of his chest. To complete the biker-hairstylist look, he wore skintight leather pants with an embarrassingly huge bulge in front, created no doubt, in the matador manner: lots of wadded-up Kleenex.

"Hi Dave," he said.

He was leaning against the frame, blocking the doorway.

"Hi Mark."

His presence was as repellent to me as the hand he proffered, with nails and cuticles bitten to shreds. I shook his hand as briefly as possible.

"Hey, the manhole inspector is here," he yelled over his shoulder. "What do you want?" he asked, his proprietary smile totally inappropriate and unnerving.

"He's here to pick me up," Miranda called. She was standing at her little sink, mostly hidden by the Chinese screen, where, oddly, she was washing dishes.

"For Thanksgiving dinner," I added.

Looking back at the screen, Mark Douglas acted as though I were invisible.

"You're going out with *him?*" he asked.

"That's right," she said.

"Yeah, well," was his comment.

He stood motionless for a moment, confused. Then picked up his snakeskin jacket and yellow silk scarf.

"Catch you later babe," he drawled.

I thought, *God.*

He waited another long moment for a response that was not forthcoming before pushing past me through the doorway.

"He's gone," I called, and Miranda turned from the sink, where I realized she'd been more hiding than working. She stuck her finger in her mouth to make a gagging gesture.

"What an asshole," I said.

"Did you see his *pants?*" she asked.

"You mean . . ."

"*Yes,*" she said. "This freak told me his buildings are just a side-line. Said he's actually a producer and asked me to be in one of his films."

"If he's a producer, I'm Marie of Romania."

"David, I might be only eighteen, but I'm not *dumb*. I told you what he said, not what I believe."

"I thought you were nineteen."

"I was." She smiled. "Now I'm eighteen."

"So I missed your birthday."

"That's right," she said, giving me a little poke with her elbow. "All the girls in the business are so young I figured I needed a little extra time to catch up, so I told Clementine I was eighteen."

"You lied to a woman who's famous for being able to tell just by *eyeballing* whether a model is five ten or five ten and a quarter — and she believed you?"

"Why wouldn't she? I gave her a phony birth certificate along with my portfolio — sort of stuck it in there with some clippings and a letter from the student film guy."

"Subtle," I said. "How'd you get a phony birth certificate good enough to hustle a hustler like Clementine?"

"You learn stuff like that at Noah's Ark."

I raised my eyebrows, preparing to ask the obvious question. But she started running her fingers through her hair the way she did sometimes when she was uncomfortable, and I backed off.

"Let's go," I said.

"I'm ready," she said as she slipped on her shoes and grabbed her coat.

"Bye Pete you vicious guard dog," she called, and blew him a kiss before double-locking the door.

2

· · ·

"I'M GLAD it's raining," Miranda said in the taxi over to Larry Owen's townhouse on Sutton Square. "I'd feel weird sitting around indoors eating on a pretty day."

"Yeah," I said. "Rain's good."

I knew I was acting antsy because I wanted to avoid talking about the unavoidable. Miranda gazed out the window quietly. I'd learned over time that she possessed finely tuned intuitive antennae. She understood that the deepest feeling is often shown in silence — or at least restraint.

And, as I mentioned before, she probably guessed about me, but still, I had to say it. In words.

"Miranda, remember that person I told you about who left me for somebody else."

"Uh huh."

"It's a guy."

"I know."

I had the oddest sense. I'm not sure if I was relieved because I didn't need to explain or defend — or hurt because maybe she could tell by kissing me — maybe there was something strange about the way I did it.

"How'd you know?" I flashed on the loudmouth bigot Dark Mouglas.

She shrugged.

"It was just a feeling," she said. "But I don't care about that stuff. You're my friend." She took my hand. "And you kiss great."

I had wanted her affirmation, and I was glad to get it. But I knew down in the darkest, most secret part of my mind — the part I only see in dreams — that this girl was a onetime thing. A gift the fates allowed; the solitary exception.

As our cab reached the corner of Sutton Square, I asked the driver to let us out so I'd have the better part of a block to give Miranda some background on the group we were about to encounter.

Larry Owen, our host, possessed luck, brains, and balls in that order. The producer of television sitcoms and suspensors, he had had at least one show in the top ten for the last fifteen years. This astonishing record brought him not only millions and millions of dollars, but the ability to behave egregiously and with impunity. All the stories from disgruntled employees about broken promises and unpaid health benefits, the plagiarism suits, the former friends, and the bitter ex-wives fueled the gossip machine and fed his ego.

His present wife, Patrice Wentworth Owen, and I met in another life when we both first came to New York and waited tables at Antonio's Tequila Tavern, a Mafia money-laundering operation that was eventually torched. The tavern vanished from memory as quickly and absolutely as did Patti Ann Woznitski, the ugly duckling from whom the swan, Patrice, emerged.

She used to be chubby and plain (not a good combination) with that unfortunate translucent skin, less than enhanced by pale brown hair, invisible eyelashes, and a smattering of freckles. Except for a weak chin, her face was okay, with reasonably regular features, so a clever plastic surgeon didn't need to start from scratch.

Patti did have irresistible energy. And her smart southern mouth was tempered by a certain sweetness. The combination generated what appeared to be charm and warmth. Therefore she made a lot of friends. Mostly men who gave her money after they slept with them. This was not, she pointed out to me at the time, like turning tricks, because she really liked these guys and why accept silly, useless gifts when what she needed was cash.

She left the tavern for good with Vincent Delfontaine, a Teamsters official who wore bespoke suits and a .38 snubnose strapped to his ankle. The fact that Delfontaine's wife, Angelica, was the daughter of

Harry the Hose Pagano, kept him married but did not prevent him from giving Patti a big allowance and setting her up in an East Eighties high-rise.

When Delfontaine got five to fifteen at Danbury (the last time we'd bumped into each other, at Bloomingdale's, Patti insisted he was *totally innocent* of those racketeering charges), she visited him on the third Thursday of every month. His wife, Angelica, visited on the first Thursday.

In all her spare time, Patti became intimately acquainted with silicone. She strengthened her chin, debagged her eyes, erased every tiny line in her face, and hiked up her newly enlarged breasts. Then she switched her hair from country mouse to city blond, hired a personal trainer, and took elocution lessons in an attempt to replace an incomprehensible Mississippi accent with something closer to English.

It was ultimately lucky, I suppose, for Patti that Angelica, in an unusual burst of originality, dropped by Danbury on the wrong Thursday. Her high spirits (she was en route to the opening of a new Loehmann's) were chilled when she learned that her husband had already seen his one visitor for the day — and frozen when she heard the visitor's description. In short order, Delfontaine was discovered bound, gagged, and chained to his bunk, with the middle finger of each hand broken and a humming dildo shoved up his ass.

Patti returned home after a pleasant afternoon at Bergdorf's to find her apartment padlocked and an eviction notice from the New York County sheriff's office taped to the lock.

But Patti's luck hadn't gone entirely bad. The stewardess who lived next door subscribed to *Forbes* magazine, which she studied religiously so she could recognize powerful CEOs as they settled down in the first-class cabin. At this point in her career, Patti already knew that only hirelings flew commercial. Serious money meant having your own G2. Naturally she didn't share this insight with her neighbor, who kept searching *Forbes* for Mr. Right-Wing.

Nevertheless, on her way to temporary quarters at the Alray Hotel, Patti stole from the doormat an issue featuring America's hundred most powerful businessmen. Number eighty-two was Larry Owen, who listed a brisk walk across Central Park as one of his daily rituals. You don't have to be an astrophysicist to figure out what happened next.

On their first date, Larry invited Patti to the Sutton Square house so he could show off his art and antiques. Evidently, she anesthetized herself sufficiently with Larry's favorite drink, the old-fashioned (indeed, nobody's ordered rye since the end of World War II), to avoid noticing the producer's shiny bald head, thick eyeglasses, and bulbous nose.

After giving her a quick tour of his garden, featuring a hothouse and a lap pool, Larry took Patti to dinner at "21," where she was the youngest person in the room by several decades. Over the first course — double portions of beluga caviar nestled luxuriously in glistening beds of crushed ice — Larry went onto autopilot, intoning his stock questions. The boring bridge to bed, otherwise known as conversation with these girls, certainly never interested him.

However, when Larry asked Patti what she wanted most from life, instead of one of the usual ho-hum answers like happiness, true love, or a really *interesting* job in television, Miss Woznitski-Wentworth replied with an ingenuous smile: "Five hundred thousand dollars, tax-free."

Larry Owen laughed so hard Walter the maître d' thought he was having a heart attack, and the headwaiter went on Heimlich alert.

A month later, Larry Owen, then sixty-two years old, announced his third marriage in Roland Tarbell's column (Malone's paramour, the aging gossipist). When Larry introduced Patti to his friends and sycophants, she was, certainly in his bespectacled eyes, and thus for all time, the beautiful, brilliantly amusing Patrice Wentworth of the Mississippi Delta Wentworths — landed gentry, recently impoverished. After all, what did Larry Owen (né Oscar Lipshitz) know from cotton plantations. All he needed to know (or so he thought until events caused a calamitous reversal) was the Golden Rule: He who has the gold, rules. He loved that tired old joke so much he created a sitcom around it, and that is how Malone first wove himself into the complicated tapestry of Miranda's story.

Considering the money these guys make, you'd think they could create a better premise than billionaire-amnesiac-running-away-from-crime-he-didn't-commit. On the other hand, the networks did get into a bidding war over the project, so impressed were they with how incredibly clever it was to recast such interesting material and to entirely redefine the sitcom drama. One of Larry's writers suggested that *situation* had theretofore meant the *same* situation: like the living rooms of Ralph and Alice, Lucy and Desi, Archie and Edith. Like the bar in Boston, the condo in Florida, and the Nantucket airport. Stag-fucking-nant, man.

Since none of the network execs are any older than I am — and even I only got "picaresque" right on the final because it was multiple choice — they thought they had something really new on their hands and committed to thirteen episodes.

Enter Malone with Roland Tarbell, who pranced him around one of Larry and Patti's famous ratfuck parties like a new pony. Naturally, Patti spotted him. Malone is very good looking, with pouty, sexy lips, an easy slouch, and a slow, silky voice. Unfortunately, I'm forced to confess, the operative word here is slow.

Patti wanted to sleep with him until she found out he was A) stupid, and B) gay. It took several trumped-up dinners for this information to rear up and smack Patti, who, in spite of her vast and ever-growing skill, turns temporarily brain-dead at the thought of anything but a self-induced orgasm. No, I'm not under the bed watching as she blows Larry every Saturday night and Sunday morning — but some things don't change as easily as the spelling of Woznitski.

Tarbell suggested to Larry that Malone would be good on one of his shows. Then Malone got lucky. And good luck, like happy families, is always the same.

Tarbell didn't fare quite so well. Malone threw him over for Louis-Michel, the sous-chef whom the Owens had recently hired straight from the Deauville estate of one of France's wealthiest families. His dazzling references somehow neglected to mention that his job had been feeding the estate dogs. The house dogs as well as the outdoor dogs. Like everyone else, Louis-Michel was full of shit. Dogshit in this case.

Furious, Tarbell decided to stay on the good side of both Malone and Owen. For the time being. Owen was rich and Malone could become famous. Should Malone flop, however, Tarbell could (and would) destroy him. Enormous patience, more than anything, is required to exact the wild justice of revenge.

• • •

So Happy Thanksgiving. Miranda and I had reached the front door of Larry Owen's townhouse. Why were we there? Because homophobia has always been rampant and rabid, and Malone the queer had been extinguished by Malone the stud. When he phoned to invite me for the holiday feast, he explained the transition.

On the day Malone signed his contract with Big O Productions, Larry Owen invited Malone into his large, dark, wombesque office and instructed him to lock the door. Malone, ever a one-note thinker, hadn't figured the producer for a fairy. Larry stood up behind his long, empty Biedermeier desk, unzipped his baggy Versace pants and pulled out his little dick.

Malone thought, Oh shit. There's always a catch.

Larry pointed to Malone's crotch.

"Take it out," he said.

"Yeah," said Malone, unbuttoning his jeans. "Let the big horse run."

Malone is quite proud of his member. He immediately started to fondle it, so Larry Owen could appreciate its full flowering.

But the producer snorted derisively, confusing Malone. He then reached for something that had to have been attached to the underside of his desk, since the desk was really a table with no drawers.

It was a gun.

Malone wilted.

To amplify the total humiliation of the moment, Malone later discovered that the gun was simply a prop — but what did Leslie Maloney, the pansy from Potsdam, New York, know from guns. Nothing.

Larry Owen smiled.

"Come on over here," he said. "Now put your hand on my cock."

Malone obeyed.

"Okay. Take it away now." The producer zipped up. "That's the last prick you're going to touch while you work for me. The star of *The Golden Rule* is not a cocksucker. If I hear you've taken a ride down the Hershey Highway, your ass is grass. I'll shoot your two-bit balls off with this little gun right here. I'll take back the money I've given you and burn your contract. Fuck your lawyer, fuck your agent, and fuck the cops — I can buy anybody. I want to see your picture in the paper with broads. Now get out of here stud — and don't forget

Thanksgiving dinner at my house. Tradition is very important to Patrice."

What about the cook, and how could Malone get away with diddling him? The answer is that when Patti hired the strapping, strutting Frenchman, she also hired his wife, Celeste, whose heinie he was forever fondling. So who would have guessed? Well, *I* would have guessed, but that's not the point.

The point is, Malone needed a date for Thanksgiving dinner, and love has no pride. Which means in spite of whatever fleeting alternate reality Miranda had created for me, and no matter that Malone had porked the disgusting Tarbell and now got a hard-on just talking about Louis-Michel, I agreed to do as he asked and show up with a girl who was meant to be his date.

• • •

Miranda kissed me on the cheek.

"Love's bad," she said.

"What do you know about love?" I snapped, testy from having confessed my feelings for Malone. It's definitely a lot easier to be a fag than a supplicant.

"Well," she said. "I know nobody ever loves you like you want to be loved."

Zing.

"How do I look?" she asked, doing a quick half turn.

To me, she looked like timelessness in a swirl of winter white. The dress she wore (on loan from her boss, Clementine Sheffield) was actually the color of heavy cream, and made from some swingy material denser than silk, lighter than wool. With her shining silver-blond hair caught up in the back, a single strand of paste pearls that looked real around her neck, and four-inch platform heels fastened by slim straps around her impossibly slim ankles, she was spectacular. And she must have known it.

(As time went by, I noticed that she usually wore all black or all white or a combination of the two. But always solid colors. No stripe, dot, star, or spangle ever interfered. Not one single time.)

I smiled. "You look like shit."

"Good," she said. "I'm going to be perfect for Malone — wait and see. He'll be okay and you'll be happy and I . . ."

"What?"

". . . won't kill myself."

"*Miranda.*"

"Just a joke."

"Some joke."

"Wait one minute," she said, and stopped walking. "All these people here, besides Larry and Patti, I mean Patrice — are they really fancy?"

"Fancy like what?" I asked.

"Like I don't know," she said. "Like high society."

The quaint phrase touched me, and for a second I thought I should get the hell away and save Miranda from the perverse roundelay waiting on the other side of the door. But I already knew that she was too vivid. Whether it was today or next week, Sutton Square or South Street, the old and the terrified as well as the young and the beautiful would be drawn to her. The dice had already been rolled.

"No," I told her. "These people are more like café society."

"What's that?" she asked.

Man, did I feel old.

"A certain columnist named Tarbell said it's like the Atlantic Ocean — good to swim in, but hard to swallow."

Just then, the heavy door swung open and we were greeted by Louis-Michel's smiling, gap-toothed wife, Celeste.

Several dozen guests were ensconced in two spectacular sitting rooms connected by an archway. Both rooms shared a wide-angle view of the East River and my favorite New York City *objet:* a huge Pepsi-Cola sign rising up across the water in red neon. On the floor of one salon, there was an unusual pale, round Aubusson; in the other, an exquisite hundred-and-fifty-year-old Savonnerie. Both rooms had classically ordered *boiserie,* fragile-looking Louis XVI *bergères* scattered around, and taffeta Scalamandré curtains held back by swags. Not to mention massive orchid plants in moss-covered pots and half a dozen large Chinese export birds, each one worth more than any house I've ever lived in.

Along with a few well-known masterpieces, I noticed several life-size Sargent portraits of stunning women. There was endless brocade, velvet, gilt, the discreet tassel here and there — dark, rich wood, and a Bösendorfer piano covered with ornately gleaming silver picture frames. God knows who the people in the photographs actually were: the sad-eyed women in Balenciaga gowns, the men on polo ponies, the elegant old fellow in a frock coat (an ambassador? a royal?) bending to kiss the hand of a tiny child with ringlets and a dotted swiss pinafore. Patti even had a photo of an elderly black woman in a simple suit, with bedroom slippers on her swollen feet, taken in what was obviously someone else's kitchen.

I imagine all this was Patti's idea of what Grandmère Wentworth's manse on the plantation would have been like if there had ever been a Grandmère, a manse, or a plantation. I inhaled deeply, expecting — what? Magnolia-scented candles. But no, there she drew the line and went with the trusty green Rigaud.

Miranda tuned me in again, spookily.

"Did you ever notice," she whispered, "that all rich people's houses smell the same? What makes them smell like this?"

The girl knew everything and nothing.

"David." With two syllables Patti communicated, *façon de parler,* volumes: You-know-my-secrets-and-I'm-terrified-but-your-life-is-worth-wormshit-if-you-open-your-mouth-because-I'm-important-now-and-you're-lucky-to-be-in-this-house-since-you're-not-rich-and-not-famous-but-I'll-open-up-a-two-way-street-take-it-or-leave-it.

"Patrice." Without pride, yes. A hypocrite, no. Or at least not in this case. I liked Patti. She was funny. And I actually understood that she had been too insecure to invite me to her house before this. In her book of life, the gossip columns, I'm nobody. However, I know I'm somebody. Ah, therapy. And the loyal ladies who read my books — the ladies who continue forgiving Cassie, my ageless heroine, and lusting after her brooding lover, Zack.

Kiss. Kiss.

A tiny shadow, quick as a bat's wing and equally dark, swept across Patti's face when I introduced Miranda. Patti was obviously thinking: She's-younger-prettier-thinner-but-I-never-heard-of-her-so-she-must-be-just-a-bimbo-I-can-use-her-at-a-dinner-party-good.

Patti smiled a perfectly symmetrical smile — which looked so much better above a solid chin. Even her teeth seemed whiter.

"You're Malone's friend," she said to Miranda (an insufferable turn of phrase that I loathe, as in: "Ahhh, David — you're Charlotte's son." *Really?* And all this time I thought I was Audrey Hepburn's son").

"I'm wild about Malone," she continued. "Let's go find him."

She linked her arm through mine and in full *droit de la princesse* led us through the small crowd.

"So what are you up to?" she asked me, barely missing a beat before describing her new venture into candle design.

"I really wanted to do something different," she went on. "But Larry hates for me to work."

I felt Miranda's finger poke my back.

But in a perfectly level voice, Miranda said:

"That must be hard — work's so important."

"I *know*," said Patti. "And I've always worked — I couldn't live without it. I have no idea what those women *do* who just do nothing. I mean, I guess they must shop all day."

"I hate to shop," said Miranda.

"Me *too*," from Patti with feeling.

No comment from me.

"What's your favorite book?" asked Miranda.

"Well, let's see . . . my favorite book . . . ," mused Patti.

I wondered idly what she'd come up with, since I happened to know that aside from Tarbell and several other tattletellers, the only things Patti ever read were astrological forecasts in the back of fashion magazines.

"Darling!"

Books would have to wait.

We looked up into one of the most photographed faces in the world. Solveig (as we've known for some time now, instant recognition of a single name, like Madonna or Secretariat, denotes stratospheric success), just twenty-five, had recently retired from a modeling career that started at ten when her Swedish mother and Japanese father sold their house in Kyoto to pay for plane tickets to Paris.

Solveig's new husband, the white-haired, magisterial game-show producer Ned Goodhue, came up to her shoulder. He could have come up to her cooey for all she cared, because (as they used to say along the Borscht Belt) standing on his wallet he was the tallest guy in the room — next to Patti's husband, Larry Owen, that is.

Patti's profound disdain for people of color had evidently disappeared along with her birth certificate. She and Solveig hugged and kissed like long-lost lovers, although they'd met only once previously. Peculiar? Never mind. On this particular party circuit in New York, money was the glue, the yeast, the catalyst; the omnipotent creator of friendships, affairs, marriages, et cetera, and zapper of same. But I digress.

Returning to that stormy Thanksgiving. Introductions were made all around. Waiters passed by with trays of drinks and hors d'oeuvres, Solveig dispensed advice to Miranda, and Ned Goodhue discussed the coming auction of Empress Josephine's jewels with Patti. Malone stood fifteen feet away beside his new boss, Larry Owen, who was involved in an awkward hug with a late arrival, John F. X. Delaney, a writer described in the tabloids, where he most frequently appeared, as hot-young-author-Jack-Delaney. Their embrace was off balance because Delaney held two bottles of 1983 Le Pin in one hand and his girlfriend, Domina Valverde, in the other.

With acetylene blue eyes, and thick fair hair which didn't disguise his black Irish heritage, Delaney, at twenty-nine, was that unusual hybrid: a darling of the literary establishment as well as a presence in the mass market. His easy charm set up the access he needed to exercise a gift he possessed more powerful than the ability to write. He could remember, and record with disarming accuracy, anything he saw or heard. But his gift was not so simple as total recall; not even close.

Jack Delaney perceived the drama of human frailty on an absolutely visceral level. He could sense the uncertainty, anticipate the conflict, feel the pain. Like a surgeon who becomes his own scalpel, he would cut and cut until he reached the dramatic essence he needed for his story. He never traveled far. It wasn't necessary. Every character he created was based on someone he knew. All his friends and lovers, acquaintances and associates, eventually appeared in the pages of his books. Certain of his contemporaries argued that this was a weakness, a fictive incapacity. Delaney occasionally responded from the lecture circuit. All his characters, he insisted, were imaginary, though imagination itself would expire in a vacuum. The friends and lovers were often furious, at first. But in time, they seemed to forget and, soothing themselves with secret thoughts of immortality, they always forgave.

His first novel, *The Wings of Night,* defined a generation. His next, *All She Loves,* while something of a disappointment compared to its predecessor, neither confirmed nor eradicated the second-novel-slump rule with its mixed reviews and fair sales.

Delaney's most recent effort, *Stations of the Cross,* published a few months before Thanksgiving, was a particularly thorough disaster because it had held such great promise. But Delaney appeared undaunted. With *The Wings of Night* he had established, not unlike Burger King, a franchise which, driven by his obvious promotional skills, was in little danger of crumbling. As the latest self-proclaimed incarnation of Scott Fitzgerald, he courted and enjoyed the sort of celebrity usually reserved for minor movie stars. He was famous for his sheer endurance; all-night binges with the boys and sexual escapades with the girls. Many girls.

Domina Valverde provided an excellent example. A Northern Italian beauty and aspiring actress, she was Delaney's current companion. She had grabbed fifteen minutes under the hot global spotlight by shooting and killing her husband, a reckless race car driver and incorrigible philanderer. Indicted in Europe but never convicted, thanks to a clever *crime passionnel* defense and several well-greased palms, she was now slated (at least by Roland Tarbell) to become the second Mrs. Delaney. The first wife — Delaney's high school sweetheart, an overweight, eternally underemployed alimony collector — was boring copy and therefore useless in the columns.

Although his reputation as writer and womanizer was widely known, Delaney was able to keep quiet his forays into the seamier side of this and many other cities. I imagine there are a few innocents left who believe if you simply snort heroin rather than shoot it into your arm, hand, toe, or whatever, you're not a junkie. Labels have never been my cup of tea, but Jack Delaney, driven by an author's guile and an addict's cunning, could score smack in the middle of the Negev at high noon on the first day of Rosh Hashanah.

Success, however, proved a more seductive habit, judging from the clever decision to go public with his addiction and rehabilitation at the very moment *Stations of the Cross* was gathering almost unanimously tepid reviews. He kicked his monkey in the pages of *Women's Wear Daily, Vanity Fair, GQ,* and *Paris Match.* Tales of this victory, also lauded on late-night talk shows, effectively overshadowed the inadequate novel and portrayed Delaney as a hero for having written the book at all.

Also with Delaney was his dear friend Peregrine Behar, the enfant terrible of contemporary British letters. His plump, permanently rosy cheeks and the round spectacles constantly slipping down his nose belied a razor mind. The mind belied a surprisingly generous spirit.

It was rumored (naturally *they* started the rumor) that Delaney and Behar enjoyed a very frequent and fascinating correspondence by fax (a new phenomenon at the time all this took place), which carried the details of their daily lives but, more significantly, clung with almost religious zeal to a single organizing principle: their abiding love of — Women? Philosophy? Politics? Fifteenth-century mystical poets? Florentine art? No. It was that into which Helen threw the drug to eliminate Paris's grief and make him forget all ills. The thing that fires us, inspires us. *Wine,* of course.

These fellows had firmly embraced the concept of waste not, want not — especially as applied to the badinage between two such clever interpreters of contemporary culture. No one had actually read any of the communications, but it was obvious to all who heard talk of this witty epistolary dialogue that there would doubtless be, and sooner rather than later, a book called *The Delaney-Behar Letters, Vol. 1,* subtitled *Wine, Dear Boy, and Truth.*

• • •

The final group to arrive was a trio of actual movie stars who authenticated the stellar circle that had become, at that moment, Patti's desired destination across the room as well as in life. Beyond dirty air, the humble and the grand of New York share very little. We all, however, have honed our peripheral vision to a fare-thee-well and consequently, while staring straight ahead, can spot a famous face a hundred and seventy-nine degrees away on the street, at a cocktail party, or in a restaurant. Some have even made pretended indifference into an art form and are able to carry on one reasonably coherent conversation while listening with hyperacuity to another discussion across a crowded room. So although all eyes were riveted on the three actors, a visitor from out of town (let's say Mars) would not have known.

Henry Garcia and his two sons, Esteban Garcia and Bobby Wilder, were a very striking bunch. Still in his forties, with a touch of gray in his black hair and an Oscar on a bookshelf in his study, Henry was an actor who paid his dues in the theater, worked for scale in low-budget message movies, and lent his name to worthy causes in which he actually believed. His youthful marriage to a gorgeous dancer called Sally Wilder was one of the few Hollywood unions to celebrate a silver anniversary, and his reasonable but not overwhelming success hit just the right key, allowing his peers to like and respect him.

Esteban was a Henry clone; slightly larger, slightly beefier, and probably not as bright. But decent.

Then there's the baby. Little Bobby with the laughing eyes, the sun-streaked hair, the crooked grin. At twenty-three, he was a bigger star than either his father or his brother was or could ever hope to be. His cinematic heritage was more like son of Kevin Costner, grandson of Gary Cooper. Descriptions always included something about his being the kind of guy women want to marry (i.e., want to screw) and men want for their best friend (i.e., also want to screw).

It was irrelevant whether destiny or dumb luck fueled his fame the day he entered Miranda's life. Her adolescence, like that of every other kid in America — rich, poor, educated, illiterate, black, white, or blue — had been informed by Bobby Wilder's bashful smile, first on the hit TV series *Sons of Guns*, where he costarred with Peter Fonda, and then in a trilogy of sci-fi flicks that shocked the movie industry by making box-office history.

I watched Patti disengage from Ned Goodhue; I watched her draw a breath so deep it pushed her new silicone breasts up against her silk charmeuse shirt. I watched her nipples get a hard-on from celebrity proximity. She swept across the sitting room, put her arm around her husband Larry's waist for a millisecond, and then with the attention to protocol of the ambassador to the Court of St. James's and the charming graciousness of the Queen Mum, she greeted the guests. (She didn't get to be hostess here by being stupid.)

First Henry.

"I'm *so* glad you could come. *Poor* Sally — I phoned the hotel a few minutes ago and Esperanza told me this migraine was really a bad one. 'Feíssima,' she said. Please remember to give Sally my love. Now you *must* meet Malone. He's Larry's new secret weapon. Malone, take

Henry right into the kitchen and ask Louis-Michel to make him a special Bloody Bull. Not one from the bar, but one of his own."

Then Delaney. To whom she gave a quick once-over with an almost imperceptible glance before she spoke.

He was dressed in what had become, during the few short years since his ascent to prominence, his trademark white suit. January or July, he always wore white suits. A brief image, straight from Hallmark, swept through my mind: Delaney and Miranda, blond-haired blue-eyed twins stunning in their winter whites, standing in a meadow surrounded by snowcapped mountains towering against the distant sky.

"Jack, you sweet thing," Patti cried. "Look at these bottles of wine. Larry, look at these. Jack, you shouldn't of."

"Oh yes he should," Larry Owen said, seizing the wine.

"Eighty-three was a good year," said Delaney modestly.

"Not as good as '82," said Peregrine Behar.

"You got me there, buddy." Delaney's voice retained a touch of the flat delivery common in the Connecticut valley, where he grew up — Hartford, Connecticut, to be exact — the only child of an insurance company executive and an elementary school teacher. These adoring parents were still in Hartford, but might just as well have lived in Pago Pago, considering the distance Delaney had put between himself and them.

Even people with nothing to hide are forced by New York to reinvent themselves, and for that very reason. What could be more boring and thus embarrassing than a conventional past?

"Larry *adores* '83!" said Patti the oenophile. "Now what's that, you naughty boy."

Patti seemed to be staring at Jack Delaney's crotch.

"Oh this." He flicked at a flat gold oval hanging by a short gold chain from his alligator belt. The word BANG! was engraved on it.

"My cousin gave it to me," he said with a sheepish smile.

Right. The cousin with the swampland in Florida.

Patti, temporarily speechless, was saved by the return of the haughty Domina Valverde, who had moved several feet away from the group to casually wash down what looked, to my hawk eye, like a few tabs of Tenuate with some *aqua still* as she pretended to examine an exquisite Magritte bottle.

"Darling, you look gorgeous," said Patti. "How do you stay so thin. I love your suit — is it Chanel?"

At times like this, my discomfort about being so close to such profound bullshit makes me want to teletransport myself to the moon. I mean, women buy Chanel because if the thing doesn't actually have those ugly gargantuan C's all over it, it might as well have. These wildly expensive, mostly unflattering outfits (the nouveau frock of choice) have redefined the concept of status symbol from Nantucket to Nashville. *So,* if somebody actually *asks* you, 'Is it Chanel,' does she think you're a moron?

"*Yes,*" sings Domina. "Jack gave it to me for an early Christmas present."

So what the fuck do I know. Except that he probably gave it to her as a distraction from his "cousin's" gift — the gold charm hanging from his belt.

Patti signals a passing servant carrying an ornate silver tray filled with glasses.

"Danny, give Miss Valverde a glass of champagne. Thank you."

So much for the glamorous girlfriend. Patti pirouettes around to Henry Garcia's elder son.

"Esteban, you are *so* handsome."

She's talking fast now, because she senses her prize slipping away. She saved the best for last, but for once her timing was off. Bobby Wilder has spotted Miranda.

• • •

Bobby stayed cool. He embraced Solveig the supermodel; she promptly introduced him to Miranda, whose hand he held in both of his for an *inordinate* amount of time. When he finally lowered it like a piece of museum-quality porcelain, Miranda was still gazing directly into his eyes with a certain look that was — depending on where you were coming from — either unnerving or enchanting in its candor, its perspicacity, its blueness. Impressed by a movie star, I thought petulantly. Maybe Miranda wasn't so damn great after all.

So who was I kidding.

• • •

I don't remember much about the rest of the party — it passed in an alcoholic vapor — except for a highlight that in retrospect was an ominous precursor of things to come.

We all sat at small round tables, and dinner was served on Royal Crown Derby china with handmade Georgian silver from London. Waiters in white jackets and gloves poured an adolescent cabernet (Larry didn't get this rich by being generous) into Baccarat glasses, and I grudgingly admit that Malone's new paramour, Louis-Michel, made delicious food. My favorite, the sweet potatoes, were superb. By the way, real men hate sweet potatoes.

After the entrée was cleared and the salad eaten (Patti pays attention and learns: no crass American first course salad for her), and before the dessert, Malone, who tortured me throughout the late afternoon and into the evening by rubbing up against me as he passed — always, it seemed, en route to the *kitchen* — stared deeply into my eyes. It was the old look. I stood up; after all, if I was mistaken, I could just be stretching my legs or going to the loo. But I was right. He stood a moment later and followed me from the room.

My heart was pounding; my cock was getting stiff; it was difficult to breathe — and to walk. As soon as we were out of everyone else's sight, he ran his hand through my hair and whispered that he'd lead the way. He was drunk, he was stoned, his eyes didn't focus, and I didn't care. My cock was fired steel.

Somewhere along the gallery wall he pressed a lavishly carved panel, which looked identical to all the others around it. A secret door popped open and we stepped into a tiny elevator built for one. Hard up against him in the elevator, I thought I would literally explode, but knew waiting held greater pleasures.

"Where're we going?" I struggled to ask.

"Patrice has a studio on the fourth floor," was Malone's hoarse reply.

"Oh," I said, "where she does all her design work. Her candles."

"You got it."

We held each other and giggled. When the elevator stopped on the fourth floor of the townhouse, we emerged onto the thick carpet of a long, dim hall. Off the hall were mostly extra guest rooms.

Patti's studio was at the end of the corridor, with the door ajar. If I hadn't been so turned on I might have heard something, sensed something. But at the time, all my senses were focused on Malone's nearly perfect body.

We burst into the semidarkness of the room, unbuckling as we went — but were stopped like statues in our tracks by the sight of everyone's favorite exemplar of fidelity, Henry Garcia, backed up against the opposite wall with his pants down around his feet. On her knees in front of him with a liplock on his unit was our hostess, Patrice Wentworth Owen.

Our timing was nothing if not perfect, because the very instant we fell upon this scene was the very instant Garcia began to come like a locomotive. Above his grunts and Malone's strangled yelp (he was no doubt thinking about a Smith & Wesson automatic aimed to maim), I managed to blurt:

"Oh God Larry, sorry. Sorry, Patrice."

Malone and I raced across the hall, down the stairway, and into the first open door on the third floor. It was an empty bedroom with an empty dressing room and bathroom attached. We ran into the bathroom and locked the door behind us.

After an hour, we sneaked through the servants' quarters, down the back stairs, and into the main kitchen. All good houses have two kitchens.

I hardly felt a pang even as I left Malone in the clutches of Louis-Michel, who reported, almost to my relief, that Miranda had gone off thirty minutes earlier with Bobby Wilder. Riding the bus on the way home, I read the note she gave to Louis-Michel's wife, Celeste, for me:

Dear David — If you do me a big favor and walk Pete and give him some fresh water and a couple of hot dogs I'll make you a bottle of White Mule. I love you. M.

She did love me. And I loved her.

3
• • •

From Delaney-Behar Correspondence:

Dear Peregrine,

Enjoyed your all too brief visit; hope you had a decent return flight.

Before buying '85 Guigal, check out '85 Hospices de Beaune Cuvée Madeleine-Collignon and '85 Romanée-Conti. Both are hundred-pointers from Parker.

By the way, it's most unattractive of you to start another book so close on the heels of your last. We have names for people who write too many books, and they are: Joyce, Carol, Oates. More importantly, where will this leave me in the race to fame?

I just picked up *Vogue* (for your review, old friend) and noticed that girl we met yesterday. Miranda. She's a beauty. Which reminds me how much I do not want to get married again. Every time I mention my reluctance to Domina (who returns to Italy tomorrow, not a moment too soon) she forgets her English.

Off to Library dinner with Nils; hope he doesn't douse his cigarette in the claret.

Yrs.,

Amory Blaine   28 Nov. New York

———

My dear John Francis Xavier,

Quite right about '85 Hospices de Beaune Cuvée Madeleine-Collignon and '85 Romanée-Conti, extolled on pps. 760 and 776 of Parker's new tome. They do, however, cost more than my car.

Surely you noticed, old fellow, that you've already won the race to fame! But if insecurity still nips at your heels like an underfed pup, you'll be pleased to know I've put aside my latest effort, which was going absolutely nowhere. Now I must find another project to keep Mr. Wolf from the door. Any thoughts?

Miranda and I spoke for a moment over the Tarte des Demoiselles Tatin at Thanksgiving. She is simply the most beautiful girl I've ever seen. Egregious grammar, but quite the little reader. Asked my favorite book, then noted it. Here's an ego-biscuit for you: she's read *Wings* three times.

Generously,

PB   London, 1st December

• • •

Fortunately, I was asleep as dawn crept into our little corner of Hell's Kitchen on stolen Nike hightops. Around noon, however, I heard a bell ringing and discovered to my horror that the exam was over and my blue book was empty. No, that was the dream. But the bell kept ringing. The doorbell. It was the day after Thanksgiving.

Just before I reached the front door, I glanced out my living room window in time to see a long black limo with black glass windows roll away from the curb. No *L* (for Livery) on the plates meant it wasn't rented. Lifetime observers learn these details.

"David — David, open *up!*" The bell-ringer was Miranda, in her white outfit from what seemed like days, weeks ago, not hours. She looked quite cheery.

"Don't tell me," I said. "You're in love."

"Yeah, for sure," she said. "Can I come in?"

"Please."

I bowed as graciously as I could in my old terry cloth robe. She sailed into the room like a duchess and threw herself onto the couch like the teenager she still was.

"Miranda," I said en route to the kitchen, "what is White Mule?"

"It's the same as white lightning," she said. "You know, moon-shine."

I didn't know; in fact I was about as far removed from moonshine as I was from the moon.

"I'll try it," I said.

"You got it," she called.

I'm not sure whether my fanatical need for organization is due to premature middle age, sexual proclivity, or excessive solitude, but naturally, my Krups coffee machine had been programmed to make a pot of French roast and keep it hot. As I poured the brew into my mother's Limoges cups, Miranda settled down comfortably and, without any tasteless encouragement from me, began talking about Bobby Wilder.

". . . Esteban is Henry's favorite; their mother — "

"Sally."

"Yes. She loves Bobby and Esteban equally."

"Fascinating — and what's *her* favorite book?" I muttered from my tiny kitchen.

"What?" she called.

"Nothing," I replied sourly as I carried our coffee back to the living room on a tray. Miranda was now lying on the couch, head hanging over the side, with masses of long hair sweeping the floor. She sat up; looked at me with those dazzling, silver-blue eyes.

"This is dumb," she said. "Why don't you just go ahead and tell me what I said wrong?"

"Aren't you being overly sensitive?"

"Me!" she said. "You're the one who's pissed off."

"I am not," I said.

"Is it about us?" she asked.

"Us?" I said.

"You and me," she said. "You know what I mean."

"I don't know what you mean," I insisted.

She said nothing.

Being coy is unattractive, but frankly I'd have gone for it if I had any talent in that direction. It was hard to explain my feelings, because I didn't understand them myself. I took her hand; I looked at the long, slim fingers, the pretty oval nails.

"I do know what you mean," I said. "And it's not about us — it's just about you and him. I guess I'm worried this guy could hurt you or something. He really is a big star, he probably has women all over the place and he's probably totally narcissistic and — "

"First of all," she interrupted, "I'm not in love with Bobby — I just *met* him — "

"Yeah, love would take at least a week."

"See, there you go again — how come?" she demanded.

"Because," I said, searching my mind, "I feel like your *father* would feel."

What I said surprised me, although I don't know what I expected.

A shadow — subtle as clouds drifting by the moon — passed across her eyes. And in a motion so small and controlled you could easily miss it, she shook her head.

"Not *my* father."

·   ·   ·

Learning certain secrets can give you a shiver of electricity, a frisson of forbidden excitement. Other secrets make your heart sink.

We were having lunch (meaning we bought sandwiches and brought them in to eat with our beer) a little later at The Shamrock, when Miranda told me her father was doing time at Leavenworth.

"He was usually in some jail — but every time they let him out, my mom would get pregnant. One time when he came home she already *was* pregnant. He beat her up good and she lost the baby. And he hates the twins, Wayne and . . ." She paused to sip her beer.

"Let me guess," I said. "Wayne and Dwayne."

"Close," she said. "I guess you got a line on white trash."

Silence was not the perfect refuge, but it was better than any alternative I could think of.

"Wayne and Noreen." She lit a cigarette and inhaled. "They were premature. Born seven months after my dad got out of Marion."

"That happens a lot with twins, doesn't it?"

"I don't know," she said. "Both of them were pretty big."

She smiled.

"Oh," I said.

"I never knew him very well," she went on. "There were so many of us kids wanting attention . . . nobody got much. And he was mean . . . I just didn't know it at first. When you're so little, if your dad hits you all the time, I guess you think that's what dads do. . . ."

"And that's what you thought?"

"Truth is, I didn't," she replied. "Maybe I thought it once. I can't remember. But I do remember figuring something was way wrong where we lived, so I decided I was going to grow up and be different, and I will."

"You already are," I said.

"Not yet," she said. "Not till I get to the top and I get enough money. Then I'll be free."

"Is anyone free," I said. Does anyone but me ever sound like such a flaming asshole.

"Ask the guys in the pen," she said.

Ben the bartender shuffled over and picked up our paper plates.

"Who was that fella you was with last night?" he asked Miranda. "He looked kinda familiar — hard to tell for sure 'cause of the shades. But I seen him someplace — he a hockey player?"

"You saw him on the tube, Ben," I said. "*Sons of Guns.*"

"Oh yeah — Thursday nights. They got reruns now on Channel 15. You like the guy?" he asked Miranda.

She nodded.

"Very interesting." He pulled a hundred-dollar bill out of his apron pocket.

"Guy left this on the bar. I figured he was drunk and thought it was a ten — so if you didn't like him I was gonna keep it — but if you did like him I was gonna keep ten and send the ninety back to him — but now I hear who he is — "

"Meaning loaded," I said.

" — and she likes him — " he said, weighing the situation.

"You get to keep ninety," Miranda interjected, "and give ten to Juliana."

"Another bleedin' heart," he said, taking a quick swipe at our table with his rag.

Having never before heard Ben string so many words together at one time, I grudgingly tipped my hat to the power of television. There was an old set high in the corner by the door. But I was surprised Ben even noticed what was on, because The Shamrock always seemed like a throwback to some other pre-TV era. Unlike the constantly changing downtown club scene, where I never felt comfortable even with friends, The Shamrock (which certainly represented a paradox in my life) stayed the same. It was fine to hang there if you were not a bleeding heart, didn't look or act gay, and knew how to mind your own business, because, among other things, the place fronted a small-time numbers operation and a more sinister loan-sharking racket. I'd heard that Mark Douglas was involved but couldn't see him getting down with the soldiers who worked for the likes of Vincent Delfontaine or Harry the Hose Pagano. Mark Douglas was a total coward. Though, I might add, scared people scare me. Of all this, Miranda knew nothing and in my view her need to know was zero.

We strolled home past the usual taxi garage, repair shop, and loft buildings. Traffic, as always, was moderate, and the few other people walking along the street looked like they'd be grateful for a destination.

"I keep forgetting to ask you why they call this place Hell's Kitchen," Miranda said.

"For one thing," I said, "nobody can remember the new name — "

"Which is?"

"Clinton," I said. "After DeWitt Clinton. He was mayor of New York once, and governor; came from a long line of Clintons in government all the way back to Madison and Jefferson. Ever heard of them?"

"I heard of Thomas Jefferson," she said. "And the governor of Arkansas's name's Clinton — maybe they're all kin."

"Nobody seems to care much about history," I said.

"They sure don't where I come from," she said. "We always used to say too bad Noah didn't miss the boat."

"We wouldn't have any problems."

"Right," she said. "Because we wouldn't have any 'we.' "

"If you believe that stuff," I said.

"Do you?" she asked.

"No," I said.

"Me neither," she said. "But I'm interested in the past, because if you learn what happened before, then you can forget it."

"You mean if you don't know history," I said, missing the point, "you're doomed to repeat it?"

"Not exactly," she said. "What I mean is what Carl Sandburg wrote — "

Too late. She paused because my reflexes were too slow to control the fleeting look of surprise on my face.

"Sorry," I muttered.

"You want to know what Carl Sandburg wrote?"

I nodded.

" 'The past is a bucket of ashes,' " she said. "I like that."

"I don't know . . . ," I said. "I have to think about it. In the meanwhile, can you at least finish telling me about the recent past, like yesterday?"

"Sure." She put her arm through mine and picked up the thread of her unfinished story about all that happened after she and Bobby left the Owens' townhouse on Thanksgiving.

". . . Then he dropped me off and drove straight to the airport. He had to go to Las Vegas — that's where he's filming."

"Think you'll hear from him?"

She smiled a little.

"I saved the best for last," she said.

"Better than the limo?" I asked.

"Much better."

"Better than he took you to the Plaza Athenée and introduced you to his mother?"

"Uh huh."

"Better than he destroyed the camera of the paparazzo who took a picture of him kissing you on the dance floor at Nell's?"

"And then paid for the camera."

"The guy was just doing his job."

Miranda rolled her eyes at my sudden attack of righteous indignation.

"I'm sorry," I said.

Why, I wondered, am I *always* the one who apologizes? How is it that I'm *always* drawn to people who, like Wallis Simpson, never apologize and never explain? The yin/yang interpretation doesn't cut it. I guess I know the answer.

"What's the matter with you now?" Miranda asked, not unkindly.

I sort of shrugged.

"Well if you can't talk, shake a bush."

"I can talk."

"Then talk."

"The truth?"

"If you know the truth," she said.

"I can't say I know the metaphysics of the truth," I said.

"The what?"

"*The Way of Truth,* by Parmenides — P-a-r-m-e-n-i-d-e-s."

She took out her little notebook and entered the title and author.

"You'll do anything to change the subject," she said.

"No," I said. "But the truth is embarrassing. I was just wishing I didn't always feel compelled to apologize and endlessly explain and explain . . ."

"I think," she said, "the only people who don't explain anything are people who don't know anything."

Miranda.

"Are you going to tell me what this best item is you saved for last?" I asked, restored.

"Piss on the past," she said. "Right?"

"Okay."

"This," she said, "is about the future."

"But what *is* it?"

"What're you doing for Christmas?" she asked.

"Oh, the usual," I said. "Psilocyban, Ecstasy, Percodan."

"Too bad," she said, "because Bobby invited me and you to go to Jamaica with him on a private jet and stay in this great big house his family has — "

"God, I don't know — "

"The house comes with a cook, two cooks actually, and a lady who does your laundry, and a lady who irons, and gardeners — "

" — why would he invite me — "

" — and they have hummingbirds and peacocks . . ." She finally glanced at me from the corner of her eye to gauge the effectiveness of her description.

"You think they have any albino peacocks?" I asked.

"Doesn't everybody?"

"Well, in that case . . ."

"Oh good — you're coming. I'm really relieved."

"Relieved?" I asked.

"I mean I'm glad you're coming and I think you'll have a good time — but if the lights go out, you'll understand."

"You didn't tell Bobby?"

"It's hard to talk about feeling like that, like you're underwater — I don't think most people get it. I mean, I don't even get it. And I just met him . . ."

"Don't worry," I said. "I'll be right there."

I did, however, wonder why she worried about being miserable in a warm, bright place like Jamaica. What makes the big difference, I later learned, is the *duration* of light — and winter days in Jamaica aren't significantly longer than winter days in New York. I imagine Miranda's fear came from her own supply of empirical evidence (I mean, Virginia Woolf wasn't even depressed when she put those stones in her pockets and walked into the water — she just sensed the illness approaching) rather than scientific documentation.

"Besides you," Miranda continued, "my one other friend who understands is pretty far away. Most people think somebody like me was born in a barn with the north door open. They say stuff like, 'Just pull yourself together,' or, 'She's faking 'cause she doesn't want to go to work,' or, 'Her family's got the bad blood, remember Kitty's mama — Pow!' "

"Pow?"

"My grandma shot herself; people remember because women don't usually favor guns."

"That's an interesting bit of minutia."

Miranda started digging in her bag.

"You know who Dorothy Parker was, right?" she asked.

"Um hmm."

She pulled her notebook back out, but naturally I had to show off:

" 'Razors pain you;' " I recited, " 'Rivers are damp; / Acids stain you; / And drugs cause cramp; / Guns aren't lawful; / Nooses give; / Gas smells awful; / You might as well live.' "

"David, how did you know?"

"Smart."

Miranda searched my face.

"Plus," I confessed, "it's not exactly an obscure poem."

But I hated that she carried it around with her; such a flimsy little hostage against fortune. Such a dim light against the permanent dark.

"Why'd your grandmother kill herself?"

"I don't know," Miranda said, running a hand through her hair. "I was little, but I remember she was sad all the time ... and one Christmas, she was asking everybody what they'd do if she wasn't around anymore. I remember I said if she took off, I'd go with her, and she starting crying. Couple of days later, she did it. I still wonder why nobody figured out what she was getting at."

"Well *you're* going to be fine," I said. "You *are* fine. I, on the other hand, will definitely expire unless I get some sun, so . . ."

"Jamaica will be great," she said.

I started whistling my entire repertoire of island music, which was, "Down the way where the nights are gay," et cetera, and Miranda danced along beside me to a reggae beat coming from somewhere inside her head.

"What do you think you're on *American Bandstand* or something?"

Mark Douglas was standing in front of our building. He just never got it right. His attempts always caved in on him. I mean, here was this fool in a mink coat over a gaping shirt and absurdly tight pants, coming on to a nineteen-year-old girl with a line about a show that was on TV before even I was born.

"So Mark," said Miranda. "Did you have a good Thanksgiving?"

"Yeah it was fabulous," he said. "You want to come over and I'll shoot some stills? I got wheels."

He motioned with his head toward a Cadillac parked about twenty feet away next to the fire hydrant. While pimps and drug dealers had taken to riding around town in the grayest, most unobtrusive cars available, this idiot had a custom Caddy painted bronze.

"Can't today," Miranda replied. "I'm just about to go for a run, and I have an appointment later." She started walking inside.

"Appointment or *date?*" the landlord demanded.

"Mark," I said.

"Not your business," said Miranda to him.

Ignoring us, he persisted: "Appointment or *date,*" as though it were a matter of life and death. Miranda stopped and frowned.

"You know," she told him. "My old granny used to say a girl is like a gun: don't fool with her. You get my meaning?"

Let's not forget that Granny knew her guns. I glanced at Miranda, who looked back innocently.

"You really scare me," Mark said sarcastically. "I like that."

"You better chill, Mark," said Miranda, undaunted, as she entered the building.

"Cunt," Mark Douglas called after the door closed behind her, then he spun toward me. "Hey I saw her in that limo," he said. "She's a butthole to hang out with rich old farts." He threw his chin up in a ticlike habit he had. "When she could hang out with rich young guys like me."

He laughed too loud and long and I couldn't resist.

"The rich old fart in the limo was twenty-three."

"Shut up, you faggot," he said viciously, stomping toward his bronzed chariot.

Dark Mouglas was always obnoxious and a pain. But his interest in Miranda and the fact that he was watching her gave me a new and eerie feeling. Where had he been when she got out of Bobby Wilder's car? Just walking by? Hiding across the street? Farther away with a telescope? Anything was possible. Including the iceberg of which all this was just the tip.

Back at work twenty minutes later, I decided that Zack would commandeer a helicopter to rescue Cassie from the burning building where she was trapped. Now all I needed to wrap *Midnight Desire* was a way for them to save their child from kidnappers in a Central American jungle before the typhoon struck. Yes, their child. In this, the fifth *Midnight* novel, my readers would discover that all that screwing was not just for fun.

From my desk, I could see Miranda jogging down the street, headed west as always toward the Hudson River, wearing earphones and her pink bandanna. Pete followed apace. I closed my eyes and imagined running along a beach in Jamaica. I imagined an endless horizon and wondered if anyone besides Cassie and Zack had ever seen the elusive green flash that's said to happen from time to time in the tropics as the sun drops into the sea at the end of the day.

When I opened my eyes I caught a glimpse of Mark Douglas's ugly Cadillac, also westbound, trailing a nasty cloud of exhaust.

• • •

From Delaney-Behar Correspondence:

Dear Peregrine,

Watched the sun come up again. Remember Elise the Dutch model? Enough said.

Nils keeps bugging me about the next book but my muses are mutinying. I could really use a big bucks movie deal (might change agents if I don't get some action on this front) or else I'll be TOTALLY tapped out, and fucked up by Domina — the original high-maintenance woman.

Wearily,

H. de Balzac   10 Dec. New York

P.S. Today's the day I leave a bid at Sotheby's for the once-in-a-lifetime 1947 Cheval Blanc. Eat your heart out.

———

My Dear John Francis Xavier,

I applaud a man who drops his bid off at Sotheby's en route to the poorhouse. Do tell the outcome because as you obviously know I'm in awe of the Cheval Blanc.

Yours,

PB   London, 11th December

• • •

In the month or so between Thanksgiving and Christmas, Miranda probably had as many bad days as good days. The bad days came in series and were reflected by her expression, her body language, and her inability to converse. I'm sure she didn't eat or sleep much or regularly, but she kept her appointments and came back and took Pete out before disappearing downstairs.

Since depression is one of the few afflictions from which I am free, I didn't recognize the enormous will and concentration required simply to go to work and walk the dog. I didn't know how to square the upbeat Miranda with the melancholy Miranda, and I kept thinking she wasn't the type. But, of course, I should know better than most — there is no such thing as a type. And, naturally, unable to stifle the officious fussbudget in my soul, I kept bugging her to see a shrink.

These were, if not exactly pre-Prozac days, at least days before everyone polished off a morning dose of Paxil, lithium, baby aspirin, hydrochlorothiazide, zinc, vitamins E, C, and slow-K with four ounces of Special K swimming in fake milk, and a slice of no-fat-no-calorie-no-bread toast with I-don't-believe-it's-butter — just in time to greet the personal trainer.

Give me half a bottle of Valium and a handful of bennies with my coffee and I'll be happy. I know I'm dating myself, but I care not.

Getting back to Miranda. She seemed to believe that fortitude was the only salve for her problem, and God knows, she was strong. But once in a while, when the lights went off, she just couldn't get out of bed; for these infrequent occasions, she and I created her so-called one and only East Coast relative, a mythical Aunt Enid in Amityville — always ailing.

Poor Enid suffered from such disgusting illnesses (like projectile vomiting brought on by ulcerative colitis) that everybody was instantly put off. Would-be suitors, photographers, Johnny Ferris, and even Clementine Sheffield (for Clementine we dreamed up dozens of suppurating bedsores complicated by a raging staphylococcus infection) were stopped cold in their questioning about a missed appointment or an unexplained absence and accepted the idea that Miranda had dashed off to Amityville to nurse Enid.

• • •

New York, need I mention, is a telephone town, and almost everyone I know keeps a second, unlisted line — for love affairs, best friends, and emergencies. These secret numbers are guarded as fiercely as Bogotá's Gold Museum and bestowed with extreme caution, especially in the ritual of let's-call-it-romance.

Back in the days when this story unfolded, fucking was far less personal than A) revealing the existence of Line Two, or B) actually divulging the digits themselves.

I had recently acquired an unpublished number, but since Malone and Miranda were the only ones who knew it, my private line was no busier than a popstand in a snowstorm. Malone called infrequently from California, preferring to torture me with long-distance silence. Miranda always called on Line One; she said she'd use the other number if something urgent ever came up.

Naturally, when my second line rang at four A.M., dragging me from a lavish dream (the details of which escaped, leaving only a sense that it was better than anything I experience in what passes for real life), my immediate thoughts were of disaster. But the voice I heard belonged to an exhilarated Miranda.

"David," she said. "You've read Ernest Hemingway, right?"

"You know what time it is?" (Don't ever believe that only girls turn into their own mothers.)

"No," she said. "But have you read this stuff?"

"Of course I've read it."

"Everything?"

"I don't think I've read every word . . ."

"I'm going to read every word."

"Tonight?"

"Not *tonight*," she said, flying past my sarcasm. "But I just finished *For Whom the Bell Tolls* and I had to tell you . . . I mean, Maria . . . her hair. *Inglés* . . ."

"I know."

"So sad," she said.

"Pilar . . . ," I said.

"Pilar was perfect . . . and the end when he makes them drag Maria back to her horse . . . and she's screaming but they take her away and he waits there by the tree with the submachine gun . . ."

I think she was crying, but I didn't say anything.

". . . I'm going to read *The Sun Also Rises* next."

"Ah yes," I said. "Jake Barnes, Lady Brett, Paris, Pamplona."

"Don't tell me what happens."

"I won't. But maybe you should start at the beginning of the work and read it in order."

"Yeah, that makes sense," she said. "But don't you think I ought to read *The Sun Also Rises* in Paris?"

What would Gertrude Stein have said?

"Paris?"

"I have to go to Paris for a shoot tomorrow — I mean today, in a couple of hours. We'll only be there a day."

"One day?" Hopeless.

"That's what Clementine told us. We're flying on the Concorde."

"I'll feed Pete."

"Thanks." She paused. Then: "David . . ."

"Yes, Miranda."

"What's the Concorde?"

Around midafternoon, after Miranda had left for Paris, Zack was assembling a group of friends from the old days when he was a mercenary, for one last mission into the jungle to retrieve his and Cassie's child. Since this was the penultimate scene in the book, and I knew where I was going, I allowed myself the luxury of monitoring my answering machine as I worked. Maybe an interesting diversion for the evening would present itself. Stranger things have happened.

Mrs. Wentworth Owen was not what or who I had in mind.

"David, Patrice here . . ."

Patrice here? Is she British now?

". . . I know you're listening, so pick up."

Patti Ann Woznitski, scam artist extraordinaire, could, as a matter of routine projection, root out just about anything tricky — from the benign, like listening in on a phone machine, to the byzantine, like, let's say, perjury. I almost didn't answer just to make a point. Almost. But her pleasant tone made me curious; it communicated either pardon for or indifference to Malone's and my stumbling onto her smarmy little scene with Henry Garcia during Thanksgiving dinner.

"Hi, Patrice — how's it going?"

"Fine. How 'bout you?"

"All right, thanks. What's happening?"

"Oh nothing special — I was just thinking of you."

Uh huh.

"Well," I said. "I'm almost finished with another book."

"That's wonderful, I've been meaning to read them."

She's warming up.

"I'll send you a set."

"Oh, don't bother," she said. "I'll get someone to run out and buy them. But I *would* like you to sign them for me."

Now she's ready.

"Sure, anytime."

"Tomorrow'd be good for me."

"Okay," I said.

Here comes the kicker.

"How's your friend Miranda? Every time I pick up a magazine I see her picture."

The fact is, although Miranda's career took off with unprecedented speed, the fashion magazines where she did most of her work operated on a three-month lead time. Therefore Miranda hadn't actually appeared in that many places, so Patti must have been paying close attention.

"She's doing very well," I said.

"Flavor of the month," Patti replied.

"I hope it lasts longer than that."

"Definitely," Patti said. "I hear she's involved with Bobby Wilder."

"I guess."

"Well," Patti went on, "I was thinking we could all do something tomorrow night — after you sign your books — like dinner. My treat. Somewhere low-key; Elaine's maybe."

Elaine's Restaurant was about as low-key as a plane crash.

"Sounds good, Patrice," I said. "But Miranda's in Paris and Bobby's in Las Vegas."

"When will she be back?"

"Tomorrow afternoon I think."

"Then she'll have enough time to pull herself together — she's only twelve years old so how tired can she be. And Bobby's got a couple of days off because his director's mother-in-law died and the funeral's in North Carolina. My dear husband says the director probably killed her himself — that's how his mind works."

"How is your husband?" I asked.

"Oh Larry's the same. Fabulous. He's in L.A. He has very high hopes for *The Golden Rule*. Says everybody loves Malone. The man is a genius."

"Malone?" I asked.

"I see you haven't changed," she said.

"Neither have you."

That'll piss her off.

"So we're on for tomorrow night?" she said.

"Why not?"

"Good," she said. "Come to my house around eight-thirty, and we'll go from there. Maybe I'll invite one or two more people to join us."

The whole point.

"Okay, see you tomorrow," I said and rang off.

•   •   •

From Delaney-Behar Correspondence:

Dear Peregrine,

Woke this A.M. dreaming of 1959 La Tâche, which is all the exchequer will allow if I don't get the cash flowing soon.

Running to *Paris Review* benefit. Why doesn't Plimpton ask me to be a contributing editor? Everybody else on earth is. Morton's a contributing editor, for God's sake — even *Nils* is.

More later,

H. Caulfield   12 Dec. New York

P.S. This wine buying is a sickness.

My dear Jack,

Wine buying is a sickness from which I have no intention of recovering; hence I have sold my soul to the Tinseltown Philistines (sounds like one of those teams you follow so zealously) who want to hire this weary Brit to write something "literary." Do you suppose they mean "liter*ate*"?

As always,

PB   London, 13th December

P.S. Are you still planning Christmas in Milan?

Dear Peregrine,

So which team are you playing for? And what's the game? Dying for details. Hope you held out for six figures, peanuts (or as they would say, bupkes) to the Left Coast Vulgarians. Advise of your schedule (they'll want meetings) so I can plan menus and inspect the cellar.

Enviously,

E. Hemingway   13 Dec. New York

My dear JFX,

The group is Norstar. The project is nothing more than reducing *Anna Karenina* to 120 pages, setting it in the present and "rethinking" the resolution. Schedule not yet done.

Dashing to Ed and Carol with magnificent '61 Gruaud-Larose in hand.

Hastily,

PB   London, 15th December

•   •   •

I was at the gym when Miranda returned from Paris and left a bottle of Stoli from the duty-free shop and a leather daybook courtesy of

Concorde inside my door. I phoned to thank her for the gifts (I was quite touched, really) and to tell her Pete had been a pleasure. She seemed fresh as mint.

"So how was it?" I asked.

"Well for one thing," she said, "*The Sun Also Rises* is the best book I've ever read in my life."

"I meant Paris, Miranda."

"You know," she said. "I haven't been to very many cities . . . yet. But Paris is my favorite — and it always will be."

"Good choice," I said, glad she couldn't see me smile. "So what did you do?"

"Mostly worked — they shot us at the Opéra and at George Cinq, and afterwards I smoked right over to the Sorbonne, and to Notre Dame — I kept thinking about poor old Quasimodo up there in the bell tower. I saw those gardens . . ."

"The Tuileries."

". . . uh huh, and where they buried Napoleon, and I loved the Metro except it made me think of poor what's-his-name on the run just for a loaf of bread."

"Jean Valjean." I wondered who turned her on to Victor Hugo and when.

"Right."

"How'd you get the time to do all this?" I asked.

"Jean Pagliuso was the photographer," Miranda said.

I had learned from the beginning that patience was its own reward with Miranda, as the logic always kicked in . . .

"And he took you around the city?"

"No, David — she's a *woman* — "

. . . sooner or later.

" — so she understood how I was dying to see Paris and she worked really fast."

Miranda's very personal logic.

"What'd you think of the people?" I asked, remembering my own awkward attempt at communicating my schoolboy French to random members of an intrinsically sophisticated Parisian populace, who invariably responded in English.

"They were okay," she said, "but none of them are ever going to drown in a bathtub. I did have this one cab driver who told me an amazing story."

"About?"

"About the fanciest people in Paris and a big charity bazaar they gave a hundred years ago."

"So what happened?"

"Just wait," she said. "They had all these booths where the fashionable ladies were selling knickknacks or whatever to the fashionable men. Suddenly a fire broke out and because all the stalls were covered with paper decorations they went up in flames. There was only one door going out and everybody stampeded."

"This is making me claustrophobic," I said.

"Do you want to hear the rest?" she asked.

"Of course," I replied.

"So," she continued, "the whole thing turned into a nightmare, with hysterical people trampling each other. A lot of them burned to death, like the queen or empress of Austria's sister. . . . After the fire, the police searched for dead bodies all night, and by morning they'd found a hundred and twenty-seven victims."

"God," I said. "What a horrible way to die."

"That's not the end," she said. "When people started talking about the fire, there wasn't a single solitary man in Paris who'd admit he'd been at the bazaar — "

Miranda was interrupted by banging at her door loud enough to hear on the phone and through my floor, meaning whoever it was had gotten past the building's outer entrance.

"Somebody's knocking," she said. "I better see — "

"Is that the end of the story?" I asked.

"Wait one second," she called to whoever it was at the door. Then, raising her voice above continuing noise: "*Guess why not one single man in Paris would say he'd been there?*"

"*Why?*" I asked as the banging became pounding.

"*Because all the victims were WOMEN,*" she yelled into the phone. Then the pounding stopped. "Somebody's still out there and that's weird, David. Nobody rang — I know because Dark Mouglas finally fixed the bell. I'm going to take a look. Did they ring your apartment?"

"No," I said, checking the empty street. "I'll come down."

"You don't have to, I've got Pete . . ."

Obviously. Pete's barking increased the general noise level but didn't deter whoever was pounding at Miranda's door again.

". . . and I can take care of myself," she added as I hung up on her.

I ran barefoot across the hall and down the dark stairs, silently cursing our landlord for failing yet again to repair the overhead light, only to find none other than Dark Mouglas himself standing at Miranda's door.

"What the hell do *you* want?" he said by way of greeting.

"How about a new light for the stairs?"

"These are *her* stairs, not yours, butthole," he said.

"So it's okay if *she* breaks *her* neck."

"I'll break *your* fucking neck, you piece of shit — I ought to kick your ass out of here — "

"David," Miranda called above Pete's nonstop barking.

"It's okay, Miranda," I called back, "it's only Mark Douglas."

I may not be the sultan of self-esteem, but I don't like to be mistreated either.

He twisted toward me, eyes bugging out.

"You cocksucking asswipe," he yelled. "You jerkoff piece of — "

Miranda opened the door.

"Mark," she said calmly, "you surprised me — I mean, you didn't buzz."

"Scared you, huh." Pleased with himself, he changed moods like an Attention Deprived Syndrome child, and smiled, showing that he'd recently lost an upper side tooth.

"I've got a passkey." He held the key up proudly, as though possessing it were an accomplishment. Any feelings I ever had toward this guy shifted regularly from loathing to pity to scorn.

"I'd appreciate if you call first," Miranda said. "Besides, I might not be here and then you'd be wasting the trip over."

"I always know when you're here babe," Mark said.

"How do you know?" Miranda asked.

"I got my ways. I got a . . . sixth sense. So you gonna let me in or what. I wanta talk something over with you."

"What do you want to talk about?" she asked.

He looked at me, clearly annoyed, but I stood my ground, and he moved closer to Miranda's doorway.

"Much as I'd hate to do this sweetheart," he said, "I got a cousin who needs a place to live — so I might hafta throw you out."

"I've got a lease," Miranda said.

"Yeah," the landlord shrugged. "A piece of paper. That's what I want talk about — *alone*."

He turned theatrically.

"Take a hike, Dave," he said.

Miranda caught my eye and nodded imperceptibly.

"Nice seeing you, Mark," I said, looking at his latest pair of crotch enhancers. "You look fan*tas*tic, I *love* your pants."

So I'm childish on top of everything else. Life holds few enough little pleasures, don't you know.

Concentrating on work was hard, with Mark Douglas downstairs obviously using his position as owner of the building to hit on Miranda. But after fewer than five minutes at my desk, I saw him out on the street, walking toward The Shamrock.

I went back to Cassie and Zack and must have gotten totally lost in that jungle typhoon, because I didn't hear Miranda let herself in with the key I'd given her or tiptoe toward me on little cat's feet. When I finally felt her presence, she was reading over my shoulder, which I hate.

"You know I hate that," I said.

"You're not going to let the baby die, are you?"

"What do you think?"

"You can be weird."

"Yeah, well if I'm weird," I said, "what do you call Nosferatu — and what'd he want this time?"

"He wants to take me out."

"Tell him you can't go until he fixes the leak in my kitchen," I said.

"I don't think this is funny," she said.

"I don't either," I said seriously. "Particularly that new wrinkle — the lease thing."

"Yeah," she said. "But I knew it was horseshit — "

"It was also coercion."

"Coercion . . ."

"Force."

"That too," she said.

"Do you want me to talk to him?" I asked.

"I can handle him — you make him defensive."

"No shit."

"He's pathetic," she said.

"I guess," I said.

"He does scare me a little," she said, just as my telephone began to ring and Bobby Wilder's voice came onto the answering machine speaker.

"Hey Dave," he said. "Unhand my woman — I know you've got her up there with you — "

"Nobody told me she was your woman," I said, picking up.

Miranda grabbed the phone to say she'd call back from downstairs.

"Bobby's here for a couple of days," she said on her way out.

But as we know I was a few steps ahead of her on this.

4

• • •

BOBBY TOLD MIRANDA that he would meet us at the restaurant; he was running late because of an interview with somebody from *Details* magazine. Just what the world needs, I thought sourly. More uninformed opinions from another postliterate, postpubescent celebrity.

Miranda changed into velvet tights and T-shirt, put a fresh gardenia in her hair, and refilled Pete's water bowl. Then, while Bobby did his part to oil the wheels of commerce by nattering on about body-part piercing and art, we grabbed a cab and once again headed east to the Owen stronghold on Sutton Square. Definitely a house built by commerce and still rife with it on every level.

"When Larry's three thousand miles away," I said, "Patti's mood improves."

"Mine would too," said Miranda.

"You don't think he's a lot of laughs," I said.

"Oh I do, and he's so good lookin'," said Miranda.

"She'll be flexing her muscles tonight," I said, "because he's not watching."

"He probably knows everything about her he wants to know," said Miranda.

"She might still have a few tricks up her sleeve," I said.

"Yeah," said Miranda, and smiled. "She's a trickster — maybe I should be scared."

"Well, forewarned is forearmed."

"Okay, Mom."

All arrivistes love excess; and Patti was to the purveyors of excess what Saint Francis was to the fur, feather, and fin dwellers of Assisi. When Louis-Michel's wife opened the front door, revealed behind her was a veritable forest of balsam firs. Each tree was carefully strung with hundreds of tiny Christmas lights and planted in what looked like a pre-Colombian pot; there were so many pots they nearly obscured the sweeping expanse of black and white marble squares that comprised the checkerboard floor of the enormous foyer.

Just as we finished navigating through the heavily scented maze, we were attacked by not one, not two, but four tiny cavalier King Charles spaniels. They wore gold-tone holly on their collars and had those buggy eyes and yippy habits of ladies' lapdogs. They preferred Miranda because they smelled Pete, or knew instinctively that she was a lot less likely to kick them than I.

"In here," Patti called out crossly.

We followed the sound of her voice to a study I hadn't noticed during Thanksgiving. Even the way the shelves were lit sang museum quality. And I'd never seen the Mirós (there were three on two walls) in any collection or book. They were all quite appealing. Which is more than I can say for Mrs. Big O, who seemed to have lost her holiday spirit.

"*Shit,*" she seethed from an awkward position on her hands and knees.

"That's what it looks like to me," Miranda said dryly. "Do you want some help?"

Patti was cleaning up a couple of pint-sized turds deposited by one of the little royals dead center on an ancient petit point rug.

"No thanks," she said. Apparently remembering who she was supposed to be, she looked up with a forced smile. "Just an accident — but now there's a spot." She gave the rug a final swipe with her wad of paper towels and dumped the whole mess in a hammered silver wastepaper basket.

"You know," said Miranda, "dogs are den animals — "

"So what does that mean?" sniffed Patti. "They only crap in the den?"

"I meant they're probably not too happy out in that big hall, or even with the run of the house; they like little quiet dark places — "

"Like some people I know," said Patti. "And where would they prefer to relieve themselves, under my bed? They were just out with Celeste for half an hour."

"The longer they walk, the less likely they are to go," said Miranda.

"That's ridiculous," said Patti.

"Miranda has a dog," I said awkwardly.

"Dogs like to go for walks," continued Miranda. "It's fun. And they're smart. They figure why should they screw up a good time. By doing what you want they basically get punished, I mean, you take them right back inside. So next time you walk them — "

"Well, *I* don't walk them myself," Patti said in a tone that suggested that walking the dogs was tantamount to slopping the pigs. "Maybe you could explain your theory to Celeste."

"Sure," said Miranda. When California falls into the sea.

"Goddammit," Patti said, suddenly noticing another little shitpile. As she bent over, the sound of her skintight skirt ripping seemed loud in the quiet room.

"Now I have to *change*," she said through clenched teeth.

"I'll get this," said Miranda, pointing to the floor. She took Patti's roll of paper towels and headed to the powder room adjoining the study just before Bobby Wilder's father, Henry Garcia, charged in with the pack of spaniels jumping at his heels.

"Patrice, get these little fuckers out of here, will you — Oh hello, I'm Henry Garcia," he said, noticing me.

"Hello, Henry," Patti said.

He gave her a chaste kiss on the cheek, and when he shook my hand I was about as successful at deleting from my mind's eye the picture of his getting blown by our hostess as I would be if somebody said whatever you do, don't think of the word rhinoceros.

"I'm a big fan of yours," I said mildly.

"Hi, Henry." Miranda walked out of the loo with a fistful of damp towels.

"Miranda," he said. "My son has all the luck."

"Is Sally in the other room?" asked Patti for our benefit.

"Oh, I thought you knew," said Henry the good actor. "She flew back to L.A. this morning. Some meeting about raising money for ambulances in Nicaragua. I'm afraid you young people are stuck with me alone tonight."

Okay, duly submitted and recorded.

"Well, I'm going to change my clothes," said Patti, bumping deliberately — and none too gently — into Garcia on her way out. "Louis-Michel will give you drinks."

"Why don't you take the dogs, Patrice," Garcia said.

She shot him a lethal glance, but made kissing sounds to the yappers, who, to a dog, ignored her.

"I'll get them out," Miranda said.

Patti hurried into the forest of firs, high heels clicking on marble.

Before any of us was forced to think what to say, Celeste came bustling in with sponges and a bucket.

"Mon Dieu," she said to the dogs. "Méchants chiens, méchants, méchants."

To us she said: "Please, Monsieur Henry, Monsieur David, Mademoiselle — Louis-Michel will bring drinks in the conservatory."

Miranda handed over the paper towels and whistled to the dogs.

I swear to God I'm *usually* in the W. C. Fields school of thought about kids and dogs. But even as one of those miserable four-legged peabrains was pissing on the side of a Hoffman chair, I knew they would follow this girl, and knowing gave me goose bumps.

"Let's go," she said, and marched them out of the room.

• • •

Later, at Elaine's, which was bedecked for Christmas, we were directed to number eight, the VIP round table in the back. Patti put herself between Henry Garcia and Bobby Wilder. Miranda, who looked so luminous in that dark, smoky room, almost lit from within, was on Bobby's other side, next to Mr. Gossip, Roland Tarbell, who pretended not to recognize me. The peerless Elaine, owner of the eponymous restaurant, joined us, taking a seat between Tarbell and me. On my right was an empty chair — a fact I chose not to recognize as symbolic.

Around midnight, a fan of Henry's sent over a magnum of champagne, which we knocked off in record time, and Elaine insisted we sample what she said was an unparalleled tiramisù created by her latest chef. I was happy enough disappearing into the act of rolling, balancing, and lighting wrapper after wrapper of amaretto biscotti and watching the thin crinkly paper flame brilliantly, burn down till only an ash remained, and then at the moment of death, lift off the table and fly up, up, up — guided no doubt by some simple, yet to me incomprehensible, law of aerodynamics — into the enveloping darkness above our heads.

Elaine's powerful peripheral vision, combined with her fabled extrasensory perception, allowed her to know and see all that was happening in every part of her saloon. Thus equipped, she was out of her chair and halfway to the door to greet Jack Delaney before anyone else noticed he'd walked in alone, wearing a rumpled white suit and a look of profound weltschmerz. He brightened a little when Elaine guided him toward our table.

She directed him into the seat next to me, and I thought I recognized the same pin-size pupils and slack smile of a few other people I knew. Surely, considering his highly publicized recovery and rehabilitation, I must have been mistaken. What was doing with his central nervous system, however, did not affect his charm.

"Elaine," he said, reaching across me for her hand, "you've got to put my dinner on the tab, love. I lost my wallet."

"Again?" Elaine asked.

"Yeah," Delaney replied sheepishly.

"Good thing this guy can afford it," Elaine said.

"I *can't* afford it," muttered Delaney.

"He'd lose his goddamn head if it wasn't screwed on," said Elaine, ignoring his comment.

"Put a rubber band around it next time," said Miranda.

"Around his *head?*" Patti laughed. "Is that like tying a string around his finger?"

"No," said Miranda, undaunted. "Around his wallet. So it won't slip out of his pocket — or get lifted out so easy."

"A rubber band," said Delaney. "Good idea. I'll have to try it." He smiled, looking across the table at Miranda. (In fact, every time I glanced at him the rest of that evening, he was looking across the table at Miranda.)

"You know so many clever little things," Patti said to Miranda. "Maybe you should give up modeling and do a column like 'Hints from Heloise.' Yours could be 'Messages from Miranda.' "

Miranda's silver-blue eyes flashed, but it was Roland Tarbell who spoke, reminding me that a spark of benevolence might live even in the darkest heart.

"Hear, hear," he said. "You can write for us anytime. Although I'd guess your dance card is already full. Don't you agree, Henry?"

"Absolutely," said Garcia, throwing in his sovereign two cents.

"Yeah," said Bobby, putting his arm around Miranda, "no quitting now. She's on her way to the top."

"To the top," said Delaney, raising an empty glass. "To the bonfires of beauty."

"May they warm your hearth," said Tarbell, "rather than incinerate your house."

"Now what am I drinking?" said Delaney.

"Hey, Roger," Elaine called to her headwaiter. She turned to Delaney, her dozen necklaces jangling. "What'll you have?"

"My treat tonight," said Patti, attempting to recover control of the table.

"Mrs. Owen," said Delaney, inclining his head. "You are a princess. How will I ever repay you?"

Garcia put his arm around Patti, whose hand slipped immediately to his lap.

"She'll think of a way," he said.

"It's only money, for Christ's sake," said Elaine.

Patti ordered more champagne. Bobby and Miranda left first, then Tarbell, then Patti and Garcia with their most recently recruited beard, Delaney. Elaine and I sat together in the mostly empty room. She offered me another drink, which I accepted, switching to framboise.

I had lugged copies of my *Midnight* novels over to Patti's just in case, and then to dinner. Naive is as naive does, and the books were still in a bag under my chair.

I gave them to Elaine, who seemed genuinely pleased.

From Roland Tarbell's column:

Once upon a time, youth was about breaking the rules; pity there are no more rules to break. . . .

While the usual oh-so-sleek battalion of boys and girls celebrated the holiday season by dashing from fête to fête, we observed a private tête-à-tête à trois, Monday night at Elaine's Establishment-To-The-Stars. Heartthrob Bobby Wilder, author Jack Delaney (where was Signora Valverde?), and Clementine Sheffield's impossibly stunning new recruit in The Race For Best Face ... chaperoned by socialite Patrice Owen and paterfamilias Henry Garcia, who starts shooting a new film with Kathleen Turner in January.

And speaking of dear Kathleen ...

• • •

The gray days of December were relentlessly cold that year, and I couldn't wait for a respite at the Garcia-Wilder enclave in Jamaica.

When the long black car with the black glass windows pulled up to our door on the brightly freezing morning of Christmas Eve, Miranda and I slipped into the back seat as though we'd been chauffeured around our entire lives. During the all-too-short walk from our front steps to the curb I squared my shoulders, lifted my chin, and secretly hoped the entire neighborhood was watching. I felt crisper, sleeker, taller.

Pete, per usual, had no collar and no leash.

Miranda looked very world-traveler. She was wearing Levi's and a white T-shirt (no bra) with boots, a beat-up black leather jacket, dark glasses, and a New York Mets baseball cap from which gleaming tendrils of silver-blond hair escaped. Even (or especially) in this getup, she was gorgeous.

She was also the only person I knew who could get in or out of the back seat of a car in one fluid motion. Like a dancer, but without the exaggerated posture and signature duckwalk of the prima ballerina — or like an athlete born to the moves.

The driver closed the door smartly after us and returned to his place behind the wheel. As he released the brake and shifted into gear, we heard a sharp rap at the window closest to Miranda.

Juliana stood outside, her thick gray hair only slightly wilder than her eyes. She was dressed, as always, in several skirts and three or four shirts; oddly, she had no coat and carried only one shopping bag.

"Julie, where's your sweater?" scolded Miranda.

Juliana inspected her torso and arms as though for the first time and looked puzzled.

"Hesitant Lady, Stone Cold, According to Chic," she said.

"That's fine," said Miranda, "but you better take this for now."

I can't pretend I didn't wince when she handed her jacket through the open window. Juliana pulled it on, then dug into the shopping bag and came up with a shoe box wrapped in red paper. Santa stickers added a festive note.

"Peace Peace Peace," she said like a magnanimous granny en route to church rather than a delusional vagrant with a rap sheet longer than our limo.

"Run the Risk, Party Boy," she added.

"Thanks Julie," Miranda said, sending up the smoky window. "Don't forget to water the plants."

Juliana smiled with sealed lips, some vestigial vanity hiding her toothlessness.

"Guilty Again," she said.

The window closed. The car pulled away and Miranda removed her dark glasses.

"Don't say anything," she said.

"Did I open my mouth?"

"I know what you were thinking."

"Want to bet?"

"You were thinking how could I let her stay in my apartment."

"Wrong."

"You were thinking how could I give her my jacket — which was old anyway."

"Nope."

"Okay, what were you thinking?"

"I was thinking you better open the box — because it's *ticking*."

Miranda held the box to her ear.

"You're right — but it's not a bomb. Too light."

"Don't tell me," I said, raising a hand. "Noah's Ark."

"It never hurts to learn stuff — you don't know when it might come in handy."

"Forgery and bomb-handling?"

I had gotten really curious about this Noah's Ark, but every time I was about to ask she cut me off.

"I'll tell you about it some other time," she said, closing the subject as she opened the box from Juliana. Inside were three items. A plastic baggie tagged Pete's Prophecy containing several cubes of red meat with the fat carefully trimmed away. Pete made quick work of his gift — an obvious success. Then there was an envelope marked A Hundred Kisses.

"A hundred kisses for you, David," Miranda said. "Look at this." She gave me the envelope, which held a two-dollar OTB slip for the sixth race at the Meadowlands from a few weeks earlier.

"Do you think she makes up some of these names?" Miranda asked.

"I used to," I said. "But not anymore. Check it out." I pointed to the *New York Post,* folded neatly along with the *Times, Journal,* and *Daily News* in the magazine pouch behind the jump seats. Miranda opened the paper to the sports page and started looking.

"Here's Peace Peace Peace in the first race," she said. "Here's Guilty Again. Here's A Hundred Kisses — he's the favorite in the seventh. Amazing . . . I'm glad she doesn't dream them up."

"What difference does it make?" I asked.

Miranda shrugged.

"I don't know," she said. "It just does."

"Maybe you like your craziness pure."

"And maybe," she said, "there's a lot of bugs around and I might wonder about some of them, like are they poisonous, but I don't have to put every one of them under a telescope."

"Microscope," I said automatically.

"How do you spell that?"

"M-i-c . . ." I stopped. Her head was bowed and she was biting her lip to keep from smiling.

"Aw shucks, you got me," I said. "I'm a pedant."

"Oh God no!" she said. "I didn't think you liked little boys!"

"Ha ha. Why don't you open your damn package?"

Miranda put the newspaper down to examine the last gift. The card read: Lady Beware. She pulled candy-striped tissue paper off a little travel clock.

"Isn't this sweet," she said. "Shit, I hope she didn't rip it off."

Although I'm no more superstitious than the next person, I'm not thrilled when I break a mirror, and I always notice if it's Friday the thirteenth. I figure it's just as easy to walk around a ladder as walk under it, and I don't discount the idea that there's a parallel universe floating around somewhere or a couple of dimensions we don't yet know about. I think maybe some people have powerful alpha waves or beta waves or whatever bends spoons from time to time.

So, a few minutes later, when the alarm on the little clock suddenly rang so loudly our driver hit the brakes and Miranda dropped *The Wide Sargasso Sea*, I began to wonder if Lady Beware was a more profound message than don't oversleep. I wondered if in her madness, Juliana had some window into the future, some narrow beam of light into the darkness of infinity — or more mysteriously, into the place where infinity ends.

I'll never know whether Juliana was psychic or simply the queen of coincidence. Her warning was certainly in order, but like the occasional spoon-benders, she had no control over the timing of her power.

Conventional thinker that I was (and still am), my mind was on the safety record of the Executive Airfleet, as the driver pulled onto the tarmac and announced:

"Teterboro Airport."

• • •

Okay. I'd never been on a private plane before. Miranda said she'd been on lots and told me about how she once took a ride on a crop duster, which I said didn't count — but she insisted it did because the pilot wasn't officially working at the time. They flew a hundred and seventy-five miles east along the Arkansas-Louisiana border to try the waterslide at a new amusement park. There was a little problem with the ignition as they prepared for their return trip — which was that the key disappeared. The flier, Miranda said, was so drunk he walked on his hands into a wall, then threw a punch at the wrong guy over a game of pool. So she just flushed the key down the toilet in the ladies room of the bar where, after the wall and pool incidents, the crop duster guy was knocking back one last boilermaker for the road, which is exactly where they wound up, hitching a ride home on an eighteen-wheeler.

Leased at about a bazillion dollars per mile, Bobby's stunning plane certainly delivered. It looked like polished sterling in the sun; a giant silver hawk with magic wings. And if a place called Central Casting still existed, the two pilots were definitely the best it had to offer. Bill was from Seattle, Bama from Mobile; both were six feet tall and tanned, clear-eyed, and shorthaired. Muscles toned, no doubt, and rippling under starched uniforms. Bill was fifty, Bama thirty; experience and reflexes — they had the board covered. Rounding out the flight crew was the stewardess, Kristin. That's all I need to say about my first glimpse of private air transportation, except money can't buy you love but *who cares?*

Bobby Wilder, leader of the Wild Ones, filmland's current crop of rebels without a clue, came bounding down the steps of the plane barefoot and blue-jeaned, grabbed Miranda off the ground, and whirled her around as I held Pete by the scruff of his neck.

"Man are you gorgeous," he said. And to the audience: "I *love* this girl!"

Then he kissed her. A long, slow, sexy kiss with his hips grinding into hers, her breasts squashed against his chest. Oh yes, he was wearing a pink oxford cloth shirt, completely unbuttoned — sort of thrown on. She of course had given her jacket to our neighborhood visionary, which left her with only a tight white T-shirt over bare skin. Obviously if you're young, healthy, hot, and hetero, a temperature of seven degrees Fahrenheit couldn't begin to chill your boiling blood.

Everybody looked the other way. The pilots fell into deep conversation; Kristin the stewardess started rooting around in her purse; while our driver got into the car, where he began a careful study of the *Village Voice*. I busied myself babbling inanities to Pete, who refused to quit growling.

After what felt like forever, a nasty (and clumsy) little worm in my heart reared its head and made me say: "CUT!"

Bobby's head snapped up, his eyes flashing anger. We all froze. I had clearly forgotten that, like happy birthday, benevolent star is an oxymoron. But the moment passed and Bobby smiled.

"Laugh-a-minute Dave," he said, coming toward me, flinging an arm around my shoulders, either ignoring or flaunting his enormous erection, at which both Kristin and I were trying not to stare.

"Let's get these cows to Abilene," he called as he turned and ran up the steps two at a time into the plane.

We followed, herdlike.

"Surprise!"

And it *was* a surprise to see Patti (I mean Patrice) Owen standing just inside the door.

It took a moment for my eyes to adjust from the bright exterior to the subdued interior — from the regular polluted air of the masses to the pressurized, rarefied, filtered atmosphere of the chosen few. Don't misunderstand: I have nothing against the oligarchy as long as I'm part of it, which unfortunately is only too seldom.

The entire plane was arranged to look more like a living room on Park Avenue than a cabin in the sky. It was all done in beige leather soft as chamois. The carpet was thick, and each seat was equipped with a discreet telephone as well as its own pale green and lavender throw of whispery mohair. There was a large video screen at the front of the aircraft displaying a brightly colored map where an airplane icon would move south little by little — kind of like a live cartoon — marking our passage.

Patti kissed Miranda and me, and slowly my eyes became accustomed to the lower light. As Kristin circulated with a tray of something for everyone: champagne, eggnog, Bloody Marys, and seltzer, I made out Larry Owen, whose jaw looked strangely swollen, coming toward us. He shook my hand and called me Dan. Close. I spotted Bobby's brother, Esteban Garcia, and two petulant-looking beauties — Jennifer and Helene — each wearing something short and tight. Larry guided Miranda over toward the others to do introductions, leaving Patti and me standing side by side.

Before we could start the usual great-to-see-you-again-you-look-terrific horseshit, the door of the cockpit flew open and a laughing little boy about four years old came racing out. He was chestnut-colored, quite beautiful, with amber eyes and dressed in a navy blue sailor suit. A young black woman, sort of nondescript, with her hair done in cornrows, chased after him, her pursuit inhibited by the red flip-flops she wore on her feet.

The child ran up to Patti and me and stuck out his hand.

"Let's shake," he said.

Patti, who'd always loathed children, hadn't changed in her latest incarnation as Mrs. Big O. She hopped back as though the little boy were contaminated.

"Okay," I replied, and gave him my hand. The series of ear-rattling noises that followed resulted of course from the trick buzzer he was palming. The kid fell on the floor giggling. It *was* funny — though not to the nanny, who grabbed him by the arm and said in a melodious but stern island patois:

"I just got two words for you Robert, *be-have.*"

I'm compelled to add here that as a gay person, I should be sensitive to stereotypes and avoid falling prey to them myself. I mean, not every forty-five-year-old man who dates a teenage girl is a dirty old creep, not every Jew is smart, not every Sicilian is vengeful, and not every young Jamaican woman in charge of a little boy in a three-hundred-dollar outfit on a private jet is an au pair. However, much as I fight it, I too am a prisoner of my experiences and have soaked up many of the very prejudices that I am dedicated to helping erase. Although I can't suffocate my thoughts, I have learned to hold my lip zipped to the count of ten. As my mother used to say quite frequently: It's better to keep your mouth shut and be thought a fool than to open it and remove all doubt.

"Mama, don't take it away — pleeeese!" The little boy struggled with the woman over the hand buzzer.

"I told you not to scare people with that thing," she said, putting the toy in her pocket.

"Daddy'll let me have it," cried the child. "*Daddy!*"

The boy's voice rose above the hum of conversation in the cabin, and I looked around trying to figure out the other half of the parentage mystery. Esteban? No way. And it couldn't be Larry Owen. Would one of the pilots bring his wife and kid along for the ride? Probably not Bama, the young southern one. Bill from Seattle?

Bobby Wilder scooped up the little boy.

"Robert, you have to listen to your mom."

"Aw, *Dad*," the child complained, "you said I could play with it later, and now *is* later."

When I sneaked a peek at Miranda she was looking so deadly calm

I realized this kid and his mother were news to her. I hardly had time to process that observation when a few feet behind Miranda a lavatory door opened and out stepped Malone.

I could barely comprehend, over the stupid beating of my heart, the pilot's loudspeaker instructions to sit down and buckle up.

Here's what I learned in the course of the flight. First, if you soak two paper cocktail napkins in warm water, wring them out so they're no longer dripping, stuff them into the bottom of two medium-sized paper cups, then take the cups and hold one over each of your ears up against your head, the moist vacuum created will relieve that terrible pressure felt during takeoff and landing.

I occasionally think of this remedy and wish there were an equally easy way to relieve the terrible pressure caused by thoughts that hide in a place far harder to reach and much more interior than the inner ear.

I also discovered that Larry and Patrice had flown to Europe recently as the guests of a Wall Street friend whose 727 was equipped with a treadmill in the master bedroom, so his big joke was he *runs* across the Atlantic.

The third thing I found out was that Henry Garcia owned a house on the beach between Ocho Rios and Port Antonio, where his whole family, together and separately, had been going for years. The first time Bobby ever visited the place alone, he invited Hyacinth Monroe, the gardener's daughter, to join him for eating lunch, smoking ganga, swimming naked, and so forth, which resulted in the conception of little Robert Jr., who was almost two years old when Sally Wilder Garcia noticed an unmistakable family resemblance.

The only thing Hyacinth's father wanted was not to be fired, which of course he wasn't. And the only thing Hyacinth wanted was for Bobby to marry her, a desire that would go permanently unfulfilled. Generous minds would believe the Monroes to be simple, decent people; the jaundiced eye, however (of Bobby Wilder's business manager in this instance), saw the last humans on the face of the earth who did not own a television set and therefore remained oblivious to the idea of multimillion-dollar contracts, residuals, backend points; in short, the incredible financial benefits cloaking the young star of *Sons of Guns*, et cetera, then and forever.

Always mindful of his percentage, the manager engaged a team of lawyers to draft a complex document making arrangements with the Monroes while protecting Bobby's finances in perpetuity. There was even a byzantine clause withdrawing all support and future moneys should Bobby ever marry Hyacinth. This, I suppose, could be called an antinuptial agreement.

Free of worry, Bobby and his family enjoyed the winning little boy from time to time when they visited Jamaica, or when they had him delivered to Los Angeles or New York, as well as the services of Hyacinth, who was not only a good mother but also a fine cook and a first-rate cleaning woman. Hip to birth control now, Bobby kept her for the night every so often when he didn't have another girl with him, and sometimes when he did.

On the plane, Bobby assured Miranda that he was simply giving Hyacinth and the kid a lift back home — by way of his house for one day, which was, after all, Christmas. Miranda (whose own life, in my book, had been pretty unusual — though I know one person's eccentricities are another person's conventions) stayed cool, but kept running her fingers through her hair, always a dead giveaway.

Larry Owen, Patrice, Malone, and his "date" (Helene, one of the cover girls hanging on Esteban) were en route to Tryall, the kind of hotel that prefers to be called a private club. They were getting a ride on Bobby's plane because Larry's second wife and second set of kids had *his* plane in Sun Valley for the holidays.

The first few episodes of *The Golden Rule* had been shot, and word was the show was aces. Larry wasn't about to let his golden boy out of sight for a solitary minute lest he get into God knows what, probably a golden shower.

When I noticed that Miranda had finished reading *The Wide Sargasso Sea* and was already lost in *Jane Eyre* I decided to avail myself of the generous picnic lunch that was elegantly laid out at the front of the cabin. Delicate sandwiches on black bread made from egg salad and bacon, smoked salmon cream cheese and Vidalia onion, roast beef and watercress dip, prosciutto and gourmandaise. They were the best sandwiches I'd ever eaten — and they made excellent sense. Thin rich people would have thin rich sandwiches.

Each of these tasty delights had been cut in thirds, and as I washed my tenth or eleventh third down with my third or fourth glass of champagne, I watched Patti a few seats away, leaning forward, chatting animatedly with Bobby, who was smiling in response.

On my way to the head I heard her say:

"You were *brilliant* in *Nogales* — you know, besides acting, you ought to be directing."

"My *dad* just directed his first film —"

"Yes, but *you* . . ."

That's all I heard; I could fill in the rest from memory. Some years earlier as we walked home after work, Patti told me she'd never met a guy who didn't get turned on by flattery, and then when the guy starts talking, if you lean way forward he thinks you're hanging on every word he says. Also he can look down your blouse. Either way or both, you can't lose. Of course, Patti was pretty flat-chested at the time — but evidently she had a handle on her future.

She looked good that day on the plane — really relaxed. No one would've guessed that she ate Librium, Xanax, and Klonopin for breakfast the way others ate Cheerios, corn flakes, and oatmeal. Nor could anyone have imagined what an effort she was making. Even in those dim, old days when we waited tables at Anthony's Tequila Tavern, she exhausted herself by charming and seducing people — some literally, some not. It always surprised me that a woman who seemed so desperate for friendship and love had no gift for either.

I hung around in the head, washing my face, admiring the hem-stitched hand towels, the triple-milled French soap, the collection of moisturizers, unopened. Naturally, I was hoping Malone would come in. But he didn't.

• • •

From Delaney-Behar Correspondence:

Dear Peregrine,

Ordered a 1982 Ch. de Marbuzet Saint-Estèphe last night — no, not even Haut-Marbuzet — *faute de mieux* on the wine list. Any residual Saint-Estèphe austerity was blasted out by the amount of fruit.

Was dining with Patrice Owen. I know you think she's a cow, but she says she can get something going between Big O Productions and me. God knows what. Larry Owen never read a book in his life. But television pays.

Yes, Christmas in Milan with D.V. And I'll see my Italian publisher. If I need to flee, will you be in London?

Merry, merry,

J. Kerouac

———

Dear Jack,

Mr. Wolf has left threatening claw marks on my door, so I'm off to Chamonix for the holidays to write a piece for that new American traveling magazine. Apparently they think I can ski. Fortunately, the Grand Hotel has an excellent wine list.

Good tidings,

PB   London, Wednesday

P.S. If you flee Milan, my key will be in its usual place, under the planter by the side door.

• • •

Landing in Montego Bay remains my most intense memory of the flight to the Caribbean. It isn't the sultry scenery, the dancing water, the soaring temperature, or the cordoned-off runway that stays with me so clearly. The memory involves Pete and my further education; i.e., if love makes the world go round, money oils the wheels upon which it turns.

Shortly after we touched down, I happened to be looking as Bobby Wilder dug into the little watch pocket of his jeans, pulled out a hundred dollars American, and slapped it into the high-five hand of the lone customs inspector assigned to our flight. Out the window — or hangar — went quarantines, vaccination papers, and yet another of my bourgeois ideas about the way business is conducted.

No matter how exotic or arcane the locales are for my *Midnight* books, what I get as a research allowance from my publisher is a subway token to the New York Public Library, where I have indeed spent many fruitful hours.

My mother dragged me to the Bahamas once, to Bimini, where I got such a bad sunburn I had to stay in the hotel reading comic books for the whole time she gambled and shopped.

I'd never been anywhere in the Caribbean before Jamaica, but even the half-dozen glasses of champagne I drank on the flight couldn't have made the island any more beautiful than it was.

We drove out of Montego Bay along the coast road toward Ocho Rios. On the left was the beach, to the right, endless blue mahoe trees, swamp palms, brilliantly colored bougainvillea, hibiscus, oleander. Wild orchids came from a pastel palette — pale pink, lavender, light green, alabaster. If you wanted, you could stop at a stand and buy a banana; the orchids were free.

Along our way, we passed Rose Hall, Flamingo Beach, Salt Gut, Runaway Bay, Oracabessa, and Port Maria. Cruising through Golden Grove, Bobby's driver flipped on the radio: Bob Marley and the Wailers were singing "Kaya."

Just before our final turn, onto the dirt road leading to Henry Garcia's house, I noticed a sign in faded red letters: WELCOME TO JAMAICA — LAND OF EVERLASTING HAPPINESS.

•   •   •

For most of us, in addition to marriage, patriotism, gender specificity, and good work being its own reward, the concept of Christmas morning was long gone into the ragbag of childish notions. Only the staff (let's not forget that servants are what make the rich different from you and me) had been up since dawn; the rest of us slept until well after noon and woke hung over, sharing the same headache — two Fiorinals away from a migraine.

I was one of the last to stumble toward the painful light of the courtyard, arriving just in time to catch those hilarious Garcia-Wilder brothers cutting up. Finally Bobby playfully shoved Esteban into the pool, and the usual madcap mayhem ensued. What else can one expect in a great big house on a pure white beach by a clear blue sea. Hormones and pheromones filled the air like ozone.

By midafternoon, the group had soaked up, besides a dozen bottles of tanning lotion and enough sun to bake a small Balkan country, at least three pitchers of mimosas and two pitchers of Bellinis. Little Robert Jr., who had, himself, belted down a bottle of mango nectar and two chocolate milk shakes, was curled up in his tiny bedlet for a nice Christmas nap.

I was reading *Middlemarch,* which I always take on vacation, to avoid losing literary perspective. Bobby was lying facedown on a chaise, with Miranda next to him, her towel spread on the terra-cotta. Her copy of *Jane Eyre* lay unopened. One of Miranda's hands trailed back and forth in the water. She too was facedown and had undone the top of her black bikini; all that silver-blond hair was tied up with a ribbon and her back glistened gold with oil.

Hyacinth walked out of the house and with no preliminaries straddled Bobby, centered herself on the small of his back, and began giving him a very professional back rub. Esteban and his companion Jennifer, lying on their chaises wearing tiny swimsuits and large dark glasses, appeared unconscious — their bodies innocent and open to the sun.

As Hyacinth dug her fingers deeper into Bobby's shoulder, she began to rock and sway, pushing her crotch back and forth stickily along his naked skin. He caught the rhythm and I stared at my book trying to ignore his low, anguished moans. Jesus.

When Hyacinth started panting and writhing and rattling the chaise, Miranda seemed not to breathe at all. I can't remember if I hoped or feared they'd come right there in front of us — but Bobby had a different idea. He pushed Hyacinth off him, took Miranda's hand, and headed toward the house. For better or worse, I was faced with the sight of Bobby Wilder's enormous hard-on a second time in twenty-four hours.

I dove into the navy blue pool, where the water was thankfully cool.

Obviously, it couldn't have taken me very long, even underwater, to swim the length of the pool, but by the time I came up for air, Miranda had returned and was standing at the other end, waiting. She didn't look happy.

"Come with me?" she asked.

"Sure," I said, climbing out and up the hot stone steps.

We walked beneath the stucco archway separating the inner courtyard from the garden, past a grove of mango trees, and down a path cut through tangled flame vines, to the sea.

Two bright spots of color had appeared on Miranda's cheeks, and she fiddled with her hair. Otherwise, she was stone calm.

"I'm leaving," she said. "What do you want to do?"

"I'll go with you," I said. "What happened?"

"Didn't you see what happened?"

Probably because as a child I didn't get any worthiness pills with my soft-boiled eggs, I try to make people like me by acting (contrary, as we know, to my true nature) nonjudgmental. This habit often backfires, causing me to look like a troglodyte. Unfortunately, bad habits are cozier than good reasons.

Making it worse I said: "At the pool?"

"*Yes,*" she said. I was grateful she didn't say yes-you-flaming-asshole-did-you-think-I-meant-at-the-Knicks-game.

"Yeah," I said. "It was embarrassing."

"Embarrassing! It was disgusting. And I don't mean just because it was a sex thing, which ought to be private. Bobby treats Hyacinth like a piece of furniture — no, like an *appliance* that he can just turn on and off — and he treats me like . . ."

She picked up a flat stone and sliced it into the sea, where it skipped three times.

"He reminds me of a couple of guys I used to know," she continued. "The big difference is Bobby does whatever he feels like with a check-book in his pocket and everybody bows and scrapes. These boys back home did whatever they felt like with a gun in their pocket, now one's dead and the other one's in the pen."

"It's hardly the same thing," I said. "Bobby earned the money in his checkbook." Mr. Prim.

Miranda turned to me, but I couldn't read a thing in those lagoon-blue eyes.

"I was talking about an attitude," she said.

"You know," I said, "some people think it's okay for artists to live by different rules, because their talent is so monumental. Look at Picasso — or your own favorite, Hemingway. I'm not saying I agree."

"Yeah — Bobby's just like Hemingway. Except he wouldn't know how to find his ass with both hands if he hadn't of been born into the right family."

She walked into the clear, shallow water, knelt down, and splashed her face a couple of times — then came back to me, and we continued at a brisk, rather military pace.

"Let's get the fuck out of here," she said.

She stalked along the shore, and although I don't think my expression changed, a moment later she said:

"What's the matter, you never heard the word before?"

• • •

By late afternoon on Christmas Day, Miranda, Pete, and I were speeding toward Tryall in a rented car.

We had phoned ahead and booked the only available house, suddenly vacant because the family that originally reserved it had canceled owing to their kids' chicken pox. And I naturally, never satisfied with dull, predictable pain, left a message apprising Malone of our imminent arrival. In those days I thought anything exquisite was best. Including pain.

Starving after an hour on the road, we stopped at a little beachside café. The lone waiter watched Miranda digging around in her tote bag and arrived at the table in two long strides, proffering cigarettes and a light, which she accepted. Apparently, though, she hadn't been after smokes, because she rummaged a bit more and finally pulled out a package the size of a cigar box done up in brown shipping paper, gauzy gold ribbon, and a sprig of silver holly.

"For you," she said, laying it on the table. "Merry Christmas."

Of course, my first thought was that it had been meant for Bobby. And why would I have such a mean-spirited, not to mention self-denigrating idea? I suppose when a person's most lucid recollections of childhood involve broken promises, forgotten birthdays, and secondhand gifts rejected by other people, unexpected kindnesses can make him preternaturally suspicious.

"Well," she said. "Are you going open it or eat it for lunch?"

"One minute," I said, and ran to the car, where I pulled her gift, unwrapped, no ribbon, out of my bag.

I daresay I was quite pleased at how surprised and happy Miranda seemed when I gave her the two leatherbound volumes of Hemingway's early works.

"Now yours," she said.

And I pulled off the paper.

"My God, Miranda," I said, opening the slim volume and turning the pages. "It's a first edition — and look, my God, he signed it!"

"I know," she said with small smile. "Pretty handwriting."

The Selected Poems of T. S. Eliot was, by far, the nicest and most thoughtful gift I'd ever received, and though I was heading downstream fast toward a waterfall of tears, I contained myself and further rose to the occasion by stifling any oh-you-shouldn't-have bullshit.

"Thank you so much, Miranda," I said.

"It's weird," she said, looking out over the flat blue sea. "I have this really good friend — Bea, did I ever tell you about her — she likes T. S. Eliot too. She has a Ouija board and she talks to him on it — she calls him Tom. But I never read any of the stuff till I got this book for you."

"And what did you think?"

"It was like . . . being in church. I think. I mean, I never went to church. . . ." She fooled with a pack of cigarettes. " 'Lord I am unworthy . . . But say the word only . . . ,' " she said just above a whisper.

Tears filled her eyes and fell down her cheeks onto the table. I pulled my chair closer and put my arm around her.

After a while we ordered a local dish recommended by the waiter for Christmas dining, washed it down with a couple of Red Stripe beers, and hit the road.

By the time we arrived at Tryall, it was dark. Not too dark, however, to see that our cottage had four bedrooms and three in help. Miranda insisted because she was beginning to make so much money we could afford this very high-ticket, high-season extravagance.

Larry Owen, Patti, Malone, and his so-called date, Helene, had left us word to join them for dinner at Lady Caroline Bell's lush estate, Palmetto Point. But before we could so much as shower and change, Miranda and I both started throwing up. The barracuda mousse we had eaten at the quaint little seaside snack shack where we exchanged gifts certainly cured me of the desire to be adventurous about food *ever* again.

Then it began to rain. And rain. Not a little — but a lot, a lot, a lot. Huge torrents, pounding sheets, an endless deluge. Ordinarily I love any kind of weather, the great equalizer. But not this time.

We stayed good and sick for three days. During this period, Pete almost never left Miranda's side. Just like the valiant collies I used to read about when I was a little boy. And dream about and ask for —

and never get. Or any other dog, or cat, or hamster, or even a fucking goldfish. Never mind.

Although I was very disappointed at the time, it probably was just as well that I didn't clap an eye on Malone once during our entire stay at Tryall. I mean, God *knows* what we might have done, causing his career to be ruined before it ever started and me to suffer from guilt the rest of my life.

Though they phoned, Miranda and I didn't actually *see* any of the Owen party because Mr. Big, still cranky from recent gum surgery, was phobic about germs and was afraid — in spite of our assurances we were suffering from food poisoning — that we might have a *virus*. Naturally he didn't want to be anywhere near us and therefore (let's not forget the Golden Rule) neither did anyone else.

• • •

The chicken poxers, having made a miraculous recovery, decided to reclaim their cottage, which was fine by us since it was still raining. Not so fine was that we couldn't book a flight home. Finally I called a travel agent friend in New York, caught him five minutes before he left for a week's skiing, and got him to set up a couple of stand-by tickets.

As early as it gets (though the latest storm obscured any morning light), three days before the New Year, with a cage for Pete to travel as baggage, Miranda and I arrived at the airport, along with what appeared to be half the population of downtown Montego Bay.

We didn't get on the seven-thirty plane, or the ten o'clock; and when we learned that the last one, at noon, was already overbooked and running on island time, I began to feel very irritable.

We had nowhere to go, with one credit card at its limit between us and about thirty dollars in cash. No way would we return to Bobby's, and I was not about to ask any favors of the newly grand Mrs. Patrice Wentworth Owen. Visiting her house with a legitimate invitation was one thing, but being even slightly in her debt was quite another. She was not what we call a generous soul.

Miranda, looking all too cheerful under the circumstances, rose from the bench where we sat. In fact, aside from her usually skin-tight blue jeans being a little loose, she looked none the worse for the last few days.

"Back home," she said, "you know what we see when lightning hits a tree?"

"God?"

"Kindling," she said just before disappearing into the crowd.

Over the drumbeats of an approaching headache, a caustic voice emerged from the darker region of my mind and began to mimic: "Down home when we get a lemon we just set ourself down and make us some lemonade."

Stifling the voice, I returned my attention to a flat soda (twenty minutes and counting until the first shot of Myers's Original Dark went into the paper cup) and an equally flat issue of *Time* magazine. I thought maybe she's a *manic*-depressive who swings regularly from baton-twirling enthusiasm to suicidal despair.

The drumbeats in my head got louder, and after about fifteen minutes, I started looking around for a pay phone. Maybe I'd just call Malone, say hello . . .

I was saved from folly by someone on the public address system directing me to the private air terminal where we had originally arrived.

Miranda was waiting in a small anteroom with an elderly gentleman who leaned on a silver-topped cane. His tailoring was British; but his hat and boots were western.

"Mr. Campbell, here's my friend I was telling you about. David, this is Angus Campbell."

As we shook hands he looked at me with unusually clear eyes for an old person.

"I'm giving you a lift, boy."

"I appreciate it."

"Who could resist such a beautiful girl," he said without a hint of prurience.

"Plenty of people," Miranda said.

"Nonsense," insisted Campbell.

"I agree," I said.

"Good boy." He looked at his gold pocket watch, and checked the sky. "My pilots say it won't take long to get out of this weather."

*   *   *

Time we know can be relative. Our ascent through a sudden barrage of thunder and an aurora borealis of lightning into a calm blue cosmos went on for an exceedingly long five minutes. Good-bye to the land of everlasting happiness. Ahead, a rosy glow suffused the cost, crime, and grime of home.

When we reached cruising altitude, Miranda was already buried in *A Farewell to Arms*. Angus Campbell and I drank bullshots and talked about gold pocket watches.

"After my father died," I told him, "about all he left was his gold pocket watch."

"You got it?" the old man asked.

I shook my head.

"What happened?"

"My mother sold it."

"Not the sentimental type, eh?"

"Hardly."

"I won this here in a poker game," he said. "At the Irma Hotel in Cody. Take a look." He handed over his watch — a beauty with a diamond representing each number, except the one and the eight, which were marked by rubies.

"Those rubies stand for aces and eights," he said.

"The dead man's hand," I said.

He raised surprised eyebrows.

"Precisely," he said. "What old Wild Bill was holding — "

" — when Jack McCall shot him down at Carl Mann's saloon in Deadwood."

Okay, I couldn't resist.

"What was the name of Bill's horse?" the old man asked slyly.

"Black Nell," I said, because I never forget anything inconsequential. "And," getting totally carried away, "although all the chambers in McCall's Colt .45 were loaded, every cartridge was a dud except the one that killed Hickok."

"How do you know something like that?" the old man asked.

"I read," I said.

No need to add researching my romance novels.

"Which is more than I can say for my no-account son, who's not getting his hands on this watch or anything else of mine either. His boy, that's a different story. He has a couple of crazy ideas, but he'll get over them — he's young, he's got all the time in the world, like the two of you. It's just too late for his father, and for me."

Miranda, with her usual sense of decorum, closed her book when Campbell began describing the bitter disappointment his alcoholic son caused him. He segued into a melancholy portrait of his late wife and finally told us he was stopping in New York to pick up a new, custom-made shotgun and a couple of Connecticut-bred Jack Russell terriers for the grandson.

"I hear these Jack Russells are all the rage back east — probably ruin the breed. What kind of dog you got there?" Campbell asked, pointing to Miranda's feet.

"A very vicious guard dog," she said. "Aren't you, Pete."

"Come here, Pete," the old man said. Pete went over and began licking our benefactor's hand.

"Very vicious indeed." The old man smiled. "My Lila had an all-white Alsatian once . . ."

By the time we disembarked at La Guardia's Marine Air Terminal, we'd heard a great deal more than we needed to know about Angus Campbell's family, his cattle operation, his cutting horses, and his passion for gambling. We were obviously the updated equivalent of strangers on a train: people to whom the old man could tell things he wouldn't dream of discussing under normal circumstances. I wondered if you always had to expect loneliness in old age — like brittle bones and cataracts.

We promised to visit if we were ever out his way.

5

. . .

ON THE BUS to Manhattan I asked Miranda how she got Campbell to take us with him.

"Remember I told you I'd been on lots of planes?"

"I remember the crop duster," I said.

"Me and my girlfriends used to hang around the private hangars at the Fayetteville Airport. They didn't have such fancy planes like the one we were just on — or the one Bobby had. They were mostly Pipers and Cessnas and Beechcraft."

"And?"

"And lots of times planes were empty, so we picked up rides."

"You mean picked up guys."

"That too."

I made a face.

"Didn't you ever pick up guys?" she asked.

"Not in airports," I said.

"It was fun," she said.

"Weren't you scared now and then?" I asked.

"Scared?" She pronounced the word as though it were part of some foreign language. "No, I love to fly. I want to take flying lessons one day."

"I meant of the guys — didn't you and your friends think twice about picking up total strangers and taking off with them?"

"We didn't worry," she said dryly. "It would be pretty hard for a guy to rape a girl and fly a plane at the same time."

"I'd worry if I were you."

"And if I was *you*, I'd be a wart on a pickle."

Even when Miranda talked like Minnie Pearl, she looked like a Doré angel.

The climate, it goes without saying, when we touched down in New York that afternoon, was perfect. Clear skies and painfully crisp air mitigated the low December temperature. For some reason this perfection annoyed me.

Having no wish to visit my irritability on Miranda, I picked up a copy of the *Times* at the East Side Terminal, where the airport bus had dropped us, and pretended to be engrossed in it during our cab ride home.

"You know," said Miranda the mind reader. "We were lucky it was raining the whole time we were sick. Just think how bad we'd of felt if the weather was perfect and we couldn't do anything."

I have to say, I wasn't in the mood.

"I'll tell you something," I snapped. "Once in a while the goddamned glass really is half empty."

"What does that mean?"

"It's a cliché."

Naturally, within two minutes I was apologizing. Miranda said forget it and we did. Or at least she did.

But I kept wondering why her glass was always full or always empty. The true Miranda enjoyed high energy and good spirits combined with that puzzling, implacable restraint. When the lights-out gloom took over, she couldn't even see the glass she thought was empty, let alone what was in it. If she could just control the contents of the glass; keep the level balanced. Maybe therapy (which I'd suggested again and she'd rejected again) or antidepressants were the ticket. Maybe she'd grow out of it. I was thinking of equilibrium as the taxi pulled up in front of our building. I hadn't considered the random acts of fate I usually feared so much. And for once I should have, I really should have.

The last light of afternoon was dying when we finally paid the cab driver, unloaded Pete, and dragging our bags inside, parted ways. But not three minutes had passed when my phone rang.

"Come down right now," Miranda insisted, and hung up. She sounded odd.

I ran out the door and down the stairs, anxiety bubbling. Her place was open; Otis Redding was singing "These Arms of Mine" on a brand-new sound system. Hundreds of white balloons dangling long white moiré silk ribbons hung from every square inch of the ceiling — and the entire apartment was filled with flowers. There must have been at least a thousand roses, anemones, lilies of the valley, orchids, lilacs, peonies, and narcissus — all pale, pale colors — in vases, urns, pitchers, and quaint antique watering cans, probably from Versailles. Next to Miranda's bed was the only primary color in the room — a dark red rose with a mile-long stem in a crystal bud vase. A note tied to it with a sparkling, channel-set diamond bracelet read: "If you don't forgive me I'll be really sad, 'cause you're so gorgeous and I'm so bad. Will you go out with me New Year's Eve? Bobby."

"Bob's certainly got a way with words."

"Is that all you can say?" Miranda demanded.

As a matter of fact, I had a good deal more to say; decided not to say it, because Miranda looked so happy. Who wouldn't be flattered by such a display? Of course for a person with Bobby's money, ordering this stuff and having it assembled is a drop in the bucket, involving a single phone call. At least Bobby made the effort to pick up the phone, indicating that maybe he was contrite.

But would he ever be good enough for Miranda? Somebody she could depend on? I doubted it. Was I bitter? Yes. Jealous? Probably.

Ben the bartender once told me, in a rare burst of wordiness, that just about everything in life was six-to-five against. I didn't always think the worst, but I had given up expecting pleasant surprises.

"It's overwhelming," I finally said to Miranda.

"I'm going to return the bracelet," she said.

"Why?" I asked, examining it, estimating its value.

All right, that was tacky. But concern about money is always with us, and most writers are fairly obsessed about where our next meal is coming from. We like to know about value. And I am no exception to anything besides sexual orientation.

"Well," she said, taking the bracelet, turning it over and over in her hands. Admiring it. "It's too much . . . I mean, flowers die, balloons pop, but something like this — I don't want to feel like I owe him anything. I don't ever want to owe anybody anything."

"How about the sound system — and see that big vase," I said, pointing to what looked like a relic from the Ming dynasty.

"Oh yeah . . ."

A few beats passed as we both looked around the room and then at each other. Suddenly a balloon popped and we started to laugh.

(By the way, I don't know where you draw the line. But she did take the bracelet back to Cartier the next day.)

After a bit, we pulled ourselves together and Miranda started shivering.

"Do you think," she asked, "Bobby had the heat turned off so it wouldn't wilt the flowers?"

"It *is* damn cold in here," I said.

"He couldn't stop the heat — could he?"

"Listen," I said, "with his money he could stop the traffic on the Triborough Bridge at rush hour and put on a musicale."

"I mean really, David."

"I don't know," I said. "I don't know who he paid to get in the place. But he's more into presentation than preservation — plus he wouldn't want you to get pneumonia. My apartment was cold too — but I can't imagine he'd shower you with flowers, beg you to go out with him, and then freeze you to death."

My actual guess was that the creep Mark Douglas had been skulking around and noticed Miranda and I were both away; since the top-floor apartment was vacant, he probably turned off our heat to save money. Which is illegal.

"Let's go over to The Shamrock," I continued, "and I'll call Dark Mouglas."

"I'll meet you there," Miranda said. "I'm gonna go for a quick run."

"It's getting dark," I said. "Didn't anyone ever tell you it's dangerous down by the river?"

"Yeah," she answered, going behind the Chinese screen. "*You* tell me all the time. But I've got Pete."

"Right," I said, "I forgot. The vicious guard dog." Who was at that very moment wagging his tail to beat the band.

•   •   •

In an hour, Miranda joined me at The Shamrock, where I was drinking a hot toddy and cooling my heels as I waited for Mark Douglas to return my call. She brought Pete with her.

"I thought dogs was supposed to live outside," grumbled Ben the bartender, setting a bowl of water on the floor.

"Yeah, who said?" Miranda asked, mock defiant. Ben didn't reply because he was already halfway to the ringing pay phone.

Holding the receiver to his chest, Ben said to me sotto voce, pointing at Miranda: "Your landlord wants to know if she's here or just you."

Miranda shook her head adamantly and mouthed "No." Within a moment Ben returned to our table.

"He says the heat's comin' on pretty soon — says there was a pipe problem."

"Right," said Miranda.

"Probably something he put in a pipe and smoked it," Ben added before moving back behind the bar to refill another customer's empty glass.

"Mark Douglas is such a pain in the ass," said Miranda.

She lit a cigarette, inhaled, and blew three perfect smoke rings into the air.

"He left about a hundred messages on my machine," she continued. "And sent me this *gross* Christmas card — with Santa Claus in a raincoat — I think he's meant to be a flasher. I'm not even sure what the card said, I threw it in the trash so fast. I really can't stand that guy."

"But you're nice to him," I said.

"I am *not* nice to him," she said, suddenly irritated. "I put *up* with him is all, because he's our *landlord*."

"Well, you can tell him off even if he is our landlord."

"*Or,*" she said grabbing her coat, "I can move someplace else. C'mon Pete."

She was out the door like a sprinter and gone.

"Ben," I called, following her. "Put this stuff on the tab."

"What tab?" he yelled toward the door closing behind me.

She was walking at such a fast clip I had to run to catch up with her.

"Hey, I'm sorry," I said.

"Forget it," she answered. "I was mad and took it out on you; it wasn't your fault."

She slowed her pace.

"I don't think," she said, "there's much room between the place where you stand up for yourself and the place where you're mean. I've just been around too much meanness. And I really hate it. So maybe it *looks* like I'm a wimp — but I'm not, not when it counts."

"I'm sure that's true," I said.

I don't know if she heard my half-assed comment or not, as she drifted back to Arkansas.

"One time," she said, "when I was a little kid, maybe ten or eleven, I was with my sister Noreen and her boyfriend Rick — in Rick's car, an old Chevy convertible. He's driving and she's in the front with him. I'm sitting in the back. They're both drinking Southern Comfort and smoking dope. It's about ten o'clock at night in a sleazy part of town and the car's zigzagging all over the street; all of a sudden we hear a siren and I get really paranoid — because I know if the cops get their hands on me, even though I'm just an innocent bystander, I'm right back in Noah's Ark."

I'd still never asked her about Noah's Ark, but obviously I was getting the picture.

"I told them to stop and let me out but they said quit griping, nothing was gonna happen to me; then I started crying but they still wouldn't stop — so I jumped out of the car."

"That was pretty brave for a ten-year-old," I said. "I mean at night alone."

She laughed, and put her arm through mine as we approached our building.

"Oh David, sometimes you're so dense. You missed the point. The car was *moving*. It was doing about forty-five when I bailed. I'll show you."

At the front steps she put her left foot up, pulled at the leg of her sweatpants, and pushed down her sock. There was a ragged scar about three inches long, running on the diagonal, up from her ankle, faded but nasty and deep.

Although I'm not particularly queasy nor am I at all prescient, something about the moment sent a scalding hook into my heart and cast an unbearable chill through the already freezing winter night.

The next night, New Year's Eve, Pete and I — sort of like Little Orphan Annie and her trusty dog — pressed our noses to my front window as Bobby Wilder escorted Miranda to his purring limo. She'd thrown a floor-length cape on over her very short, spangled dress, and Bobby was wearing — perhaps as penance — a coat and tie.

Although she had lost a few pounds during our Jamaican poorlies and seemed fragile as a sylph wrapped in black velvet, her beauty left a permanent imprint on my memory. I can close my eyes right now and recall the image of her face, of the black velvet hood like a dark halo around her silver-blond hair. The driver opened a rear door, but Miranda, apparently having forgotten something, turned and ran back into the shadow of the building.

Since I couldn't see straight down from my window, I couldn't tell what she was doing in the darkness. She was back, however, in a flash, and the limo sped off into partytown.

When Juliana emerged from the shadows to watch the departing car, I realized she had been the object of Miranda's brief detour. She wore her usual multilayered attire, now accessorized with a black velvet purse and long black velvet gloves, which she was pulling on over her fingerless mittens.

I cut up a nice hamburger for Pete, poured myself a double shot of Courvoisier, and settled down in front of the television to watch the hordes at Times Square. Pete and I were both asleep long before midnight. What did we care.

• • •

Wild oats may be a lousy long-term crop, but they must make a good breakfast cereal.

The next morning when I took Pete, my new best friend, out for a walk, Bobby was downstairs in Miranda's apartment. I knew this not because I saw Bobby, or because the black limo was at the curb, or because Miranda called. Nor do I have the proper vocabulary to describe a dialogue with a dog. Trust me though: Pete said the Son of a Gun was there — and he was right.

By the end of New Year's Day, pissed at Miranda for assuming I was just good old dependable David upon whom she could dump her dog because I wouldn't have any important plans for the holiday, I had worked myself into a real swivet. What was I meant to be anyway — the only friend she had who was unconditionally reliable?

Well, yes.

Nevertheless I was feeling like a dog myself — specifically, a dog in the manger. *I* didn't want her (not in *that* way anyhow) but I still didn't want *him* to have her.

Pete and I went for another long, melancholy walk around eight in the evening. It was frigid outside, no moon and no stars. There are never any stars above New York City.

We had drifted over to Twelfth Avenue near the Passenger Ship Terminal, where ghosts of the *Liberté, Queen Mary,* and *Andrea Doria* shimmered into mind and probably distracted me from the most important piece of business on the streets at night, which is perpetual vigilance. I don't know how long Pete had been growling deep in his chest when my own inner alarm sounded.

Over my shoulder I caught sight of two guys behind us. They were still almost a block away, but the vibes were not good — even back then, before every twelve-year-old kid had his own Glock 17.

On the street, I knew to go with my instinct. If something felt weird it always was, and the two guys were closing the distance between us. As I moved faster, so did they. The shadowy sidewalk ahead was empty, and the bass drumbeat of my heart shut out all other sounds.

The loft building to my right was boarded up, covered with graffiti. The old piano factory across the street was deserted. I looked back again and they were catching up. There was nobody around and nowhere to hide, which left only one choice — and I went for it.

With Pete galloping along at my side, I ran.

• • •

Miranda was lying on the couch in my apartment reading *The Old Man and the Sea* when we got back, having lost our would-be assailants by dashing in front of a bus on Tenth Avenue straight into the downtown traffic.

"Hey," she said, smiling. Then she checked us out and frowned. "You okay?"

"We're fine," I said, pulling off my coat and scarf.

She marked her book, and picked up a travel folder titled "Ruidoso Downs" from the coffee table.

"Where'd you get this?" she asked, holding it out to me.

"Oh that's with a pile of research stuff I never used," I said. "From when I was thinking about setting up Cassie and Zack in the Southwest — but then I put them in Montana. What's Ruidoso anyhow?"

"A track in New Mexico," she said. "One of my stepfathers took us all down there when I was seven or eight. They have a big quarterhorse race every Labor Day."

"*One* of your stepfathers," I said.

"Well none of them," she said, "were actually my stepfather, because my mom never married any of them; she was always married to my father who was always — "

"Away," I said.

"Yeah. God what a bummer. . . . Now try this, I made you a drink," she said, passing me a dark concoction in one of my four hand-me-down brandy snifters. "It's a flamingo; Sally showed me how to do it last night."

Interested as I was in knowing more about the unsavory tangle of people from whom Miranda had escaped, I clamped a lid on my curiosity since she was so clearly changing the subject. As she always did.

"I thought flamingos were pink," I said.

"Well the red stuff's in there, but I had to mix it with something else because you didn't have any gin."

"I don't have gin because juniper berries make people crazy," I said.

"Do you have a theory about *everything?*"

"I have a few opinions."

"More than a few."

"So," I said, joining her on the couch. "You want my opinion on calling Bobby's mother *Sally?*"

"*No,* thank you." Her silver-blue eyes opened wide with emphasis.

"Okay, okay," I said. "But tell me about New Year's Eve anyway."

And she told me all about the evening — almost. I was grateful that she treated certain details with circumspection.

The whole family got together to celebrate. Sweet. First caviar and smoked salmon chez Garcia-Wilder at the Plaza Athenée, with Henry, Sally, Esteban, and his date, Jennifer, who had survived the Jamaica cut. Then they all went on to dinner at the Café Carlyle and spent midnight at the Waldorf being photographed, signing autographs, and picking confetti out of their hair. One dance at the Rainbow

Room and a couple of uptown parties — then home to Hell's Kitchen. Very L7 if you ask me — but nobody did.

I built a fire, scrambled some eggs, and settled down with Miranda to discuss the future. We decided to devote the next few months to hard work, good health — particularly mental — and to saving every penny we had so A) we could move to a better place, and B) maybe we could rent a summer house (we were just dreaming, so why not) together at the beach on Long Island.

As I threw another fake log into the fire, Bobby Wilder was already winging back to Nevada to finish his film and scheduled to start another right afterward in Spain. He'd invited Miranda to visit, but she wanted a place of her own, which was wise since, for no discernible reason (or so I thought at the time) beyond the vagaries of youth and fame, Bobby disappeared into the New Year like a stone into a bottomless well.

• • •

As the weeks went by, Miranda ignored Bobby Wilder's absence. She was either indifferent about not hearing from him or too proud to mention being upset. I certainly didn't miss him.

Malone (yes, I continued to delude myself by assigning him the role of my sweetheart) was basically living in California. He was booked solidly into a shooting schedule for *The Golden Rule* as well as the start of *his* first movie, a so-called erotic thriller in which he would be playing the lead opposite one of the only three bankable females under thirty in the entire world. Ah show biz, it never disappoints.

He came east only once that winter, during a brief hiatus in production of *The Golden Rule*. Big O flew him to New York for an appearance on a late-night talk show, reserved a suite at the Mayfair, and provided a car and driver.

Larry Owen's publicity people choreographed Malone's every move to maximize his momentum. The strategy was simple: he was ordered to make the scene, keep his nose clean, as it were, and return to the West Coast fully photographed and amply interviewed.

Unfortunately for Malone, who had the attention span of a gnat, part of this plan involved attending the opening of a play that once would have been called a tragedy. (I don't know why we still have comedies but no tragedies.)

This is where Miranda and I came in. Being a counterfeit hetero-sexual in Los Angeles on the cusp of the moment when power replaced sex as everyone's most desired objective, Malone had been able to find girl companions. No female framework had been set up for him in New York, and none was in the works, as he apparently had mentioned to his handlers that he was very close to Clementine Sheffield's hottest model, who would go anywhere on his arm. Comments like this always return to haunt you, like the lunch dates you make so far in advance you think they'll never actually come around.

I have every reason to suspect that Malone invited me to join them at the opening of the play only because Miranda insisted. So there it is. But I went anyway, and we (I basking in reflected beauty) looked pretty good as we set out, on foot. Unfortunately, Malone's limo had died at a red light coming crosstown, so we were searching for a cab.

God knows there were probably eight million more unusual stories in the naked city on that February night alone — but a small gesture of kindness from Miranda resonates in my memory as powerfully as what happened later during the high drama into which we were so precipitously plunged.

You can't get a generous spirit as a gift or a trade. You can't buy, imitate, or make one up. You're just born with it, like curly hair. It's the sort of spirit that informs kind behavior with or without an audience. And if you don't count Malone and me (I don't), no one was looking as we turned a corner onto Ninth Avenue en route to the theater.

"Oh God," murmured Miranda.

"What's the matter?" asked Malone.

"Look," said Miranda, and we followed her gaze.

"So?" said Malone, still a New Yorker in his heart. Plus he didn't want to be late.

"We know her," I said.

On the sidewalk ahead, Juliana was half sitting, half lying against the side of a coffee shop. Her several skirts were flared up, exposing naked thighs and a sparse patch of pubic hair.

Miranda went over and said in a low voice: "Julie, cover up, okay? It's too cold to sit around like this — and it's not nice."

Juliana ignored her. Miranda waited.

"Come on, Miranda," Malone said impatiently.

"In a minute," said Miranda, kneeling down. "Julie, please."

Still no response. And as Miranda tried to fix the bag lady's skirts, a flying fist came out of nowhere and Juliana slugged Miranda in the middle of the chest. The blow caught Miranda by surprise and nearly knocked her over.

"Hey," shouted Malone, and we both stepped forward.

"It's all right," said Miranda, motioning us away. She regained her balance, stood, and patted Juliana, who was now covered, sitting up against the wall of the coffee shop, arms clasped tightly around her knees.

"It's okay, Juliana," she said.

"Sinned to Win."

We made it to the theater in plenty of time for Malone to preen and be duly photographed with Miranda.

The play was about a woman who by a tiny accident of fate lost her family, friends, and career and wound up living in the street. Despite good reviews, it had a short life on Broadway.

•   •   •

From Delaney-Behar Correspondence:

Dear Peregrine:

Hope yr. Xmas went better than mine. Am sending this by snail-mail (as Nils has begun to call anything nonelectronic) because nobody here has a fax machine.

Bah humbug,
Charles Dickens   30 Dec. Port'Ercole

———

Dear Jack,

Received postcard from Port'Ercole, but where on earth are you *now?* Have fired off enough faxes to paper your sitting room walls.

Phoned everywhere. Got an hysterical maid in Milan (*no parla Inglese*); your answering machine is full, your friends don't know anything, neither does your agent. Morton rang Nils and even he has no idea. We stopped short of calling the ex Mrs. D.

If you've vanished, with whom will I share the Millennial Quaff? Seriously,

PB   London, 12th January

———

Dear Peregrine,

Didn't mean to worry you; Xmas a disaster. Was hiding out near Barcelona. Isabel Loperena lent me her house. Couldn't find a decent bottle of wine anywhere. More later.

Jack   14 Jan. New York

Dear Jack,

Domina phoned this morning with a bizarre tale about Port'Ercole. What the devil's going on?

Before I rang off, she said she would call again. So you see why I had to leave the house — an act eventuating in the purchase of a case each of 1982 Lafleur and 1982 La Conseillante, for which I think it only fair that you pay half the storage.

Faithfully,

PB   London, Tuesday, 20th January

Dear Peregrine,

Just posted a check for my half the storage of the Lafleur and the La Conseillante.

Leaving Port'Ercole (me at the wheel), D. and I were in a car wreck. We had argued at lunch, the upshot being my refusal to make the commitment she wanted.

After the accident, she dealt with the police because I don't speak the language. For some bloody reason she thought I'd change my mind about our relationship if she told the police she was the one driving the car, not me. Naturally I had no idea she'd martyred herself.

Later she blew up when I failed to show sufficient appreciation for her act of love and sacrifice — the whole notion of which was fucking insane, as the wreck wasn't our fault.

Here's the rest: Although the elderly couple from the other car left the scene unharmed, the old woman died of an unrelated heart attack twelve hours later. Her family's filing suit against D., whose police record, you recall, is not unblemished.

D. has not exactly threatened to go back to the police with a revised story, but she has already demanded two hefty "loans," which I've sent, hoping this will all blow over.

Wines notes a little thin this week.

All the best,

Jay Gatz   22 Jan. New York

•   •   •

Winter went on forever. Each morning I worked on *Midnight Passion,*
the sixth — and what I was determined to make final — book in the
Midnight series.

I watched with my usual surprise as the pages began to stack
inexorably up. Back in L.A., when Malone got bored on the set of *The
Golden Rule,* he would call to gossip. He told me, among other things,
that Patti Owen's affair with Henry Garcia had become quite blatant,
at least as far as his source, the Owens' couple, Louis-Michel and
Celeste, were concerned.

Once Celeste had walked in on them in the tub, cavorting around
making dolphin noises. Another time, quite drunk and/or stoned,
Patti had buzzed Louis-Michel, directing him to make two hot fudge
sundaes and bring them up to her bedroom on a tray, toot sweet.
When a giggling Patti opened her door to receive the ice cream, she
wore nothing more than spike-heeled mules and a peekaboo nightie;
Louis-Michel was also treated to the sight of Henry's evenly tanned
butt as it dashed, not quite in the nick of time, into Patti's stippled-
peach dressing room.

•   •   •

During these cold, gray months, Miranda was working hard. Apparently unfazed by the ever-increasing attention and adulation coming
her way from the power brokers of fashion and advertising, she
continued to display the cool detachment of an experienced professional. I wondered occasionally if this detachment was a result of
inner tranquillity or if it came from what the shrinks call disassocia-
tion. When I was drinking out of the full cup I marveled at her calm;
when the cup was cracked and leaking, I considered something more
off center, almost comatose.

Except for an isolated episode when the sun couldn't make its
way through the sleet for a week, I rarely saw Miranda in a totally
despondent mood after the first of the year. She once said something
oblique about how being miserable didn't give a person any special
rights and I disagreed, but that was it. And although the lights went
out now and then, she and I were both more circumspect. When she
felt bad she wanted to be alone; she wanted to sleep. I respected her
wishes.

But even when I didn't see her, Miranda, like Cordelia the bright absentee, distracted me. At the time I didn't have a proper vocabulary for depression (now called unipolar illness), but I figured that Miranda, operating on only three cylinders, had to be summoning enormous discipline to battle the nameless, faceless, sorrowful darkness that occupied far too much territory in her mind. She almost always kept working, running, hanging out with me at the movies or the ice skating rink or The Shamrock until a weekend came. Then she'd crash. She'd put a Fayetteville Sheraton "Do Not Disturb" sign on her door, and I didn't. But there was always a deadline on my self-control, like Saturday-at-midnight, or Sunday-by-the-end-of-*Sixty Minutes,* or if-it-starts-raining.

When Miranda slipped into the abyss where it really was dark, she couldn't or wouldn't (one learns after a while there's no distinction) open letters or listen to phone messages. Since she always turned down my offer to find help, saying nothing did any good (hopelessness is another symptom of this pernicious illness), there was nothing for me to do but pick up her mail, check her answering machine, and respond accordingly, usually by invoking Aunt Enid on the verge of expiration in Amityville.

During the one almost week-long episode, the usual mail arrived and the usual people called. With one exception: a woman who seemed to know Miranda well and whose messages reflected a growing concern.

On the first day she said: "It's Bea and I'm still waiting to hear from you — if you can't talk, shake a bush. Maybe you didn't get that postcard I sent a couple of weeks ago telling you the new main number: 875-6000. Same extension: 401."

"Miranda," she said around the third day, "I think you're down that old rabbit hole with the lights out, so you just better call and tell me everything's okay."

Later that day: "Girlfriend, it's Bea again and I'm getting worried. Remember what you promised."

The next day: "I hope you're listening, Miranda, because I'm telling you to haul ass out of that bed *right now* and go run around for a couple of miles. Always makes you feel better. Folks up there gonna think you're not playing with a full deck."

Day five: "Okay Miranda — you want me to mess up, quit my job, lose my benefits, 'cause I got to come up to that godless city and hold your hand so you don't do anything stupid. I told you not to read that damn Sylvia Plath. But you never listen."

There's only one area code in Arkansas, so I didn't have to waste any effort guessing.

The number rang about twenty times before a weary, nasal voice twanged an incomprehensible greeting.

"Excuse me," I said.

"What extension?" the voice asked.

"What did you say?"

"I said what extension do you want?"

"I mean before that."

"I said like I always say: Southern State Correction. Now what extension do you want?"

"Four-oh-one."

"That extension is busy."

"I'll hold."

"It's up to you."

"Can I ask you something?"

"Go ahead."

"What is Southern State Correction?"

"You got the right number?"

"Yes."

"It's a correctional institution — for minors. You know, reform school — jail. That extension is still busy."

"Can I ask you one more thing?"

"I got two more calls coming in now."

"Where are you located?"

"Noah, Arkansas, please hold."

Bea's line stayed busy for a long time, and I had to take a rare call from my agent. I phoned her again a couple of hours later, but nobody picked up her extension.

I didn't have much appetite for dinner, though God knows we all need sustenance, so I ambled over to The Shamrock where, ignoring Ben's disdain, I drank several brandy alexanders, my personal version of nursery food.

Back home, I followed part one of Joyce's dictum to write drunk and edit sober. But Cassie and Zack were not speaking to each other or me, so I was busily staring out the window when Bea called again.

"She's told me a lot about you," Bea said after we'd dispatched the preliminaries.

"Really?" A typically asinine response as I flew through a range of emotions from vanity (I was so interesting, such a fine friend) to regret (Miranda didn't feel close enough to tell *me* about *Bea*).

"And you sound like a normal person," Bea said.

Ho, ho, I thought. Then I reminded myself that this woman was phoning from a prison where she was either an employee or an inmate.

"What can I do for Miranda?" I asked.

Static crackled over the line as Bea sighed.

"I'd give my pension for the answer to that one," she said. "You know, I used to think if it wasn't for bad luck, that child wouldn't have any luck at all. Now she tells me her life is good, but maybe a person can never get shed of the past."

"What happened in the past?" I asked. "I mean, I know some of it, but is there some terrible thing I don't know?"

"I like your books," said Bea.

I was taken aback.

"What I'm saying," she continued, "is you have quite a feel for drama, but in this case there's no one thing, just everything . . ."

"Like?"

"Like her daddy's in the penitentiary and has been doing time most of her life."

"I guess I knew that."

"It's very humiliating for a child in a small town when everybody knows your daddy's in jail, and your ma's kind of a . . ."

"I understand," I said, although how could I.

"What's worse," Bea said, "was her mama didn't want her. Kept having kids, didn't want any of them; farmed 'em out to relatives, in-laws, neighbors. These men Kitty always had — that's her name, Kitty — not all at the same time, but one right after another, Lord knows, these men didn't want the kids either."

"That's a relief," I said. "I mean — "

"I know what you mean," Bea said. "And I'll tell you — where I work I see a lot of beat-up kids. Kids who've been violated in the worst way. Miranda didn't get hurt sexually, or physically — well, maybe she got knocked around a little — it was more mental."

"And emotional."

"Both of 'em," said Bea. "Kitty kept sending Miranda off to some foster home — "

"God."

" — and Miranda was always in trouble, 'cause she'd run off, even when she was a little bitty thing. One time she got as far as the Missouri state line . . ."

"But what about now?" I asked. "What do you think about the weather, I mean not having enough light?"

Bea sighed again, and I think I could have heard that sigh without benefit of the telephone.

"Hell, I don't know," Bea said. "I think it's hogwash."

Not what I expected to hear, but being neither intuitive nor even a good guesser, I find many people in my life outside fiction quite unpredictable. I could hear Bea being summoned over an intercom, and we promised to resume our conversation another time.

The next morning Miranda climbed out of the rabbit hole, at least for the time being, and therefore I had no excuse to call Bea.

•   •   •

Just as Miranda anticipated before Thanksgiving, the lights went out less frequently even as a frigid March wind blew us around in circles and icy tides of April rain chilled us to our bones.

People liked Miranda and were drawn to her, but she kept a distance from the other sizzling young models who made up her peer group. I didn't examine the reasons she chose me to be her closest friend, because as Miranda said ominously about various objects and subjects: If it ain't broke, go ahead and break it, see what happens.

One thing we did agree needing breaking, though, was her lease. That dim, miserable pit Miranda called home could have made Pollyanna sing the blues. She decided to find out if she could rent the empty apartment above mine.

I'd been up there a couple of times, and not only was it commodious but sunlight streamed in through the various windows at all hours of the day. Perfect for Miranda's problem, which goes by the name of Seasonal Affective Disorder, taking its place in the oral and written history of the mind with King Saul's melancholy, Blanche DuBois's despair, Churchill's Black Dog, Thomas Skelton's sadness-for-no-reason, Holly Golightly's mean reds, Seymour Glass's last day, and Hemingway's life story.

The place upstairs had been vacant for nearly a year since Mark Douglas with a stinginess of spirit even more disgusting than his dirty hair and repugnant fingernails, evicted, for habitual late payment of rent, a young couple and their nine-day-old baby.

"He wants me to come to his apartment tonight and talk about the rental," Miranda said over China tea at my place on a particularly cold day during the last week in April.

We never have spring in New York. Six months of winter are followed by six months of summer, maybe a week of fall, then winter again.

"What's there to discuss?" I asked, knowing the answer.

"What do you think?"

She rolled her eyes at my apparent naïveté. Ah, the subtleties of human intercourse: she failed to notice my pretending not to understand what I didn't care to consider.

"Want me to go with you?"

"No thanks," she said. "Seeing you would just piss him off — he'd probably think we were cooking up a conspiracy to screw him. I can handle myself — I mean, the guy's bent but he wouldn't *do* anything."

"I don't know," I said. "He worries me."

"Listen, David," she said. "Didn't your daddy ever tell you the boys in the big hats are the premature ejaculators? A person like Mark is all gurgle and no gut. Believe me."

Miranda's impoverished background, the down-home authority with which she spoke, not to mention that overwhelming beauty, often seduced me into believing what she said — even when her cup was so full it was spilling all over the place. However, I was older, more experienced, infinitely more cynical, and damn it, I *was* the man here. And this time I didn't agree with her.

"I'd feel a lot better," I said, "if you'd let me go with you."

"Sometimes," she said, looking past me, "I used to worry so much I'd feel like I was really *doing* something. But nothing got done; I didn't have anything to show for all that worrying except more . . . what?"

"Anxiety," I said.

"That's it," she said. "Being sad half the time was enough. I didn't need extra anxiety. It was like paying interest on a debt that would never come due. So I quit worrying."

"Just like that?" I asked.

"Yep," she said.

She got up and went to the kitchen.

"Where'd you put the sugar?" she asked.

"In the cabinet over the sink," I said.

Her back was turned to me as she searched the shelves.

"At Noah's Ark," she said, "they would tell us two things all the time. One was if you touch shit, you are shit — and the other thing was we all got trouble and it's dumb to run away from it because if you treat it like a friend, you can learn about it and get to know it. So after a while, it doesn't sneak up on you anymore, but if you do bump into it you can walk right through it because you know the way."

"Sounds very born-again to me," I had to say.

She'd found the sugar and was spooning some into her tea. I was still talking to her back.

"Noah's Ark," she said, "was a place they sent you from Juvie Detention if nobody wanted to take you in to be their foster child. It was down near the Texas border in a town by the name of Noah, Arkansas — alongside a swamp."

She turned, tensely, and looked straight into my eyes as if searching for a hidden response.

I had no idea what to say but naturally was not deterred.

"I didn't think you had swamps in Arkansas."

The tension evaporated so fast it may have lived only in my

imagination; she returned to the table, and sat down looking wistful.

"We do have them — with nasty crocodiles and huge poisonous snakes. *Not* a perfect place for children. But Noah's Ark is for kids — kids who aren't old enough for real jail. It's a reform school . . . but some of us got thrown in there because there wasn't anywhere else to go."

"Who's Bea?" I asked.

"She's a guard."

"A prison guard?" Mr. Whitebread.

"I guess."

"She cares about you."

"Yeah," Miranda said. "I ought to call her. She wasn't too happy about me coming to New York City."

"Why?"

"She thinks modeling sucks."

I said nothing.

"You and Bea would love each other," Miranda said.

"I don't think modeling sucks," I said.

"You just think it's stupid."

"No I don't," I said.

"Oh bullshit," she said. "You think it's a stupid job for stupid, vapid people who were accidentally born looking like . . . like I don't know what, but that's not the only thing you and Bea have in common."

"We've got you," I said.

Miranda looked past me toward the bookshelves that lined almost every wall of my apartment. And then she seemed to be looking past the bookshelves, far away.

"Bea turned me on to books," she said finally. "The first time I got sent to Noah's Ark I was a little kid — the youngest kid in the place. She wasn't supposed to, but she read to me. And sometimes she made up stories; like we'd be sitting on the steps of the dorm and she'd pretend we were on a ship crossing the Atlantic Ocean. . . . We'd meet all these interesting people on the ship. Then we'd go to London and to Paris and we'd take the train, the Orient Express, and we'd meet more amazing people . . .

"*Rats.*" She interrupted herself. "Check out the time. I've got to get over to Dark Mouglas's and look at those papers, sign the new lease or whatever, and" — she held up her hand to stave off what she knew I was going to say — "I've already asked Donny to pick me up there, if that'll make you happy."

She blew me a kiss as she ran out the door.

6

· · ·

WITH BOBBY WILDER MISSING and (I imagined) presumed guilty, Donny Redding was the new blip on Miranda's romantic screen. He was also the Mets' biggest bet in the pitching sweepstakes. A prelaw graduate of Stanford, he was part black, white, and Asian, with a ninety-nine-mile-an-hour Zen fastball and the kind of great good looks only mestizos are lucky enough to inherit. Supposedly a decent guy as well — but there's always a wrinkle. Redding had just broken up with his wife of eighteen months, a model for Clementine Sheffield's biggest rival, the Dirk Agency.

Somebody's favorite book, *The Power of the Transitional Woman*, was the latest in a loathsome string of bestselling self-help volumes. And Miranda was an equal opportunity reader. She decided power or not, she didn't want to be Redding's or anybody's transitional woman. She adjusted her attitude toward him accordingly, and needless to say Donny Redding fell madly in love with her.

Miranda's photograph had already been in the *Daily News* once with Redding, though her head was turned away from the camera and she was identified only as "Pitcher's Mystery Girl." There was a blind item in Roland Tarbell's gossip column too, but Miranda seemed intent on avoiding the press glare as much as possible, since she thought it embarrassing to be written about just for showing up at a party or being somebody's date.

Her innate understanding of how sleazy it was to sling oneself into the rapacious arms of the paparazzi and prostitute oneself for a few lines of ink in a newspaper that would be lining someone's birdcage the next day, was classic Miranda.

And if you think I'm an opinionated snob vis-à-vis privacy, understatement, and restraint, a snob who thinks it's just fine to appear in the paper three times only — at birth, marriage (not of course in my case), and death — you're abso-fucking-lutely right.

• • •

From Delaney-Behar Correspondence:

Dear Peregrine:

Dined last night with Nils (and therefore stayed at the lower end of the wine list, though I managed to find the '85 Fonsalette Cuvée Syrah, which Parker gives a 92), who was kind enough to show me a picture of you and Morton shitfaced at the Groucho.

Nils is getting apoplectic as I finish writing the *New Yorker* piece — he'd probably expire if he knew how much time I've spent trying to come up with something for Big O Productions. But every time D.V. stamps her cloven hoof, I can hear it straight across the Atlantic. Must settle with her once and for all.

The only bright spot in my day was bumping into the rather mysterious Miranda as I crossed 6th Avenue. Wilder's out of the picture, but now I hear she's seeing Donny Redding, a pitcher for the Mets (baseball). I could be smitten with this girl! Why don't I learn what's unattainable today is unendurable tomorrow.

Onward,

A. Chekhov   New York, 19 April

• • •

I was packing up a chicken sandwich and a copy of Richard Price's novel *Ladies' Man* (I *write* trash, I *read* good stuff) for a short walk to The Shamrock, where I planned to spend a quiet evening alone with my supper, my book, and a couple of Dos Equis.

Before leaving, I went to the bathroom. I tell you this only because even when I am alone in my own house, I close the bathroom door. This habit results from having grown up with my mother's lifelong open-door policy, which applied to every door, drawer, and letter. She loathed privacy.

So, with the bathroom door closed, I couldn't hear my phone ring or the answering device playing the caller's voice on monitor. But as I was walking out of the apartment, some atavistic peripheral vision made me notice the blinking light on the machine and play back Miranda's whispered message:

"David, I called line two but no answer — hope you come back soon — I'm in the bathroom at Mark's with the portable phone — Donny's not getting here for another half hour and I'm a little scared. This guy's acting weird, really weird — he's wired out of his skull on blow — "

I could hear the sound of knocking in the background.

"I'll be right out, Mark," she called. "David, come and get me right now — I mean *right now.*"

More knocking was following by Miranda disconnecting.

God.

I raced out of our building, heading south toward the giant new apartment complex where Mark Douglas lived. Fortunately for me it was one of a kind in Hell's Kitchen, several years ahead of any other gentrification. I couldn't remember the exact street or the exact street number, but I knew more or less where it was. I cursed my lousy memory as I ran; cursed my bathroom door, my mother, and myself for once again lacking the courage of my convictions or any courage at all.

Why had I let her go off by herself, right into that pig's own pigpen? How much time had elapsed since she made the call? What would he do when he saw her walk out of the bathroom with the portable phone? Maybe she hid the phone in the bathroom before going out. What'll he do when he finds it in there later? Who gives a shit. Miranda and I should both get the fuck away from this guy.

There it was. The enormous high-rise fronted by a circular driveway, half-assed fountains, and a couple of marble columns. I dashed by the doorman in his red-and-gold uniform to the lobby with its banks of North and South Wing elevators. How was I going to get past the concierge and the elevator operators? I'd figure a way — I'd handle it. I'd —

"David."

I whirled around. Miranda came out from behind what looked like a mutant ficus tree. Her face was calm but she was walking fast, and when she got near enough, she grabbed my hand.

"Let's get *out* of here," she said, pulling me along.

I took a quick look over my shoulder at the cavernous foyer, which had about as much charm as La Guardia Airport on a rainy Friday.

I guess I was expecting Mark Douglas to materialize, swinging from one of the fake French chandeliers or pounding on an elevator door for not opening fast enough. But he was nowhere in sight, and within seconds we were out on the street in a cab going —

"Where to?" asked the cab driver, a middle-aged, heavyset black man.

"Just drive," Miranda said — a line I'd been hoping to use all my life and never had.

"Fine by me," the driver said.

In those days, most New York cab drivers were English-speaking American citizens who knew the way to Wollman Rink, Madison Square Garden, Christopher Street, and West Broadway and wouldn't get mad at *you* if *they* didn't recognize one of these addresses. Off the point yet again. But I really hate the point.

"So what happened?" I asked. "I got there as fast as I could."

"That guy's crazy as a bullbat!" she said.

"What'd he do this time?"

She was still holding my hand, sitting as close to me as she could get. Slowly, she breathed in through her nose, turning her nostrils white with the controlled effort. Then she exhaled, through pursed lips, with relief. After a while, her breathing returned to normal.

"First," she said, "he wanted to take my picture. And I told him I was totally booked with work and I wasn't into film stuff at the moment and so if he was thinking about his movies, it was a waste of time — maybe next year or something.

"But he started dragging out all this camera equipment anyway — and I was trying to explain to him, like, I said I get paid a lot of money for posing these days and that's why I can afford a better apartment.

"I'm not sure what pissed him off — I don't even think he heard the apartment part — he started carrying on about weren't we friends and how could I talk money for my pictures — it was so creepy.

"Then he went in the bathroom — came out with toot all over his face — didn't offer me any either, not that I wanted any. And he's sweating like buckets. So he gets some baby powder and starts shaking it into his shirt. It was *gross* — and it gets in his dirty hair and he looks totally insane.

"So I say, 'Okay, just take one picture and then let's talk about the apartment.' So he goes '*Smile*' — which I can't, I can't stand listening to his obnoxious voice — so I'm not smiling and he comes over and puts his arm around me — and that was it, man. That's when I decided I was out of there, but I saw he'd locked all the locks on his front door including the police bar and I had a feeling if I asked him to let me out just then, he'd go nuts — so I went to the john and called you."

"What happened when you came out?"

"He saw the phone in my hand and started yelling about was I calling somebody and who was it and how come and a lot of other bullshit and I just made a break for it. I got to the kitchen and ran out the back door and down the fire stairs for about three floors and got in an elevator with a lady and her kids. Then I stood behind that tree till I saw you come in."

"Jesus," I said.

I held her hand tightly and looked out the window as the cab sped down Seventh Avenue approaching the Village.

"What about Donny?" I asked.

"Oh my God," she said, rapping on the plastic partition between the driver and us. "Hey stop, turn around, we've gotta go back where we came from! Fast!"

"No problem, miss," the cabby said as he calmly ran a red light and dangerously gunned the car across three lanes, cutting off half a dozen honking, cursing drivers. He made that right turn and we were immediately careering back uptown — going I don't know how fast, since I closed my eyes when the speedometer needle hit seventy, and Miranda said tightly:

"Can you please go a little faster?"

We bounced over a giant pothole into the circular drive, and skidded to a stop at the entrance to Mark Douglas's building.

"Jesus Fucking Christ," I said.

"I don't believe it," said Miranda.

"Hey, is that Donny Redding?" asked the driver as he, too, looked through the big plate glass doors into the lobby. It was indeed Donny

Redding who stood there engaged in what looked like casual conversation with Mark Douglas.

"Let's get out of here," said Miranda.

"No, wait a minute," I said. "Donny doesn't know what happened; he obviously went in to find you."

"I'm not going in there," she said.

"I guess I'll go," I said with something less than enthusiasm.

"*I'll* go," the driver offered hopefully.

I got out of the cab and went inside. Mark Douglas ignored me as I approached, and Redding didn't know who I was because we'd never met, so he didn't acknowledge my presence either.

"Excuse me," I said to Redding.

"Yes?" said Mark Douglas imperiously, as though he'd never seen me before.

"Miranda's outside." I pointed toward the cab.

"Got to jump," said Redding to the landlord, who gave him one of those playful little punches on the arm.

"Let's get together," said Mark Douglas to the pitcher. "You and Miranda, me and somebody."

"Yeah, sure," said Redding, following me out the door.

In a moment he and Miranda climbed into the Car Service Lincoln he had waiting and sped off. I got back into the cab.

"So is Redding a good guy?" asked the driver.

"I hope so."

"I picked up Sandy Koufax one time at the Odeon Restaurant. He was a good guy. You getting out here?"

I looked at the meter. It read $12.25.

"No," I said.

"Okay, pal," said the driver. "Where to?"

Miranda was okay; Dark Mouglas was at bay, and maybe Donny Redding would turn out to be a good guy. Earlier in the day, I'd finished a chapter, and Malone actually called me three times. So how come I felt bad?

Much as I admired T. S. Eliot, I never bought April-is-the-cruelest-month. That is, people grow gloomy when everything like flowers and grass is being reborn and they're not. I think a much more suicidal time of year is fall, when everything is *falling*, like leaves, hair, jowls, even hems. But fall was far away, so why did I feel clammy with foreboding?

If only I could have figured it out.

"Just drive," I said.

•   •   •

The next week was unseasonably warm, and one evening after I knocked off work I went out to the stoop to read a copy of the *L.A. Times* entertainment section Malone had sent me because it featured a piece about him on page one. I was more impressed that Malone had gone to the trouble of mailing it (well, having someone at Big O Productions mail it, but still) to me than I was by the story, which was quite good.

At the end of the piece, I looked up and noticed Miranda about a block off, returning from her usual run with Pete prancing along behind her.

When Juliana appeared like a poltergeist from God knows where, Miranda slowed to a walk and put her arm around the bag lady. As they drew closer, I could see that they were deep in conversation, and they were still talking when they reached the stoop. Miranda was saying:

"So then this photographer said, 'Honey, I *am* the eighties.' "

"Shoot to Kill," said Juliana.

"Exactly what I thought," agreed Miranda. "Then the other model says, 'I'm not painting my tits blue if you're the entire twentieth century.' "

"Miss Iron Smoke."

"Hi girls," I said. "Getting thirsty?"

"Bad Debt."

"It's okay, Julie," Miranda said. "David's buying."

Five minutes later, in what was probably no less peculiar a foursome than could be seen anywhere else in New York that night, Miranda, Juliana, Pete, and I entered The Shamrock. Ben started shaking his head the moment he saw Juliana, but Miranda, undeterred, took her arm and guided her toward a table.

Even after my first 10 High, I couldn't find a way to converse with the only homeless person extant walking around in Susan Bennis and Warren Edwards boots (Miranda claimed they were left over from a shoot), and I was relieved when Juliana finished her Bristol Creme, said, "England Expects," and departed The Shamrock. Dinner no doubt with the Duke of Bedford.

"Okay," said Miranda, smoking a Gauloise (from her Paris trip) and working on her second pepper vodka. "What do you say we both move? I really want to live upstairs from you or next door or whatever — but after the other night, I don't think I can stand anything to do with that jerk Mark, even if it's just sending him a rent check every month. I guess he's trying to be important and doesn't know how — but he's bad luck walking, and I think we should get away from him."

The issue I faced was not exactly a moral dilemma, but it was a tad sticky. I loathed Dark Mouglas and wanted to be near Miranda, but I loved my place.

"Well," I said, waffling. "Let me think about it."

"Yeah, too bad for us, but we've got time," she said. "Because I don't have enough money yet to get a good apartment."

The modeling business was notorious for endless delays in payment. A six-month lag was more the rule than the exception. Still, it occurred to me that Miranda never seemed to have a sou, and I wondered darkly whether her generosity toward Juliana extended beyond the occasional pair of boots, gloves, or jacket. Whatever the true source of her apparent impoverishment was, I was secretly relieved that we could postpone making a decision about moving. So it was easy to say:

"Fine. When you feel like you have enough money, let's sit down and discuss it again."

The matter temporarily settled, we ordered another round.

• • •

Several weeks passed, and the memory of her nasty encounter with Dark Mouglas had faded when, from a field box behind the Met dugout at Shea Stadium, Miranda and I watched Donny Redding take to the mound against Chicago.

I tried not to forget who I was, or frolic too much, or get singed by the flame of reflected glory when I was out with Miranda. In her usual blue jeans and T-shirt, with her shining silver-blond hair and impossibly perfect body, she caused the kind of stir, hum, and buzz rare in workaday life. Although she was still relatively unknown, the sheer power of Miranda's beauty caused even the most jaded New Yorker to catch his breath as she passed.

Fit and good-looking, with the restless grace of a matador, Donny Redding fired up the fans with a flashy array of fastballs, breaking balls, and off-speed pitches which kept the Cubs unbalanced and scoreless for eight innings. The only problem was the Mets were also scoreless.

At the top of the ninth, one of Donny's famous inside sliders was fisted down the line and should have been caught by the left fielder, who misplayed it, putting a man on second.

When Don walked the next batter, the lights at Shea Stadium seemed to blaze more brilliantly than usual. The pitcher pulled at his hat and chewed on a wad of gum. The Met manager popped from the dugout, and the crowd roared like an ocean. Miranda sat stone still, showing she was alive only by running her fingers through her hair a couple of times.

As the manager slowly marched to the mound, furious Met fans started stomping and booing the idea that our boy might be lifted. A bunch of assholes behind us kept throwing beer cans and wadded-up newspaper until a couple of security guys materialized. The debris stopped but the shouting didn't.

Catcalls finally turned to cheers when the manager, after some quick words, gave Redding a pat on the ass and headed back to his perch beneath us. Obviously psyched, Donny retired the next batter by fielding a sacrifice bunt and throwing the guy out at first. Meanwhile, the baserunners advanced to second and third.

I'd finished a six-pack by the time the next hitter lofted a flyball to medium right field, where Eddie Dwight snagged it and fired to the plate, nailing the runner from third who'd tagged up on the flyball.

With two outs and a new runner on third (he'd moved over from second on the sacrifice fly), Donny had already pitched a masterpiece. But he'd thrown a hundred and thirty-two pitches and was clearly tired. Head down, he stepped away from the mound, took off his hat, and wiped the sweat from his face. Then he looked up — directly at us. I mean at Miranda.

She lifted her hand and said in a normal voice, barely audible over the din: "Go for it, you can do it." I didn't see any response or acknowledgment from Redding, who just stood there, staring.

Silence shot through the Queens night like an anesthetic. I could hear the wind blow. My hands began to tremble — and I don't even give a shit about baseball.

The hush held and grew until Redding, after another moment of staring, returned to the mound, disposed of the last batter for the third out, and moved the game to the bottom of the ninth.

Even though Donny was credited with the victory when the Mets won on a home run slammed a few minutes later, the high point of the game for me (as if you didn't know) was that half minute away from the mound followed by his knocking off the last Cub.

"What I don't like," Miranda whispered in my ear, "is somebody always has to lose."

I felt the same way, but I suppose some retro machismo prevented me from saying so.

Down on the field, a wide white grin flashed across Redding's tanned face just before his frenzied teammates mobbed him in one of those All-American-male all-skates where because the frenzy is for sports and not for sex the hundred million or so people watching could care less that these guys are practically humping each other to death on national TV. Do I sound jealous? Never mind.

Miranda joined the rest of the fans, shouting, screaming, jumping higher than gravity normally allowed. Something — my interest in what's going on along the periphery of an event or, and more likely, my claustrophobic need to know a way out of theaters, elevators, or in this case the stadium — made me turn and look behind us. Whereas most of the fans were still cheering, a few had begun moving, starting their long walks out to the parking lots or public transportation.

The face was far off and thus indistinct. But I was too familiar with the passing image to be wrong. Even half-hidden by oversized aviator glasses and a baseball cap, there was no mistaking that the person I spotted pushing through the crowd was Mark Douglas.

Both Freud and the Zen thinkers have written that there is no such thing as coincidence, and they're right.

More's the pity.

*   *   *

Yeah, the party after the game was great. And it was wild. Remember, this was in the days before all those sex scandals started tearing sports apart — before a guy looked cross-eyed at some chick and got hit with a rape charge. Am I an unsympathetic, misogynist homo? No way. I happen to know for an eternal verity that we're all potential victims the minute we're born.

I also know it's harder to be a woman, because even if she's got an IQ of 160 and a heart rate of 75, a woman's muscle density is not equal to that of most fourteen-year-old boys and therefore most women can be pretty easily overcome with physical force. Per usual, I digress.

Donny had mineral water at the party. Miranda and I both got drunk on J. W. Dickel, and as the ballplayers and their girls started pairing off like minks, I meandered out into the city looking for love.

• • •

Early the next morning, alone and hung over, I tried but couldn't remember the nightmare that woke me.

Only a very powerful work ethic I got from I don't know who or where kept the vodka out of the tomato juice I was washing down four aspirin with as the doorbell rang through every fiber of my brain and body.

Plus ça change, plus ça la même chose — meaning there's still no combination like youth and beauty. Miranda stood outside my door emanating such radiance I thought the sun was in my eyes. The same Miranda who'd been knocking back shooters of Kentucky's best a scant few hours earlier.

"I'm double-booked till midnight," she wailed. "I've got to ask you a big favor."

"What happened to everybody's All-American?" I asked. Hey, I never said I was charming in the morning. But Miranda, always an elegant person, let it go.

"I know you don't like to be interrupted," she said, unaware that writers *crave* interruptions.

"Just go to work," I said. "I'll walk Pete."

"It's a little more than that," she said as she came through my open door lighting a cigarette. "And Donny'd do stuff for me — he's not too grand. But they're going on the road this morning."

"You want a cup of coffee, a glass of tomato juice?" I asked.

"No thanks," she said, shaking her head. "Listen, I'm worried."

Now this was unusual.

"Hey, Pete." She whistled once through her teeth and the big dog appeared out of the dimness in the hall. "He's been acting funny, sort of no energy . . ."

"Lethargic," I said, quickly considering rabies and distemper, the only dog diseases I'd ever heard of.

"And you know," she said, "how he'll eat anything that doesn't eat him first."

"All too well."

"For the last few days, he hasn't had much of an appetite and — well, feel this, David," she continued, putting my hand on a small bump hidden under the fur behind Pete's left ear. "Do you think it could be a tumor?"

"You're asking the wrong guy."

She dug a crumpled slip of paper out of her pocket.

"Here's the address of a vet in the neighborhood I got from Clementine yesterday."

"God," I said. "Is there anything that woman doesn't know?"

"She doesn't know how old I am," Miranda said.

We both laughed for a second, lightening up the atmosphere a little.

"Laurel Greel, D.V.M.," I read, checking out the location of her office. "With this address, she'll certainly need the business. I can probably get her to see Pete before noon."

"Thankyouthankyou!" said Miranda, and kissed me on the cheek. Then she pulled back, crossing the first two fingers of her right hand.

"There's something I keep meaning to ask you," she said. "Do you think I should get an unlisted number? I mean, I've been getting a lot of hang-ups and . . . I better go or I'm really going to be late."

"Is there something else?" I asked.

"No . . ."

"Just tell me," I said.

"I think maybe somebody's following me," she said. "Isn't that dumb?"

"Juliana follows you once in a while," I said.

"It's not Juliana."

"Doesn't Pete bark or growl?" I asked.

"It's when I don't have Pete," she said.

"Maybe different guys follow you . . . ," I said.

"Yeah, but I just don't have time for this shit," she said angrily. Why should I have been surprised. I frequently used hostility to hide anxiety myself.

"Okay," I said. "Start by getting a different number — unlisted. And take cabs. Don't walk around here without Pete or me, and I'm going call a Realtor and check the paper for new apartments — for both of us. In the Village or on the East Side. Someplace safe."

She smiled and, as in my stories about Cassie and Zack, everything changed. The brilliance of her perfectly even, perfectly white teeth, her shining hair, and her silver-blue eyes warmed me, lifted me, filled me. She kissed my cheek again, and the smoke from her cigarette did nothing to detract from the sweet scent of spring rain enveloping me as I held her, wanting to keep her with me. Keep her forever. My heart suddenly took up all the space in my chest. I couldn't breathe.

The early morning's forgotten dream came clear all at once. Miranda and I were running along a slippery street, running away from a giant bronzed Cadillac bearing down on us. The harder we ran, the slower we went; the slower we went the closer it came. I shuddered.

In real life she was already flying out the door. I hadn't told her about seeing Mark Douglas at Shea Stadium. After all, maybe I'd been wrong. And as it turned out, I was very wrong, but not about who I saw at the baseball game. If you think I'm a harsh judge of other people, I can assure you, I'm a lot harsher home alone.

"Got to work," she called over her shoulder as she ran down the front steps.

Pete and I walked to an open window and watched her hit the street.

"Don't smoke," I yelled.

"*Okay,*" she yelled, flicking the cigarette butt off her thumb and middle finger like an Arkansas coal miner, into an enormous arc, causing it to land two inches from Juliana, who materialized, leprechaunesque, from behind a banged-up car illegally parked in front of our building.

"Reckless Life," she said to no one.

Indeed.

• • •

Because the real world outside my own head is so profoundly treacherous, so unjustly ruled by willful demons who seem to prefer total chaos above all else, I choose to write so I can be in charge of something.

In my work, I know what's going to happen — because I make it happen. I like to choreograph the variables, tie up the loose ends; to explain the character flaws and correct the plot flaws. To be in control.

I stayed at my desk most of the morning, and after mapping out what I'd write following lunch, I left Cassie and Zack in a hailstorm high in Montana's Bitterroot Mountains with a gang of transplanted 'Mung warriors.

I went down to Miranda's apartment, got Pete, and headed off to see the veterinarian. As we strolled past one burned-out building after another, I considered the proximity of the Lincoln Tunnel and the Port Authority Bus Terminal. Both these famously sleazy sites brought together the meanest specimens of humankind, carrying on every kind of human business.

I wondered for the billionth time where, if anywhere, I fit in.

Ringing the buzzer at Dr. Laurel Greel's office, it occurred to me that I'd never seen Pete around any other animals, and I hoped I'd be able to control him without the help of a leash and collar, which of course Miranda didn't own.

I shouldn't have worried, because when a youngish black man around my height wearing white bucks, baggy chinos, and a faded plaid shirt opened the door, I could see that the waiting room behind him was completely deserted.

"Can't buzz anybody through," he said by way of greeting. "Neighborhood gets worse every day. This Pete?" He started scratching Pete's ears.

"Yes."

"You're late," he said.

My natural inclination toward sarcasm didn't suddenly metamorphose into a cloud wafting up out of my head and away — but I didn't say anything about the vacant waiting room either.

Pete followed Mr. Nice Guy past the empty reception area and into a short hallway.

"Where's the doctor?" I wanted to know.

"Doesn't he have a leash?"

"Why don't I just explain everything to the vet?" I asked as we entered a clean white examining room.

"I'm the vet," he said. "Jonathan Loring. Dr. Greel went to Idaho, where she's reconsidering her life. I'm looking after her practice for the time being. Do you know her?"

"No."

"Good vet."

He handed me a clipboard with a printed form to fill out while he examined Pete, very slowly. Maybe he was careful — probably he was a Dull Normal.

I sat on a stool jotting down what little I knew, which basically amounted to Miranda's name, address, and phone number.

"What about that lump?" I asked, getting a little impatient.

"You know there's a leash law in New York."

I'd had it.

"Listen," I said, "we came here about the lump, not the leash. If you have a problem with that we can leave."

"The lump's got to come out," he said obliviously. "But he'll be fine. Pick him up in the morning around ten."

"Are you sure?" I asked, suddenly worried about Pete. My question, evidently beneath contempt, did not elicit an answer. Jonathan Loring continued the unhurried, presumably conscientious examination, which may have reflected well on his technical skills but left his interpersonal ones hopelessly stranded.

"I'll be going now," I said. I patted Pete's rump. "So long, buddy."

"Be sure and close that outer door," said Jonathan Loring.

What an asshole. But since he was Clementine Sheffield's asshole, I imagined he knew what he was doing dogwise. Though it was no wonder his waiting room was empty.

Well, not quite; as I walked out, I almost collided with two little boys carrying a basket between them which held a bunch of tiny, mewling kittens. Some clientele.

*   *   *

Back home, I called the photographer's loft where Miranda was meant to be doing a shoot and learned I'd missed her by a few minutes.

Then I got lost in a few hours' research about the discovery of gold at Grasshopper Creek, which eventually led to the creation of the Montana Territory. By the time I arrived at the Battle of the Little Bighorn, I was parched and nipped out for a six-pack of St. Pauli Girl.

When I returned, the single message on my machine was from Miranda, between gigs, advising me that she'd called the vet and Pete was recovering very well from his minor surgery. In the great tradition of self-pity, I considered how many people would care if *I* were recovering from minor surgery. Would *anybody* care? I spent the last hour of my workday planning the details of my funeral right down to a recitation of "The Lake Isle of Innisfree" and "Ash Wednesday" and a gospel choir singing "Swing Low, Sweet Chariot" and "Sinner Man." I also noted who would and would not be allowed in the door of the church.

Cheered by an ethereal image of Malone and Miranda, all in black, standing by my grave weeping, I decided to go to The Shamrock. I'd stop at the deli on my way and pick up a big corned beef sandwich for dinner. And some cole slaw.

I rang Miranda at the studio where she'd scheduled her final appointment and discovered the phones were out of order.

The Shamrock, as always, provided a comforting respite, and when I returned shortly before midnight, I was a few steps behind Miranda, who was just getting home. She looked untouched by the day's occupations — or maybe I couldn't see straight. I'd run into a couple of guys from the old days at Antonio's Tequila Tavern and by eleven o'clock I had one too many, followed by two too many, et cetera.

"David," Miranda said mildly. "You look like you're walking on broken glass."

"Yeah, well watch this." I, who couldn't do the box step on the best day of my life, suddenly decided to become Baryshnikov. I leapt through the air, executing a drunk's idea of a grand jeté, and landed on the sidewalk at Miranda's feet.

She helped me up, then up the stairs to the door and into my apartment. She off-loaded me in the darkness of my bedroom and sat on the edge of my bed.

"Get some rest," she said, patting me gently on the shoulder.

"Miranda," I remember muttering.

"What?"

"You're not going to go running now are you?"

"Too bad you're never gonna be somebody's mother," she said.

"Does that mean no?"

"Yes."

"Yes, what?"

"It means yes mom I'm not gonna go running late at night down by the river without Pete because it's too dangerous."

"Good."

In one swift and silent move, she lay down on top of me. Her breasts pressed into my chest and her sweet, heavy hair brushed my cheeks. She kissed me long and deep, and I could feel my heart beat in every part of my body.

Then she was gone.

But she didn't go home. She closed the bedroom door and from my living room called the one doctor, dentist, lawyer, or, in this instance, veterinarian in the recent history of New York City who answered his own phone and lived above his own shop. Because Dr. Jonathan Loring was an insomniac, he was awake at one o'clock in the morning, reading. He gave in to Miranda's appeal and agreed to let her come by and pick Pete up.

• • •

The only reason I know all the details of what happened next is that some of it is public record, and when she finally could remember, Miranda told me the rest, and I wrote everything down in my journal. When I feel awkward, or nervous, or scared I start making notes — to have something to do, or to look like I'm doing something. Now and then, I scribble a word or a phrase or an idea I can use later in a story. I never would've guessed that this would be the story for which I'd be using some of those scribbled words.

If only I could undo the words and the paper they were written on and the events that caused me to put the words on the paper, I'd gladly sit in a million restaurants waiting for the guy who never comes, or a million offices where the editor lights his cigars with my manuscript, or a million bus terminals chewing on my tie with my thumb up my ass and nothing to do but watch drunks puke in the corner and the clock tick my life away. If I could undo the words.

7

. . .

DESPITE HOW SHE LOOKED to me (and as we know, because I'll never forget, I was drunk), Miranda was worn out. She'd worked two lengthy sessions back to back, and when one of the photographers, nearly old enough to be her grandfather, started hitting on her, she told him off and he flipped. With schedules so tight, and everybody running late, there was never time to reshoot. If she came out looking tense and shitty in the pictures, the agency would blame her.

A message from Clementine Sheffield caught Miranda just as she and another model were leaving for their first meal of the day at nine P.M.

Clementine had set up a ten P.M. meeting with the chairman of a major cosmetics firm who was searching for someone to embody his most elegant and expensive line in all media advertising. The lavish one-year contract, renewable for another two years, would ordinarily go to an established model, or to a figure from films or sports. But the chairman had noticed a picture of Miranda, had called for her portfolio . . .

The episode with Mark Douglas, followed by the incident with the photographer, had frightened Miranda, and she expressed her uneasiness to Clementine, who agreed that it was unusual to meet in the evening. The requested meeting was very spur of the moment; and normally an executive or an executive team handled this kind of interview. But cosmetic endorsement deals were stable, lucrative, and few.

Clementine had insisted that if the CEO wanted to see Miranda on the Jersey Turnpike at two in the morning, she should go. This meeting she had scheduled, fortunately, was set for the Grill Room at the Four Seasons. A limo would drive Miranda home afterward. Miranda was torn between hesitation and hope, but Clementine allowed no wavering. Plus Miranda was certain that Clementine's obsession with business stopped short of funny business, simply because it no longer paid.

As it turned out, the chairman of the cosmetics company was neither obnoxious nor lewd; he was purely eccentric. But when the interview was over, Miranda had little sense of whether or not the meeting had gone in her favor.

Tired but restless after she left my bedroom, she knew she wouldn't sleep, thought how much she missed Pete, and, as I said, called Jonathan Loring, the vet.

Before she left his office, Loring offered to get her a cab for the short ride back and when she declined he offered to walk with her.

She said there were still people on the street and cars and besides she was safe with Pete. Loring watched them walk away and returned to the book he'd been reading.

• • •

Halfway home, Miranda hit a deserted stretch of Tenth Avenue. There were no other pedestrians on the sidewalk and only a few cars passed, one of them crawling by a little too slowly. But it eventually accelerated past broken streetlights and disappeared into the darkness.

A cold rain began falling, and Miranda thought about how much she wanted to get back to her apartment. She was exhausted and her leg was beginning to cramp. She'd drink orange juice as soon as she got in; the potassium always worked on her leg. And she'd give Pete some chopped sirloin. Thank God he was okay. Maybe Clementine would call in the morning with good news from the cosmetics company. Miranda could hear the sound of her own breathing become amplified, probably because everything else was so quiet on the dark, empty streets with their blurry, swaying shadows.

When Pete began growling deep in his chest, Miranda tried to choke down her fear. She ran through memories of sleeping in the

Arkansas woods, of outsmarting sadistic guards at Noah's Ark, of successfully hiding from her mother's boyfriend — the one who would yank off his belt and start cracking it against the kitchen table. She was tough. But she picked up her pace anyway because her palms and armpits were sweating and the cramp in her leg had turned into a burning knot.

Pete growled again, louder and more menacing this time, and Miranda knew she should turn around but she didn't dare.

She heard something faint from a distance. Footsteps. No, she thought — it was her own feet hitting the pavement. Yet the sound had a different rhythm; it was another set of footsteps for sure. Pete's growl intensified, making her certain someone was behind her, coming closer. The muffled footsteps were gaining on her. *Turn around,* she told herself, and *see*. It's just another tired person wanting to get home. But why is Pete growling like that . . .

She finally forced herself to take a quick look back. Two men were bearing down on her, one of them carrying a tire iron.

Miranda ran.

One of the men yelled, "You goddamn bitch," and they both took off after her. Inexplicably, Pete slowed down, stopped, and curling his lip, drew back his mouth and snarled at the approaching men, who didn't break their stride.

Miranda kept running and called for Pete to come. She knew if she could just make it to the corner, she'd be okay. And the corner was up ahead, in clear sight. Around that corner, there was a little bodega, open all night. She'd get there and be safe. She yelled for Pete again and he galloped up to her. She could hear the radio, the one they kept on the counter in the bodega, faintly playing in Spanish. So the door must be open. Miranda and Pete were almost home free.

But the men were gaining on them, grunting as their feet hit the cracked cement. Flying forward, Miranda screamed into the dark, empty street for help as she unbuckled her backpack and let it drop. She was twenty feet from the corner when the first man jumped over the backpack and tackled her; as she hit the sidewalk he fell on top of her and pinned her while his partner smashed Pete with the tire iron, knocking him out. Miranda tried to call for help but she was too terrified.

They dragged her across the street, where it was darker still, behind a fence built up at the site of a burned-out building, and while the bigger man, panting hoarsely, held her, his ramrod stiff cock pressing through his pants into her buttocks, the other man started hitting her face again and again. Finally she found her voice and began to scream and the smaller man stuck his fist in her mouth to shut her up. She bit him as hard as she could and he punched her in the stomach. She gagged and her knees buckled. The bigger man dropped her.

It wasn't until she was down on the filthy ground, with the blackness of the night pouring into her, blotting out memory and hope, fear and love, that she felt her own hot, sticky blood in her eyes and in her mouth.

The men ran back across the street; as the shorter of the two passed him, Pete, just coming to, sprang high in the air, all white fur and bared fangs. He sank his teeth into the shoulder of the man who had hit him with the tire iron and the man's shriek of pain reverberated through the ruined landscape.

Pete probably could have held on forever, but he needed to get to Miranda. So he let the man go and dashed into the street toward the building site where she lay, curled in the dirt, losing consciousness.

Just then, a police car came barreling around the rain-slicked corner, driven by an officer from Brooklyn. A few hours earlier, this cop discovered that his wife had run off with his partner. So this cop, who'd been AA for seven years, started drinking again. He hit a few bars, then stopped at a liquor store and picked up a pint of Gordon's. Too loaded to care about Internal Affairs, suspension, or professional disgrace, he thought only of deception and betrayal. A sorrow more powerful than anger or the desire for revenge took him over. Certain he could never replace what he'd lost, he blamed himself for being unworthy in some way he didn't understand. Hot tears blurred his vision as he stepped on the gas, remembering his wedding day, when the bride had been so happy and his partner had been best man.

The cop missed hitting the big white dog who sprang out of nowhere like a terrifying phantom, but when his patrol car fishtailed onto the sidewalk, it dislodged from the blacktop a sharp piece of scrap metal that catapulted through the air at a brutal velocity — piercing the big dog's skull, killing him instantly.

PART TWO

. . .

8

. . .

WHEN JACK DELANEY walked into Miranda's hospital room, her life changed as irrevocably as it had the night of the attack.

He was wearing his trademark white. A linen suit, rumpled so elegantly, to press it would diminish its style. A crisp white shirt. No tie. An alligator belt with silver buckle and a pair of bespoke shoes. No socks. He carried a big bouquet of snow-white snap-dragons, which he handed to me as he pulled a chair next to Miranda's bed.

"Remember me?" he asked, picking up her hand.

"Sure." She smiled.

Sure, I thought. Your picture's in the paper every thirty seconds going to some party. Hard to miss for anyone whose reading isn't limited to the *Christian Science Monitor*.

As Delaney bent to kiss Miranda's fingertips, his long fair hair fell across his forehead into his bright blue eyes.

"You need a haircut," she said.

What a dumb thing to say, I thought with hostility. Can't she see his hair is part of the whole mannered presentation.

But when Delaney blushed at her remark, I caved, because you can't make yourself blush any more than you can make yourself levitate. And despite whatever life experience I've been able to process, I'm always a sucker for the tiniest sign of humanity.

"I've been thinking about you so much since you got hurt," he said.

"I was thinking about meeting you at Thanksgiving, and about that dinner we had at Il Cantinori."

"I've been thinking about you, too," said Miranda.

"Excuse me," I said. "I'm going to get a vase for these flowers." I went into the hall.

What dinner at Il Cantinori!? Miranda had dinner with Jack Delaney sometime between Thanksgiving and the hospital and didn't tell me. I couldn't believe it. I felt betrayed, angry, dizzy, nauseous. Naturally I'm not proud to confess that for an instant I actually felt worse hearing *this* news than I did when I learned of the attack.

During a trancelike walk to the so-called visitors' lounge across from the nurses' station, I bummed a cigarette (big fucking deal) off a passing orderly. This, thank God, was in the days before smoke-free hospitals, when a sick old lady, sneaking a short respite from the reaper in the comfort of a Camel Light, might blow herself up with a spark to the oxygen tank.

Soothed by nicotine, my personal drug of choice, I tried to clear my head of small-minded bullshit. I loved Miranda but I didn't want to make love to her. I didn't want to marry her. I didn't want to own her. Maybe what I wanted was exclusivity. But that was absurd. I began to think darkly that the reason I was such a loyal friend was because if one can't offer great brains, wit, money, beauty, sex — there was always loyalty, like a dog.

Though regret is as familiar to me as my own face in the mirror, it's never a feeling I pursue. I didn't want to lose Miranda. If I loved her, then I'd want the best for her. Who was the best? Wilder? Redding? Jack Delaney? I didn't know.

• • •

My anger and jealousy abated along with the dizziness and nausea, leaving me exhausted and miserable. My fatigue was so profound, I remember thinking on the way home a little later that death would be the only cure.

But instead of committing suicide, I tortured myself by going back to the night Miranda was attacked and replaying the events that led us all to the hospital.

*   *   *

I had been sleeping for I don't know how long after Miranda left my bedroom when Juliana's screaming invaded my dream and captured it.

"SUNDAY BLOODY SUNDAY. BALANCE OF TERROR. OUT OF LINE. FIRST TO STRIKE. FAMOUS BEAST. SUNDAY BLOODY SUNDAY!"

Juliana was wild and ranting, banging at the outer door of our building. With my head pounding as loud as her fists, I ran to let her in and she threw herself at me, collapsing on the floor, clinging to my leg. Her clothes were washed in blood.

"My God, Juliana, what happened to you? Try to tell me."

"Sunday Bloody Sunday," she sobbed. "Flagrant. Balance of Terror."

I didn't know what to do.

"Can you stand up?" I asked, trying to get a good look at her. She shoved me away, pulled herself to her feet, and turned in a circle to show that she was all right.

"Last Chance, Last Chance." She wept, pointing an arthritic hand toward the street. Then she pushed me toward the door — hard.

With icy rings of fear speeding my steps, I ran where she directed — away from demons, toward demons. I ran for several blocks before I finally heard the sirens wailing and realized they had been in the background the whole time, drowned out by Juliana's more immediate screaming.

I slowed on a sparsely populated section of Tenth Avenue and saw a clutch of cars ahead, not parked, just stopped at crazy angles. The EMS was there and a couple of police cars — one of which was up on the sidewalk.

Headlights left on provided an otherworldly pool of light in the darkness and the rain. A cop in a slicker yelled into a bullhorn, but I couldn't understand what he was saying. Then two mounted police officers came trotting out of the night on a matched pair of bays, and all I could think of was how horses used to pull the slaughterhouse wagons along this very route.

The paramedics stood out from everyone else because of their white uniforms; as I drew near, I watched them lifting a stretcher. The person on the stretcher was clearly unconscious, almost totally covered by a blanket, so all I could see, glistening with rain and blood, was the face.

It was Miranda's face.

In the movies, they always let the boyfriend or the brother ride along in the ambulance. In real life a young cop notices the blood all over your pant leg, cuffs you, and drags you down to the Midtown South Stationhouse, where your literary agent, who also happens to be a nonpracticing lawyer, is very unhappy to come and get you out.

The paramedics took Miranda, who regained consciousness on the way, to a hospital which naturally was not the nearest but rather the one where 911 pickups from that quadrant on the Manhattan grid went.

Since every private emergency room cubicle at Sisters of Mercy was in use, two interns sliced off all her blood-soaked clothes without the benefit of so much as a curtain. Miranda remembers sitting dazed and naked in front of several dozen gawking patients and orderlies while somebody looked for a gown.

Finally the interns put her in a torn hospital robe and lay her down on a portable table. Then she passed out again.

By this time, she had lost twenty percent of the blood in her body.

It was dawn when I finally got to the hospital and went straight to admissions, where in spite of my wanting simply to ask a question, I had to wait in line as the five people ahead of me were processed through the system.

When my turn came, they said Miranda was still in the emergency room, a horrendous notion considering how many hours had passed.

I was wild — racing to emergency, demanding to see Miranda right that instant. Unfortunately the demandee was an orderly who didn't speak English.

"A la chingada, pendajo," he said.

I got his meaning.

Surely there is nothing in contemporary urban experience to equal the profound but impotent rage felt when confronted by the icy indifference or defiant insolence of the overburdened, undercompensated personnel in a big-city emergency room.

Everyone I approached was too busy to talk to me; would have been even if I'd opened a vein on the spot. As there were no empty seats, I leaned against the nearest wall and closed my eyes in an attempt to calm down, which failed because I was so tired, wired, and scared.

Naturally, seconds after I seized the shoulder of an equally tired nurse, two cops materialized by some kind of cop magic, grabbed me, and marched me outside to the street. Luckily they happened to be more sympathetic than the earlier guys, who were hoping I was the perp.

Admissions was wrong; Miranda had already been in and out of the operating room. The cops said they were under orders not to discuss her case but directed me up to the third-floor office of Justin Paige, M.D.

Paige was tall, tanned, and so mellow I had to sneak a look at his pupils. Here was Narcissus in gold chains, huge cuff links, and a Rolex studded with diamonds. Some plastic surgeon. Except for the watch, he looked more like the headwaiter at a trendy Tribeca restaurant.

"Sit down," he said, motioning toward a chair beside his desk. "You are — ?"

"Miranda's friend. Her closest friend. She doesn't have any relatives in the city."

"Um hmm."

The phone in front of him buzzed.

"Dr. Paige. . . . Um hmm. . . . Um hmm. . . . Ten milligrams Valium. . . . Okay."

He rang off and turned to me.

"Have you been to Europe?" he asked.

"Yes," I said.

"How old were you when you went?"

"Let's see," I said, trying to restrain my impatience. "Twenty-two."

"Did you go to Florence?"

"Just Rome and Venice."

"You know," he said, "I was nineteen the first time I visited Florence. I went to see Michelangelo's David at the Accademia. It was at that moment, the moment I saw the statue, I decided to become an artist."

He played with the fancy Rolex, opening and closing the clasp.

"Art takes many forms," he went on, "many directions. I am a sculptor. My tools are scalpels — and instead of clay or stone or bronze, I work in bone and flesh. I love beauty. I'm in *awe* of beauty, so

I try to create it, maintain it, or in the case of your friend, restore it. But I'm afraid in this instance there were some insurmountable obstacles . . ."

• • •

With the exception of Bedlam, I don't think I've ever seen any pictures of nineteenth-century hospitals, but Sisters of Mercy reminded me of one anyway. People always talk about that puke-green institutional color. This was worse: a kind of ugly oatmeal, cracked, chipped, graffitied, and mottled with layers of city soot. The existing lights (many were burned out, creating random spots of darkness) were the cheapest fluorescent available, insuring that if you didn't enter the hospital sick, you would *look* sick no matter what. I'll just skip the smells.

That Miranda's room was on seven, I thought, emerging from the interminably slow elevator, was a good sign. Lucky Seven. Seventh Heaven, Seventh Son, Seven Sages of Greece, Seven Wonders of the World. But as I walked down the long, dark hall, I began to dwell on the Seven Years' War, the Seven Deadly Sins, and the Seven Sorrows of the Virgin.

My mind was abuzz with magical thinking when I opened Miranda's door and saw her lying unnaturally still, hooked up to various intravenous devices, face half hidden by bandages. She looked so fragile, so much smaller; I didn't dare touch her.

The other bed in this semiprivate room was at least temporarily empty, so I lay down and immediately fell into a deep sleep. When I awoke several hours later, Miranda was still asleep or unconscious and hadn't moved at all. I called her name. No response. I rang for the nurse. I went to the nurse's station. I asked to see a doctor — then demanded. Everybody was too busy to talk.

Miserable and frustrated, I went to the cafeteria, where I pretended to read the New York Times and drank three cups of coffee. Returning to Miranda's room, I sat next to her bed and looked through a tattered issue of Sports Afield I'd borrowed from the visitors' lounge, which was a euphemism if I ever heard one.

I don't like hospitals. Nobody does.

Miranda began to stir.

"NO!" she screamed. I jumped, spilling what was left of my taste-less coffee all over the floor.

"No, no, no — please don't put me with Rocky." Her voice became a whimper. "I'll be good, I promise. Please, don't lock me in there."

"Miranda," I said. "No one's going to hurt you. I'm here. It's David."

"He'll kill me, like he killed that little girl from Lewisville — I know he will. Those bars won't hold. Bea, help me!"

"Miranda, listen to me, please — you're safe." I sat on the edge of her bed, stroking the arm that wasn't linked to the IV machinery. But she pulled her arm away, and hugging herself with it, began to sob. I ran down the hall, searching for a nurse, and when I couldn't find one, dashed back and discovered Miranda sitting up in bed.

I put my arms around her and felt again like a traveler on the bright landscape of love. But the emotion Miranda invoked in me could never be neatly categorized as sexual, filial, paternal, or romantic. The mystery of it confused me then and haunts me still. At the very least it was a lesson. *Le coeur a ses raisons que la raison ne connaît point.*

"What happened?" she whispered, touching her face with her finger-tips. "David, don't cry . . . oh, don't cry, David. Take a look at me, I'm in one piece. Don't cry, sugar."

She leaned forward awkwardly and kissed my tears of relief and release.

"Hey," she said, "this ain't no hill for a stepper."

"I'm sorry," I said, embarrassed.

"Tell me what happened, okay? I can't remember anything after I picked Pete up at the vet's — and we were walking home and . . . and it was dark . . ."

"Somebody attacked you."

"Why?"

Why.

"I don't know why. The police don't either. Not yet, I mean. Whoever it was left your backpack — "

"Oh my God." She shrank into the pillows, her face white beneath the white bandages. "They didn't . . ."

"No, no, no. You weren't . . ."

"Raped?"

"No, you weren't raped."

I felt sick saying it. And couldn't believe that overnight we'd entered a world where we had to be grateful Miranda was beaten, maimed, and nearly killed instead of something even worse.

"My eye . . ." She touched the bandage covering her left eye. "Can I see with it?"

"Yes. Definitely. You've got a cut running from your forehead, through your eyebrow, and down past the corner of your eye. A nerve was severed next to your eye, so the doctors wanted everything to be quiet and heal properly. That's why they covered your whole eye. But you can see perfectly."

"So I was lucky."

I looked at her crooked smile. I was *not* going to let myself cry again.

"Damn right," I said. "You could be blind."

"Or deaf."

"Or paralyzed."

"Or puke across the room like Aunt Enid."

"Or all of the above."

"Then you'd be stuck with me."

"God forbid."

We started to giggle like we were high; our laughter had a manic edge, but it was a hell of a lot better than crying.

• • •

"Miranda, excuse me."

A skinny woman about thirty-five, wearing high heels and a lab coat over a beige suit, walked in and shut the door firmly behind her. I was pretty sure I hadn't seen her in the hospital, though she did look familiar.

"Are you my doctor?" Miranda asked.

"No, but I wanted to see how you're doing."

"I'm fine thanks."

"Excuse me," I said.

As you know by now, suspicion is my middle name.

"Can I do something for you?" I said. "Are you with the police?"

"What's your name?" the woman asked me.

She remained poised; perfectly confident.

"I'm sorry," I said. "But I think it's more appropriate if you tell us *your* name."

"No problem," she said.

Never taking her eyes off Miranda, she sat at the edge of the bed and kept talking without missing a beat.

"You're as beautiful as they all said," she persisted. "I can tell even with the bandages. Do you have any idea who attacked you?"

"Just a second," I said. "You still haven't given us your name — and we don't know what you're doing here."

"I'm Tansy Stoner from the *New York Post.* I want to tell Miranda's story."

"Just get out," I said, taking her by the arm.

"It's okay, David, I'll talk to her."

"Miranda, you don't have to talk to anyone," I said. "You haven't even seen your doctor yet."

I glared at Stoner.

"How the hell did you get in here?" I demanded.

"With that doctor's jacket," said Miranda, turning to the reporter. "And I bet you have a phony ID. Can I see it?"

"No, I'm for real, and so's my press card."

"I meant your phony doctor ID," Miranda said. "In your pocket."

This woman might work the street beat for the *Post,* but it's still a long way from Vassar College to Noah's Ark.

Tansy Stoner made the right decision; without hesitating, she pulled a laminated M.D. photo identification badge complete with clip from the breast pocket of her white jacket and handed it over. Miranda glanced at it without comment, gave it back. Suddenly she looked even more pale and very tired.

"Could you go now, for God's sake," I hissed.

"Can I come back later?"

"Sure," said Miranda wearily. "Come back later."

"Can I ask just *one* question?"

"Okay," said Miranda.

"Do you know who attacked you?"

"No."

"You've been in the city less than a year — how does this attack make you feel about New York?"

"Listen," I snapped. "You said *one* question."

I opened the door.

"I love New York," Miranda said. "You can get beat up anyplace."

"But you weren't just *beaten,*" Stoner said. "Your *face* was *slashed* with a *razor.* You'll be scarred forever — your modeling career is finished, your — "

I dragged her out the door.

"You fucking bitch," I said, and gave her a push, harder than necessary.

When I went back in the room, Miranda was trying to move out of bed.

"Hey, get back in."

"*What* did she say?" Miranda whispered.

"I'm going to make sure she can't come anywhere near you again," I said, grabbing the phone.

"David," Miranda said. "Put the phone down. First tell me what she was talking about. What razor?"

"I don't know what she was talking about," I said.

Lame's the name; denial's the game.

"*Goddammit,*" Miranda cried. "You're fucking worse than her!"

"Oh thank you," I said. "That's very nice."

I'd much rather start an argument than tell Miranda what she wanted to know.

"Sit down," she said. "And quit trying to trick me; you're not making me feel better. Just *say* it, I can take anything."

"I don't really know that much," I said.

"Then bring me a mirror," she said.

Maybe I was in some kind of shock. I felt everything slow down; my head was filled with glue. I couldn't talk. I didn't move.

"*David.*"

"There aren't any mirrors," I said.

In fact, there was a small mirror hanging on a side wall where a print of Honolulu at sunset should have been.

"You're such a shitty liar," she said, and forced her feet over the side of the bed, stood up, swayed for an instant — then collapsed on the floor, ripping the tubes out of her arm. She was unyielding when I tried to pick her up.

"Just get that fucking mirror."

I took the little mirror down and brought it over. She was still on the floor, sitting now, leaning against the bed. When I tried to hand it to her, she turned away.

"I can't look," she said.

"Okay," I said.

"But I have to."

"Do it later," I said.

"I have to do it now."

She took the mirror out of my hand, but still didn't look.

"The only fucking thing they ever gave me," she said, "was this fucking face. It was gonna be my ticket out of the shit . . . but I was too stupid."

"That's absurd," I said.

She fiddled with the mirror, balancing it on one corner.

"I know why you write your books," she said.

"Why?" I said. Anything to postpone the inevitable.

"So the good guys win."

"That's probably true," I said. "But if you think the good guys lost this time, I can tell you the story isn't over yet."

"It's over," she said.

Slowly, she turned the mirror around and held it up.

"Oh no," she whispered. "I didn't believe it before; I could feel the bandages, but I didn't *believe* it."

As she looked at her face — battered, bruised, half swathed in bandages — I watched the chill flame behind those silver-blue eyes go dead.

"No, no, no," she cried again. She put down the mirror carefully and curled in a tight ball on the floor, arms locked around her knees. I couldn't move her so I pulled the cotton blanket off the bed and covered her. I walked slowly through the door and closed it quietly behind me.

Then I ran for all I was worth to find help.

• • •

Racing down the hall, I almost collided with Justin Paige, the plastic surgeon, who hurried back to Miranda's room with me, where we found her still curled like a fetus on the floor.

Paige touched her shoulder. She didn't respond.

"Miranda," he said.

Nothing.

"You're going to be all right," he said.

Still nothing.

He lifted her onto the bed and reattached the IV tubes she'd yanked out. Then he sat next to her and began calmly describing her injuries and their treatment.

Considering the guy's egomania, I hoped his operating skills matched his rap, but since surgery had already been performed (while I was sitting uselessly in jail) I was grateful at least for his gentle tone.

He talked about skin, nerves, sutures, antibiotics, healing, cleansing. He mentioned a new technique being developed by a Dr. Hutton at Massachusetts Eye and Ear. His calm voice, almost a monotone, was soothing, and I started to unwind for the first time since Juliana woke me with her screams.

Finally Miranda asked:

"What about scars? Will I have scars for the rest of my life?"

Paige's pause seemed to grow and fill the room.

"*Will I?*" she insisted.

"It's too early," the doctor replied. "I can't really say."

"*Try,*" she said.

"Miranda," said Paige, "I'm a scientist — "

"Thought you were an artist," I mumbled.

"What's that?" he asked.

"Nothing," I said.

"Go on," Miranda said to Paige. "You're a scientist and what?"

"And although medicine is an imperfect science," he continued, "we try for specificity. So until I know something definite, I'd be doing you a disservice if I guessed at the outcome."

Miranda paused; long tangles of silver-blond hair obscured her face as she bowed her head.

"I *want* you to guess," she said. "I'm strong, I can take it."

Oh sure.

"Please," she said.

I thought Paige would prevail here; but obviously fatigue had killed my remaining brain cells and I forgot the effect — even in bandages — Miranda had on men. Including men who were supposedly unsusceptible, like queers and doctors.

Now it was Paige who paused, staring at his Rolex for a response or a reason to leave.

"I'd say you'll have some scarring," he finally said.

"But you can fix it, right?" she asked.

"I don't know," he said.

"You or the doctor you said in Boston, with the new technique."

"Maybe," the surgeon replied.

"Maybe's not good enough!" Miranda's voice turned shrill, and I felt a quick dart of pity for Paige, who was no psychotherapist.

"We can talk about this again," the doctor said, standing. "I'll check in on you later."

As soon as he left the room, Miranda began to cry.

"I'm fucked," she said. "It's finished."

"Nothing's finished," I said.

"Oh yeah, right," she said. "Why don't you just pee on my back and say it's raining."

•   •   •

While Miranda slept fitfully, I paced the room; then I paced the hall. I ran into an old queen who used to live around the corner from the Tequila Tavern. He was en route to visit his lover in the cardiac care unit and gave me a Xanax, which I washed down with some more disgusting coffee from the cafeteria.

When Miranda woke up, she asked for a painkiller, and the nurse who gave her the injection told me she'd be out for hours, probably all night. I needed air, if only New York's most polluted, and decided to head home for a shower, a drink, and some sleep.

As I walked quietly to the door of Miranda's darkened room, she called my name.

"Don't forget to feed Pete."

So sue me. I didn't have the heart.

"Sure," I said, and closed the door.

I'd tell her when she was a little stronger.

Next morning on my way back to the hospital, I picked up a couple of newspapers.

SLASHED MODEL STILL LOVES NEW YORK screeched the ninety-six-point headline in the *Post,* over a photo of Miranda snapped in the emergency room, accompanying a story bylined Tansy Stoner. The *News* and *Newsday* weighed in with equally large type and lurid details.

Although what happened to Miranda was the biggest thing in my life, it took time to absorb the idea that the entire city was also stunned. And people beyond the city.

Good editors and producers know the mix is the thing. And I guess the mix of Miranda's beauty, her upbeat position on New York, the vicious and apparently gratuitous crime, in combination with a slow news week, created a frenzy in the press that lasted considerably longer than I or anyone else could have anticipated.

• • •

From Delaney-Behar Correspondence:

Perry Old Pal,

Finally told Sherry Lehman to send over a case of '85 Rausan-Ségla. Recommend you phone your fellow in London and do the same. Parker's not wild for it, but everyone else touts it as a return to early grandeur.

Went to see Miranda at the hospital and I must tell you that after what she's gone through, her ruined beauty has taken on an ethereal, almost mystical quality. I can overlook the trailer park aspect of her past, because though lacking education, she's quite bright. E.g. to the *Times:* "Everyone has scars, mine show." Not a bad line. The fucking mayor called her!

Yr. friend,

Bill Faulkner   28 May New York

———

My dear John Francis,

Why shouldn't the fucking mayor ring? He's a crafty chap and Miranda's story gets the old tear ducts welling and piping. It's all over the papers everywhere.

My French publisher was wild to hear all the grisly details — you know how those Frogs love the macabre. Fixed dinner for him last night. Porcini risotto, assorted antipasti, and an '82 Renati Barolo — a tad austere.

Took your advice on the Rausan-Ségla.

Faithfully,

PB   London, Friday, 29th May

P.S. Question of the day: Can oenophilia and egalitarianism coexist peacefully in the same heart? Time will tell.

• • •

The surprise publicity around the attack on Miranda made me steel myself for a crowd, but when I reached her room, the door was closed with a NO VISITORS sign on it. The hall beyond was quiet. Assuming the sign didn't mean me, I knocked and went in.

Miranda was sitting up in bed, pushing away a tray filled with untouched, nasty hospital food — all white punctuated by lime Jell-o.

"Don't tell me to eat," she said.

"I won't."

Trying to find a vase for the little bunch of carnations I'd bought at the greengrocer's next to the newsstand, I noticed there were no other flowers in the room.

"Who put up the NO VISITORS sign?"

"Me," she said. "I mean, I asked them to. I don't feel like seeing anybody."

"Did you talk to anyone this morning?"

"Just the nurses," she said. "A cop came over, but I told him I was too tired to talk — why?"

"I figured people would call."

The newspapers I'd brought were still in a plastic bag on the floor.

"Nobody called."

"Maybe you have messages," I said. "Let's check."

I picked up the phone and dialed the hospital switchboard.

"I don't want messages," said Miranda.

This attitude was distressing, but who could blame her.

As it happened, since no one had requested that the phone be activated in her room, of course it hadn't been. I told the switchboard operator to turn it on, thinking well-wishers would create a cheering effect. Indeed, the very moment I hung up, the phone rang. Miranda surprised me by answering.

She was silent for a few moments, frowning above the bandages.

"What?" she asked. "What are you talking about?"

Pause.

"You're *crazy*," she said, and dropped the receiver back on the cradle.

"That," she told me, "was an insane woman talking about how God would forgive me for my sins, for whatever sin it was made somebody mad enough to hurt me — she said the minute she read about me in the newspaper she started praying for me. Did you see anything in the paper?"

Then the phone rang again and it was Clementine Sheffield.

"Fine, I'm feeling fine," Miranda said. "No I'm really much better already — I should be back to work in a couple of weeks. I'm a fast healer — "

She listened for a few seconds.

"Well no, he didn't say exactly how long."

Miranda was nodding slowly at what she was hearing.

"It's okay with me, I guess, but if another doctor comes in to look at me, I wouldn't want Dr. Paige to get the wrong idea. I mean he — "

Pause.

"Oh yes, they got here this morning, thank you very much. Yes, I love phalaenopsis orchids too."

She looked over at me and shook her head.

"Okay, Clementine, Dr. Don Baldwin. I'll be expecting him. No problem. Thanks for calling. No don't worry, I know you hate hospitals . . . and I'll be out soon. . . . Okay. . . . Bye."

Miranda dropped the phone in its cradle and leaned back on her pillows with a sigh.

"Clementine wants to send in another plastic surgeon for a second opinion."

"That makes perfect sense," I said, wishing Clementine's motives could be pure. "Everybody around here gets second opinions. Clementine Sheffield would get a second opinion about a hangnail. And I've read about Baldwin in *New York* magazine; he's supposed to be the best."

"I just want somebody to fix my face," said Miranda. "I don't like a lot of fuss."

"Yeah, well take a deep breath."

I pulled the newspapers out of the bag and lay them on her bed.

She was enormously surprised by all the attention, particularly the front-page play. At first she couldn't imagine how they came by the pictures, but then she remembered a photographer in the emergency room who got off a few shots before being kicked out. She read each piece dispassionately between phone calls. And the phone calls, having started, seemed never to stop.

Clementine Sheffield's right hand, Johnny Ferris, called; Ben from The Shamrock, Bea from Arkansas, Malone from California, Donny Redding from Georgia, where the Mets were playing the Braves, a girlfriend from Texas and another from Oregon. Miranda heard from the crop duster pilot, from her boss at the insurance company in Fayetteville, and even from Juliana, who apparently knew how to panhandle quarters and use the telephone.

One time I answered and someone told me the Justice Department was calling, which I thought was a joke.

"Don't hang up," said Miranda. "That must be Lynne."

Lynne Huffman, it turned out, worked for the attorney general in Washington. She had been Miranda's best friend at Noah's Ark.

Miranda chatted about her life in New York, her work, her stalled romance with "can-you-believe-Bobby-Wilder — no-I'm-not-putting-you-on," and finally the attack, a few more details of which she was beginning to remember. Lynne, on her boss's recommendation, offered to give Miranda the name of a New York lawyer in case she needed help, and after about fifteen minutes they said good-bye, promising to stay in touch.

"Why would *I* need a lawyer?" Miranda asked me.

"Maybe you can sue somebody."

"I don't want to sue anybody — I want to put them in jail."

"Well the attorney general obviously knows who's who — so just get the name in case you ever need a lawyer."

"The only time I ever needed a lawyer before, what I got was a social worker — mean as a snake too."

• • •

From Roland Tarbell's column:

. . . just back from a long weekend with Wales, et al., to take her place at the starting gate of the summer social season. Baby sister Buff (they never did share the same taste, except in husbands) plans to stay at Lyford Cay until the first hurricane. Such a brave girl.

In a more serious vein, our thoughts are with Clementine Sheffield's most promising star, who lies alone this day, in a darkened hospital room, her face bandaged, victim of an unspeakably brutal attack. As the poet said: "Beauty more than bitterness, makes the heart break." Our heart goes out to you, dear Miranda.

Note to an East Side lady and her Western paramour (you know who you are): Love may be blind but everybody else is watching. . . .

• • •

In the cafeteria, checking out the gruel of the day, I wondered why no one in Miranda's family had called. And if she heard from Bobby Wilder, she didn't mention it.

While Miranda napped, my mystery meat lunch was made tolerable by the discreet addition (from a small silver flask I'd found at a Columbus Avenue flea market) of some eighty-proof Mount Gay to my watery Coca-Cola.

I felt pretty good after a couple of these clandestine colas, and at the nurses' station on Miranda's floor, I stopped to admire a cartful of flower arrangements, far more lavish than the usual hospital variety. An aide I hadn't seen before came around the corner, took charge of the cart, and turned it toward the staff elevator.

"They something else, ain't they," she said, pointing to a large fragrant basket of peonies and lilacs.

"They been comin' in by the bushel for that poor model what got her face cut. She told us take 'em up to the peoples in the psycho ward — ain't no flowers up there, I can tell you that."

"How come she doesn't want her flowers?" I asked.

"Dunno," the aide said guilelessly. "Guess she figures flowers won't do her no good when her life's wrecked."

"But her life's not wrecked," I said. "I mean, she's got her arms and legs and her brain. She's got friends, she's smart — "

"Listen, honey," the aide said with surprising passion. "I recognize that girl — even sliced up like that — I seen her on the cover of *Cosmo,* and on the cover of *Smart,* and in one of them shampoo commercials on TV. When she ever gonna be such a big deal again or make that kind of money? Never's when, and if she so smart she probably already got it figured out. Then there's the other thing . . ."

"What other thing?"

My innocent act, patience, and alcoholic good humor were all disintegrating into the aura that precedes a migraine headache. The space in front of me narrowed. One of the duty nurses noisily hung up her phone and looked over at us.

"Nothin'," said the aide, and pushed her cart toward the elevator.

I sat with Miranda for the rest of the day. My headache never reached maturity. It was still just a throbbing behind my eyes hours later, when I finally left her in the hands of Dr. Donald Baldwin who, if he wasn't then, is certainly now the single preeminent plastic surgeon in New York.

Returning to Hell's Kitchen, I decided The Shamrock could live without my business for another night. After I got home, I called Malone in Los Angeles. He was out God knows where or with whom or doing what for how long.

Juliana strolled by as I dropped my blackout shade, and I was almost happy to see her. I washed down a couple of Restoril with a shot of Appleton's minus the cola and passed out.

• • •

From Delaney-Behar Correspondence:

Dear Peregrine:

I think your friend Mr. Wolf has decamped London for New York and is currently ensconced on my doorstep. Am avoiding him, Nils, and my agent while trying to cope with the latest sortie from Milan.

Domina, unbelievably, has bribed a waiter in Port'Ercole to swear I was drunk when we left the restaurant the day of the car wreck. She also claims the old man (from the other car, whose wife later died) saw me at the wheel and she's threatening to take her story public. All to extort as much money as possible from me. I don't need a scandal at this point. On the other hand, I'm going broke.

Ever,

F. Dostoyevsky   30 May New York

My dear John Francis,

Terribly sorry to hear the news from Milan. Can't fathom D.V. going so far. Fax or ring if there's anything I can do.

I know this is dreadful for you. So dreadful, in fact, you won't have time to study pps. 9–12 in the Christie's catalogue . . .

Water divides, wine unites,

PB   London, 1st June

––––––––

Peregrine you old sot,

You beat me to the punch with that case of '70 Mouton-Rothschild from Christie's. But I forgive you because I'll get the next one. Looks like good news for the exchequer. DON'T TELL MIRANDA, but Patrice Owen just saved my sorry ass.

Cheers,

F. S. Fitzgerald   2 June New York

P.S. I heard Sony made an offer for Norstar. You better develop a taste for sake.

––––––––

My dear John Francis Xavier,

Throw a lucky man in the water and he comes up with a fish in his mouth. I certainly can't tell Miranda if you don't tell ME. Please send details.

Racing to lunch with Sabrina Guinness (of the banking lot, not brewing) — divine girl.

Yours,

PB   London, 3rd June

P.S. I loathe sake.

––––––––

Dear Peregrine,

I knew my luck had changed when I took Patrice Owen to dinner and discovered a 1980 DRC Romanée-St.-Vivant on the wine list for considerably lower than the retail price.

This is the deal: DON'T TELL MIRANDA, but I'm writing her story. World rights to Big O Productions. They'll package the novel, produce the movie, everything. I've gone global.

Ad astra per aspera,

Gore Vidal   4 June New York

•   •   •

After the Tansy Stoner episode, Miranda refused to give interviews or see anyone from the press. What's the point, she asked, and since we shared the same feeling about publicity for publicity's sake, I certainly couldn't think of any. Her decision, however, didn't stop the huge media snowball. Hordes of reporters kept phoning and hanging around the hospital; they came from television, from the news-weeklies, and from the daily and weekly tabloids. The rhinoceros-skinned Stoner wouldn't say die and continued ringing several times a day though Miranda always hung up on her.

All the attention amazed Miranda. But the bottom line remained stationary: the police were getting nowhere in their efforts to locate whoever attacked her.

The only journalist for whom Miranda made an exception and granted an interview was the one from the Great Gray Lady. By way of explanation, she said: "Well David, it's the *New York Times!*"

But of course.

Even when she found several inaccuracies in the story, which appeared as a big front-page human interest piece, she said: "I'm sure that reporter has plenty of things on his mind."

"Oh yeah," I said, "like the Yankees score, like is he going to eat dinner at Runyan's or the Palm, and would you go out with him if he ditched his wife and kids. You're such a Pollyanna."

"And *you're* so contrary," she said. "If I threw you in the river, you'd float upstream."

"Maybe I'd just walk across the water."

"Yeah, more likely," she said.

"But you'd never get me in the water," I said.

"I guess you forget how strong I am," she said.

I walked over to the bed, rolling up my sleeves.

"Go ahead, hotshot," she said, lifting her free arm. "Try to pin that arm."

So we arm-wrestled, and I didn't insult her by not trying. Even under those circumstances, the girl was surprisingly powerful, and it took longer than I guessed to get her arm down.

We were both thinking the same thing, but I waited for her to say it. She ran a hand through her hair and put her head on my shoulder.

"I'm strong, David. But there were two of them. I remembered that this morning. I still can't remember much of anything else. I hate having a big blank."

"It'll come back to you," I said, half hoping it wouldn't. "Miranda, who's Rocky?"

"The movie?"

"I don't think so," I said. "It was somebody you were dreaming about. You were saying something like, 'Don't lock me in with Rocky — he'll kill me, like he killed that little girl from Lewisville.' "

She smiled a sad little smile.

"You're a good detective," she said. "I bet you thought maybe Rocky had something to do with the attack."

I shrugged.

"I suppose," she said, "people's minds are always working, making connections, no matter what. Rocky sure was an attack artist — but he never got me."

"Was he a guy from Noah's Ark?"

"He was a bull at Noah's Ark."

"As in . . . guard?"

"We had bull dykes too," she said. "But I'm talking four-legged male animal with two huge horns. They had a dairy farm down there at Noah's Ark . . . a lot of cows, I can't remember how many. And he was the stud. All the cows lived in the barn . . . and he lived nearby in a big pen with a fancy indoor area attached. It looked like a little house. If you went in the door from the outside, not the pen side, you were in a little room with no windows, just these bars separating the room from the covered part of the pen. If a kid was bad, the guards would lock him or her in that little room alone all night. Rocky liked to charge the bars and rattle them with his horns . . . and of course the kid would get scared to death."

"What about that girl from Lewisville?"

"Poor little thing. All she did was sass this one guard on a bad day, and they locked her in there . . . and the frame around the bars came loose, and Rocky got into that room with no windows and killed that little girl."

"Jesus," I said — but I don't think Miranda heard. She'd lain back down against her pillow with her free arm over her eyes. She was far away, by the edge of a south Arkansas swamp.

• • •

I gave Cassie and Zack a vacation as the hospital became my routine. But it was a strange routine. Time expanded and shrank like Alice after drinking the magic potion, and my circadian rhythms went crazy.

So one afternoon while Miranda was undergoing a series of tests on various floors, I went home, had a hit of some very excellent hash I'd been hoarding for a rainy day, and passed out. The chronically depressed are not the only ones who know where to find refuge.

I slept that daytime kind of sleep in which dreams are unavoidable. In the midst of a particularly lurid episode along a bombed-out Fifth Avenue of the future, featuring Miranda and Malone, both with hair chopped off and dyed black, the doorbell woke me.

No one ever rings the doorbell in New York. I don't mean as opposed to knock, tap, or break it down. I mean people never drop by. And people rarely visit. Because, as I've said before, the city runs along telephone circuits.

9

• • •

JACK DELANEY was at my door.

"Hey, sorry I woke you up," he said. "But I was thinking we could talk. I mean, I need to talk to you. You want to have a beer?"

"A beer?"

"Or, you know, whatever." He was uncomfortable — and in the space of a moment, this handsome young writer for whom I felt simultaneous envy and disdain, seemed oddly exposed. Not because, like many straight men, he didn't know how to treat a fairy — and thus slipped into some unfamiliar mode meant to underscore his own masculinity. No, this guy was famously hetero (albeit of the hetero type that prefers sipping Ch. Petrus with Peregrine Poohbutt to swilling brewskis with the boys), and his discomfort came from somewhere else.

"Give me a couple of minutes," I said, leaving him in the living room while I headed for the shower, where I was more interested in clearing my mind than cleansing my body.

When I emerged a little later in fresh clothes, I found Delaney studying my bookshelves. Turning to me he recited by heart, from Jim Harrison's *Legends of the Fall*:

" 'Cochran held her tightly in his arms remembering how light a dead bird felt when he picked it out of a thicket in the Indiana woods. He spoke again in a rush trying to keep her alive by the power in the energy of his words: it was as if his brain had split open and he plunged, raked, dug, mining any secret he might hold to bring her to health.' "

My throat closed. I was afraid I'd cry.

Having created a heavily fraught atmosphere, Delaney immediately set out to change it.

"I see you have all Harrison's books," he said. "And McGuane's. I do too."

"I think," I said, relieved to be back on solid ground, "with all due respect, McGuane's the best writer under fifty in America."

"Top five," said Delaney.

"Who else?" I asked.

"Styron, Matthiessen, Cormac McCarthy.

"All over fifty," I said.

"Okay — Joan Didion," he said.

"She's over fifty."

"Picky, picky," he said. "Richard Price."

"Are you counting movies?"

"I don't know — what are the rules?"

"No rules," I said.

"Bret Ellis," he said.

"Under fifty," I said. "Not under twenty."

"He's almost our age," said Delaney.

"I know, I know."

Delaney and I strolled over to The Shamrock, discussing contemporary American letters, and I (the not-so-secret snob) became more and more impressed with his wide-ranging, idiosyncratic education and knowledge. Or maybe it was his concentrated interest in me. Thinking back now, I can't really tell.

Incidentally, just as I would never look at a child as a sex object, I never look at a straight man — except in a passing fantasy — as a sexual possibility either. Not that they're inviolate like children, but life's too short.

When we reached The Shamrock, Ben, who manned the bar seven days a week for as long as I'd been a patron, was absent. A big guy with shaggy hair and pallid skin told me, in a thick Irish brogue that didn't invite further questioning, Ben was "out" and would be back "soon." Too much was going on for me to explain to Delaney how strange this little nuance was.

Delaney ordered us a bottle of California zinfandel, probably the only wine in the place he considered potable. After wrinkling his nose and raising one eyebrow at the first sniff — but without comment — he guzzled down a glassful and quickly refilled.

"So," he said, and lit a cigarette.

"So," I replied. "You and Miranda are friends."

It was the best I could do in spite of the passage he'd chosen from *Legends of the Fall,* which had touched my heart and muffled the ever-present sounds of skepticism in my head.

"Sort of," he said. "I took her out to dinner a couple of times."

A *couple* of times.

"And?" I asked, not generous enough to let him feel entirely comfortable.

"And I really like her."

"Everybody likes her."

"I mean I couldn't get her out of my mind after that Thanksgiving party at Larry Owen's."

"Life is lived at parties."

"Sometimes it is."

"I guess," I said. "But what happened to your girlfriend?"

Ordinarily, I'm afraid to ask a question that even knocks on the gate of somebody's personal life. These, however, were unusual circumstances requiring unusual behavior. Plus I knew the answer because I'd read it in the gossip columns.

"Domina?" he asked, as though perhaps I was referring to some other girlfriend.

"Yes, your fiancée."

"She's at her sister's house in Milan. First she was recuperating, now she's waiting while her apartment is redecorated."

"She was sick?"

"We had an automobile accident. It was in the papers."

"Oh, I guess I missed it."

"That's amazing," he said. "I mean, the press from here was driving me crazy — and I was in Italy. And the Italians — forget it. The word paparazzi didn't get to be global for nothing."

"What happened?" I asked.

"The usual," he said. "They called, they hung out at the hotel, they — "

"I meant the accident."

"The accident, of course, the accident. I was over there to see my Italian publisher. It was raining, but for some reason Domina wanted to drive. She's a lousy driver, but I was still jet-lagged so I said okay. We were out in the boonies on the way back from Port'Ercole and I figured what could happen?"

"What did happen?"

"The car skidded, she lost control, and we hit a car coming in the other direction."

"God," I said. "You're lucky to be alive."

"The other car was going slowly — we weren't going that fast either."

"But Domina was hurt?"

"Broken collarbone," he said. "A couple of cracked ribs. All I got was some bad bruises."

"How about the other car?" I asked.

Delaney looked at me over his glass as he took a long drink of wine.

"A couple on their way to Monte Argentario," he said. "Shaken up, scared; their car had to be towed, but they walked away all right."

"That was lucky too," I said.

He turned toward the bar.

"What kind of brandy have they got here?"

"Nothing too interesting."

In fact, the only choice was the ghastly Christian Brothers, which the temporary bartender gave us in double shot glasses.

"By the way," said Delaney. "I'm not engaged to Domina. That was just something the press picked up and ran with — it was never real."

"It looked real," I said. Pathetic.

"It was about appearance and reality," he said.

"I'd say more about truth and consequences."

I was, of course, drunk.

"Yeah, well — " He shrugged.

"Miranda would say twenty-four wells make a river."

"Oh," he said.

"Why are we here?" I asked, boozily out of character.

"Because we both care about Miranda, because we both want to help her."

"You barely know her," I said.

But I could hear the ice cracking under my skates. Maybe he knew her a lot better than I thought.

"I guess that's true — but I want to get to know her; she's an incredible girl. And so beautiful."

I was moved by his faith that she was still beautiful.

"And," he went on, "it's obvious that you're closer to her than anybody, so I — " He shrugged again and stared into his brandy.

Suddenly I saw Delaney as a gallant friend, not a heavy-handed flatterer. And in some place I couldn't summon up sober, I was relieved. The flip side of wanting Miranda all for myself was having no one with whom to share the burden of her attack. Although I knew my virtues, whatever they were, sprang from weakness rather than strength, I had been prepared to carry the weight alone. But here was Jack Delaney, holding out his hand.

Actually, at that moment, he was holding out his glass for another refill, but you get my point.

•   •   •

Day became evening in a blur of brandy at The Shamrock; we phoned Miranda, who was half asleep but sounded happy that Delaney and I were out together. Later, just as we finally decided to pay the tab, Mark Douglas walked into the bar.

More foul and unwashed than ever, his dirty hair was loose from its usual ponytail, his eyes were bloodshot, and his shirt was almost entirely open, revealing a small pot belly which, on his skinny body, looked as if it were occupied by an alien being. Jack Delaney didn't exactly draw back in horror, but he shifted around uneasily in his seat as the landlord approached us.

"Dave," the landlord said, "who've you got here?"

"A friend."

"A friend, huh. How about I join you guys?"

He started pulling up a chair.

"We were just leaving, Mark," I said, standing.

"Yeah," said Delaney. "It's been a long day. Sorry."

He moved toward the door.

"Speaking of friends," Mark Douglas said, "how's your friend what's-her-name?"

What's-her-name? Why did the question chill me? The boozy

warmth I'd been feeling was suddenly replaced by icy bands around my heart, squeezing, as I searched for the answer just beyond my grasp. Could Mark have been involved with the attack on Miranda? Yeah, the butler did it. At this rate I was ignoring skepticism, pausing at suspicion, and diving directly into paranoia; next stop, the loony bin.

"She's fine," I said, and followed Jack Delaney to the door. Outside, we parted with a promise to talk the next day.

At home, there was just one message on my machine — from Detective Mike Romanos of Midtown South, saying they had picked up one of Miranda's assailants, a young man by the name of Dooley Kincaid.

• • •

My doorbell rang early the next morning, for the second time in two days, practically establishing a trend.

My caller was Jonathan Loring, the rude veterinarian. Since The Shamrock wasn't open at that hour, I made him a cup of coffee, although he looked so uncomfortable a drink might have been better. Probably has no idea how to handle himself outside his little animal fiefdom, I thought sourly.

"Now," I said, at ease in my own little fiefdom. "What can I do for you?"

Something about this guy made me contentious.

"Ah . . . ," he said, looking at the floor.

I waited. He took a sip of coffee.

"I need to ask your friend Miranda a question . . . and I haven't done it yet."

"Why not?"

"Because," he said studying the floor again. "It was too hard, but . . ."

"But what?"

"The cops," he said, finally looking at me, "released the remains of the dog to me and I have to ask her what she wants done — but I was afraid to disturb her or upset her."

I felt like shit — about Miranda's attack, about Pete's death, about this guy who reminded me of my frequent inability to get people right on the first pass — but most of all because several days had now passed and I still hadn't told Miranda about her beloved companion.

"What are the choices?" I asked.

"Same as people, basically," said Loring. "She can have him buried, or cremated — but time's going by, and some decision should be made."

"Well, I haven't told her yet," I confessed. "I just couldn't assault her with the news. She was in and out of it at first because of pain-killers and all that. Then she was so weak. But she's getting stronger. I still don't want to tell her — but I guess I have to."

"You want me to come with you?"

When Loring and I arrived at Miranda's room half an hour later, we found Jack Delaney sitting next to her bed reading aloud from Emily Dickinson.

I was afraid that the moment she saw Loring she'd know we brought bad news — but apparently she didn't recognize him.

"Detective Romanos came by," Miranda said.

"They arrested one of the assailants," Delaney added.

I told them I'd heard, and introduced Jonathan Loring, who surprised me by smoothly inviting a puzzled Delaney for a sandwich in the cafeteria, so I could be alone with Miranda.

"That was the veterinarian we took Pete to," I said.

"My God," said Miranda. "He was the last person I saw before ..." She ran her fingers through her hair. "I can't believe I don't remember him."

"It'll come back," I said. "Other things are already coming back."

"Guess how the cops got this guy Dooley Kincaid," she said.

"I have no idea."

"Pete bit him so hard the bite got infected, and he went to the emergency room at Bellevue, and a nurse who'd read about Pete in the paper had a funny feeling. . . . Did you see anything about Pete in the paper?"

"Yes."

"But you didn't read me that part."

"Miranda . . ."

"He's okay though," she said. "Isn't he?"

"Let me tell you what happened."

"He's alive, David, isn't he?"

"I'll explain — "

"*No*," she said, holding out her hand, palm perpendicular to the floor.

I cleared my throat.

"You see . . . ," I said. Then I had to close my eyes.

"No," she whispered. "No, no, not Pete, please — *please*."

Miranda decided to have Pete cremated, and two days later Jonathan Loring came by the hospital again to deliver an ebony box filled with ashes — all that was left of Miranda's big, white, prancing dog.

Loring was still with Miranda and me when the police detective, Mike Romanos, called. Dooley Kincaid had fingered his cousin Lester Bartholomew as his accomplice in the attack. Bartholomew had skipped but was most likely hiding out with other relatives somewhere around Mobile, Alabama. The Alabama authorities promised it was just a matter of time until they got their hands on him.

Kincaid and Bartholomew's motive, which they said was robbery, satisfied nobody because A) Miranda's bag, which contained cash, was left behind, and B) the slashing didn't jibe with anything on Kincaid's or Bartholomew's long rap sheets.

•   •   •

Miranda finally began feeling better. The bandages were reduced to three strips across her forehead, eyebrow, and cheek. Out of bed and sitting in a chair, she was talking to Johnny Ferris when I walked in carrying watercress soup and sandwiches for our lunch. She was telling Ferris that Paige, who did the original surgery, and Baldwin, whom Clementine called in to consult, agreed it was too early to know exactly when they could restore her face. But it would be soon.

Unfortunately, this was the glass-overflowing account.

I'd been with her during Baldwin's last visit, and Miranda was far too smart to misunderstand. Even as the soft-spoken young surgeon described ambitious research in Boston, Tel Aviv, and Buenos Aires and imparted an evenhanded hope for the future, he had explained, with impressive compassion, the likelihood of scarring, and spelled out the absence of foolproof techniques to fill or erase the scars.

"These cuts," Miranda was saying, "are gonna heal fast."

"How do you know? asked Ferris.

"Because I'm a fast healer," she said.

"I hope so," he said petulantly. "Clementine's suicidal about that endorsement deal, and all your bookings canceled except one."

"But I was booked through Christmas!" said Miranda. "I can cover the scars with makeup, then Dr. Baldwin can fill them in or that guy in Boston — how could Clementine let this happen?"

"Darling," said Johnny Ferris, suddenly conciliatory. "Don't get bent out of shape. You know Clementine, she's a control freak. She goes wild if she's not in charge. She can't dictate how long your face will be . . . whatever. She had to put other people into your spots. She just wants you to rest."

"Oh bullshit, Johnny," said Miranda.

"What can I say, Miranda?"

"Who didn't cancel?"

"*Bazaar.* Cat Kelly said she thought you'd be okay."

"Well that must mean something to Clementine," insisted Miranda. "I'm supposed to do the September cover — the biggest issue of the year."

"I *know* what it is," said Johnny.

Miranda closed her eyes for a moment.

"I'm getting tired," she said. "How about let's talk later."

Looking relieved to be off the hook, Johnny Ferris, with an awkward hug for Miranda and a nod in my direction, hurried out.

Miranda turned to me.

"He and Clementine both think I won't be able to work anymore," she said.

"Ferris and Clementine don't think," I said. "They only react — like reptiles."

Just then, Johnny came back into the room.

"Forgot my bag," he said, grabbing a L'Uomo satchel he'd dropped by the bed. After giving Miranda a quick air kiss, he left again.

"Well," she said, blowing a kiss at the closing door. "If you're gonna kiss a rat, kiss him good-bye."

"He's a creep," I said, squelching my uglier thoughts. "Here, I brought something to eat. Take a look."

"They're not the only ones . . . ," Miranda said.

"I know, I know," I said. "We could have had BLTs, or chicken salad, or minestrone — or an omelet." Pathetic.

"You know what I mean," she said.

"Okay," I said. "What other ones are you talking about?"

"Before the attack," she said. "I was talking to a couple of TV people — "

"Something you failed to tell me."

Although I can be as asinine an egomaniac as anybody else, in this case I was trying to distract Miranda. But she wasn't buying.

"Because I wanted to surprise you," she said. "Besides, it was just cable."

"*Just* cable," I said. "Like HBO, MTV, and CNN."

"*Local* cable," she said. "Do you want to hear this?"

I nodded and started unpacking the lunch.

"So I met these two really smart girls at a party," she said. "They were putting together a new kind of talk show — new format with four hosts, two women and two guys. There was one place left. We had some meetings, we did some test videos — they offered me the job and — "

"What?" My heart was sinking.

" — and I called them this morning. They said they were sorry and they hope to talk to me in the future, but for now they're going in a different direction — "

"Their deal probably fell through," I said. "They probably never even had a deal."

"They're starting production in a month — and this one girl said she *knew* I'd understand, but the *reality* was the audience would look at my scars and miss the content of their show. She said I should give them a buzz next year — or sometime."

"But not sometime soon," I said.

"Like never," said Miranda.

I often think no matter how tough I get, I'll never catch up to the way things really are.

"Try this soup," I offered.

"It's green."

"So's grass, money, and emeralds," I said. "All things you like. Now this is good. Eat it."

"I'm not giving up, David."

"Well that's a relief," I said. "You're already so skinny if you turn sideways you disappear."

"I don't give up," she said, ignoring me. "I haven't even been in the hospital that long — and these people act like I'm finished. I am *not* finished — I've barely started."

I tried not to let on how grateful I was that she'd either forgotten or changed her initial response.

"Yeah, well start your soup," I said. "What channel was this alleged show going to be on?"

Miranda took the remote from the bedside table and clicked on the television.

Like an unfriendly ghost, the image of Tansy Stoner appeared, her long face and flat chest filling the screen. Although I'd never seen it, I remembered that several years earlier her tabloid columns had given birth to a local talk show.

Evidently her appeal as the lowest common denominator in the mass market insured her continuing midday slot. Indeed, she may single-handedly have inspired the spate of tabloid shows that followed, but was unable herself ever to make the leap out of New York cable to any major or minor network since she couldn't overcome conventional broadcast wisdom, which called for expunging from on-camera a homely squinter with a nasal whine. Miranda thought Stoner was a disappointed person and therefore bitter. I thought she was just born mean.

Whatever the case, overbearing is an understatement to describe Stoner's interviewing persona. She made her reputation, such as it was, by literally chasing ambulances and asking the unaskable, like: "How does it feel to see your children splattered all over the road?"

"Today," said Stoner through her nose, "we're going to discuss a vicious crime. A heinous crime. One of the ugliest crimes we've seen here in New York in a long time. And we've seen them all, haven't we?"

She leaned forward to stress the importance of her words.

"But there are two sides to every story," she continued. "And we're going to explore both sides of this story today through the eyes of two women who care the most. The mother of the victim and the mother of one of the alleged perpetrators."

She bowed her head for an instant. Then snapped it up.

"I am talking," she mewled, "about the recent reprehensible slashing of a beautiful young model who still lies in the hospital battling to recover from face wounds that required *one hundred and seventeen stitches.* One *hundred* and seventeen stitches."

A photograph of Miranda in a bikini taken for a *Cosmopolitan* magazine cover flashed across the screen, followed by a bootlegged photo from the hospital with her face swathed in bandages.

"With us today," twanged Stoner in voice-over, "is Miranda's mother, as well as the mother of Dooley Kincaid, who stands accused of participating in the attack and is currently incarcerated at Rikers Island. We'll be right back."

"I can't believe it," Miranda said. "My *mom* is *here* — "

"No," I said. "They must have a hookup to some television studio in Arkansas."

" — and she didn't call."

"She's not here," I said, fiddling with the volume control.

The mouthwash commercial ended and we watched Tansy Stoner reappear. Miranda's mother, Kitty, was sitting next to Stoner, dressed almost entirely in pale blue (someone probably told her this color worked well on camera), which made her long, dyed hair look even blacker. Everything about her was curved, from her pug nose to her plump hands. It was amazing that she and her daughter even came from the same planet, and unbelievable that the progenitor of Miranda's perfect cheekbones, classic jaw, and exquisite ankles was languishing at Leavenworth.

Or perhaps Miranda's father was really a film star who spent a month or two in Arkansas on location — or possibly a European aristocrat whose Lamborghini broke down as he drove across America the summer before entering Oxford to read history.

No, my mind's playing games — one of those was *my* father.

"Kitty, I know this has been devastating for you," said Tansy Stoner onscreen. "But can you tell us a bit about your daughter? About how the attack affected her — and the effect it has had on you and your family."

"I'll try my best," said Kitty, reaching into her purse for a tissue, dabbing at her eyes the way women do when they don't want to mess up their mascara.

"Go ahead, it's all right," Stoner urged.

"Miranda," said Kitty, "is a good girl, a nice girl — very pretty. She was a comfort to me after her daddy passed on."

I looked at Miranda, who smiled a crooked smile and waved her hand dismissively.

"She always pretends he's dead," Miranda said. "I bet if they ask her about the kids, she won't mention my brother Eugene either — she hates him."

Kitty was dabbing at her eyes again with a fresh tissue.

"You have several other children — " said Stoner.

"Six," said Kitty into her tissue.

"Six children," said Stoner, "that's quite a lot of work."

"Not as bad as seven," said Miranda.

"Besides Miranda, there's Raymond, Tiffany, Wayne, Noreen, and Raymond."

"You already said Raymond."

"I know," said Kitty. "We call the baby Little Ray. I just love the name."

"I guess you do. But I'm a bit confused," said Stoner, checking her notes. "I thought you had seven children."

"Who told you that?" said Kitty.

Stoner acted bewildered.

"Well, there's Eugene," said Kitty. "His cornbread's a little soft in the middle."

"I never heard that one before," I said.

"Stick around," said Miranda.

"All those children," said Stoner. "And one of them . . . well. What a responsibility."

"Miranda used to help out with the younger kids," Kitty said, "before she come east."

"So you have a close family."

"Yes, we're all very close."

"Yeah, right," said Miranda. "She kissed me maybe twice in my life. She'd always say there were too many of us to kiss."

"You're still a single mother?" asked Stoner.

"Yes."

"And what do you do to support your family?"

"Welfare," said Miranda.

"I'm a hostess in a dining establishment."

"She was a waitress at a bowling alley," said Miranda.

"So," continued Stoner, "all the money Miranda was making as a top model must have come in pretty handy."

"Whatever she sent us went to the younger children — but that's finished now, I guess." Some extraordinary force of gravity seemed to be pulling at Kitty's mouth, shoulders, and head.

Tansy Stoner nodded in sympathy.

"I don't give a flip about the money," said Kitty. "All's I want is *justice* for my little girl." Kitty was no fool.

I glanced at Miranda, who stared straight at the screen. As usual I had no clue to her thoughts, but regarding money, I did know that modeling agencies — like their older and more powerful relatives, publishing companies and movie studios — were notoriously slow to pay.

Except for our cottage in Jamaica and a few pieces of eccentric clothing, Miranda seemed, almost a year later, as destitute as she had been when she arrived in the city. I simply assumed she was still owed a lot. Now I realized that although quite a bit of pay was probably backed up in the pipeline, whatever she'd received had been fired straight out to Arkansas.

"I'm sure," said Stoner, "you do want nothing but justice — as we all do — so this is a particularly tough question, Kitty, but I have to ask it — and I'd like you to answer as candidly as possible."

"As what?"

"As truthfully."

"Well of course I would."

The ferret-faced interviewer paused melodramatically before leaning forward and lowering her voice. Her body language was a travesty. But her query worked disastrously well. From the moment Tansy Stoner posed the issue, it took on a life of its own, settling into the darkest reaches of more minds than I could have imagined at the time and growing like a tumor.

"Kitty," demanded Stoner, "*what* did Miranda *do* to bring this attack on herself? I mean — they didn't try to kill her, they didn't steal from her. But they did deliberately *disfigure her for life*. What anger did she inspire in the alleged perpetrators Dooley Kincaid and Lester Bartholomew? What was her *relationship* with these young men?"

"She didn't have no relationship with my son," said Dooley Kincaid's mother, Chawna Basset, who'd been sitting off-camera to Kitty's right.

"We'll get to your side of the story in a moment, Chawna," said Stoner. "But let's finish this first."

She returned her attention to Kitty.

"Miranda must have done *something*," she said. "I mean, did she dress provocatively? Did she drink excessively? Anything like that?"

"I don't *think* so," said Kitty with some uncertainty.

"That's great," Miranda muttered.

"As we all know," said Stoner, "Dooley Kincaid is being held at Rikers Island under suspicion of aggravated assault. So far, his family has been unable to raise the fifty thousand dollars bail required to effect a temporary release. Let me remind our viewers that our legal system is built on the following premise: a person is *innocent* until found guilty — but I'm going to ask *you*, Kitty, if in fact Dooley Kincaid *is* convicted, how would you like to see him punished?"

"No question," she said. "He ought to just be killed."

Her lack of affect was startling.

"Yeah?" said Chawna Basset. "Well your kid made him do it. She must of gave him drugs."

Stoner swung around in her seat, drilling the woman with her squinty little eyes.

"So," she said. "You *do* feel that Dooley committed the assault."

"I didn't say nothin' of the kind!" Chawna insisted. "I said *if*."

"I see," murmured Stoner. "All right, let's get back to the punishment question in response to what Kitty said a moment ago. You know, Kitty, in New York State we don't have the death penalty."

"Well," said Miranda's mother, "then I think they ought to lock him up for the rest of his life in the psychic ward of Sing Sing. You got that in New York State, don't you?"

Tansy Stoner stared myopically into the camera.

"We'll be right back to continue our interview," she intoned. "Next we'll talk to Chawna Basset, mother of Dooley Kincaid — don't go away."

"That's perfect," said Miranda. "The psychic ward."

Miranda clicked the remote control; the screen went black in the middle of a root beer commercial.

"I hate root beer," she said.

10

· · ·

A WOMAN in street clothes, but wearing the ubiquitous Sisters of Mercy ID card pinned to the breast pocket of her severe, pinstriped suit, knocked and entered Miranda's room. She was Idelisse Maldonado, one of the hospital's chief administrators and probably, I thought, another of the in-house crowd trying to use Miranda for self-promotion and hospital publicity.

"I hope you're doing better today," she said to Miranda. "Are you up to having a guest?"

"Is it my mother?" asked Miranda.

"Your mother?" Idelisse Maldonado was uncomprehending.

"Forget it," said Miranda. "I am feeling better, but I don't think I can talk to any reporters right now."

"Oh, this isn't a reporter," said Maldonado.

"Who is it?" I asked abruptly — suspicious of everyone since Tansy Stoner's initial full-court press.

"Mrs. Vonseca would like to meet you," said Maldonado.

"I don't know any Mrs. Vonseca," said Miranda.

Vonseca, Vonseca. Definitely a serious name in what remained of authentic New York society, a shrinking group now primarily defined by ennui and exclusion, particularly of wealthy and desperate naïfs who, mistaking boredom for elegance, lobbied tirelessly to gain admission, always succeeding.

But who was *this* Mrs. Vonseca?

"She's very nice," Idelisse Maldonado continued, "and a big supporter of this hospital — she gave us our new burn unit. It's state-of-the-art. We'd be grateful if you'd see her."

"Okay," Miranda smiled her crooked smile. "Why not?"

Then I remembered.

The year I came to New York, when I was waiting tables at the Tequila Tavern, there was a terrible fire in a townhouse on Fifth Avenue. The townhouse belonged to Alison Vonseca, who must have been about thirty-five at the time.

Shortly after she flew to Vienna to be with her ailing mother, a five-alarm blaze, the origins of which remain in permanent dispute, broke out in the middle of the night, and by the time firefighters arrived, the whole interior of the old limestone mansion was enveloped by flames. Despite reportedly Herculean efforts of the firemen, there were no survivors.

Thorpe Vonseca, Alison's husband, was found on the back stairway, trapped between two floors, his five-year-old daughter and six-year-old son in his arms. The Vonseca's thirteen-month-old son was asphyxiated in his crib, and the Swiss nanny died on the floor of the bathroom between her bedroom and the nursery. The rest of the staff was off. It was Thursday night.

Alison went through a long period of mourning and seclusion. During that time (I discovered only recently) she tried to kill herself. The suicide attempt would have succeeded were it not for the fortuitous presence of a young bayman illegally haul-seining off the Vonseca's East Hampton shore at dawn the day Alison walked into the water with no intention of returning.

After the young man pulled her from the sea and wrapped her in his jacket, the two sat on the beach sharing his thermos of hot coffee under a gray sky flattened out by grief.

He was the son, grandson, and great-grandson of baymen who had always fished these shores with nets. He was risking fines and the revocation of his license because, he said, as long as there were fish in the water, he and his family wouldn't accept food stamps. Plus one of his kids was deaf and needed a special school that cost money.

Alison Vonseca had the kind of money that grows exponentially. Like other things one inherits, say, brown eyes or perfect pitch or an irregular heartbeat, she'd never given it much serious thought — until that morning.

The bayman's deaf son would go to school; the bayman's family would eat, always.

And many other people — no one knows how many — would, as time went by, eat, sleep, go to school, and benefit from the latest medical technology thanks to Alison Vonseca's vast but anonymous generosity.

She also quietly funded a pyrotechnic think tank, hiring inventors, scientists, technicians, and advertising wizards to create the most sophisticated smoke detectors, fire alarms, and information systems available in the world.

Idelisse Maldonado called into the hallway and a moment later Mrs. Vonseca entered Miranda's room. She stood over six feet tall in low heels, had pink-and-cream skin devoid of makeup, pale blue eyes, and blond hair going gray swept up in a loose French twist.

She shook hands with me first, then introduced herself to Miranda.

"I'll be leaving now," said Maldonado, going out the door.

"Me too," I said. "Lunchtime."

"Don't go, David," said Miranda. Her voice was calm; no discomfort or fear.

"Do stay," added Mrs. Vonseca politely.

"I'm just going to get a sandwich at the cafeteria and take a walk around the block. Would you like me to bring anything back?"

Alison Vonseca was already sitting on the edge of the bed, holding Miranda's hand in both of hers. Miranda was looking up into her eyes.

Wearing sneakers, I walked to the door and beyond without making a sound.

• • •

When I returned after forty-five minutes, Alison Vonseca was on her way out. She nodded to me in passing, but it was impossible to read those pale blue eyes.

Miranda, who must have been exhausted from the long visit, looked asleep, one arm flung over her eyes. I turned to leave.

"David," she said, barely moving a muscle. "You are *not* going to believe this."

"Good or bad?"

"What do you think?"

"Smart money bets good."

"Smart money wins again. She's paying my hospital bill — she's paying my rent. She's even going to send a check home for me — until I can go back to work again. It's like a miracle."

Suddenly Miranda sat up, wincing with pain.

"Oh my God," she said. "Did I dream all that?"

"Probably," I said. "Demerol dreams. I could use some of those myself."

"I wonder what she wants from me," Miranda went on.

"In addition to permanent servitude, eternal gratitude, and access to your snow-white body?"

"She said," Miranda continued, ignoring me, "that nobody should know about this money and I shouldn't discuss it with the media — fat chance — or anyone."

"What am I, chopped liver?" I said.

Miranda looked at me for a long moment, and for the first time in days I saw the light return to her silver-blue eyes.

"Very finely chopped with a soupspoon of onion."

"*Soupçon.*"

●　●　●

An hour later, even through the heavy, closed door to Miranda's room, we could hear a commotion growing in the hall. But as it got louder, the undertone seemed more about giggling than panic.

"I imagine," I said, pretending to read the editorial page of the *Times,* "you think all that noise has nothing do with you."

"We both know you're dying to see what's happening," said Miranda. "Go take a look."

"I don't care," I said.

"Yeah, really," she replied.

A muffled scream. Hysterical but not afraid.

"Go *ahead,*" Miranda said.

In the hall, a gaggle of nurses and nurses' aides, patients, and assorted other females, having picked up the drumbeat, had somebody surrounded and were apparently trying to suffocate the victim.

Bobby Wilder was the object of this uproar, and his admirers had actually torn the sleeve of his shirt.

"*Dave*," he yelled. "GET ME THE FUCK OUT OF HERE!"

"Sure thing, asshole," I muttered as I dove into the throng.

Just exiting the elevator, Jack Delaney, white-suited as usual, barely stood out in the flock of white uniforms. Since the celebrity–hysterical woman combo was his specialty, he could easily appropriate the situation, I thought darkly as he elbowed me aside to reach Bobby Wilder.

I became point man when the three of us finally pushed through Bobby's fans to the shelter of Miranda's room. She greeted us sitting up in bed wearing the pale pink quilted bed jacket Alison Vonseca had given her. She looked fragile but, despite the bruises and bandages on her face, luminously beautiful.

Bobby, clearly revved by so close a brush with his public, raced across the room, sliding to a stop on one knee next to Miranda's bed. He grabbed her hands and buried his head in her sheets.

The tenderness of people who don't love us can be so moving.

Even as she stroked Bobby's famously sun-streaked hair, Miranda was looking at Jack Delaney. And he was staring back with eyes nearly as blue as hers.

The force field they created made me feel dizzy, because I saw an unmistakable message flash between them, powerful in its silence. A sensual message of hope, promise, infinite possibility.

On the other hand, I do have a busy imagination, and maybe I was just getting the flu.

After a moment on his knees, Bobby pulled himself together and took charge of the telephone. Soon a series of delivery people from the Mayfair, Salou, Sherry Lehman, Petrossian, Delices de la Côte Basque, and Barney's began to arrive.

The comings and goings of these messengers was facilitated in the usual way. Bobby, who like JFK rarely carried cash, pulled a single check from the back pocket of his blue jeans and made it out to the Sisters of Mercy Development Fund; then in a clever coup de grâce, insuring impunity, he posed for photographs with Idelisse Maldonado and several members of her staff.

Buying off the hospital took about twenty minutes, and within an hour and a half Miranda's room was filled with magnums of Cristal, pounds of beluga, hundreds of pink orchids, a make-it-yourself ice cream sundae bar as well as a regular bar. Bobby opened a big matte box and dumped an array of beautiful nightgowns and robes onto Miranda's threadbare, hospital-issue counterpane, creating a pale profusion of silk, satin, and chiffon.

"Looks like Jay Gatsby's shirts," Delaney said.

"Whose shirts?" Bobby asked.

"The Great Gatsby," Miranda said.

"Right," replied Bobby. "Put some of this stuff on, you'll look gorgeous."

"Go ahead," added Delaney.

"Which one, David?" she asked.

"I don't know," I said. "Daisy Buchanan was wearing white the first time we meet her."

"How can you remember a thing like that?" asked Delaney.

"Jordan Baker was wearing white too," I said.

"Why don't *I* remember that?" complained Delaney.

"I like white," Miranda said.

"Whatever you want," said Bobby. "You look good in everything."

Unconsciously, Miranda put her hand to her cheek for an instant. Then she chose a floor-length ivory-colored T-shirt made of some magical mystery material and headed for the bathroom to change out of her hospital garb.

Departing from my infantile urge to compete with Delaney, I wondered what, if any, changes the attack had wrought on her self-image.

Not so many years later, it seems as though this entire country spontaneously reinvented the old sixties idea of group therapy. Besides painfully detailed confessionals, solipsistic spirit-fests, and infinite variations on the original Twelve-Step program, we have support, advisory, and advocate groups for every imaginable type of victim. Not to mention victimizer.

But at the time her face was slashed, Miranda, unfortunately, was quite alone in much more serious ways than the selection of a peignoir.

Bobby fired up a joint; the sweet smell of reefer filled the air as he switched the tube to MTV and raised the volume. He uncorked a bottle of ancient port pronounced perfection by Delaney, who was busy arranging an armful of orchids when Miranda finally emerged from the bathroom with her hair (which I'd helped wash just a few hours earlier) draped over the bandaged side of her face.

The clinging opacity of the long number she'd put on was quite fetching and made her look like she belonged to an earlier time and topography in the spiritual birthplace of our generation: Los Angeles. She extended a long, slim arm and opened her hand for a glass.

"I'll have champagne," she said. Very Veronica Lake.

Good sign, I thought.

Delaney filled two fragile flutes, passed one to her then touched her glass with his.

"To you," he said, looking into her eyes. "To us."

"Hey," Bobby said from the other side of the room.

"Hey what?" asked Delaney.

"She's *my* girl," said the Gun Son.

"*Was*," said Delaney.

"Hang on," said Miranda. "I don't *belong* to people — never have, never will." Her festive tone of righteous indignation was generally ignored.

"I *believed* you were my girl," said Bobby theatrically.

"Put a sock in it," I said.

"Yeah, cram it," said Delaney.

"Put a pillow in it," Bobby said, and snatched one off Miranda's bed which he threw at Delaney, who caught it on the fly with a fork from the nearby smoked salmon platter, causing feathers to cascade across the room when he heaved it back at Bobby. Bobby threw that pillow at me and grabbed another to fling at Delaney, who was advancing, fork in hand.

The Stones sang "Start Me Up" in the background, and naturally none of us noticed the door opening, or Miranda's mother walking in on the arm of our landlord, Mark Douglas.

"Nobody looks too sickly in here," Kitty said, peering through the smoke. "Wait a sec — is that *Bobby Wilder?*"

It was Bobby Wilder, blasted.

"In the flesh," said Bobby. Literally. His shirt was unbuttoned all the way and hanging out.

"Oh my *God*," said Kitty. "I love *Sons of Guns*! I watched every single episode — and I watch the reruns, unless I'm working, and I saw *Nogales* three times, where you play the young sheriff — "

"Ma," said Miranda. "What are you doing here?"

"Well what do you think I'm doin' here, baby? I come to see you."

"And go on TV?" Miranda asked in a quiet voice.

"They gave me a free plane ticket — else how could I *afford* to get here, now that . . ." Kitty's words trailed off into silence.

"Now that the gravy train got run off the track?" said Miranda.

"You're looking hot, Miranda," said Dark Mouglas. "I can see right through that thing you're wearing. You like to turn the boys on, don't you?"

His voice, always discordant, this time set my teeth on edge. Particularly in light of what he was saying. The weirdness of the scene and the fact that Delaney, Wilder, and I were stoned slowed our reactions.

"That's enough, Mark," said Miranda.

"You gonna introduce us to your friends?" asked Mark Douglas. Without waiting, he walked over to Bobby, chewed-up hand extended.

"*Us?*" Miranda hissed at Kitty.

"Well, Mr. Douglas" — she smiled over at the landlord — "was kind enough to let me into your place, just in case you needed anything."

She moved close to Miranda and lowered her voice.

"I found a bum in there — some old lady talking crazy. I made quick work out of her, but God knows what she already stole."

Miranda groaned, and Kitty poured herself a glass of champagne, noting that Alexis (from a nighttime soap of that period) drank the same kind.

"Mr. Douglas said don't call the cops," she continued, "because you are *acquainted* with this woman. All's I can say, Miranda, is if you let people like her in your place, ain't no wonder — "

"Ma," Miranda begged.

"Don't 'Ma' *me,*" cried Kitty, pointing her finger at Miranda. "Just look at you sittin' around with movie stars and champagne — who the hell do you think you are, Mrs. Jesus Christ?"

Delaney and I exchanged a glance.

"She's a cock-tease," said Dark Mouglas. "That's who she is."

"You better go," said Delaney. He grabbed the landlord's arm and started moving him out of the room as I did the same with Kitty, though she tried to shake me off. Oddly, Delaney had an easier time with Mark Douglas. But the landlord couldn't resist a parting shot.

"See babe," he said. "If you stuck with me, this wouldn't of happened. You should've acted nicer. I would've taken care of you."

Delaney crowded the landlord out the door and I followed, pulling the prodigal mother. Without a word to Kitty, Mark Douglas took off down the hall, bouncing on the balls of his feet.

"David," Miranda called from inside her room.

"Go in," Kitty told me, "and say her mother wants to talk to her privately."

Then she turned to Delaney with a flirty little smile. "And who exactly are you? We didn't get introduced."

• • •

Miranda decided to deal with her mother sooner rather than later, so we ushered Kitty back inside the room and left the two alone — since Bobby was by then basically unconscious.

Delaney and I paced the hall for not more than a few minutes before we heard Kitty's voice rise to a dangerously high decibel level.

When I yanked her back into the hall again, I decided it was for keeps or at least for the rest of that day. No point in letting her make trouble just as Miranda was beginning to feel stronger.

Kitty's indignation at being dragged out of the hospital room melted in the heat of Delaney's celebrated charm. He offered to buy her a cup of tea while I went to confer with Miranda regarding disposition of the errant mother.

When I went in, Miranda was on the phone and signaled me not to speak.

"That's impossible, Johnny," she said. "I'm still in the hospital, for God's sake. The plastic surgeons aren't even sure exactly — "

Then: "But I *told* you they're going to *fix* the scars."

The knuckles of the hand in which she held the receiver were white.

"You do *not* know. You wouldn't know beans if the goddamn sack was open! Let me talk to Clementine — *please.*"

Those silver-blue eyes burned, and although taking care of business requires a cool head, I figured anything, including hostility, was better than the psychic paralysis from which Miranda often suffered.

"Clementine," said Miranda, regaining her persistent calm, "Johnny says you've dropped me. . . ."

She paused while Clementine Sheffield spoke.

"Well, whatever you call it," Miranda said. "It amounts to the same thing. . . ."

She listened for a moment with her eyes closed. She opened them again before speaking just above a whisper.

"But if you won't advance me any money, I'd say you don't expect me to be working."

Again, she listened briefly.

"What do you mean bad publicity?"

Then a long pause.

"Clementine, how can you even *ask* me that? I didn't know those guys, I didn't do anything to make them attack me."

Twenty seconds passed.

"*What?* . . . And you just listen to some escaped maniac before you listen to me. . . . Fine, I'll check it out. . . . Oh sure, call me."

Miranda replaced the receiver quietly and ran her hand through her hair a couple of times.

"What happened?" I asked.

"Clementine dropped me."

"She's crazy."

"Yeah, like a fox with a pack of dogs on its ass."

"I can't believe it," I said with more conviction than I felt.

"Believe it," Miranda said. "I asked the agency for an advance so I could send my mother home — Stoner's show only gave her a one-way ticket — and Johnny Ferris told me I was off the books. Then Clementine got on the phone all fake apologetic and said she was really sorry, but like I already knew, there just won't be any work for a model with scars and what's the point of wasting her time and mine pretending. She said the sooner I could accept the *truth* the better for me and I ought to start getting on with my life. Plus the cops in Alabama just caught the other guy — Lester Bartholomew — and he said they met me in a *bar* and I came *on* to them and invited them home then changed my mind. Clementine said it was all over the news."

The one day in a hundred I hadn't picked up the papers.

I switched the tube from MTV to CNN, but they were in the middle of the international weather.

"We better handle your mother first," I said. "I'll book her a ticket" — Miranda tried to interrupt but I wouldn't let her — "and you can pay me back *later*."

"I'll get her a ticket," Bobby said from where he was lying on the floor, half under the bed. "Hell, I'll get her a plane — get her whatever she wants."

"I don't like this," Miranda said.

"Let's just get Kitty out of here before she drives you nuts," I said. "Then, with all due respect to her famous expertise, I say fuck Clementine, she's been a total bitch. You can go to work for Ford or Dirk or anybody else in town tomorrow. And one other thing."

"What?"

"You better talk to a lawyer."

"I don't *need* a lawyer — I was the *victim*."

"Everybody needs a lawyer," said Bobby.

"And if you get a lawyer," I said to Miranda, "he can respond to bullshit like what Clementine just told you — I mean like that freak saying he met you in a bar."

I nudged Bobby with the toe of my shoe and helped him from under the bed.

He, Delaney, and I escorted Kitty out of the hospital to the Regency (she'd read Elizabeth Taylor stayed there when visiting New York), where Bobby had booked her a room for the night. En route to the hotel in Bobby's limo, Kitty said she'd come to New York on such short notice she didn't have a single thing to wear.

Right.

First stop Macy's. Her choice. Bobby picked up the tab. At that point I'm sure Delaney and I would have donated our life savings to outfit her at Valentino just to be free.

When we finally arrived at the Regency, Bobby told her a car would pick her up in the morning and the driver would have her ticket back to Arkansas.

The Regency doorman opened the door of our limo. Kitty didn't make a move. The anticipatory grin vanished from Bobby's face as he tensed up and started tapping his foot ominously.

I took Kitty's arm and kind of pulled her awkwardly out behind me onto the walkway in front of the hotel. She was pouting — not the best look on a middle-aged woman.

"What's wrong?" I asked.

"*Just* a *car* and *driver?*" she snapped. "No chauffeur and limousine because I ain't *good* enough — now that Miranda's *ruined* and I'm a little too *old* for any of you boys."

She unconsciously smoothed her dyed black hair.

"Kitty," I said, "when somebody like Bobby says car and driver, he *means* limo and chauffeur, okay?"

"Oh," she said, and her eyes suddenly filled with tears.

Shitfuckcrap.

"I don't feel well," she said.

Get me out of here.

"There was too many kids," Kitty said as I guided her away from the curb. "I couldn't handle Miranda. But she's a good girl. She didn't do nothing to make them cut her up. When she's little I told her treat her body like a nice guest towel. The more men wiped their hands on it, the dirtier it'd get."

The horn on Bobby's limo started honking. Kitty and I had reached the entrance to the Regency.

"Everybody must be sayin' I'm the world's worst mother," she sniffled.

"Nobody says that," I said.

"Yeah, well you don't get no prizes for lyin'," she said, and waved a wistful good-bye.

The instant she was into the hotel, I ran back to the waiting car.

I probably should have kept running.

• • •

My new best friends and I went to dinner at Lucky Will's, where all the waiters were transvestites. After Delaney conferred with the maître d' about wine, Bobby found a second wind.

"So what the fuck happened with Miranda?" he asked.

"She went to pick Pete up at the vet —" I said.

"At midnight," added Delaney. "And two black guys followed her, grabbed her and cut up her face, then left her in an empty lot and took off."

"Did they . . . ?" Bobby couldn't say the word.

"No," I said.

"Well did she *do* something to, you know, piss them off, or turn them on or . . . I don't know," said Bobby. "Maybe they were working for somebody."

"Of course she didn't *do* anything," I said. "She didn't do shit except mind her own business. As *always*. But you wouldn't know about that because you were such an *asshole* when we were in Jamaica and where have you been lately anyhow?"

Did I mention I'd had more than a couple of shots of Maker's Mark in the car, definitely not your everyday bourbon.

"You all went to Jamaica together?" Delaney asked.

So there was one thing Miranda neglected to tell him. Probably by mistake. I wondered if he knew about Noah's Ark.

"Dave . . . ," Bobby whined.

"Fuck off," I said, not unpleasantly. "You'll never get another girl like her."

"If you weren't a queer," Bobby said evenly, "I'd say you want her yourself."

"I like being a queer," I said.

"Yeah, for sure," Bobby said.

"Guys, guys," said Delaney, opening his arms grandly. "We're all queers, we're all straight, we're all brothers." He'd had his share of Maker's Mark too.

"We're all queers," Bobby repeated. "We're all straight, we're all brothers. Hey, I read for the part last week — can you believe they made me do a screen test? But everybody wants to play Jamie. Oh man, I forgot — *Wings of Night* — that's your book. How come you didn't write the script?"

"Because," Delaney said, "I'm too close to the material."

Which means they wouldn't give him the job, which probably went to a producer's son who thinks syntax is a punishment and cliché a suburb of Cannes. Movie executives don't read; they don't like books, and they don't like authors. Quite simply, they don't like words. They like moving pictures.

•   •   •

Later we hit the Palladium, the China Club, Area, and Nell's, finally dropping into an after-hours spot where Delaney was clearly a regular. The kohl-eyed girls and skinny guys playing blackjack were too cool to acknowledge Bobby's presence, let alone his identity.

Delaney definitely appeared to have quit drugs, but somebody at this place displaying all the obsequious aggressiveness of a dealer without the threatening antagonism of a spurned dealer was hanging around. I can't say for sure.

Specious thinkers seem to believe that gay people know everything about perversity, particularly regarding marginal behavior and illegal activity. But knowing the nature of secrecy is a lot different from knowing specific secrets.

I don't remember much of what we talked about that night and into the early morning. I do recall a kind of macho passing of Miranda's torch from Wilder to Delaney, and their desire for my blessing on the deal. Since I was both offended (on Miranda's behalf) and flattered (all right, there's the embarrassing truth), I took the low road, talking inconsequentialities.

I was drawn to these guys, and although I tried to numb my brain by diving down deep into a lake of booze and exhaustion, naturally I still knew they didn't care what I said. This was theater and I was a good audience.

We decided to have breakfast at The Shamrock, which meant buying donuts and eating them there. Ben was back behind the bar serving shooters to a couple of guys on their way to work. Since his early career was wrestling, not boxing, I didn't think he'd stepped back into the ring. But his face was beat to shit. Maybe a car wreck.

"Morning, Ben," I said. "You got tomato juice?"

He nodded.

"We'll have three," I said.

"With vodka," he said.

"No, just straight," I said. "What happened?"

"What're you talkin' about?"

"Your face," I said.

"Nothin'."

"*Nothing?*" Bobby cut in from where he was slumped in his chair, with his long blue-jean-clad, cowboy-booted legs sticking straight out in front of him. "Your face is a *mess* man — "

I thought: I'll kill him if he asks what the other guy looks like.

"Ben," I said, "remember Bobby Wilder — you know *Sons of Guns*. Miranda brought him in here, I don't know, before Christmas — remember that tip?"

Ignoring Bobby, Ben leaned forward and placed his big, red hands on the bar.

"How's Miranda?" he asked.

"Great, much, much better," Delaney jumped in.

As though he hadn't heard, Ben kept looking at me.

"She's okay," I said. "She'll be out of the hospital pretty soon."

Ben nodded and went about some glass polishing, which required turning his back to us.

After a bit, Delaney said he had to go return phone calls; Bobby said he too had pressing business elsewhere, and we all walked out together.

● ● ●

From Delaney-Behar Correspondence:

Perry Old Pal,

Got fried with Bobby Wilder last night. Ran into him at the hospital. He's a pretty good guy but identical taste in wine, alas, to Nils: none.

Patrice thinks he'll want to play me in Miranda's story. What I want is for Patrice to concentrate on moving my check.

Miranda's in all the NYC papers again. London too?

As always,

S. Maugham   6 June New York

———

Dear Jack,

Went to banker friend at the weekend. Observing all those lithe young girls dash about playing grasscourt tennis raised a thirst that was handily quenched with 1986 Leflaive Bâtard-Montrachet followed by a 1983 Latour Corton-Charlemagne. Concluded my day over the snooker table sharing a bottle of 1971 Latour which was a tad awkward and burnt. Rather a disappointment.

Miranda continues to be front-page news over here. What does she say about your project?

Always,

PB   London, 8 June

• • •

I stopped by the newsstand before going home to sleep. Extraordinarily, Miranda was again on page one of both daily tabloids and on the front page of the *Times* metro section.

SLASHED MODEL'S ATTACKER #2 PICKED UP IN DIXIE, read the *Post* headline.

Inside, Tansy Stoner was at it once more, with a rabble-rousing column in which she began reaping the harvest from the poison seeds she first sowed on her talk show with Kitty and Dooley Kincaid's mother, Chawna Basset.

The very unsisterly columnist pounded out a dangerously misogynous diatribe portraying Miranda from the point of view of Lester Bartholomew, the poor, put-upon, hounded cousin of Dooley Kincaid.

Why, she demanded, would these two young men who need every ounce of energy they possess to escape from the ghetto and emerge from the underclass, participate in this crime? Did they steal from Miranda? No. Did they rape her? No. Was it a racial incident? No.

It must have been *something else.*

If they committed a crime, had they been *provoked?*

(I remembered the nurse's aide with the cart of flowers talking about "the other thing," which I now realized meant provocation.)

Yes. Miranda *must* have incited them. After all, she's a model — and what's a model who sells her face and body to the highest bidder, but a prostitute by another name.

Stoner neglected to mention Bartholomew's two-hundred-dollar-a-day cocaine habit or the fact that Dooley Kincaid had been on probation for a violent felony robbery.

Disgusted, I threw the *Post* in the trash. Flashing lights no one but I could see signaled a new entry to the Headache Hall of Fame, and I moved mechanically toward home only to find Juliana sitting on the stoop. The flashing lights didn't increase my patience — but I did notice Juliana anxiously twisting and kneading her hands.

"Lego My Lady," she said.

Presumably she was asking about Miranda.

"Miranda's getting better," I said, trying to go past her up the steps. "She should be back soon."

Juliana seemed uncomprehending, upset, or both. Frowning and chewing her lip, she began to tear at the hem of her outermost skirt.

"State of Rage," she said.

"I agree," I said.

Juliana angrily ripped her skirt from hem to waist, got up, and stalked away. Ten minutes later, I was in my bed, dead to the world.

● ● ●

I slept till four in the afternoon; and when I woke I knew why Miranda had been attacked.

Before my head cleared, the phone rang.

"I just figured it out," Miranda said.

● ● ●

I slammed the door behind me, tucking my shirt in as I ran down the street. I had to find Juliana, whose comings and goings were hardly predictable. Halfway through a mental map of the neighborhood, I saw her sitting on the curb by the fire hydrant folding paper bags.

"Juliana," I said, "come with me, I need to talk to you."

She shook her head in the negative.

"Fateful Beauty," she said.

"Yes exactly," I said. "I want to talk to you about Miranda."

"Eastern Love, Sullivan's Soul, Enjoy the Silence."

"I'll give you money," I said.

"Go Quack, Pay Me Now."

I came up with a ten-dollar bill, which disappeared into one of her many pockets. But she didn't move.

"Please," I said. "It's important."

"Track Gossip, Zero for Conduct."

She shook her head again.

"Come on," I said.

I took her elbow and gave it a tug. She surprised me by standing and gathering her things. For an instant, I thought she was going to run off, but she simply stood still, looking at me like a cat waiting for dinner.

When Juliana and I entered The Shamrock, there was only one other customer at the bar.

"Get her outta here," Ben snapped, spotting my companion.

"We want to talk to you," I said.

"What 'we,' " Ben said. "She don't talk."

The intense quiet was punctuated by a fly buzzing, and when Ben smacked it dead on the bar as hard as he could with a folded newspaper, the lone customer left some money by his glass and scuttled out.

"She talks," I said.

"She talks bullshit," Ben said.

"What happened to your face?" I asked, realizing that I sounded like a character out of one of my own novels. What if Ben decided to walk around that bar and break my arms?

"Get the fuck outta here Dave and take the loony with you."

He turned his back and started polishing glasses. As we know, I'm not brave. But I wasn't frightened. Early summer sun was pouring through the windows of a place I visited nearly every day of my life, illuminating the short neck and big, sloping shoulders of a man I saw just as often.

I'm not sure how much time passed, but when an unwitting drunk ambled through the door, Ben dashed from behind the bar, kicked him out, and put up a rusty CLOSED sign I'd never seen before. Then he poured shots of Cuervo Gold for himself and me, and a shot of Bristol Creme for Juliana. After we all knocked back our drinks, Ben bowed his head as if in prayer. When he looked up, his eyes were filled with tears.

"I should of told you before," he said.

• • •

I went straight from The Shamrock to the hospital, where I found Miranda dressed in street clothes and seated on the edge of her bed watching the local news.

" — anonymous tip," reported Chuck Scarborough, "sent Detective Mike Romanos back to interrogate each cousin one more time. Despite Lester Bartholomew's contradictions, it was a sworn statement from Dooley Kincaid that finally led police to make the arrest at dawn this morning. Another anonymous call to our studio, perhaps from the same source, alerted us, and our cameras were on hand."

The screen filled with videotape of Mike Romanos and two uniformed police officers hustling a handcuffed prisoner who hid his face into an unmarked car. As the door shut behind him, the prisoner turned toward the window.

It was Mark Douglas.

Miranda clicked off the television.

"We were looking for jackals," she said. "So we missed the snake."

"Un-fucking-believable," was all I could say as the screen went blank.

"But why?" Miranda asked. "*Why* did he do it?"

At that moment I guessed both of us probably knew as much of the answer as we would ever know.

The phone rang with a call from Miranda's friend Lynne in Washington. Attempting to respect her privacy, I walked out. Being anxious, hyper, and nosy, I stuck my head back in the door a minute later. She waved me inside.

"Well what if he's too busy?" she asked. "Or I can't afford him, which I'm sure I can't."

She twirled a pencil; I paced.

"Okay," she said. "I'm writing it down."

She scribbled a name and phone number on a scrap of paper.

"Thanks Lynne," she continued. "Don't worry, you know me."

It took Lynne almost a minute to respond to that last comment, during which time Miranda passed me the scrap of paper. The name she'd written on it was Terrence O'Mara.

"Let's go," she said right after she hung up.

"You can't just walk out a day early."

The silver-blue eyes blazed as she looked at me for a long moment; I flashed on a hundred pictures from several lifetimes, hers and mine, discarding all but the one of a little girl locked up with an angry bull.

"Learn or be taught," she said. "I'm out of here."

Having already said her good-byes to the staff, Miranda — with only a couple of slender bandages covering the worst slashes across her cheek and eyebrow — put on a pair of dark glasses and a wide-brimmed hat I'd never seen and led me directly to a freight elevator. The elevator carried us to the subbasement where, without a misstep, Miranda followed a labyrinthine path to daylight at the end of a delivery ramp.

We walked around the corner, hailed one of the last of the big old Checker cabs, and once inside the car I didn't even ask how she'd learned the route we just took out of the hospital, which was becoming smaller and smaller in the rearview mirror, if not in memory.

Nor did I remind her as she lit up, that smoking impedes healing. And who am I to judge life's little addictions? Exactly.

"Do you want to talk?" I asked.

"About . . . ?" She made a small gesture with her hand.

I nodded.

"I don't know if I can even talk to this lawyer — I feel like — I'm so angry."

But the flaming silver had left her eyes. Or maybe it was just a trick of light and shadow. I hoped so.

"Do we have an appointment?" I asked.

"Lynne's boss called."

Only in America.

There was just enough time to tell Miranda what I'd learned from Ben before we reached our destination.

Entering the building at Park and Fifty-first under a June sun bright as it ever gets, I thought about how entirely our lives are ruled by random events and haphazard acts.

I was wondering if there actually was a fault running the length of Central Park when an elderly woman carrying a pile of yellow legal pads greeted us at Terrence O'Mara's reception area. She punched a combination into a sophisticated security system and opened a pair of double doors onto a hall at the end of which lay her employer's inner sanctum.

11

. . .

TERRENCE O'MARA was too young to be a legend, but at forty-one he was more famous than most trial lawyers half again his age. His dark hair was beginning to go gray, and his eyes, behind tortoiseshell spectacles, were as green as the Emerald Isle where he kept a stone cottage with no telephone. Fourth-generation American, yet Irish to the core of his heart, he was blessed by an astonishing intellectual clarity and probably cursed by the same thing. He had become well known defending former Black Panthers and Weathermen. Then he moved on to accused gunrunners, dope dealers, mobsters, and murderers.

He was stunning in court and mute elsewhere. So personally low profile and unwilling to discuss anything besides the current client and current case, the press nicknamed him the Shadow. The more successful he became, the more frequently he was criticized and the more his legend grew. He rarely responded to shrill voices braying about wealth he'd amassed as attorney to Mafia chiefs and tax evaders.

Privately, he'd calmly explain that all citizens have the right to a defense. But even in private he never mentioned his huge load of pro bono cases or the fact that he never had and never would defend a person accused of rape or of a crime against a child. He laughed at the stories of his packing a piece, eating prairie oysters for breakfast, and holding a black belt in karate.

He was standing at the window behind his desk, looking out, but turned to greet us as we walked through the door. He went directly to

Miranda and took both her hands in his, a theatrical gesture which, coming from him, seemed sincere and reassuring.

In a voice so soft it was just above a whisper, he said, "We have a lot of work to do."

O'Mara explained that during the last two hours, Mark Douglas, with the help of relatives, had made bail and was free pending his trial, the date of which had not yet been set. The relatives had hired an expensive criminal lawyer, who immediately issued an indignant denial on the landlord's behalf, concluding with a carefully but deliberately worded suggestion that Miranda had brought the attack on herself and deserved what she got.

Even more disturbing, Dooley Kincaid, charging police brutality, had rescinded his statement implicating Mark Douglas, and Douglas's lawyer was already trying to get the case against the landlord dismissed.

"So," O'Mara said, "I need to assemble the facts."

We all sat at a small round table in one corner of his office, sipping iced tea from tall Waterford glasses. At O'Mara's request, Miranda delivered a brief autobiography, which included Noah's Ark and extended to the present. Then she looked at me.

"David, tell about Juliana and Ben," she said.

I described them to O'Mara, who listened impassively until I got to the night of the attack, at which point he folded his hands and bowed his head as if to memorize every word.

"Nobody came into The Shamrock after eleven-thirty that night," I said. "Ben swept the place, washed some glasses, locked up, and started walking home — he lives in a tenement near the Port Authority."

"Alone," Miranda added.

"Yes," I said. "Nobody saw what happened later. Anyway he's walking along Tenth Avenue and he hears these blood-curdling screams and decides to find out what's going on although he knows better."

"Meaning?" asked O'Mara.

"Meaning," I said, "you want to stay out of trouble in New York, you hear screams you go the other way."

"Maybe he recognized the voice," O'Mara said.

"I asked him," I said. "He doesn't know."

"So," said O'Mara. "He followed the screaming and — ?"

"And when he got to the corner where it happened, he saw a police car and Miranda's dog — "

"Pete," said Miranda.

" — Miranda's dog, Pete, yes," I said. "And he saw Juliana kneeling on the ground shaking Miranda, who was unconscious, and he saw the cop just kind of sitting in the car with his head in his hands."

"Anything else?" O'Mara asked.

"Yes," I said. "He thought he saw Mark Douglas's car — a bronze Cadillac — pull out from under a broken streetlight on the other side of the street and take off."

"Tell why Ben left," Miranda said.

"Because," I continued, "he was afraid Mark Douglas saw him; he knows Mark's crazy, and although he claims he's not personally involved, he does know that Mark and a couple of other guys use The Shamrock as a base for some illegal activity."

"You don't believe the bartender's involved," O'Mara said.

"That's what he claims," I continued, feeling foolish. "After he saw the cop he took off because he was scared."

"He was right to be scared," Miranda said.

"Yeah," I went on. "A few hours later, two guys with guns broke into his place — "

"Kincaid and Bartholomew?" asked O'Mara.

"Maybe."

"Go on," said O'Mara.

"They put Ben in a car," I said. "Drove somewhere on the other side of the Lincoln Tunnel and beat the shit out of him. They said he's a dead man if he opens his mouth."

"And," mused O'Mara, "he figures even if they don't kill him, his job is history and maybe he's looking at a couple of years in Dannemora."

I said yes.

"And he has an eighty-five-year-old mother," Miranda said.

That was news to me. How does she know these things?

"But," said O'Mara, "this Juliana witnessed the entire attack."

"We think so," I said.

"Do *you* think so?" the lawyer asked Miranda.

Miranda nodded slowly.

"I remember hearing a scream," she said. "And Juliana follows me a lot. I never paid much attention, because she's harmless and it kept her busy. Sometimes I'd notice her and sometimes she'd just pop up next to me on the other side of the city."

"Okay," O'Mara said. "Let's get her up here and I'll see if I can persuade her to talk."

He saw the glance Miranda and I exchanged.

"We have to try," said O'Mara.

"I know," said Miranda.

O'Mara stood, signaling the end of the meeting. We followed him to the door of his office.

"Where will you be staying?" he asked Miranda.

She and I hadn't discussed it, but I already knew the answer. Knowing, however, didn't mitigate my sudden sinking feeling — as though the normal power of gravity had just increased tenfold.

"I'm going to stay with Jack Delaney," she said. "The writer."

"Yes," O'Mara replied. "*Wings of Night.*"

On the street, I'm proud to say, I managed not to remind Miranda that she could also stay with me. I have my problems, but looking for new ways to suffer is not one of them.

I dropped her off at Delaney's loft on Broadway and West Fourth Street.

• • •

From Delaney-Behar Correspondence:

Dear Peregrine,

Thanks for the call; that was D.V. on the other line. She received the money I wired (just about cleaning me out, as I've still not received 1st payment from Big O) and has settled down, at least temporarily, which is good because Miranda is about to move in, at least temporarily.

Haven't quite told M. about the script yet. Since you're adapting *Anna K.* and Hollywood is nothing if not imitative, I said I'm adapting *Bleak House*. A little boost for the always underrated Dickens, plus, if you recall, the character Esther Summerson was permanently scarred, so I see a segue here. I'm sending you the prologue.

Parker gives the 1985 L'Evangile 95, Coates 18.
What do women want?
S. Freud   9 June, New York

———

My dear Jack,
    Just finished reading the prologue. Very impressive — still resonating. Is this material true? Is it fiction, or as T. Capote first said, faction? Whatever the case, old fellow, her life is the wellspring and therefore you *must* tell Miranda.
    The 1970 Petit-Village is good middleweight well-balanced stuff, but I prefer the 1981, let alone the 1982. '85 L'Evangile all right as a punt.
    Having a touch of trouble with Vronsky.
    Ever,
    PB   London, Wednesday, 10th June
P.S. Walking in France 12th–19th

•   •   •

I was closing up shop on Cassie and Zack for the day, and planning my evening. First the gym, then the Angelika to see *Red River* with a friend from high school; afterward dinner and undoubtedly a nightcap at The Shamrock. Not exactly thrilling, but better than hanging around worrying about Miranda with a bottle of Porfidio and the late show for company.
    I heard a noise at the front door and my heart raced. Recent events had put my internal warning system on red alert. Each shadow, footstep, or car slowing down carried new significance. And now some interloper was at my apartment. I grabbed my letter opener, which whoever was about to break in would probably use to stab me.
    "Hi, David."
    Miranda had opened the door with the key I gave her.
    "You scared the shit out of me," I said.
    "I'm sorry," she said. "I thought you'd be working and I didn't want to bother you, so I used my key. That's pretty." She was pointing to my letter opener.
    "Oh yeah, thanks, I was . . . just going through some mail."
    I dropped the erstwhile weapon on my desk and put my arms

around Miranda. When I began to move away, she held on and I knew she was crying. We stood like that for a while.

"I'm glad to see you," I said.

"I'm fucked up," she said. "Don't say no you're not."

"No you're not," I was saying simultaneously.

We both smiled.

"Go sit down," I said. "I'll be right back."

I phoned my high school friend from the bedroom to cancel, then made a Campari and soda for Miranda and a negroni for me.

We sat on the couch with our feet up, and Miranda put her head on my shoulder.

"So tell me what's wrong," I said.

"You know I like Jack," she said.

This was not the moment for a smart mouth, so I just nodded.

"I couldn't go back to my place," she went on. "And I didn't want to crowd you."

According to Einstein, the formula for success is $a = x + y + z$. X is work, y is play, z is keep your mouth shut. So I did.

"Jack has a big loft and when he invited me, I thought it would be okay. I mean, I thought it would be good."

I'd been repressing the whole concept. For example, where did I think Delaney would sleep? In the tub? At the Forty-seventh Street Y?

"Um hmm," I said.

"Only I've changed," she said, tears filling her silver-blue eyes. "I can't let him near me; I don't want him to touch me. And it's not him, it's me. I don't think I can ever touch anybody again."

Even as she said this, she was holding my hand against her scarred cheek in an unconscious gesture beyond sexual intimacy.

I kissed her fingers and gave her a tissue.

"You're wrong, Miranda," I said. "Anybody would feel like this."

"I'm scared," she said.

"And anybody would be scared ... Amelia Earhart would be scared," I said. "Isak Dinesen would be scared." I couldn't think of any women warriors.

"Who's Isak Dinesen?" she asked through her tears.

"Have you got your notebook?"

I was so relieved, when she pulled it out of her bag, to see consistency in the form of those tattered spiral-bound pages. The notebook had been in her backpack the night of the attack and was in her purse now. She hadn't felt the need to discard it for a new one. Or stop using it. Or stop writing down titles. This must mean something good.

She added *Out of Africa*.

"Wasn't there a movie . . . ?" she asked.

"From the book," I said. "It was good too. Why don't we rent it, send out for Chinese food, and you just stay here."

"I hate to do this to you," she said as my answering machine played an incoming call.

"David, it's Jack. Have you heard from Miranda?"

"Can I pick it up?" she asked.

"Sure," I said. "Just push that second button on the right."

She ran over and grabbed the receiver. When they began to talk, I went out for the paper and stayed out for about twenty minutes. When I returned, Miranda was lying on the couch.

"I'm going back," she said. "You don't mind, do you?"

"Of course I don't mind," I replied. "And you can change your mind and come back here anytime."

"I think it'll be okay," she said.

I wasn't so sure, but I followed Einstein's advice. As a man and a writer I might be mediocre; as a friend I could try to be first-rate.

After Miranda left, I finished my negroni and wondered what had made her decide to go back to Delaney's.

I didn't wonder for long. Not much later in the evening, I discovered that Miranda had apparently hit the wrong button on my answering machine and inadvertently recorded their conversation.

Miranda: Hi, Jack, I'm here — let me just turn this off — wait a sec — okay.

Delaney: I was worried about you, I couldn't find a note or a message on my machine. Are you okay?

Miranda: I'm fine, I didn't mean to get you upset — oh, David just left to buy the paper, but I know him, he wanted to let me talk in private.

Delaney: He's a discreet guy. . . . Listen, is something wrong? Did I do something?

Miranda: No Jack, you've been great, but last night . . . I just couldn't . . . I'm sorry, I guess I gave you the wrong idea —

Delaney: No Miranda —

Miranda: — so I thought it would be better if I moved in with David.

Delaney: Miranda, listen to me for a minute. If you want to move in with David, that's fine. You should do anything that makes you feel comfortable. But I've been at his place and it's small, and it's right above, you know, your old place, which must have some bad associations. What I want you to understand is I care about you — a lot. And *I* probably gave *you* the wrong idea; I mean, when I asked you to stay with me, it was no strings attached. I can see what you've been through on one level, but I'm sure there are levels only you can feel, so we'll go at your pace. You have your own room, and I'll do whatever you say, whenever you say. I just want you to get well. It's okay if we never have sex.

Miranda: (Laughs.) Jack —

Delaney: (Also laughs.) Well, maybe someday. Seriously though, I mean everything I said. Let me be your friend.

Miranda: You're a good friend.

Delaney: And I'm a good cook.

Miranda: And you've got good wine.

Delaney: The best.

Miranda: (Sighs.)

Delaney: So come home.

Miranda: Okay.

•　•　•

The next day Malone asked me to visit him in Los Angeles. Surprised? So was I. I knew he was having a fit of boredom, laced with insecurity and seasoned by nostalgia, but I didn't care.

•　•　•

I returned from my short trip, the details of which are best forgotten, to find that Miranda and Delaney were not in the city and had left no way to get in touch with them. My curiosity was already doing a tango with my imagination when I received a letter from my friend Perruchio, the stylist who was in the studio the day Miranda washed off all her makeup and stood on the plumber's shoulders.

Yellow Knife
Thursday or Friday
Holá David,

I'm in Canada freeze my butt. They no hear its summer already.

I send the stuff you want about Caracas and the Maracaibo. And Mama say thanks for the book. Say she want to learn English to read about Cassie and Zack. Buena suerte.

Last week I'm dead from work so I travel alone (muy triste) to Country Inn in Massachusetts I find in New York Mag. Quiet, big rooms, nice.

Now I whisper you something that old maricón Tarbell give his eyetuck to hear. ¿Who was at the inn? Miranda and Jack Delaney! Bad boy David, why you no tell me this gossip. She looks fantastic still, but her career is finish. This norteamericano idea of perfect is to me always so boring. Scars are sexy, Dios me mata.

Miranda don't recognize me and I no say nothing. All the time they stay alone, hold hands, read poems. But here's the kick: *separate bedrooms.* And no just for show. My room is next to his room. Interesting, no?

This guy screwing every model in the city then adiós chica. Pero quién sabe, maybe is different with Miranda. I hope.

Abrazos,
Perruchio

Adiós and arrivederci. I didn't like to think about all those models (not to mention actresses, editors, aging debutantes, and other people's girlfriends — didn't the guy ever *sleep?*) and I wondered what had actually happened between Delaney and Domina Valverde. The story he told me at The Shamrock seemed like the first layer of an onion. I figured there were many more layers as well as attendant tears.

I suppose I could have asked Delaney again, because five minutes after I read Perruchio's letter he and Miranda called to say they were back and invite me to join them for dinner.

• • •

We met uptown at Mortimer's, where each table was filled with people I knew intimately through Roland Tarbell's column. They were glamorous (I suppose enough money could make a Komodo lizard glamorous) but they were old. Miranda's precious few years, along with Delaney's and mine, barely reduced the median age in the room to sixty-five. Nevertheless, Delaney kissed as many cheeks and shook as many hands as he had at Nell's.

Out of eight million people in New York, there are probably five thousand who fix the pace, set the trend, say when it ends. Delaney evidently knew all five thousand, including the headwaiter, who waved us to a power table and delivered the wine list, which Delaney ignored, ordering Dom Perignon Rosé.

Miranda, in a starkly elegant off-the-shoulder little dress, looked lovely and seemed perfectly comfortable; the lights were on, her mood was high. I sensed I was sitting just outside an erotically charged circle where she and Delaney danced a sparkling pas de deux. How far this dance had gone, only they knew.

While I tried to study the menu, Delaney gazed indulgently at Miranda, his face taking on a goony, spaniel-like cast.

"How do you like my girl?" he asked. "Isn't she beautiful?"

My girl?

"She used to look like a boy," I said.

"Really," replied Delaney. "I love androgyny; I guess you do too, Dave."

"How are Cassie and Zack?" asked Miranda.

"You don't need to change the subject," I said.

"I know I don't — but how are they?" she repeated.

"They're okay," I said.

"Are they androgynous?" asked Delaney.

She ignored Delaney's question but held his hand, so one gesture canceled the other.

"Where are they?" she asked me.

"They're still in Montana," I said.

"*Who* are they?" Delaney wanted to know.

"Nobody," I said.

"They're David's characters — in his books. Haven't you read them?"

"Men don't read romances," I said quickly.

"But they read their friends' work," Miranda said.

"They definitely do," Delaney agreed. "And I will."

"Please don't bother," I said.

"Speaking of books," Delaney said, searching through a big leather bag he'd hung over his chair, "I have something for you Miranda . . . now where is it?"

"He loses *everything*," said Miranda.

His search was interrupted by a waiter taking our order, but he finally found what he was looking for.

"Here it is," said Delaney, handing her a fine leather-bound copy of *Bleak House*.

"Jack," she said. "Thank you, it's beautiful. Now I'll finally get to read what your screenplay's about. He's been very secretive."

"My God," I said, "that's a long book to adapt."

"Well," said Delaney, "they want me to focus on Esther Summerson's story line."

"What is her story?" Miranda asked Jack. But he didn't answer because we had visitors.

"Excuse me."

Nesui Hamid was standing at our table. As cool as Elvis, or Ray Charles, or Miles Davis, the mythic rock 'n' roll entrepreneur who put more musicians on the map than anyone before him or to this day had walked over with his agelessly beautiful wife, Nicole, and his famous protégé Chris Bradshaw.

At seventy, the droll Hamid, with a tan from the sun, a perfectly groomed goatee, and the best clothes I ever saw, was as nonchalant as Nicole was elegant. She owned a distinguished Soho gallery and was probably the only woman to appear consistently on the Best-Dressed List without trying.

And there were almost as many stories about the notorious Bradshaw as about his mentor. About the record label he started at sixteen, about his movie company, his string of hotels, his women, and about his escapades as an incorrigible nomad who did business from a compound in the Turks and Caicos or from the phone in his back pocket.

Delaney and I had gotten to our feet as Nesui Hamid bent forward, took Miranda's hand, and kissed it lightly. The fact that the Hamids and Bradshaw didn't know or didn't acknowledge Delaney gave me an unnatural boost.

"My dear," Hamid said to Miranda, raising his eyes to her chest, "you are a brave . . ." His eyes moved to her face. ". . . and stunning young woman."

"I wish all that was true," Miranda said.

"Listen to me," said Hamid. "It is true." Then he whispered something to her and she whispered back. Meanwhile, other activity accelerated. Waiters swooped, plates and silver were moved about, more wine materialized, several groups of diners came by the table.

Naturally, we invited the Hamids and Bradshaw to join us, but they declined, and when our food arrived they decided to take their leave. Hamid pulled an engraved calling card bearing only his name from an onyx case and handed the card to Bradshaw.

"Christopher, write my number down there, will you," he said. "I can't see a damn thing without my glasses I left in the car."

Bradshaw had already outdistanced Hamid his surrogate father, in terms of net worth, by several zeros. Perhaps because I knew how much power the younger man wielded on several continents and how many people depended on his businesses for their livelihoods, I smiled to myself as Bradshaw followed orders like a good secretary. When he finished writing he gave the card to Miranda.

"My private number," said Hamid. "If I can ever do anything for you, my dear . . ."

"Thank you, Mr. Hamid," said Miranda.

"Nesui," said Hamid before walking away.

"*Nesui,*" mimed Delaney.

"To me," whispered Miranda. "*Mr.* Nesui to you."

"He certainly likes girls," muttered Delaney.

"So?" said Miranda.

"Almost everybody does," I added.

"Yeah," said Delaney. "*Almost.* I hear Bradshaw swings both ways."

"I never heard that," I said.

"You mean he only does guys?" asked Delaney innocently.

"I mean he just likes women," I said. "He's been married twice."

"I didn't know you were so tuned in, Dave," said Delaney.

Just gay Jack.

"What's the matter with you Jack?" asked Miranda.

"Nothing," said Delaney with a quick smile.

Except Bradshaw and his careless sangfroid. His scruffy sneakers, his long, unruly hair; Miranda asking his favorite book and his reply that he didn't read. His oblivious disregard for Delaney's most cherished convictions.

I watched Hamid move slowly to the door, leaning heavily on a silver-handled walking stick, then I turned to Miranda. Despite her current good mood, to me she seemed as fragile as all the other diners seemed invulnerable, their authority permanent.

Live and learn, Dave: apparently the only thing that stays intact is change. Beyond the aroma of coq au vin and the breezes of Joy in the restaurant that night, I didn't notice the cloud of spiritual and literal bankruptcy moving in, which eventually rained down ruin on many of the fun-seekers in the room.

When Delaney went to the loo, Miranda opened the book he'd given her.

"What *is* this book about?" she asked me.

"I'm trying to remember," I said. But I couldn't. Obviously a gap in my education.

"*Bleak House,*" she said, candlelight dancing in the silver and blue of her eyes. "Good thing June twenty-first's in spitting distance."

"Longest day of the year, isn't it," I said.

"And the most light," she said. "My favorite day."

Delaney returned, we drank our espresso, and dinner concluded smoothly. Except for one thing: I got stuck with the check, as Delaney couldn't find his American Express card.

Ordinarily I wouldn't even remember such a commonplace piece of business unless of course it was a precursor of things to come.

Leaving Mortimer's, we decided to walk awhile and went west across Lexington Avenue through the cool evening, to Madison.

Just down from the Whitney Museum, we paused in front of Books & Co., which, with its dark paneled wood, winding stair, and cozy atmosphere, fulfilled everybody's fantasies of what a bookshop should be. Though it was way past closing time, a party was going on inside.

"I want to stop one minute," said Delaney. "Jeannette will let me in."

Naturally he knows the owner. And he can't miss a party, I thought with some hostility, even though Miranda said she wasn't in the mood for another crowd. She and I strolled around the corner to a deli, where she bought cigarettes and I picked up the paper. When we met Delaney a few minutes later, Miranda immediately checked his big leather bag.

"Look David," she said, "*Midnight Passion, Midnight Fire, Midnight Confession.*"

Wrong again.

Later, lying in my bed, staring up at the glow-in-the-dark stars I'd once pasted on the ceiling, I was suffused with new feelings of bonhomie toward the sensitive Delaney.

Most people I know are either essentially illiterate like Malone, or hyperliterate like Jack's buddy Peregrine Behar. So none of them ever read my work. In fact half the ladies who do read my stories put those plastic book jackets with fleurs-de-lis all over them on the paperbacks, not to protect the books but to hide the raunchy covers from the other people on the bus.

I was drifting, almost asleep; the air conditioner hummed in perfect counterpoint to my warm thoughts of brotherhood. I hadn't felt this good since long before the attack on Miranda. Delaney really surprised me . . . we'd probably wind up close friends . . . he was one great guy . . .

With shit for brains!

Suddenly I was awake, remembering what happened in *Bleak House.*

It was her *face.* Esther Summerson's face was permanently disfigured.

• • •

From Delaney-Behar Correspondence:

My dear JFX,
    Dashing to dinner. Morton claims to have two '61 La Chapelles. Act
One brilliant! More later.
PB   London, 23rd June
P.S. But do get a grip dear fellow, you simply cannot call the girl
Daisy.

•   •   •

A few days after our dinner at Mortimer's, on a morning made vivid
by clean air for a change, a comfortable temperature, and the tiniest
hit of Acapulco Gold, I strolled along Broadway beneath a hundred-
and-sixty-foot woman stretched out across a billboard advertising
Calvin Klein panties. I passed the peep shows and porno parlors, triple
X-rated film houses, and head shops; zigzagged through the flesh,
bone, and blood peddlers; and left them all behind.

When I reached Fifth Avenue I turned north. To my left was
Central Park, where flowers, grass, and trees serve as botanical
boundaries of 10021 territory, home to the greatest concentration of
personal wealth in New York City, a bit of trivia that becomes more
interesting when one realizes there are two hundred and ninety-two
other zip codes in Manhattan alone.

I met Miranda at my favorite oasis of temporary tranquillity, the
old mansion turned museum on Seventieth Street that houses the Frick
Collection. Delaney was off doing some kind of research for his script.
I was impressed at how fast he had gotten a deal, and I figured with
Behar on *Anna Karenina,* Delaney on *Bleak House,* and several Edith
Wharton novels in the works, Hollywood was moving my way. So I
called *my* agent, who got back almost instantly with the news that A)
Middlemarch was already in development for public television, and B)
I should stick with Cassie and Zack.

"Jack and I are still in separate rooms," Miranda said as we looked at
Monet's *Vétheuil in Winter.*

"That's good," I said.

"Do you really think so?"

"I mean it's good if that's what you want."

"I don't know what I want," she said. "But Jack's been great. We stay up late and talk and he never pushes me or asks me for anything. I can't figure where he gets this reputation about women. People don't know him. He's really very sweet."

"Maybe he's just patient," I said.

"Like the wolf waiting for Little Red Riding Hood?"

"Yeah."

"Did you know," she said, "that some guy rewrote a bunch of those children's stories. 'Little Red Riding Hood' was from the wolf's standpoint."

"Don't tell me," I said. "He was just misunderstood."

I was on Miranda's right as she executed an effortless kick with her left foot in a mysteriously backward and side motion, nailing my ass with the toe of her shoe. The two old ladies en route to lunch at the Colony Club barely noticed.

As we moved on to Fragonard's *Progress of Love,* Miranda said she and Delaney had discussed *Bleak House* (he told her he'd had the idea for months, since Peregrine started his script) and Esther Summerson, whose irreparable scars came from smallpox. Miranda decided to put the book aside for the time being, but wasn't hers a gorgeous edition and didn't I think Delaney was a thoughtful guy.

Well . . .

And, oh yes, he's already read the first half of *Midnight Passion.* Well, yes.

• • •

From Delaney-Behar Correspondence:

Peregrine:

We may not agree about claret, but you were on the money about Bradshaw. This guy (who must be well over 40) had the balls to phone Miranda at *my* place (I'll probably have to change my fucking number again) and ask *me* to have her call him! That message went straight to the round file.

Jack   New York, Friday

———

My dear John Francis,

Aren't we lucky that I go for the fat floozie clarets whereas you prefer the ones who won't kiss before the fifth date. Makes for a good cellar spread between us.

Don't worry about Bradshaw. He'll never stay in one place long enough to seduce your woman.

Shall fax notes on Act One by Friday latest. Have you told Miranda?

Cheerio,

PB   26th June, London

• • •

My reservations about Delaney were quickly buried under the fast lane where I often followed him, and not so reluctantly, during those long, light evenings at the end of June. And I confess I liked the screenings and parties and openings to which Delaney tirelessly trekked, his arm draped protectively around Miranda.

The roles we assumed — Famous Writer, Tragic Heroine, Best Friend — were about as accurate a reflection of reality as Classic Comics are of the stories they tell, but I was seduced by the romance of the moment. Also, people who spend their lives on the outside looking in, love being part of a group. Even a group of three.

• • •

When the last bandages came off, Miranda's vicious scars looked the same. Although the perfection of her beauty had been permanently compromised, its power grew.

To me, of course, the enchantment of physical beauty has always been with the flaw. Obviously others prefer a numbing symmetry. Unfortunately for Miranda, those were the people who promised her an extraordinarily lavish way of life, then rescinded the promise and with it her livelihood. All of them were gone before she left the hospital. Jobs canceled, assurances countermanded, excuses made.

Clementine Sheffield, the first rat overboard, went on vacation in Tuscany. The constant calls from bookers, photographers, and advertisers were replaced by calls from freaks, lawyers, journalists, and the low-rent hawkers of every sleazy product from Miracle Mark Scar Remover to Guns for Girls, Inc.

During this period, Miranda was so bent on getting out and having a good time, she ignored or repressed the disintegration of her career. Normally I would have seen her uncharacteristic behavior as a danger signal, but when I jumped on Delaney's merry-go-round for my one ride, I got dizzy enough to suffer from blurred vision.

Cat Kelly of *Harper's Bazaar* was the one person who remained as good as her word, sending Miranda to pose for a cover in accordance with an agreement made several months earlier.

The shoot took place as planned. Almost. The attack had changed the rules.

I guess we all knew this would be Miranda's last job, so when Delaney said he wanted to watch her work, I realized I'd never once seen her in front of a camera and asked if I could go also.

Will Rubino, the photographer, was not known for warmth, but he, too, picked up on the aura of finality around the situation, greeting us cordially and offering us coffee and sandwiches.

I hate to say this, but Miranda was born to be photographed. As Rubino lifted his camera, she dropped her off-duty veil of restraint and segued effortlessly from gravitas to mirth; from waif to vamp. Her performance was so very good, I realized with sickening certainty, that she could have been one of the few to succeed in making the switch from magazines to movies. Could have been.

"Will, Will, Will," said Cat Kelly, whom I hadn't seen come into the studio. "Get rid of those shadows — let's see her *face*."

A black shirt and jet jewelry set off the slim fashion editor's prematurely white, signature bob. She marched over to the photographer's side and allowed her winning smile to soften the edge of the imperious instructions she continued to give.

Rubino, who'd been putting Miranda in profile and discreetly lighting all the other shots, fiddled interminably with his meters.

"Okay Miranda," he finally said. And shot her straight on, full face.

"Good good," said Cat Kelly at the end of the session. "Just what we wanted. Miranda dear you're brilliant. You too Will. I know I'll get something wonderful."

And she did. But to use what she got, she was forced to put her job on the line. The relatively powerful, though intellectually challenged, corporate authority to whom she reported felt that Miranda was a symbol of violence. He feared that advertisers would be deterred, newsstand sales would suffer, subscribers would cancel. He ordered Kelly to prepare another cover, featuring a different model. She refused. Trouble ensued, followed by a showdown. At last, they reached a compromise.

When the striking black-and-white cover appeared a few months later, it became a collector's item for people who follow such things. Miranda's last fashion photograph was a stark and beautiful profile, rendering only the pristine, undamaged side of her face.

• • •

As the unforgiving heat of early July descended on us, the charges against Mark Douglas still held. But the Manhattan DA called Terrence O'Mara to warn him that the state's case was coming apart. Since Ben stubbornly maintained he couldn't (or wouldn't) *swear* to having seen the landlord at the scene of the attack, O'Mara insisted on interviewing Juliana, who he said was now the only person standing between Mark Douglas and freedom.

It took a while, but we managed to track down Juliana, who had made herself scarce just when we started looking for her. Miranda got her bathed, shampooed, and dressed in one layer of clothing and proper shoes for the crucial visit to O'Mara's. When Delaney volunteered to go along, Miranda accepted his offer.

Thus the four of us entered the Park Avenue office promptly at ten in the morning and passed a departing man, whose face I recognized from the heavy media coverage of his money-laundering trial.

O'Mara, dressed in a polo shirt and khaki pants instead of his usual dark suit, offered coffee, juice, and sweet rolls, to which Juliana helped herself without reservation. Maybe this was a good sign. No one else had an appetite for anything but getting on with business, so after a few minutes O'Mara directed us to his round table and placed Juliana between Miranda and himself.

O'Mara metamorphosed before our eyes. He became loose, avuncular, dear.

"Juliana," he said. "What a lovely name. I'm Terrence O'Mara. Miranda's friend."

"The Wild Irishman," said Juliana.

A tiny spark of hope began to glow in my heart.

"Not so wild," said O'Mara. "But determined to help Miranda. And I know you want to help her too, because you're also her friend."

"I Do, I Do."

The spark grew. Miranda and I exchanged a quick glance. O'Mara continued speaking softly, clearly, slowly.

"Now," he said. "On the night we're talking about, it was late. . . . Miranda went home . . . then she decided to go pick up Pete at the veterinarian. . . . You probably followed her that night to make sure she was okay. Because it was so late to be walking around alone, right?"

Juliana didn't say anything.

"When Miranda got hurt, Juliana," O'Mara proceeded, "were you there?"

The bag lady tilted her head. I couldn't call it a nod.

"Good. That's what I thought," said O'Mara. "I knew you were there."

He moved his chair a little closer to Juliana.

"But," he went on, in a lower, even kindlier voice, "you couldn't protect her, could you?"

"Fortune Wand," said Juliana.

"I know," said O'Mara. "It was very bad luck."

The spark flickered; O'Mara was undaunted. Juliana's lips began to quiver, then she started to cry.

"Oh Julie," said Miranda.

"What can we do?" asked Delaney.

"Missed the Storm," said Juliana, and sniffled loudly. When she blew her nose on the hem of her skirt, defeat etched itself into Delaney's face, but O'Mara was unaffected.

"There was nothing you could have done against two men," he said to Juliana. "But I'd like you to try and remember the men."

"Monster Order, Nake the Snake."

She was trying.

"*Good*," said Delaney, and we all looked at him. He cleared his throat and said, "Sorry."

"It's okay," said Miranda.

"Juliana," O'Mara went on, "I know you can answer my next question. I want you to say 'yes' or 'no' and I know you can do it."

The bag lady stared at him.

"Sure you can," Miranda said, smiling and nodding.

Juliana slowly nodded in concert with Miranda.

O'Mara pulled a photo of Dooley Kincaid from a folder on the table. He put it down in front of Juliana.

"Did you see this man?" he asked. "Did he hurt Miranda? Just say yes or no."

"Miss Smart, Gotta Be Tough."

O'Mara took a picture of Mark Douglas out of his folder and showed it to Juliana.

"What about him?" he asked. "Was he in his car watching the men hurt Miranda?"

Miranda bowed her head and closed her eyes.

"Explosive."

"This is very important Juliana," said O'Mara, gently tapping the photo of Mark Douglas. "We all think you can tell us yes."

Juliana folded her hands.

"Ace Deuce."

Miranda looked up and said, "Ace Deuce no use."

Later, as we walked toward what was then the Pan Am Building, Juliana gave us the slip, and I was just as glad, because Miranda's disappointment had suddenly turned to fear.

"There goes the case," she said. "Now they'll be on the street again and Mark Douglas probably wants to kill me."

Delaney put his arm around her.

"I'll take care of you," he said.

Oh sure, I thought, Lancelot in a white suit. What's he going to do, stick his fountain pen in their eye?

• • •

Worries about the case didn't keep us from heading downtown that evening to a new restaurant called Alice on Dominic Street, which was meant to have a superior wine list. There, like everywhere else we went, Delaney was accorded star treatment. Although several years had passed since its publication, *The Wings of Night* remained an active part of the group consciousness, because in the downtown clubs and restaurants, night was still the most important part of the day.

*Some*how, the press always learned Delaney's itinerary. The more he complained about being harassed, the more he showed up in gossip columns, fashion pages, or city magazines' celebrity sections. It was clear to anybody (except Miranda) with a particle of sense, that Delaney craved attention, sought it, loved it. And Miranda's presence by his side considerably increased the wattage of the spotlight.

She'd resumed her original indifference toward the media, but with a wariness and a wiliness new since Tansy Stoner first sneaked into the hospital. Miranda didn't solicit or encourage the continuing fascination. But since she didn't avoid it either, I wondered whether this adjustment was made to suit Delaney's unquenchable thirst for ink — or if Miranda had a need to put her scarred face on display to the world. Was she subtly showing her anger toward Mark Douglas — building a case against him in the hearts and minds of the public? Where did she put the anger that wasn't so subtle? I'd never seen it.

"Now *this* — if it's as good as I think — is a bargain," said Delaney, pointing to a '79 Pichon-Lalande priced at eighty dollars on Alice's wine list. He called the waiter over and ordered a bottle.

"I bought a car one time for eighty dollars," said Miranda.

"A car," said Delaney. "God — my gym shoes cost eighty dollars."

Only a third of what the soft Belgian loafers he was wearing must have set him back. Not to mention the white suit. And bespoke shirt. Unfortunately my idea of pulling it all together is a navy blue blazer from Brooks Brothers (I wouldn't want to be a black guy who couldn't throw a ball either, but there it is).

Together, Delaney and Miranda looked particularly arresting that night, she in her black jacket with a cropped white T-shirt, pleated micro skirt, and necklace of beads and charms assembled and sent by a fifth-grade class in Brooklyn.

Two young women with lots of eye makeup, dark red lipstick, and five or six earrings in each ear, swooped down on our table with pens and paper in hand. They ignored Delaney, who had turned to them smiling graciously; Miranda was their quarry. After she gave them each her autograph and they departed whispering, Delaney pretended — my guess is it wasn't hard — to sulk.

Miranda jollied him past this pout and we checked out our menus, idly discussing the changing and relative values of goods and services and segueing into what had become a familiar litany from Delaney: art undervalued, writers underpaid; particularly good writers particularly underpaid, and he himself the most sinned against of all.

At the end of our first course, the wine had breathed sufficiently to distract Delaney, who tasted and approved it. Before dessert, we'd knocked off three bottles of the Pichon-Lalande and were into the fourth. Delaney was telling a story — about a bar fight he'd managed to avoid which involved a friend's estranged wife, a Hell's Angel, and a giant misunderstanding — when a young woman who would have been pretty were she not so chalky-looking and chubby, presented herself at our table.

"Jack," she said in a loud, shrill voice. "You really are a bastard."

Overbleached hair hung down almost to her big hips, where she'd placed her hands, clenched into fists. Her eyes had a special look — validated by the white residue around her nostrils. A twitching jaw eradicated any doubt about her condition: she was definitely cranked. And she'd taken Delaney by surprise.

"Courtney," he said. "I thought you were in L.A."

"Don't you wish," she seethed.

Obviously uncomfortable, Delaney tried being conciliatory.

"Pull up a chair Court," he offered. "I'm glad you're back. Meet my friends."

"You are *so* full of shit Jack," she fairly shouted.

But she did pull a chair up and fell heavily into it. Delaney motioned toward Miranda and me.

"This is — "

"I know who they are," said the young woman. "America's favorite victim and her walker. Cute."

"All right, Courtney, that's enough," said Delaney, taking her arm.

"It's okay," said Miranda.

Not with me, I thought.

"What's your problem?" asked Miranda.

Her composure was the real thing, not the terrifying calm I'd seen at times when just the opposite emotion was appropriate. Miranda could handle this girl, who was swiping at her runny nose with her sleeve. Then an odd sound, something between derision and pain, escaped from her.

"What's my problem," she mocked. "Ask your *boyfriend*."

Delaney shook his head, impatience growing. His usually pleasant face was taking on a dark cast.

"I asked *you*," Miranda said.

"I'm thinking about suing you Jack," Courtney said. "My father's lawyers are the best in the city, *Jack*. Aren't you going to answer me?"

She reached for a half-finished glass of wine and drank it in two gulps, heedless of the port-colored clown smile now adding to her disheveled look.

"Guess not," she said. "Well Miss Miranda, you better watch out — because you know what you are to this Jack-ass? *Nothing*. Like me, like his wife. He used *her* up fast. Then he went on to Gaby Sebastian — you know, Abe Sebastian's daughter. He owns CBS or NBC or one of those. She fell apart when he dumped her for Domina Valverde. Now she's in the loony bin."

"She is not," Delaney said wearily, "as you so eloquently put it, Courtney, in the loony bin."

"Okay, she went into a convent."

"An ashram," said Delaney slowly.

"Whatever," said Courtney. As she waved her hand in a sloppily dismissive gesture, she knocked a glass of wine onto Miranda's white shirt.

"Dammit Courtney," said Delaney, standing.

He looked about to grab the girl. But switched gears and bent over Miranda, kissing the top of her head. Then he ran his hand lightly over her wet breasts.

"Are you okay?" he asked. Without waiting for a reply, he tilted Miranda's chin up and kissed her. "Can I get you some soda water — or it salt?"

"Why does everything happen to *me*?" wailed Courtney, her eyes filling with tears. Evidently she forgot who was the spiller and who the spillee.

"Don't bother," Miranda said to Delaney. "It's just a T-shirt."

"Half a T-shirt," he said, smiling.

Miranda turned those piercing platinum-blue eyes toward Courtney.

"So what's your point?" Miranda asked.

"Well," Courtney whined, "I mean, he said he was going to marry
me."

"*Jack* marry *you?*" I said, in a tone suggesting that such a concept
would destroy the first law of nature.

I am not a walker.

"All of you can just go to hell!" said Courtney, her voice trill-
ing with malice. "Jack-*ass* Delaney is the biggest liar I ever met in
my life."

She shifted her attention back to Miranda.

"He'll dump you," she said. "Like a *dump,* and flush you down the
toilet the minute he finds somebody he likes better."

Jumping up awkwardly, Courtney turned over her chair. The noise
made no difference since everyone in the small boîte was speechless by
then, watching this little scene unfold. When she ran toward the
restrooms, finger already up her nose, the whole place exploded in
loud chatter as though by stage direction.

At the same time, Alice Birch, the owner, whose sweet teenage
appearance belied a well-documented business sense (to me, running a
good restaurant is as mysterious as betting soybean futures), came
striding out of the kitchen. She made a beeline for our table where,
needless to say she greeted Delaney with a kiss, but didn't waste time
fawning over him before addressing herself to Miranda.

"As if you haven't been through enough," said Alice.

"I'm fine," said Miranda. "But for a second I thought I'd have to
smack that loudmouth brat."

"I'd like to take a shot at her myself," said Alice.

"I'm sorry we disrupted the place," said Delaney.

"We all know how much you hate dramatics," said Miranda,
taking his hand.

"I see you've got his number," said Alice.

"Hey — " said Delaney.

"Hey, you're a lucky guy Jack," said Alice, "and my customers got
some theater with dinner, so everybody's happy. Come in the kitchen,
Miranda, and we'll try to get that wine out."

"Oh shit," said Delaney. Courtney was emerging from the ladies room.

"I'll handle her," said Alice. "Excuse me."

By the time Alice reached Courtney, the three of us were hurrying out of the restaurant into the heat and traffic and noise of the summer night. Miranda and Delaney turned left into the dark shadow of an awning next door to Alice's, and though I didn't mean to separate myself from them, in my haste escaping the idiotic Courtney, I turned right, into a little alleyway next to the restaurant.

"We're safe," I heard Delaney say.

"Where's David?" asked Miranda.

I was about to walk out of hiding when Delaney said, "Poor Dave."

"What do you mean 'poor Dave'?" asked Miranda.

"Nothing," said Delaney.

"No, what did you mean?" she asked again.

"I think it's obvious — he's crazy about you."

"Jack," she said. "You are one tricky buckaroo. First of all, David is crazy about Malone, not me. And second of all, you'll say anything to get off the subject of that bitch Courtney. Who *is* she?"

"I'll tell you about Courtney," said Delaney. "Once upon a time she was a nice enough kid — but she was *always* pissed off about one thing or another. Now what's left of her brain is really fried. I'm sorry about all that stuff she said, and I'll get you a new shirt."

"I don't want a new shirt," said Miranda. "I want something else."

"Okay," he said. "How about something in precious metal?"

"No," she said. "I'm not fooling around. I want a promise."

"Anything."

"Promise to tell me the truth."

"I promise," he said softly.

So throw me in jail, I'm a voyeur.

"I promise," he said again as he pulled her close and kissed her scarred cheek lightly, again and again. Then he folded her into his arms, caught her shining hair in his fingers, and kissed her parted lips long and hard. Returning his kisses, she stood on tiptoe, arms wound around his neck, her whole body pressing into his.

"Oh God," he said, his voice catching. "I love you Miranda." He pushed the jacket off her shoulders, slid his hands under the wine-soaked T-shirt and began to kiss her breasts.

At that moment, I felt a stab to the heart more piercing than my father's absence, Malone's faithlessness, or my own mediocrity. I imagined a universe created before my very eyes, with its own rhythm and its own rules. A cosmos with a passion and a beauty so effortless that all would want to enter but none would be allowed. A galaxy with space for only two stars — whose light would never shine on me.

I was wrong, but as we know, this is nothing new.

Fused at the hip, Miranda and Delaney walked around the corner and out of sight.

"He'll fuck her over."

I whirled so fast I nearly fell. Somehow, Courtney had gotten into the alley from the other end and was standing directly behind me.

"Scared you, didn't I?"

"I'm fine," I said, and stepped away from her onto the sidewalk, where I immediately hailed a cab.

"Did you ever fuck a girl," she called after me. "You're cute for a fag, you want to fuck me?"

• • •

Late the next afternoon, while I put my orderly desk in further order, Miranda sat cross-legged on my living room floor, reading my *Diary of Anaïs Nin* and finishing my bag of chocolate chip cookies. It was almost as if nothing had happened and nothing were different. Except when she looked up from the book and swept away the mass of silver-blond hair obscuring her face. The contrast between her pale white skin and the obscenely livid scars seemed even worse than the scars themselves.

I feared that her high spirits, so far out of sync with recent events, sprang from a dubious source.

"I've never felt like this before," she said.

As if the tableau outside Alice's on Dominic Street hadn't been enough, Anaïs Nin should have tipped me off. But I was hiding out in the dangerous sanctuary of denial.

"There's something about his face, his hands . . ."

I hummed a little tune in my head. De de de de. De de da da.

". . . his body."

De da de de. De da de de de.

"David," Miranda said. "Are you listening? I can only tell this to you. . . . Last night when we went home . . . he put candles in the bathroom and filled the bathtub for me . . . and when I was taking a bath, he put his hand on my face and said: 'Matter too soft a lasting mark to bear.' . . . I think the pope said that."

"Not *the* pope," I said. "It must have been *Alexander* Pope, the poet."

"Okay, it was some Pope," she said. "Then he floated rose petals on the water. He sprinkled *rose petals* all over me and into the water . . ."

"Rose petals," I said, taking a deep breath. I could feel my heart heading south. Who was this goony Miranda, and what had she done with *my* Miranda?

"And when he touched me — "

"Do I want to hear this?" I asked. Maybe she was a Passing Miranda.

"I don't know," she said. But she didn't care whether I wanted to hear or not. She wanted to tell.

"Go ahead," said kindly Mr. Superego.

"I couldn't say this to anybody else," she said.

Why must she keep reminding me?

"But when he touched me," she went on, "it was so . . . exciting, really exciting, but I felt safe too. It felt like I had always known him."

"Good," I said. And cleared my throat. The charm of infatuation, of course, is that it creates a past in minutes; all other affections require history.

"Could I have some of that iced tea?" she asked.

"Sure," I said, and poured.

"Have you got more cookies?"

"I'll take a look," I said, and walked into the kitchen.

"What do you know about orgasms?" she called.

"Orgasms," I said. Now she thinks I'm one of the girls. "I assume you mean female?"

"Uh huh."

"I know absolutely nothing," I said, which was true.

There were no cookies, so I returned to the living room with a box of Carr's biscuits.

"Is somebody having a problem?" I asked. Somebody indeed.

"Oh no," she said. "Just the opposite."

"Have a cracker," I said.

"I didn't mean to embarrass you," she said.

"Don't be ridiculous."

"But all of a sudden I feel like a different person with Jack, and not because of the attack, but because of him."

Yes ma'am. *We Are Renewed.* Right up there on the Falling-in-Love Top Ten. Jumping from Number Nine with a bullet last week to Number One today. And *here, in person,* the White Knight himself: *Jack Delaney!*

He did come by just about then, tieless in an alabaster jacket, with dark glasses hiding his eyes but somehow making him look even more handsome. He and Miranda — like refugees at the border, winners of the prize, parents of the newborn — kissed immediately. Her skin grew rosier and so did his. God knows mine probably did too.

Everything was suffused with a kind of pink light.

Like rose petals.

12

• • •

Per usual, the Fourth of July afforded some spectacular fireworks, but none so sensational and unexpected as those that took place at LAX shortly before the holiday began. Our sources report that when mega-producer Larry Owen pulled up in his mile-long limo complete with chilled Cristal, a bright red rose, and an equally bright red leather box from Cartier to greet his wife, socialite Patrice Wentworth Owen, who arrived via the couple's new Falcon jet to spend the long weekend with him doing the requisite roundelay of parties, he was met by news far more explosive than a sky full of Roman candles. The third Mrs. Owen gave him (as we used to say in gentler times) the gate. Copious tears (his and hers) fell, there was much hand-wringing (his and hers), but in the end, determination (hers) to leave prevailed over desperation (his) and she nipped back onto the plane bound for New York. Mrs. Owen did not return our phone calls. A spokesman from Big O Productions said: "Mr. Owen has every hope for a reconciliation." Late on the Fourth of July, Larry Owen was spotted with a tight knot of supportive friends at the Malibu beach party of agent Ron Meyer. There's nothing worse than a broken heart, but maybe Mr. Owen can find some comfort in the fact that his latest show, *The Golden Rule,* starring Les Malone (who's destined for *People*'s Sexiest-Man-In-The-World cover) shot right to the top of the ratings chart, where it apparently has found a happy home.

Meanwhile in Newport . . .

• • •

I never found out what and who happened in Newport because I dropped the paper to pick up the phone. Malone was calling from Santa Monica.

"Did you see Roland Tarbell's column?" he asked.

"Just now," I said. "So what really happened?"

"I think Roland was only playing with me — nobody knows who's gonna be the sexiest man till the last minute."

"I mean what happened with Larry and Patti?"

"Oh yeah. It was what you read — she gets off the plane and tells him she wants out. I was in the car."

"You're the 'sources.' "

"Well . . ."

"I don't care — did she say all that stuff in front of you?"

"No, they were standing outside."

"And you rolled down your window."

"Half an inch."

"So?"

"So he asks her right off the bat if she's seeing another guy."

"And she says — because truth is the best lie, right — of course I'm not *seeing* another guy."

"I don't get it."

"She's not seeing somebody, she's *fucking* somebody."

"But she has to see him to fuck him."

"Forget it."

"Well I think it's Bobby Wilder she's got the hots for anyhow. Whatever it is, no way is she gonna cop to her thing with Henry Garcia — but Larry starts crying anyhow."

"Jesus."

"Dave — Larry's one tough motherfucker. *Believe* me, those were alligator tears — if he's not sticking a gun in your cajones he's bawling. He always gets what he wants."

"Not this time."

"I don't know. He's a sneaky sonofabitch — "

"Believe *me,* I know. After I shook hands with him I counted my fingers. But I still don't think he's as sneaky as she is."

"Vamos a ver."

"What does that mean?"

"It means I've been studying Spanish."

"Humping a Mexican."

"David."

"You're a prick, Malone."

"But you love me."

"Keep dreaming."

● ● ●

Terrence O'Mara's relentless (and pro bono) damage control on Miranda's behalf became more necessary, as the tabloids, led by Tansy Stoner and with a uniquely American fickleness, turned on Miranda. She who had been their darling only a few weeks earlier was suddenly, gratuitously, portrayed (within libel limits) as a liar, a seductress, and a slut.

At the same time, like the true deus ex machina that she was, Alison Vonseca, having decided to visit friends on the coast of Turkey after attending a conference in Vienna, insisted Miranda use her house in the country. Miranda invited Delaney to go along. She also invited me.

We set off a good four hours before rush hour in the little gray Mercedes Delaney had leased. But trying to second-guess New York City traffic is like trying to outsmart the house in Vegas. It never happens. Within minutes, we were stopped halfway through the Midtown Tunnel (not one of my favorites on a list that includes all tunnels, bridges, and elevators) while police and tow trucks dealt with a collision at the far end.

I sat scrunched in the back trying not to hyperventilate while Delaney fiddled with the tape player until Miranda finally rewound the Jimmy Buffett tape he wanted and put it on. Then she went back to *Tender Is the Night.*

Delaney got out of the car a few times, returned fidgety, tapping the steering wheel.

"Do you have to read?" he asked.

"Something wrong?" Miranda asked.

"Nothing's wrong," he said. "I just want you to pay attention to me."

She closed the book, kissed his cheek, ruffled his fair hair.

"No problem," she said. "Now what'll we do?"

"Wish I had a phone in the car," he said. "Everybody in California has a phone."

"Thought you wanted attention from *me*," Miranda said, and laughed.

"I do, I do," he said, drumming his fingers on the dashboard.

"Jack," she said. "What's your favorite book?"

"You never asked him before?" I said, surprised.

"Yeah," said Delaney. "I've heard you ask other people. You asked Elaine Kaufman — "

"I didn't know you were listening," said Miranda, pleased.

" — and you asked that guy with the Hamids, I can't remember his name."

Right, Jack.

"Bradshaw," I supplied.

"Yes," said Delaney. "The scruffy-looking record guy. You asked *him* and you never asked me."

"I'm asking you now," she said.

"Okay," he said, "but I'm going to ask you first. You're always reading — which is good — what's *your* favorite?"

"That's easy," she said. "It's *The Sun Also Rises*."

"No," he said, shaking his head.

"What do you mean 'no,' " she said. "What's wrong with *The Sun Also Rises*?"

"It's *my* favorite book," he said.

Oh, for God's sake.

"What difference does it make?" she asked.

"It makes a difference to *me*," he said.

"Why?" I asked.

Why can't pigs fly? Why do fools fall in love?

"Jack," she said.

"*What?*"

"The truth is," she said, "I really liked *A Farewell to Arms* better. I had *The Sun Also Rises* in my head because I just read it in the hospital."

The hospital on the Champs-Elysées.

"You know something — " I said, and Miranda fired me a look armed with silver-blue daggers.

"What, David?" she asked.

I was about to say they were both insufferable and I was getting out of the car there and then. But the traffic began moving, and silence once more proved to be the better part of valor. Also, the old scar on Miranda's leg affirmed that you can get hurt jumping from a moving vehicle.

We drove for an hour and a half before leaving the permanent reconstruction of the Long Island Expressway at Exit 70 for Route 27, where even I could tell that many of the drivers, clearly city people on vacation, should register their cars as lethal weapons or take the bus.

As we motored past the few remaining potato fields of Water Mill, Bridgehampton, Sagaponack, and Wainscott, I started thinking about our destination.

Alison Vonseca's East Hampton shares nothing in common with what has become known as "the Hamptons," not even geography. The enormous double dune over which her turn-of-the century, gray-shingled, Lutyens-designed house looks, is a natural phenomenon running for only a few short miles along the shore. Protected in perpetuity by the Nature Conservancy and affording a grand and sweeping view out to an endless sea, the double dune makes the Further Lane property behind it even more valuable than the better-known Lily Pond Lane and the glitzier West Way.

Alison Vonseca, like most of her lifelong friends and neighbors, treasures privacy. Her East Hampton, revolving entirely around the Maidstone Club, the Devon Yacht Club, and the Garden Club, conducts its business in the City and its social life behind towering hedges and generations of decorum. The captains of industry and finance and their wives who people Alison Vonseca's East Hampton play their cards close to the vest and always have. Their activities may surface occasionally in the *Wall Street Journal* and *Business Week* — but are never seen on Tansy Stoner's type of tabloid television or chronicled in columns like hers or Roland Tarbell's.

Although Mrs. Vonseca's singular tragedy cast her briefly into the public eye, she managed thereafter to keep her messianic cause and philanthropic bent largely quiet. Her personal life and that of her friends read like the discreet signs scattered here and there on their land: PRIVATE, KEEP OUT.

• • •

"Not bad," said Delaney, turning right at the sign, which read simply, A.V.

We drove through the privet, onto a long, hard-packed dirt drive bordered by Kwanzan cherry trees, past a shuttered guesthouse in the style of the main house, empty stable, tennis court (so brilliantly designed, sunken, and surrounded with trees, it appeared to have no fence), and black tiled swimming pool with pool house in the same mode as the other two houses.

An allée of three hundred evergreen trees, each twenty feet tall, made a stunning sweep straight down the middle of the lush eight-acre lawn, creating a landscaping statement rarely seen anywhere outside the south of France and certainly never seen anywhere at all by me. The allée ended at the entrance to a sunken garden where Alison Vonseca grew at least three dozen varieties of roses.

Scores of fragrant cutting flowers, multitudes of vegetables, and every imaginable herb filled several other gardens. I noticed a rhubarb patch, a raspberry patch, and a stand of pear trees. Not to mention a Calder stabile by the little reflecting pool.

Beyond the reflecting pool and gardens, on the other side of the house, the lawn gave way to half a dozen different types of exotic sea grass, which in turn stopped in a vast tangle of beach plums, rosa ruberosa, and scrub pine, fanning out on either side of the long path down to the ocean.

We pulled up under a porte cochere and stopped the car just as a man in a starched white jacket and unlikely gold loop in one ear stepped onto the porch. This was Evandi, Alison Vonseca's major-domo, who helped take our bags out of the Mercedes and lug them inside. He explained that before leaving the next day on his annual holiday, he would get us settled, demonstrate how everything worked, and answer any questions.

A quick look around confirmed that Mrs. Vonseca collected good art and loved English and American antiques, and that she apparently had no interest whatever in central (or any) air conditioning, micro-wave ovens, cable TV, or superfluous telephones.

Since there were endless guest rooms and no instructions about where we should sleep, we got to choose. I couldn't decide between a monk's cell with bare walls, polished floor, single bed, desk, and chair, and an L-shaped room done in Anglo-Indian style which included an elegant daybed for reading, a four-poster bed for sleeping, and on the wall across from the armoire, a Gauguin watercolor — for inspiration. While my self and soul engaged in dialectics, Delaney took a large second-floor suite.

His bedroom, which Miranda would share, was done up in a pleasing combination of blue and yellow and white matelassé. The suite's sitting room was square-shaped and bright, with faded floral couches, comfortable chairs, and a big, beautiful George III kneehole desk where Delaney could put his equipment. Since he was technologically hopeless, Miranda promised to set up his computer, printer, and fax.

(I once took a course in word processing, but people like Delaney don't bother with such mundanities. On the other hand, while I wrote about Cassie and Zack, he wrote *The Wings of Night* . . .)

For herself (as well as for the sake of any reports the departing Evandi might make to his employer) Miranda chose an all-white aerie on the third floor with a view due east and a sense that one was riding the prow of an ocean liner.

Figuring I was already sufficiently ascetic, I went for the Gauguin.

• • •

Having been in East Hampton no more than three hours, Delaney was able to gather a group of midweek gambolers for a dinner party.

I wondered idly who would show up. Most of Delaney's friends and acquaintances were writers, artists, arbitrageurs, and the actress-model, producer-researcher girls he called hyphenates. They all seemed to think good luck was a guarantee and good times were their due, so they swooped in and out of parties, games, jobs, and marriages expecting and experiencing nothing less.

They were so good looking, accomplished, and well connected they appeared unreal, at least until late at night when the booze and drugs took over. Then they became too real.

However much they whirled, twirled, drank, and snorted, the group stayed small and tight, like the eye of a storm, and did not welcome outsiders. However, they ignored Miranda's preference to remain outside. Fame as we know was the shiniest coin in their realm, and when she made the ultimate leap from posing for magazine covers to being the subject of magazine covers, she surrendered her privacy. They demanded access. They wanted to peel away whatever layers she had left and find what made her mysterious. Touch it, feel it, devour it.

•   •   •

Coming down the stairs, showered, shaved, and feeling summery, I could hear music drifting in from the terrace. Delaney was playing Sinatra's "I've Got You Under My Skin" — Malone's favorite song. Not exactly the cutting edge of contemporary sound, but it hadn't held any of them — Sinatra, Delaney, or Malone — back. Maybe there was lesson for me . . .

"You're certainly making the scene these days."

The unexpected voice startled me.

"Patrice!" I said. "What are you doing here?"

She had just walked through the front door.

"Is that how you greet your old friends?" she asked, and dispensed two air kisses. "Jack called a little while ago and invited me. I'm down the beach."

She pointed, but I still barely knew where we were.

"I had no idea," I said.

"Well, it's Larry's house; he thinks I can't get it or any of the other houses because I signed this prenuptial agreement."

"Isn't that the purpose of a prenuptial agreement?"

"They're made to be broken," she said breezily. "But I'm not doing anything at the moment."

"Oh," I said.

She was always doing something.

"Larry's stuck in California with more gum surgery."

A look of disgust swept across her face, signaling the end of any residual affection she might once have persuaded herself to feel for her husband.

"He said," she continued, "I could use the house to think things over. He wants me to change my mind."

"Will you?"

She shrugged, laughed, and leaned close to me, so I could smell her very expensive perfume and, had I been interested, get a good look at her tits.

"Henry's on his way out from the city," she whispered. "Don't say anything — it's a secret."

Patti's idea of a secret — telling one person at a time — hadn't changed.

"I wanted him to meet me here," she continued. "But he wouldn't. I mean, he could've said he was Jack's friend, or your friend — "

"For sure."

" — or even, you know, the one who had a thing with Bobby."

"Miranda."

"That's right, Miranda." She took my arm. "Aren't you going to offer me a drink?"

We walked around until we found a bar set up in a small sitting room facing the sea. Patti poured herself a big-girl glass of vodka over two ice cubes and added a twist.

"So what really happened with Miranda?" she asked.

Obviously I was stuck in this conversation for the moment, so I flipped the top off a bottle of Corona.

"Didn't you see the papers?" I asked.

"How could I help it. You'd've thought World War III broke out from the attention she got — even on the West Coast."

"Then you know what happened."

"I can't believe that's all there was to it," said Patti.

"I'd say that was enough."

"Well," said Patti petulantly, "I think she's taking advantage of the situation. She was in the news every single day for *weeks*. She got this house out of Alison Vonseca, and God knows what else she hustled."

Irritating as these remarks were, there was no point in chastising Patti, who saw duplicity in the eyes of her most loyal friend because she herself was deceitful, or envy in a stranger's contented heart because she was the jealous one. Her own crippling solipsism would eventually be punishment enough.

"Do you want anything else?" I asked.

"Could you ring for some — what do I want — macadamia nuts."

"Ring?" I asked dumbly.

"You know, on the intercom."

I glanced over at the phone.

"I don't think there is an intercom," I said.

"Damn," she said, annoyed. "These old WASPs are so cheap."

"I thought *you* were supposed to be an old WASP."

"Oh shut up, David," she said. "Let's go check out who's here. Jack said there'd be eight for dinner; maybe I can talk Henry into coming over."

We walked into the big square central hallway just as Miranda came skipping down the stairs. The hem of her undershirt-type dress was a lot closer to her waist than her knees.

"*Miranda*," said Patti, stepping forward. "I'm *so* sorry about what *happened*."

She kissed Miranda and Miranda sort of kissed her.

"Thanks, Patrice," she said. "I'm feeling a lot better now."

"Those *disgusting* men!" said Patti. "They ought to get put away forever."

"We're working on it," said Miranda.

"Now, have you agreed to any network interviews?"

Patti, always friendly to women she didn't like and very friendly to ones she couldn't stand, was being downright hearty toward Miranda.

"I can't handle interviews right now," said Miranda. "But I've been meaning to call some of those TV people who left messages . . ."

"Well," smiled Patti, "*you* must know what they say back home."

"What's that?" asked Miranda.

" 'Mean to' don't pick no cotton. My husband knows everybody in that business. I could get in touch with the heavy hitters for you."

Theo Alexander and Ned Augustus, two of Delaney's buddies from South Carolina, saved Miranda from further officiousness by charging through the front door, bearing enough shopping bags and cake boxes to feed the Confederate Army at Fort Sumter.

"We brought y'all a little food," said Theo Alexander. "So Jack could just concentrate on choosing the wine. Where's the kitchen?"

An hour later, Delaney sat at the head of the table, with Miranda at the foot. He put Patti on his right but seemed to argue with her throughout the meal. She'd been up and down several times to the phone and finally excused herself before dessert to go meet Henry Garcia. The rest of us sat around till midnight, when we left the candlelit dining room for the moonlit terrace.

Somebody took the obligatory swim and somebody else produced ecstasy. A visiting tennis pro who in his spare time obviously pursued more compelling interests than improving his ground strokes, pulled out a hefty bag of cocaine, went inside, and started chopping on one of Alison Vonseca's rosewood card tables.

Ozzy Osbourne's "Suicide Solution" was playing so loud no one could hear Delaney and Miranda quarreling, a dozen feet from me. Evandi interrupted them with a phone call from Terrence O'Mara for Miranda, who said she'd take it in the library.

I happened to be passing the library door when she emerged.

Liar, liar, pants on fire.

I happened to be pacing and hovering at the library door, and when Miranda came out, I saw that her breathing was ragged and her scars stood out against skin gone colorless. She dropped down on a bench under a Childe Hassam landscape and pulled a pack of cigarettes from her pocket.

"What happened?" I asked.

"Terrence O'Mara said the cops picked Mark up on a drug charge. He was dealing. It didn't have anything to do with my case. But because of it, the judge revoked his bail."

"I know that's good news," I said. "Kind of."

"I didn't tell you the good news yet," she said. "If you can call it that."

"Which is?"

"Mike Romanos — "

"The detective."

"Yeah, he went to see Dooley Kincaid. When Kincaid heard Mark was on his way back to Rikers, he changed his story again, and really nailed Mark."

"So now Douglas, Kincaid, and Bartholomew are all at Rikers Island," I said.

"And they set two trial dates," she said. "The first one's in September."

Miranda went to tell Delaney the news. About twenty minutes later I saw her slip upstairs carrying Zelda Fitzgerald's *Scandalabra*.

Giddy with release from my usual solitude and glad Dark Mouglas was in a cell, I stayed up till dawn with Delaney, his friend Alexander, and a couple of the hyphenates.

• • •

From Delaney-Behar Correspondence:

Dear, Dear Peregrine,

Prepare to get your pale white butt over here immediately. Miranda and I are ensconced in the comfy and commodious digs of Alison Vonseca, whose family was fried in a big fire on Fifth Avenue a few years back. I'm sure Fleet Street picked it up. The old girl has trundled off to the Old World, leaving us with the key to the cellar. Apart from swooning over the aforementioned, I'm working, Miranda's healing, and her buddy David (he's part of the package unfortunately) is doing whatever he does.

As we say in Hollywood, later for you, babe.

D. Hammett   Wednesday, 15 July
                                                                      East Hampton

---

My dear John Francis Xavier,

Am sending these notes overnight air express, as you neglected to give me your new fax number.

Act II extremely affecting. You've got a winner. Do tell Miranda at once. Truly.

Uncorked Léoville-Poyferré today. Exquisite harmony.

Late for lunch. Shall fax pages with notes in the A.M. if you send your fucking number!

Cheers,

PB   London, 17th July

P.S. I don't know about "Mandy" — isn't there some odious song by that name? I suggest "Mary." You'll keep them on their toes with the bifurcated religious implications. Heigh-ho.

• • •

By sleeping late, Delaney and I missed most of the next morning. A benevolent sun and clear sky gave no hint of the deteriorating ozone layer; and it was easy to forget the icy darkness just beneath the shining surface of the sea.

When we finally shuffled down to the beach, we found Miranda, proscribed by her doctors from running or sunning, under a huge umbrella reading *The Last Tycoon*. She wore dark glasses, a black bikini, and bright red polish on her toes.

"You look great as usual," Delaney said, throwing himself down next to her. "Unlike me. I look like a corpse, don't I?"

"I'd guess you've been dead about seventy-two hours," she said.

"Oh that's good," he said. "Is she always like this, Dave? I can't get her to be nice to me."

"I'm very nice to you," said Miranda, returning to her book.

Delaney lay back on the sand with a towel under his head and his arm shielding his eyes.

"I don't think you like me anymore," he said.

"I like you," she said.

"You don't like my friends," he said.

"I like most of your friends," she replied.

"Ah ha!" he said, his regression into early adolescence complete.

"I didn't like what's-her-name last night with the gray teeth," she said.

"Si*by*lla," he said. "She's a child."

"She's older than *me*," said Miranda.

"There's no comparison," said Delaney. "And besides I've known Sibylla forever."

In this context I'd learned that forever meant at least a year.

"She had her hand on your crotch," said Miranda.

"She was drunk," said Delaney, turning over.

"I thought she was always like that," said Miranda.

"Bitchy, bitchy," said Delaney, his voice muffled in the towel.

"You got it," she said, and poked him rather hard with her foot.

Delaney sat up, seamlessly switched gears, and started caressing her ankle. She smiled as he kissed the bottom of her foot.

"Good afternoon," said Evandi, who materialized like the genie he resembled.

He was carrying a huge picnic basket.

"Ah, Evandi," said Delaney.

This was the life.

"I brought a going-away gift," he said, placing the basket on the beach. "I am going away this afternoon, as I said. And this arrived for you."

He handed Delaney a letter, and while Delaney first searched for his sunglasses then read his letter, Miranda, Evandi, and I unpacked the wicker hamper. We laid out simple Spode china, plain Jensen silver, hemstitched linen napkins each the size of a tablecloth, and a festival of crudités, pâtés, tea sandwiches, cheese, fruit, and tarts. Bubbling water, still water, iced tea, and a chardonnay at which Delaney nodded positively when he saw it come out of the cooler.

We thanked Evandi, wished him bon voyage, and watched his white jacket disappear behind the dune. Suddenly we all started to laugh, obviously feeling like kids out of school, home alone with parents far away. Not that any of us, except Jack, ever spent too much time at school, and none of us grew up in anything as nice as Alison Vonseca's pool house, and in point of fact none of us, except Jack, had parents who showed a modicum of interest in keeping track of us then or now. Ergo, according to the books, Jack should have been the most together of our little group.

This is why I prefer fiction; it's a better reflection of the truth.

• • •

Although there were floods in Asia, forest fires in California, hurricanes in England, shipwrecks in the Pacific, and giant plane crashes everywhere, not to mention the spectre of the first trial coming in September, I was lulled by the sound of the sea, the warm sun, the food, the flowers. The garden path.

After packing the remnants of our lunch back into the wicker basket, Jack and I went for a swim cut short by the strong undertow. Soon we settled back down on either side of Miranda, who was still reading *The Last Tycoon*.

Delaney asked what she thought of the book.

"I like the way he's writing," she said. "Too bad he didn't get the chance to finish it. . . . The movie business sounds pretty raunchy even back then."

But already Delaney wasn't listening.

"I've got to get those assholes in L.A. to pay me," he said.

"They'll pay you," said Miranda.

"*When?*" demanded Delaney as if she knew.

"Soon," said Miranda.

"If they don't pay me *this* week — " said Delaney, searching for the appropriate threat.

"You just tell 'em," said Miranda, "to take their screenplay and stick it where the sun don't shine."

"You think this is *funny?*" Jack asked.

"No," she said. "But why worry about the mule going blind before you load the wagon?"

"Oh fine, that's fine if you're a *hillbilly,* for Christ's sake," said Delaney. "But in my business, *first* they pay you, *then* you work."

Miranda hit Delaney with a blast of silver blue by removing her dark glasses. I hid behind the *New York Times.*

"I don't know much about your business," she said. "But in most *other* businesses, first you *work,* then you get paid."

"Are you suggesting I don't work?" asked Jack, sitting up, his body growing rigid.

"You got a good imagination," she said.

"Goddammit," he shouted. "I postponed my next book to do this. I turned down other projects."

He jumped to his feet.

"What do you know about work anyway?" he yelled. "You don't know shit about responsibility or worry or — "

In an unbroken motion she stood, replaced the dark glasses, and headed toward the path. As soon as she got there, she started to run.

"She's not supposed to run," I said, no doubt in precisely the nasal whine you imagine.

"*Miranda!*" Delaney called after her. "Shit," he muttered, kicking up a little sandstorm, half of which landed on me.

"Don't say anything," he said.

Okay, I thought, I won't *say* a thing, but since I'm not a ninety-seven-pound weakling, what I'm going to *do* is break this asshole's head.

Yeah. And I'm also king of the esprit de l'escalier. I gathered my things and followed Miranda up the path.

• • •

We were all so resilient; our hair, our skin, our moods. By 6:30 Miranda and Delaney were in the shower together. Incidentally, I am not a peeper: they announced their bathing intention like a bit of late-breaking news as they dashed up the stairs hand in hand.

By 7:30 they descended. Dressed for what Delaney, striking in his white dinner jacket, had suggested (repeatedly) would be the ne plus ultra party of the summer, the year, or maybe the decade.

For sheer electricity, no fictional character could possibly have come close to Jack and Miranda that night. She was nothing less than mesmerizing in an Armani black satin bustier and billowing ballroom skirt of black silk taffeta with God knows how many petticoats. No jewelry, no accessories; nothing but the scars that stopped her life.

After Delaney and I agreed to meet the next morning on the tennis court, I kissed Miranda and picked up the keys to the station wagon Evandi said I could use. Though Miranda should have swept off in a coach and four just then, they left in the gray Mercedes.

They went to Southampton; I went to the Swamp.

•   •   •

From Roland Tarbell's column:

. . . and although set in bucolic Southampton, where "cottages" have no fewer than fourteen bedrooms, this birthday soiree with its lavish appointments and hagiographic guest list dazzled us in the tradition of dear (R.I.P.) Truman's fabled Black and White Ball.

On the wings of an al fresco first course, five hundred snow-white doves were released into the perfect sunset. Three dozen ushers, dressed in ebony-and-gold uniforms designed for the occasion, escorted the celebrants inside, whilst helicopters swooped from the sky to remove tables and chairs lest any guest peer out at a blemished vista. En route to dinner, the revelers were treated to the pièces de résistance — several series of alcoves, constructed for the event by our favorite architect Jeremy Campion. Each alcove held a tableau featuring live models. Outstanding among them: Ingres' "Turkish Bath," Manet's "Olympia," and Eric Fischl's "Bad Boy." If any of you art mavens have, perchance, forgotten, these are all famous nudes. La.

The guests, however, were dressed. To the nines, as we used to say in the olden days. Among the celebrants, that madcap icon of elegance, the truly original Jane Winter with husband Jann; darling Cynthia Hayes-York just back from Barcelona with Mike Kennen, the America's Cup contender; George and Sarah Ames; Peggy and Cooper Conrad of the D.C. Conrads as if you didn't know; writer Joan Caraganis and golf great Johnny Jakobs; Lenora Baratelli and Scott Kilkare — and many others too glamoroso to describe.

The Athos, Porthos, and Aramis of the younger crowd — Nick Roberts (computers), Thomas Hunter (commodities), and Tari Farm-afarmian (the peacock throne) — danced the night away with beauteous Annie Price, Genevieve Hudson, and Olivia Connor. But it was on the arm of D'Artagnan (author Jack Delaney to you) as well as at the center of a bitter legal battle and media brawl, the most ravishing of all, despite the tragic badge she bears . . .

• • •

The next few weeks went like wild strawberries in the spring. With Alison Vonseca in Turkey and Evandi on vacation, the house was gloriously ours, and even the weather held. Half a dozen gardeners constantly came and went; but very quietly as if slipping in from Mexico without papers, which all of them had probably done at some point.

The days were long, so Miranda's interior lights stayed bright, giving her some respite. She had finally gained a couple of pounds, gotten a bit of color in spite of the hats and dark glasses, and remembered more details of the gruesome attack. But the scars weren't fading, and she never mentioned Pete.

I worked on Cassie and Zack's latest adventure in the mornings, and Delaney worked on *Bleak House* in the afternoons. He was oddly secretive about his material, and Miranda told me he said nobody (including her) could see one single word until it was finished. At the time I figured his behavior was nothing more than idiosyncratic.

The three of us usually met for lunch on the terrace or in the sunroom. Somebody had always stopped for food at the nearby Farmers Market, where, if I went out for the newspapers early, I would see summer vacationers standing in a long line waiting to buy coffee. They would take their coffee and sit three abreast on one of the benches around the market, most of which offered a view of Route 27.

Meanwhile within easy walking distance, undisturbed by human sounds or scents, busy mice skittered, harmless snakes slithered, and happy seagulls swooped along the most spectacular seashore on the east coast of America.

Taking advantage of Mrs. Vonseca's big, beautifully equipped kitchen, I started cooking. It occurred to me that when an author writes something stupid, he must live with the permanent humiliation of print, whereas a chef can feed his mistakes to the dog. Maybe I'd switch careers.

Early one afternoon over my ceviche and an '81 Mondavi Chardonnay Reserve from the cellar, Delaney announced that Peregrine Behar was coming for a brief visit.

• • •

From Delaney-Behar Correspondence:

Dear Jack,

The Philistines sent a round-trip plane ticket with layover in NY. Arriving Tues. P.M. by car from JFK. Suggest we test Pomerols. I still think '81 is underrated.

Wine gives strength to weary men,

PB   London, 1st August

P.S. Bartender at the Groucho looking through *Vanity Fair* (with Morton's piece) saw photo of Patrice O. and swore he once worked with her in the States at some saloon the mob burned down. Now we have a £10 bet.

———

Dear Peregrine,

Good news from Italy for once. Port'Ercole lawsuit was just dropped. The old man died and nobody's in the mood. I'm off the hook!

Big O's business affairs dept. is processing my check; script almost done. All's right with the world.

Decanted 1978 Beaucastel for one hour yesterday; liked it better than you and Morton. It was big and burly all the way. Not as fruity, though, as the '78 Rayas we drank when you were here in November.

Have arranged tasting with local wine merchant.

Godspeed,

T. Hardy   2 Aug. East Hampton

P.S. Tell the barkeep he owes you £10. Am sure Patrice was at boarding school in Switzerland (or maybe Virginia) and then traveled.

———

My dear Jack,

Delighted with your news. Perhaps, under the circumstances, you should reconsider your project (a copy of which in its entirety I have placed on the black walnut secretaire in my study). Put it aside perhaps. If you do press on, you *must* tell Miranda.

Will read Act III on the plane.

Rushing to Heathrow,

PB   London, 4th August

•   •   •

Behar's imminent arrival put Delaney in the shopping mood. Not to mention Miranda's kind but firm reminders about replacing the wine we'd taken from Alison Vonseca's cellar. Fat chance. I personally had imbibed a few vintages that probably no longer existed outside some canny Bordeaux vintner's personal hoard.

He decided to take Miranda on a pilgrimage to Amagansett, a hamlet where the average income, ordinarily low enough to require food stamps, jumps during the summer like an eventer at the Hampton Classic. It's also the site of Amagansett Wine & Spirits, which despite its location offers the best selection of wine within a hundred miles of New York in any direction. Delaney knew the way to places like this the way other people know the way home.

I'd just put away what was left of the ceviche, and was thinking I'd bike into town to see an exhibit of Peter Beard's photos, when the phone rang.

Over a poor connection with a lot of static, the overseas operator asked for Delaney.

"He's not here," I said. "But he'll be back — who's calling?"

"Milan," said the operator, and at the same time, someone, no doubt Domina Valverde, began sobbing and talking nonstop in Italian. Suddenly she stopped crying and switched to English.

"Tell that sonofabitch to call Domina," she screamed, "that prick."

The connection broke, but I got the message, and when Miranda and Delaney returned, I passed it on to him privately. He asked if I'd keep Miranda occupied while he rang Domina, and at the time I didn't think I was doing wrong by agreeing. But he was on the phone long enough for me to start questioning my judgment and worrying about the upshot of the call.

*   *   *

Artists from everywhere have always come to this little strip of Long
Island to paint in the stunning clarity of the North Atlantic light,
which was just fading into dusk when Delaney, carrying a bottle of
wine and looking mysteriously sunny, finally joined us in the rose
garden.

Miranda clipped Coeur d'Amour, Harrowband, and Landora. I
followed with the basket, and Delaney sampled the Lafleur Pomerol
he intended to serve during the first course of our first dinner with
Peregrine Behar.

"How is it?" asked Miranda.

"Perfection," said Delaney. "They only produced three hundred
cases. Behar had a case. But it disappeared when he moved to a new
flat last year. He thinks the movers nicked it."

Perhaps they left it in the lorry or the lift.

"Let me taste," said Miranda. She swirled, sniffed, swizzled the
wine around in her mouth and swallowed.

"Um," she said. "A very witty, kinky wine. Curvaceous too. I see
why Parker compared it to '47 and '59 and gave it a 98."

Delaney grabbed Miranda around the waist.

"Hey," he said. "*You're* curvaceous — the wine's monumental.
And how do you know about Parker?"

I suppose Delaney thinks he's the only one who can read the best-
known wine critic in the world, and in point of fact she's *not* curvaceous.

"You keep talking about him," she said. "So I got a couple of
his books. Here, David, what do you think?" She handed me the
glass.

"Definitely curvaceous," I said.

"Oh, for God's sake," said Delaney, taking back his glass, "curvaceous does not exist in the lexicon of wine."

"Kinky does," I said.

"Kinky is real," he replied.

"So's curvaceous," I said.

"To us," Miranda added, and threw her arm around my waist.

"You're quite a pair," said Delaney, finishing the wine, pouring
some more. "Now let's plan the guest list for Behar's dinner."

"Bobby's going to be here," said Miranda.

"Bobby Wilder?" asked Delaney. "Who told you that?"

"He called me," said Miranda.

"He called you?" asked Delaney.

"Um hmm," she said.

"He *called* you," Delaney repeated.

Yes Jack, I thought, on the telephone, not unlike the way Domina just called *you*.

"Have we got an echo out here?" asked Miranda. "Yes, he called me, we're friends."

"Some friends," said Delaney, his good cheer disintegrating into sarcasm. "When did he call?"

"The other day," she said. "When you and *your* friend *P*atrice were out buying *pâté*."

"Patrice *is* my friend."

"I'll alert the media," I said.

"What's *your* problem?" Delaney snapped.

"Sorry," I said.

"I didn't say she wasn't," said Miranda.

"When's he coming out?" asked Delaney.

"Tuesday morning. Larry Owen asked the whole family — Bobby, Esteban, Henry, and Sally — to come and help talk Patrice into getting back with him."

"He asked *Henry?*" demanded Delaney.

"And they're all coming," said Miranda. "Except Sally because she's in Europe."

"You're kidding," I said.

"It's true," said Miranda. "They're coming."

Delaney finished with his wine, put the glass in my basket, and headed toward the house.

"Where're you going?" asked Miranda.

"I'm going to invite *everybody* to dinner Saturday night," he said over his shoulder.

Twenty minutes later, he popped out on the porch, rubbing his hands together. Mr. Conviviality had returned.

"They'll be here," he said. "Eight-thirty. Larry's bringing his French couple out, and Patrice said they can help us with dinner."

13

• • •

IT WAS MIDDAY and the sky, sea, and fog just rolling in were all
the same color — known in my books as gunmetal gray — differing
only in texture, when a Town Car (writers don't get limos) from JFK
deposited Peregrine Behar beneath the porte cochere. Delaney, Miranda, and I descended the front steps to greet him, and after we all
shook hands, he lifted his chubby fingertips to Miranda's face to touch
the deepest scar on her cheek.

"I'm so sorry," he murmured.

"It's okay," she said softly.

Behar blushed. Delaney studied the skyline and I cleared my throat.
Then Behar bent over a bag at his feet and came up with a bottle of
port.

"For you, old man," he said. "Not bad, eh?"

"Cockburn '55." Delaney smiled. "Not bad at all."

We repaired to the sunroom at the back of the house to try Behar's
port with some Stilton. As the two friends caught up on international
literary gossip, Miranda and I settled down side by side on the couch.
In the odd, dull light, her hair was more silver than blond, her eyes
more silver than blue.

"So, old buddy," Delaney said eventually. "I'm glad you finally got
a beat on Vronsky. I was having the same problem with Bucket."

Behar knocked over his glass reaching for a napkin.

"So sorry," he said, "terribly sorry — "

"Forget it Peregrine," said Miranda rising. "It didn't amount to two drops, I'll fix it."

She mopped up port with a cocktail napkin.

"Thank you so much," said a chagrined Behar.

"As I was saying Peregrine," Delaney continued, "I'm all right now; I'm just following Esther's narrative."

"Just so, old man," said Behar, twiddling his heavy thumbs. "Just so."

The fog had evaporated, and magically the day became brightly beautiful.

"Let's get Peregrine settled," said Miranda. "And go to the beach."

Patti Owen (after the usual flurry of phone calls) came by from the airport, where she'd deposited her houseguest Roland Tarbell, who was going back to his burrow.

She wore a lot of designer chiffon, unheard of at the beach and too dressy for daytime anywhere else east of Los Angeles and north of Houston. It did, however, achieve the desired effect, which was to show she had a body while obscuring most of its flaws.

Delaney had whipped up a batch of peach daiquiris, which we brought with us as we strolled down the path to the ocean. Miranda in a tiny bikini and Panama hat tilted over her face, Delaney in tennis whites, Patti with flags of orange chiffon flapping, and Peregrine in a tie and sweater vest. My beach attire was predictably bourgeois: a swimsuit.

We had barely spread our blankets and tucked into our first daiquiri, before the two authors launched a battle of literary one-upmanship reciting sea lore, sailing back and forth between the popular and the arcane. Having taken turns with the Bible, Conrad, Coleridge, Walt Whitman, Lord Byron, and of course Masefield, Behar came up with:

" 'There is *nothing* — absolutely nothing — half so much worth doing as simply messing about in boats.' "

"I know," said Delaney. "That's from *The Wind in the Willows*."

"But who said it?" asked Behar.

"You mean who is the author?" inquired Delaney.

"No, I'll give you the author — Kenneth Grahame — "

"I knew that," said Delaney.

Patti yawned.

"I'm asking for the *character*," said the Englishman.

"Let's see . . . ," said Delaney, stalling.

"Maybe you know, Miranda," said Patti. "You're always reading."

"I never heard of it," said Miranda.

"*All* children read *The Wind in the Willows*," declared Behar.

"I guess I missed it," said Miranda.

"That's all right," said Behar. "It was the Water Rat."

"I have the best one," Delaney said. " 'Full fathom five thy father lies; / Of his bones are coral made; / Those are pearls that were his eyes — ' "

" 'Nothing of him that doth fade,' " chimed Behar. " 'But doth suffer a sea-change / Into something rich and strange.' "

" 'Sea-nymphs hourly ring his knell,' " added Miranda, concluding Ariel's song.

"Very impressive," said Delaney, more surprised than patronizing.

"So what is all that?" asked Patti impatiently; her pretensions never ran to the intellectual.

"It's from *The Tempest*," said Miranda. "By Shakespeare."

"Tell me," said Behar. "Were your parents big fans of the Bard?"

"Who's the *Bard*?" asked Patti, knocking back her third peach daiquiri.

"Shakespeare," said Jack. "And the heroine of *The Tempest* is called Miranda."

"No, Peregrine," Miranda said, answering Behar. "They didn't even have a nodding acquaintanceship with Shakespeare — I'm not named for the girl in *The Tempest*."

"Serendipitous coincidence, what," said Behar.

"I'm named for Ernesto Miranda."

"I see," said Behar.

"You do?" she asked.

"You never told me that," Delaney said to her.

"It's not something I ever think about," she said.

"All right," said Patti, "who the hell is Ernesto Miranda?"

"Miranda versus Colorado," said Delaney. "Around 1963."

"It was Arizona," Miranda said, "1966."

"Oh of course," said Behar.

"Is somebody going to tell me who this person was," demanded Patti, working on number four.

"He was a rapist," said Miranda. "Because of the Miranda decision cops have to say, 'You have the right to remain silent — ' "

"Oh yeah," said Patti. "Whatever you say can be held against you and all that. On TV the cops are always saying did you *Mirandize* the suspect. But why did they name you after a rapist?"

"You really want to know?" asked Miranda.

"Americans are always surprised by *my* name," cut in Behar, attempting to change the conversational direction. "And if they've ever heard it before, it's always in connection with the peregrine falcon. The word actually means traveler."

"Well I have to travel home," said Patti, staggering to her feet. "And get ready for Mr. Big O. Cover up Miranda, you don't want to be scarred *and* burnt."

Delaney stood and took her arm, none too gently.

"I'll walk you up," he said, half dragging her away.

• • •

Patti never liked her, but what I didn't understand as time went by, was why so many other women were hostile toward Miranda. Maybe they held her personally responsible for destroying beauty's promise of happiness. Maybe the attack on Miranda, as she walked alone at night, reminded them how vulnerable they were, and their anger hid their fear.

Some women considered Miranda an adversary with a special advantage because her ruined beauty was still hypnotic. But now she had the scars. And the scars sent a signal of helplessness to men. The scars showed that she had been weak, she had been down, she could be overwhelmed. The scars aroused in men a sense of power, a desire to protect — without risk. They didn't need to fight off her assailants or wipe up her blood. Men saw a victim and wanted to save her. Women saw a rival and wanted to destroy her.

• • •

Early the following morning, less than a day after Behar's arrival, a Federal Express truck pulled up with a letter for Delaney, the contents of which put him in great good spirits. It was the payment he'd been waiting for from Los Angeles. We spent the rest of the morning and half the afternoon on preparations for the dinner in honor of Peregrine, who'd gone off to Montauk to visit a friend from Cambridge.

I remember standing at the kitchen window watching the gulls and trawlers far off in the distance when Michael Cinque, owner of Amagansett Wine & Spirits, phoned to say he'd gotten the '61 Château Latour Pauillac. Delaney was out of the house like a shot and back almost as fast.

"*Miranda!*" he bellowed.

"She said we needed shallots — " I explained.

"Have you seen my fucking wallet?" he demanded.

I hadn't seen his fucking wallet, and against my better judgment I gave him my American Express card.

He wasn't gone ten minutes when Miranda returned. She strolled into the kitchen carrying a small grocery bag in one hand and Delaney's wallet in the other.

"Can you believe this?" she said, dropping the wallet on the table.

"Jack's wallet?"

"He's hopeless," she said with an indulgent smile. "Where is he, I saw the car was gone."

"He went to buy wine and pick up Peregrine," I said, looking down at the wallet.

"You should have seen the people at the Farmers Market today," she said, running a hand through her hair.

"What about them?"

"Like I was standing in line next to this little kid who says to her mom, 'What happened to that girl's face?' and the mom stares right at me, then says to the kid, 'She was in an accident.' And the kid says, 'In a car?' and the woman says, 'Yes.' Then the kid asks if I was wearing a seat belt and the mother says she doesn't know, so the kid turns to me and says, 'You should always wear your seat belt.' "

"The woman recognized you?"

"What do you think?"

"People are strange."

"Some of them get really strange around me," she said. "They don't know what to say or how to say it; sometimes I think my face is like a crazy mirror for them. But I don't really understand what they see."

I didn't either, nor did I know how to soothe her. I picked up Delaney's wallet.

"Where'd you find this?" I asked.

"Right in the middle of the porch," she said.

"So are we going to see what's in it?" I asked.

"*David*," she said, mock shocked, and I think a little shocked for real.

Here's the thing: I've looked through the occasional medicine chest, and I found a guy's wallet one time on the bus so obviously I looked in it to see where to return it. But I don't go through people's drawers, and ordinarily I don't look in their wallets.

"If you look where you're not supposed look," Miranda said, "you always see what you're not supposed to see."

"Do you actually think there's something in there you're not supposed to see?" I asked.

"No," she said. "But it's his . . . it's his private wallet."

"Well," I said, "you're living with him, you're sleeping with him. What could be that private?"

"David," she said. "Is there some reason you're being so weird?"

"No," I said. And that was true up to a point. Clearly there was a reason; I just had no idea what it was.

"Okay, I'm going to put it on the tray in the hall," she said.

"Fine," I said.

We both stood in silence for a moment. Then Miranda picked up the alligator wallet, pulled the credit cards out of their slots, and dumped the rest of the contents on the table. There was a hundred-dollar bill and two tens. A New York driver's license, various calling cards, a couple of receipts for wine, and a corporate check from Big O Productions (with an asterisk after which was typed: *per Patrice Owen*) to Delaney via his agent. The usual information — sum, date, taxpayer ID number, et cetera, was filled in, as was the following:

First payment for screenplay, draft, and set
(Title) DON'T TELL AMANDA —
THE SLASHING OF A SUPERMODEL
(Working title) BLEAK HOUSE

"What does this mean?" asked Miranda, pointing at the title, tapping her foot on the kitchen floor.

"I have no idea," I said.

"You're the worst liar I know," Miranda said. ". . . But now we know who's the best, don't we?"

"I guess so," I said.

"Do you *see* what he's done? He *promised* to tell me the truth. And he *promised* not to write about me," she said. "He doesn't care about *me,* he's just been using me. He was so nice, so patient, because there was a *payoff.* And it wasn't making love — it was making *money.*"

She kept staring at the check, running her hand through her hair. "I'll be right back," she said.

"Where're you going?" I called after her, but she didn't answer.

I took out the sharpest knife I could find and tried to kill the shallots.

I suppose if you're strolling along the streets of Beirut on a quiet afternoon, you can't call sudden gunfire unexpected. I was waiting for something. It turned out to be the sound of breaking glass.

I took the stairs three at a time. Raced down the hall to Delaney's room. Miranda was sitting on the floor sobbing, under a broken window, blood all over her right hand and arm.

I had never seen a woman put her fist through a window; nor for that matter had I ever seen a man put his through a window, a wall, or anything else, except in the movies.

She was clutching a stack of paper as I picked her up and carried her to my room, where I washed her hand and realized that miraculously stitches wouldn't be needed to close up the cuts. I was grateful on several counts, not the least of which was escaping the poison pen of Tansy Stoner, who would have grabbed this tidbit (no doubt she had a snitch in the local emergency room) and run with it to the tune of: *SUICIDE!!! MODEL'S GUILT OVER CAUSING WRONG-FUL INCARCERATION DRIVES ATTEMPT TO TAKE OWN LIFE . . .*

Half an hour later, in my bedroom, with curtains drawn against a pitiless sun, I held the hand I'd bandaged as Miranda talked.

"I can almost get Mark Douglas," she said. "I mean, it's easier to understand somebody who's crazy, because you can accept that a lot of stuff doesn't add up. Mark was an accident looking for a place to happen. And it was my bad luck. If it hadn't been me, I think it would be the next girl who pissed him off."

"I can see that," I said. "And I can see why it was you, because you were the most unattainable . . ."

"But Jack's worse," she said, blinking back fresh tears. "Because he's not crazy. He's just got no . . . right or wrong. I mean, he doesn't have a conscience."

"He's a monster," I heard myself saying, as if from some extreme distance. The word, which is not in my repertoire of epithets, gave me a chill.

She laughed and tears ran down her face.

"And you don't even know what he *did*," she said.

"I know what he did. He lied," I said. "He told everybody he was adapting *Bleak House* when he's really writing a movie about you, which he promised he'd never do. . . . Is there something else?"

"Yes, there's something else," she said. "Stealing my life wasn't enough. Changing it and twisting it wasn't enough — my God how could anybody do this — look what he wrote, look at *this!*"

She threw a stack of pages on the floor.

"But," she said. "Us pathetic self-destructive *Okies* always know some things — probably part of our *genetic* heritage we keep stored in our little pea brains . . ."

I flashed on her grandmother and the gun.

"What are you talking about?"

"Remember that stupid bitch in the restaurant, the one who said Jack was going to *dump* me?"

"I remember."

"Well he did worse than that — " Her eyes filled with tears again.

"Miranda — "

"I'm okay, because like I said, there's plenty of stuff I know," she said getting up. "Like where to find the town dump."

She ran out of my room down the hall and back to Delaney's room. She yanked Delaney's computer off the desk and, refusing both advice and help, in two trips had loaded it into the old station wagon along with his disks, his files, fax machine, and every scrap of paper in the room. Except for a pile of Delaney-Behar faxes that I filched the first time she went downstairs.

I also picked up the crumpled top page of the stack she'd originally thrown on the floor, which turned out to be a recent entry in the Delaney-Behar correspondence. I smoothed it out and read:

Perry, Perry, Perry,

Don't bother looking for '82 Petit-Village. Just bought three cases.

Had two '85's last night — Brane-Cantenac and L'Angélus; advise you to lay some in. '85 clarets in general are your kind of wine. Flirty and fruity without that fifteen-year chastity belt of hard tannins. The Margaux are quite good now too.

Here's the Third Act. Could you take a quick look? I didn't want any on-stage sex, but Larry insisted. He and Patrice both say this can be to the nineties what *Wings* was to the eighties.

Something has always been missing. But I think I've found the solution. The story needed an extra jolt, and I finally figured out what to do. Works right in with the second plot point. It's heavy — so fasten your seat belt. And for God's sake, DON'T TELL MIRANDA.

I'll explain everything to her at the right moment, which is not now.

Best as always,

Jack   1 August, East Hampton

• • •

With all Delaney's equipment and material loaded in the car, Miranda roared down the long driveway and just missed colliding with the gray Mercedes as it wheeled in from the road. She laid on the horn, but Delaney, instead of moving out of the way, jumped from his car and ran over to see what was wrong.

Ignoring my usual nonintervention stance, I raced outside, because frankly I was scared. Miranda was angry beyond reason. No one could understand her anger better than I. But what if she had a knife in the car. What if she'd learned dangerous moves at Noah's Ark. Maybe she knew how to kill somebody using the heel of her hand to smash his nose back into his brain. Anything seemed possible at that moment.

By the time I reached the end of the driveway at a dead run, Delaney and Miranda were screaming at each other. As bad as this confrontation was (and it was very bad), I felt a trill of delight and relief watching Miranda let go in a way I'd never seen before.

"I *was* going to tell you — "

"When? Next month, NEXT YEAR — "

" — today — "

"TODAY? You're totally full of shit Jack; you lied to me about every single thing. And you're a THIEF. You came in and STOLE my life. But I guess the story wasn't good enough for you — "

"What're you talking about, Miranda, you're hysterical — "

" — so then you thought YOU'D just change MY life. You'd just turn me into a little whore and liar who got cut up as PUNISHMENT for coming on to some asshole, and then *LIED* IN COURT!"

"She lied to insure their punishment. . . . It's fiction for God's sake — "

"*Bleak House* is fiction — THIS IS MY *LIFE* — "

"IT IS *NOT* — "

"Oh you think you made it okay when the girl *confesses* to the junkie that she'd actually been sleeping with the landlord and he got mad because she called it quits — "

"Are you crazy? He's not a junkie — "

"Are *you* crazy? I didn't *do anything!* Oh, but did I just say *junkie?* I guess I meant journalist; this bimbo confesses her sins to the *journalist* after *HE* fucks her — "

"Miranda please — "

"You broke your word Jack, you lie about everthing. And I can tell you right now what's gonna happen to your career too — "

"I don't have to hear this crap."

He started to move away, but Miranda's voice suddenly became hushed. She was speaking slowly, just above a whisper, and he was drawn back to face her.

"You steal other people's stories," she said. "Like a cat who sneaks in at night and steals the baby's breath and kills the baby. But when *you* blow out the breath, it's not air anymore, it's poison.

"You're a good writer, Jack, but you're never gonna be a great one. Because the great ones have a heart. You're the best at looking around with the evil eye, but you don't know how to look inside your own head, so you don't know a fucking thing about yourself, which means you can't ever know any true thing about anybody else."

Delaney's face was deep red beneath his suntan; a vein stood out at his temple.

"So the mannequin expounds," he said. "I've heard of jailhouse lawyers, now we have a jailhouse critic. What a joke. You can barely spit out a simple declarative sentence."

"You got my meaning, didn't you?" she said.

"I happen to think what I wrote *was* true," he said. "You're just a low-rent little slut, and all you ever had going was your face. I think you *did* come on to that landlord — "

"You're right, Jack," she said in a very low voice, as if speaking to herself. "*My* fucking face. *My* scars. *My* life."

I remember the next thing in slow motion, but it actually took only a split second. First the blue vanished from Miranda's silver-blue eyes and the silver went flat like stainless steel. Next, her bandaged right hand tensed into a fist as she drew back her arm and bent her knees like a skier; then she shifted her weight, bringing the arm around to deliver a blow as powerful as it was unexpected — catching Delaney on the side of the head, by his ear, and knocking him right off his feet.

Miranda walked slowly and deliberately back to the station wagon, hit the gas, and aimed straight at Delaney, who rolled away just in time. Before reaching the main road, however, she did manage to smash the back fender of the Mercedes and tear off the bumper.

• • •

In the fall, there were two trials. One for Mark Douglas and the other for Dooley Kincaid and Lester Bartholomew. They were all convicted. The day after the last sentence was handed down, Miranda and I bought a couple of sandwiches and took them to The Shamrock for lunch. It was a sad little pilgrimage. The leaves on the trees were long gone, and winter chilled the air.

Ben was absent, we learned, at his mother's funeral, so we ate our tuna and drank our beers under the gaze of a temporary bartender who turned up the volume of the TV on the wall.

"Do you want to talk?" I asked.

"Not now," she said.

"When?"

"Someday."

"What are you going to do?" I asked.

The only light in the room was coming from those silver-blue eyes.

"I don't know, I'll find something to do."

"I know you will."

She lit a cigarette.

"I need to figure out my life."

"Well," I said. "That ain't no hill for a stepper, is it?"

"I guess not," she said. She picked up her copy of *The Catcher in the Rye* and put it in her bag.

"I love you, Miranda."

"And I love you," she said.

She smelled like rain.

The next day she was gone.

EPILOGUE

. . .

How many loved your moments of glad grace,
And loved your beauty with love false or true,
But one man loved the pilgrim soul in you,
And loved the sorrows of your changing face.

W. B. Yeats

TIME DOES NOT heal all wounds. Though time does pass and wounds do heal, time cannot erase the worst scars — and should not.

Memory is infinitely mysterious: eyewitnesses are unable to remember colors, clothing, or topography. We can recall terrible physical pain only as a concept. Our memories protect us. They blaze, spark, sputter, and blaze again; they never burn with a steady fire or we would surely perish.

Here's what happened to everyone.

Mark Douglas, Dooley Kincaid, and Lester Bartholomew are each serving five to fifteen years in the state penitentiary at Ossining. Parole has already been denied once to Douglas and Kincaid and twice to Bartholomew.

Terrence O'Mara filed a civil suit on Miranda's behalf against all three of her assailants. She was awarded the largest settlement in the history of New York State. It was recorded in the *Guinness Book of World Records* and stands to this day. Unfortunately she got nothing, since none of the three, including Mark Douglas, has any money.

I still live in the same place. After the trial, Mark Douglas's relatives sold the building (and the rest of his property) to a small German-Japanese financial consortium, which went bankrupt two years ago. My current landlord is a Russian émigré who once ran a state-owned sable business in Siberia and managed to skim enough cash to get himself started in U.S. real estate. The rent is up but at least he turns the heat on in winter.

Our cancellation of the Behar dinner struck a chord in Patti, who called off the Owen-Garcia-Wilder confab and flew to Rancho La Puerta with Larry to repair their marriage. After confessing her infidelity, she phoned Henry Garcia to come and rescue her from a furious Mr. Big O — but Garcia never showed up.

Ben had a heart attack and retired, which is probably a good thing, because The Shamrock has become gentrified, with little checked tablecloths, fancy mixed drinks, and a bartender who went to college. I still go there sometimes, but needless to say, it's not the same.

Larry Owen filed for divorce and announced the decision to marry his periodontist.

• • •

From Roland Tarbell's column:

> . . . and parties are being planned everywhere in preparation for Turkey Day, one of the few times when many of Gotham's glitterati can be found tending the close-to-home fires. Queen Tralala, the shero of Soho, will be hostessing a strictly fruitarian do with a trompe l'oeil turkey of avocado mousse. Meanwhile, on the ohso elegant East Side, Larry Owen and his young (and brainy) bride of two months (who said it wouldn't last!), Dr. Betsy Owen, will entertain a group too beautiful and famous to mention. I myself will be going over the river and through the woods to Grandmother's house or something like that. . . .

• • •

Henry Garcia and Sally Wilder renewed their wedding vows in the presence of three hundred guests at a Bel Air gala and adopted a ten-month-old baby girl from Mexico City. They sold the place in Jamaica, feeling the island had become unstable.

Bobby Wilder's directorial debut won second place at Sundance two years ago. Esteban was associate producer.

On the south side of the Conservatory Garden in Central Park, there's a dark green bench that faces a creamy sea of fragrant daffodils and hyacinths every spring. A small brass plaque is affixed to the bench, engraved:

Pete
Death Shall Have No Dominion

The plaque, given anonymously, is what one receives for a ten-thousand-dollar donation to the Central Park Conservancy. Alison Vonseca told me over spiked tea at the Plaza one rainy afternoon that her secretary's brother, office manager for the Conservancy, said the donor was Terrence O'Mara.

Cat Kelly recently started her own magazine.

Tansy Stoner was hit by a taxicab on Third Avenue, dragged for two blocks, banged, broken, bruised, but too mean to die. She's still recuperating, and I have no doubt she'll be back, like a locust.

Everyone says Peregrine Behar will win the Booker Prize this year, with his latest work, *Anna*.

Jack Delaney never submitted the screenplay. O'Mara wrote him a letter on Miranda's behalf which I didn't read but can imagine. Also, after Miranda destroyed the disks and papers in East Hampton, and because Delaney hadn't ever sent pages to his agent, to Patrice, or to Big O Productions, there was only one remaining copy. In Behar's London flat. I happened to be in London when that last copy disappeared under mysterious circumstances. . . .

Delaney lived with Patti for about a year after Miranda left him and Garcia left her, but during a visit to Montecatini they ran into Domina Valverde. Delaney's Milan marriage was duly reported by Roland Tarbell. He remains in Europe, where his work is very popular.

Patti returned home alone from Italy and eventually moved to Santa Barbara, where she gave up candle design and started playing golf. She now lives with a golf pro.

Big O Productions keeps churning out hit shows, but *The Golden Rule* is over. Malone was hoping he could start production for another season when he died. Killed at thirty by an arrow he shot at twenty-five.

Jonathan and I took care of him at the end. Jonathan Loring the veterinarian. We got to know each other pretty well after the trials. He's in Kentucky right now, as his expertise is Thoroughbred horses.

Juliana hasn't been around for about a month. A long time for her. I phoned Detective Mike Romanos, who said if a missing person is dead, there's always a body. He checked everywhere and there was no body. Maybe she hitched a ride to Hialeah. I hope.

I'm writing my ninth and definitely last *Midnight* book. While they're still young and beautiful, Cassie and Zack will join the ranks of Butch and Sundance, Thelma and Louise, Héloïse and Abélard — caught in amber for all time, never having to endure the indignities of midlife or midlist; to lose a race or a chance or a child. Never having to grow old, to suffer, or to die.

For over a year after she left New York, I got infrequent and perfunctory postcards from Miranda. Then I received this letter.

A yellow stick-it note was attached to the first page:

David,

I wanted to wait till I had some news before I wrote to you. If you start thinking this letter looks like a long walk for a short beer, it's not, because I've got really good news. But it's at the end, so keep reading. xxxooo, M.

———

Dear David,

I'm not much of a letter or any other kind of writer but I think of you all the time. I hope you forgive me for leaving like that. I just hate saying good-bye because it spooks me.

So I went down to Florida to visit Alison at her place in Boca Grande. Very grand (so what else is new as everybody in NYC says). We talked a lot. She helped me think through what I should do next, tho I still haven't figured it out totally. She's an amazing woman. Changed by fire. I think she can see right through people to where everyone is the same.

She gave me a jeep. I woke up one morning and found out she'd flown back up north and left an envelope with the keys, registration, etc., and a note basically telling me to go home and deal with my family before I made any big decisions. I don't know how I'll ever pay her back.

I went to Kitty's to see all the kids. My brother Raymond's in jail. Kitty says it's my fault because he got into a bar fight defending my honor. She left out the part about the bar fight happened an hour after he ripped off a liquor store. Probably my fault too!

I drove to Kansas to see my Dad. That was no fun I can tell you. When I was there, I read in the Cattleman's paper that Angus Campbell died and I decided to go up to Big Piney for the funeral. It was real sad.

Finally drove to Noah's Ark (which believe it or not was a lot more cheerful than any of the other places I went after Florida) to visit Bea. You two have got to meet soon because you and her are definitely soul mates. Five more years till she retires and then she's hot to start a school. I wouldn't mind going in with her on it, but who can think so far ahead.

There was a doctor in Zurich who said he could fill in my scars. Dr. Baldwin and Dr. Hutton (from Boston) both said it was too early but I wanted to see this guy anyway. So I sold the jeep and flew to Europe.

Well, I didn't like the doctor and I hated Switzerland. Women couldn't even vote there till fifteen or twenty years ago and it's no joke they're so famous for their clocks. I mean you could be laying in the street dying and they'd rather run you down than be late for lunch. Yech.

I figured as long as I was there I mine as well smoke over to Paris where I could live forever. I was going through all my junk and found this card Nessoui Hamid gave me that night we met him. The other guy, Chris Bradshaw, was supposed to write Mr. Hamid's number, but he wrote his own number — three of them! One in London. So I figured I'd call him.

I'll cut to the chase. That's the wrong word because I'm already caught. DON'T WORRY. I'm at Chris's house out in the country now. This is a guy who doesn't talk that much, but he could blow Bobby, Donny, and Jack (who's been hounding me trying to apologize, fuck that) out of the water, with about five words. He is REALLY smart. And he doesn't even notice the scars.

But I'm leaving here soon because Bea turned me onto a college. I'm sure you've heard of it — St. John's, where they've got the Great Books Program. *Four years* of learning the greatest books ever written. My idea of heaven.

I didn't tell Alison because this is something I have to do myself. AND THEY ACCEPTED ME WITH A SCHOLARSHIP!!! I can't start right away because I need a couple of high school courses I never had (like *algebra*) but I'm going to take them there in Maryland where the school is. And I expect you for Thanksgiving, Christmas, all my birthdays (ha ha, I told them the truth) and vice versa.

The lights are more on than off.

I see Chris coming up the road now. He's with his new artist, Junior Miles. We're going to have lunch pretty soon.

Angus Campbell's grandson (who I don't think is exactly a chip off the old block) said his grandfather wanted you to have what's in the little package. The other package is mine, I'm sending it to you for safekeeping.

Did you know Zelda Fitzgerald wrote a book too? *Save Me the Waltz.* When I think of you and me (you know what I mean) I think of this line she wrote:

"Nobody has ever measured, not even poets, how much a heart can hold."

Miranda.

I was stunned when I opened the small package. There was Angus Campbell's pocket watch from the poker game in Cody, Wyoming. With the diamond numbers, except for the ruby one and the ruby eight.

I set the watch, put it in my pocket and opened the second, larger, package.

It was the ebony box that held Pete's ashes.

•   •   •

I never pray. In fact, I'm still an atheist. But somewhere along the line I decided to embrace Pascal's Wager. The bet is about trying to live a decent life. If, at the end, heaven is your reward, you've won. And if, as reason dictates, there's nothing beyond death but the eternal void, what have you lost?

Since I met Miranda, I see things a little differently; I think a little differently. I think we smother fear and call it courage. And although we persist in confusing beauty with goodness, lost beauty with lost goodness, we endure. We're weak but we hang on. We keep struggling. Struggling through the night, reaching for the light.

ACKNOWLEDGMENTS

• • •

The author is deeply grateful to Terry McDonell, without whom *Half Crazy* would simply not exist. There's a full moon over Tulsa.

To Libby Behar — the paradigm of unconditional love — for a lifetime of loyalty.

And to Ed Victor for his gracefulness, guidance, and dearest friendship.

• • •

The author also wishes to thank Fredrica S. Friedman for her relentlessly inspired editing; Anne McCormack for her wisdom; Judy Hudson, Joan Jakobson, and Jane Wenner for keeping the lights on.